CALLED TO GOBI

Books in The COIL Series

Dark Edge, Prequel
Dark Liaison, Book One
Dark Hearted, Book Two
Dark Rule, Book Three
Dark Vessel, Book Four
Dark Zeal, Book Five

Books in The COIL Legacy Series

Distant Boundary, Prequel
Distant Contact, Book One
Distant Front, Book Two
Distant Harm, Book Three

...†...

Other Books by D.I. Telbat

Arabian Variable
COIL Extractions: Short Story Collection
COIL Recruits: Short Story Collection
God's Colonel
Soldier of Hope
Leeward Set: Fury in the Storm, Book One
Leeward Set: Tears in the Wind, Book Two
The Legend of Okeanos
The Steadfast Series: America's Last Days

Coming Soon

Last Dawn Trilogy

CALLED
TO
GOBI

A CHRISTIAN END TIMES CHRONICLE

D.I. Telbat

In Season Publications
USA

Printed in the United States of America

Called To Gobi/D.I. Telbat. – 1st ed, updated 9/2018
Christian Fiction, End Times

ISBN 978-0-9864103-6-9

Book Layout ©2013 BookDesignTemplates.com
Cover Design by Streetlight Graphics

To my Dad
Regardless of the mountains,
the valleys, and deserts,
he continues to prove worthy.

Acknowledgements

When I was a child, a missionary visited
our church as he was on his way to the mission field.
He had a heart for a far-away land called Mongolia.
This book was inspired by that man, Drew Robinson.
And, as with all of my books, this manuscript
would have remained on the shelf without the
extensive help and input of many people.
I especially thank Dee, for her dependable
attention to detail; Jamie, for her proofreading
assistance; and my brother, whose adventure
in Mongolia added key insights to the terrain
and lifestyle. May God be glorified by this work.

Character Sketch

Andrew "Pond" Foworthy – bold, daring, 6-foot native of NYC; called by God to Mongolia; spends time with two different clans—a Mongolian clan and a Kazakh clan

Duulgii – Lugsalkhaan's half-Russian brother-in-law in the Kazakh clan

Dusbhan – Gan-gaad's nephew and gunman in Mongolian clan; adopted brother of Zima

Gan-gaad – Mongolian clansman chief who hates foreigners

Jugder – a large Kazakh with only two fingers on his right hand

Li Chong – Chinese interrogator

Lugsalkhaan – head of a Buddhist shaman Kazakh clan

Luyant – Gan-gaad's brother and mute clansman in Mongolian clan; owner of Zima

Kandal – an elderly Kazakh nomad

Manai – Orphaned 5-year-old boy in Kazakh clan

Randy Erickson – American missionary for 20 years to Eastern Mongolia

Rex – American pilot from Eastern Turkey

Sembuuk – a skilled Kazakh hunter

Sergeant Xing – Chinese infantry officer

Zima – A Russian-Kazakh woman, owned by clansman Luyant in the Mongolian clan

Western Mongolia

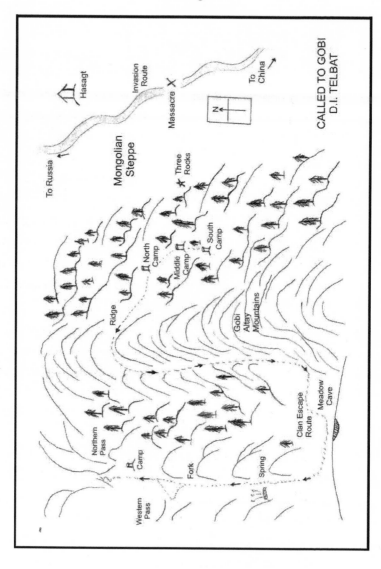

CALLED TO GOBI
D.I. TELBAT

...✝...

Andrew Foworthy crawled through the darkness and rain. The cold soothed his bruises from the latest beating delivered by his foster father. As a young child, he didn't know such abuse was abnormal since he'd never known life any other way. Abuse and neglect were Andy's norm.

Moving across the backyard, he squeezed through the neighbor's fence. Too late, he remembered the ferocious mutt that ruled the property. The dog was upon him in an instant, teeth barred, growling inches from Andy's face. He ducked his head under the hot breath of the canine.

For one minute, then another, he shivered under the territorial fury of the animal. Still growling, the dog nuzzled Andy, perhaps seeking a reaction. Passively, Andy remained still. The only thing worse than his foster father's fists, he imagined, were the slimy teeth of the neighbor's mutt.

Finally, the canine stopped growling and sniffed at Andy's damp clothes. Through the rain, the animal had smelled the stick of jerky Andy had stolen from his foster brother. He figured it was a fair trade if the beast didn't eat him alive. Tearing the stick in two, Andy shoved one half into his own mouth, then fed the other half to the dog.

Andy felt confident enough to continue his slow crawl

after that. He had to get out of the rain. The animal sniffed at his clothes for more food as Andy climbed through the opening of a dog house. The dog followed him inside the small enclosure and licked his face.

"You stink!" Andy wiped his face, but the cold forced him to tolerate the smell of the wet fur and rancid dog breath. He wrapped his arm around the animal as it settled with a groan next to young Andy.

Toward dawn, Andy woke to his own cries. No, it had just been a dream. He was safe with the angry dog. The canine licked his salty tears, and Andy snuggled closer to the only friend he'd ever had. In those quiet moments, he named the dog Asia. At school, he'd learned that Asia was on the other side of the world. Asia was the farthest place he could think of away from there. If only he could go to Asia . . .

...✝...

CHAPTER ONE

At the age of twenty-two, I was being chased by police through the boroughs of New York City. Until that day, I'd lived most of my life on the streets—no family, in and out of foster homes. There wasn't a classroom that could hold me. I was a problem child, plain and simple. It certainly didn't seem very likely that I would become a missionary to Mongolia.

Through my teenage years, I was a man of the world. At sixteen, I'd hitchhiked across the States to the West Coast, then stole cars on my way back east.

There's simply no point dwelling on the mistakes of my troubled youth, because it all led to me getting tackled by eight police officers south of Houston Street. My sins had caught up to me. As it turned out, the middle-aged man I'd beaten and robbed at an ATM ten minutes earlier, was a precinct detective. The judge gave me nine years, then promised I'd do every one of them—and more, if I didn't learn my lesson.

Needless to say, I didn't learn my lesson right away. As a youngster in a big prison outside Albany, I thought I had something to prove. Since I was tall and strong—a lean 200 pounds and a little over six feet—I took to fighting. I fought just about everyone from inside or outside the city's five boroughs. During my second year, when I was twenty-four, a few fellas grew tired of my attitude. Three healthy boys from the Bronx put me in the prison infirmary for two months.

With my jaw wired shut and my leg in traction, I lost forty pounds. That liquid diet just about killed me. But since I couldn't speak or fight, I was forced to watch and listen to the small bit of world I could see and hear. I learned to play chess and began to study for my GED.

It was during that time I met three men who changed my life forever. The first one was Gino Palucii. He was a pastor of Ridgewood Community Church, and if you know anything about Queens, where I'm from, then you know Ridgewood is an Italian neighborhood. Italians are a proud people—proud of both culture and heritage. Though most are devout Catholic, or at least baptized into the tradition, one would think Gino Palucii would've gone the way of the saints and sacraments. But there he was, a Protestant and ex-mobster himself, in the heart of Ridgewood, preaching the Gospel.

Gino would tell you I was the most stubborn man in the prison infirmary. He didn't care, though, and I couldn't protest his company verbally. I knew what he was, and initially, I wanted nothing to do with him. That first day, he asked if he could sit with me awhile. I shook my head, but he sat down anyway. More than once as a juvenile, I'd had the cross thrown in my face. I didn't know what it had to do with me. Before I knew it, Gino was giving his testimony. Every part of me wanted to run away, but I couldn't. God had seen to it that my leg was broken in three places and my jaw was wired shut because there was no other way I would sit still and listen.

It wasn't long before I'd become riveted to Gino's life story. His youthful years were as ugly as mine, and his journey down mobster lane wasn't too pretty, either. It was as if Gino had read my criminal file, understood every piece of my life, and knew I hated it. He'd lived the same way. Yes, I was tired of fighting the world. Yes, I was lonely. Yes, I was afraid of the future—though I didn't admit it to him that day.

Two weeks later, Gino came back as I was using crutches to hobble my way out of the infirmary. It was then that I met the second man who helped change my life— Randy Erickson, a thirty-eight-year-old father, husband, and missionary to Mongolia. Gino introduced us, but because I was still another week from losing my jaw wires, Randy did most of the talking. He spoke of sacrifice and love and service in a brutal Asian country I knew nothing about. And he told of a proud warrior people who still rode horses and snared animals for their fur—and communists that spied their every move.

Randy told me his life story, too. It was much different from Gino's story. But I connected with this missionary— his quick eyes, ready smile, and excitement. His left shoulder slumped stiffly, but it didn't bother him as he used his entire body to emphasize and explain the hard steps he'd taken to become a missionary for Christ in the distant land.

Then he said something that truly struck me. He said, "Andy, can you believe that even though Jesus died for the whole world, some people haven't even heard His name?"

This seemed so absurd to this spectacular speaker that I felt guilty for not knowing more. By this time, Gino had given me a study Bible to read myself, and after they'd left the prison grounds that day, I went to my cell, abandoned my GED studies for a week, and dug into the Bible. Gino had given me passages to read. I read John, then the three other Johns. Then I went to Genesis and read spellbound through the creation of man, the birth of civilization and empires, and into the depths of the Old Covenant.

When Gino returned the next week, he was alone, but my jaw was finally unwired. I had a thousand questions—so many that my brand new jaw hurt for two days from talking so excitedly. Referring to scribbled notes, I had questions for Randy Erickson, too, but Gino said he'd already flown back to Mongolia to continue the ministry he'd begun over a decade earlier.

Gino was slow and methodical as he answered my questions, making certain I understood each issue before we moved on. Gradually, I came to understand deep inside why it was so important to Randy—and to Gino—that everyone had the opportunity to hear the Good News.

A couple more weeks passed, however, until my list of questions were answered. Then, Gino asked me his own question.

"You've had the facts laid out for you, Andrew. God doesn't take our lives lightly and neither should we. Do you believe you're ready for that step?"

For once in my life, I was speechless. I knew I was on the edge of the greatest Truth ever known—with a choice that would determine my eternal destiny.

"If receiving Christ is step one, what's step two?" I asked.

"Step two is maturing as a believer in this one true faith. Step three is sharing it with others."

"Well, I already know who I want to share it with," I said, decided even then. "When Randy was telling me all about it, I knew. I'm going to Mongolia."

I, Andrew Foworthy, received Jesus Christ into my life that day in the state prison. And though I still had seven years left of my sentence, and assured by the judge I would serve every day, I didn't complain. Rather, with a purpose now in my life, I realized I had much work to do before I was ready to be kicked back out to the streets again. Without a doubt, I would need every day of my sentence to mature in Christ.

The next seven years were a blur as I delved into my studies. What began as excitement didn't fade, but it grew into something that wasn't mere excitement at all. I had an urgent passion, a longing, and a love that tested even Gino's patience at times. Though he lived and preached in Ridgewood, he drove inland at least once a month to visit me. Every time he came, we discussed the Word, and he challenged me to constantly grow through knowledge of the Bible, God's gift toward and beyond salvation. We prayed together each time, our heads bowed in the prison visiting room, with people staring. But we didn't care; we were talking to God.

When I was discharged from prison, I was thirty-one years old. Gino kindly accepted me into his home—but only because it was temporary. He had a son, a daughter, and a wife to think about, and I understood that.

While I was in Ridgewood for that month, Gino kept a

firm, fatherly hand on my lifestyle. Though God was a force in my life, the flesh still managed to pull at me with temptations. Gino was there to make sure I didn't wander back down to my old neighborhoods and life of crime. By the grace of God, I didn't stagger again into my past. My heart was fixed firmly on what I believed God had set before me to do, which was plenty for a young man fresh out of prison.

After the month with Gino, I hitchhiked down to Atlantic City and walked into the office of Asian Missions of America. AMA was a mission board that managed missionaries' practical needs while they were in the field.

It was the beginning of June, but I wore a long-sleeved collared shirt. During my rebellious years, I'd gotten a tattoo of a scorpion on my left forearm. Now, I was ashamed of it, so I kept it covered.

"Mr. Schumacher?" I asked with anticipation as I peeked into an office. My blond hair was trimmed short and my appearance was tidy, even after hitchhiking. "I'm Andrew Foworthy. We have an appointment."

Richard Schumacher, a thin, middle-aged man with glasses, had a poker-face, I'd say—one I couldn't easily read.

"Of course, Mr. Foworthy. Come in." He straightened his desk, we shook hands, and he motioned to a chair across from him. "I'm surprised to see you at all, actually. I thought you were still in, uh, prison."

"Nope. Done with that scene permanently." Briefly, I glanced about the office. There were pictures of men and women with natives from all over the Eastern Hemisphere.

"I was told I was meeting with a committee today. Am I early?"

Schumacher fidgeted in his chair. He was uncomfortable. I could read that much.

"I didn't think they'd be necessary." He leaned back, opened a cabinet, and selected a file with my name on it. "The last thing I want to do is discourage you from any phase of the ministry, Mr. Foworthy."

"Andy, please."

"All right. Andy. I, uh, took one look at your application and realized you don't have a financial plan whatsoever. If you had a dozen churches behind you to support you in a civilized country, I'd welcome you with open arms. But Mongolia? You're going to need some source of support."

It was my turn to fidget.

"Well, I'll have a little money when I get over there. I had a job in prison and saved every penny. It'll be enough until I find work there."

Schumacher nodded, his face blank. He studied my appearance and I felt the room temperature rise. Without thinking, I started to roll up my sleeves. I suddenly stopped with my scorpion exposed, then rolled the cuff back down. But it was too late. Mr. Schumacher had already seen the tattoo.

"What kind of special skills do you have, Andy?"

"Um. I wrote them in the application. Nothing specific. Just a lot of little things. I worked as a barber for a while. I'm pretty good at sewing, fixing things, stuff like that. I'm pretty well-read, so I know a little about a lot of things. Most importantly, I have a heart for the Mongolian people.

Ever since I heard Randy Erickson talking—"

"Oh, you know Randy?"

"Yes, sir. He and Gino Palucii led me to Christ seven years ago. They were the first two important men in my life. They introduced me to Jesus, the third but most important Man in my life now."

Schumacher shuffled through my file.

"Yes, I saw a letter of recommendation from a Gino-somebody."

"Gino Palucii. He's been discipling me over the years. He's an honest man of God."

"Andy . . . Mongolia . . ." He sighed with frustration, the same sigh Gino had given at my stubbornness. "You have no infrastructure. No money. No emotional support, except this Gino, of course, who is a dedicated, godly man, I'm sure. But you just got out of prison. You need—"

"Mr. Schumacher, listen: the money issue is not a concern. I can adapt over there. I'm sure of it. I'm staying with Randy and his family to start with. And I don't need you to manage my finances, only the other stuff. I've been writing Randy. He's the one who's been helping me put this together. Once I have a job and I'm set up, I'll be sending for Bibles and flannel graph materials and things that Randy says you guys know how to get into the country for teaching purposes."

"So, you'll be working with Randy in Ondorhaan?"

"Initially, but my heart is pulling me west and even south into the Gobi."

The man gasped and tried to cover it up with a cough, but he was noticeably surprised. His poker face disappeared.

"Okay, brutally honest?"

"Please."

"You've got no skills, Andy. No money, nothing. You want to go to one of the worst places on earth inside one of the toughest countries on earth—alone. What I suggest you do, is get your bearings now that you're out of prison. Speak in some churches. Raise some support. Gain some preaching and teaching experience. And most importantly, learn the language."

I forced a patient smile. Sometimes my juvenile temper rose up through my exterior, but I held it back this time.

"If you would've read my application, you would've seen I'm fluent in Mongolian at the conversational level."

Schumacher paused a few seconds in surprise, then flipped two pages.

"Oh. I see. And you read and write Cyrillic?" He narrowed his eyes. "You learned this in prison?"

"A Russian guy we called Russ taught me Cyrillic. I learned Mongolian from twenty-four cassette tapes. It's taken me seven years, Mr. Schumacher. I'm not merely an ex-con. In a way, I've been in Bible school getting trained and ready for all of this. I've been taking classes and reading everything I can get my hands on about Mongolia. And can you imagine people's response if I went to their churches asking for money and support? Not all of them, but many would be just like you. They wouldn't read my material and all they'd see is a big scorpion tattoo."

Schumacher had gone pale, which was not my intention. He stuttered a couple of words then shut his mouth. I rose to my feet.

"I'm sorry to bother you, Mr. Schumacher. I wouldn't have come except Randy asked that I meet with you before I left."

"Left? Um. When are you leaving?" He stood and straightened his tie.

"Tonight, on a container ship bound for Istanbul. From there, I'm hitchhiking to the Air Force base northeast of Adana to find a flight over the Caucasus Mountains, the Caspian Sea, and Kazakhstan—avoiding China as much as I can."

"And you're staying with Randy?"

"That's right, but it'll take me the better part of June and July to get there."

"Right, right. Well, you seem to have the boldness for it. You're really going for it then, huh?"

"It's a calling I can't shake."

He scratched his chin.

"Well, seeing that you know the language and seem to have some miraculous survival skills, which you'll need, I'll push your application through. Just make sure you stay with Randy and listen to him! He's been doing this for twenty years. Why you guys picked Mongolia, I'll never understand."

"I didn't pick it." I smiled. "God did."

"Of course. Well, welcome aboard, Andy."

And we shook hands.

...✝...

CHAPTER TWO

I had purposely chosen a Russian container ship to take me across the Atlantic Ocean so I could practice my Cyrillic writing. Mongolian Cyrillic had derived from Russian Cyrillic in the 1940s when Russia stood as a communist country beside Mongolia. The two languages were close enough for me to get some extra hands-on practice from someone besides Russ on the prison yard.

Gino met me at the harbor with my small pile of gear: a duffle bag, a backpack, a bicycle, and a uni-haul—a one-wheeled sort of trailer that attached to my bicycle seat. It was all I owned in the world.

Gino set the bicycle before me and admired its mechanics.

"There it is, Andy. It would take more than a sledge hammer to break those welds, I think."

He was right. I had designed the frame, and a welder from Gino's congregation had done the rest. The frame looked like a squashed, inverted *Y*, and the welds were as bulbous as fists on the aluminum alloy frame. It was a three-speed with one hand brake for the rear wheel. Extra precautions were made regarding maintenance. Once in Mongolia, a bike shop wasn't something I wanted to locate—though I'm sure there were parts shops in the larger towns. The frame was solid, though still sleek, with no adjustable parts that could rattle loose. The seat was welded in place, premeasured for my height. The wheels had been the trick for a low-maintenance machine. They were mags—hard, black plastic, with titanium sealed bearings. No lubrication would be needed. And the tires were solid poly. I didn't want an air tube patch kit to bother with or even a spoke wrench. The bicycle was essentially tool-free.

"She's beautiful, Gino!" I ran my hand down the frame.

"I still wish you would've let us paint it. It's a junkyard on wheels, if you ask me!"

"No, no." I flicked a finger at a metal flake. "That's the look I need. At a glance, nobody'll bother to consider stealing it. Besides, if it's painted, I might baby her. I don't want to do that."

"But you insist on calling it a 'her,' huh?" He laughed. "You've come a long way, Andy. It's been some years in the making. Just look at you. Off to Mongolia!"

I took a deep breath.

"You've been like a father to me, Gino, and then some."

"Come on now." With a wave, he hushed me, and dug into his breast pocket for a hard-bound leather booklet with a sturdy pen attached on a thin string. He handed it to me. "I want you to write in this every day. Write to me. You can't imagine what obstacles the devil will throw in front of you. He'll mess with you, tempt you, Andy. You're human, so you'll feel alone at times. That's what the journal is for. We'll call it your *A-J*—your accountability journal. After you fill a few pages, stick them in the mail to me. It'll help you keep your heart and your head straight because it'll also be our way of fellowshipping. A believer needs that, Andy. The church will be praying. Count on that. Trust the Spirit to lead you, and use the wits God gave you. The rest is easy."

Our parting was difficult. I didn't start living until I'd met Gino, and I'd been his project, so to speak, for seven years. Later, I found out he'd accidentally wandered into that prison infirmary the first time we'd met, when he was supposed to be on visitor status on his way to the chapel. God knows what He's doing!

...†...

I'd never been on a container ship, but thirsty Russian machinery doesn't discriminate. Though I'd signed on as a crewman, I had no idea I'd be an oiler for twelve hours a day. After stowing my bike in a locker on deck, I dropped my bags in my cabin, which I shared with three other crewmen. In the belly of the beast that was as long as two football fields, I greased any mechanical joint that moved. It was my first job outside razor wire, but I was happy to be on my way east. As for my Cyrillic studies, there was little time. My oiler companion and I worked for twelve hours, then collapsed in our bunks as the two others from our cabin took the day shift. As a beginning grunt, I pulled nights.

Not a night passed in those three weeks that I wasn't covered in grease from leaning over machinery to reach a joint or movable arm. I've wondered if American ships are cleaner in the engine room. To this day, I still feel that brownish-black silk under my fingernails.

When I wasn't sleeping or working, I was studying my Bible or on the top deck growing accustomed to riding the bike. There was plenty of length to the deck, though the containers filled most of the center deck space. The bike's center of gravity was higher than a normal two-wheeler, and I do admit to several crashes toward the stern. But I'll blame those wrecks on the sea spray and the roll of the ocean.

A ship that size is a small city, though I stayed to myself mostly. There were fifteen other crewmen throughout the giant tower that rose nine levels above to the bridge and control room—the cook, the two engineers, the navigator, the captain and his two mates, four oilers, and four deckmen. I never saw the deckmen do anything but lay around, so I developed a sneaking suspicion they were stowaways of some sort. When I tried to approach them, they avoided me like radioactive waste—after they got one look at the Bible in my hand. Thus, my socializing was confined to quarters with Lokva, my shift's second oiler.

Lokva was an older man of fifty, though he appeared to be sixty. Since he spoke slow Russian naturally, I didn't have to ask him to repeat himself. His mouth wasn't the only slow part about the gentleman. Most nights, he found a place below decks where he could just sit and oil a joint at arm's length. He was a tired, old peasant from Tomsk, he said, which was a state in Russia he hoped he never saw again. So, I oiled for the two of us and when we took breaks, we talked of his days in Tomsk. One night, he claimed to have seen God on a road once outside Novosibirsk and he said he hoped to never see Him again. All other advances about the Word or Christ were scowled away, so we settled into less important conversation to pass the time.

One morning, in the mess hall on the third level, I prayed aloud over my meal, and Lokva heard his name from my lips. He stewed about that for two days and nights until he finally approached me.

"It was not a curse, was it? It was a prayer for well-being, da?"

"Of course." I smiled. "Well-being before God for all eternity."

"Da, da! Who wants to live forever?" Then he stalked away.

Istanbul is a majestic old city, rich as any other with culture and heritage and pollution of both land and soul. It was a hub of all sorts for three continents. Since Asia Minor was such a focus for Paul, John, and other first century leaders, I would've thought it to be more Christ-oriented. It was quite the contrary, however, for though Turkey boasts tolerance for any religion, even its Christian landmarks, it's a traditional Muslim state—though a very worldly one.

I set my bike on Istanbul's thousand-year-old streets and peddled eastward. Twice, I had to ask for directions to the small pita bread shop where I'd arranged to meet Jim Beckley, a missionary serving the Istanbul area. He was about my age and he had some good advice for me.

"Don't be afraid to learn in silence," Jim said. "Where you're going, they have a violent dislike sometimes for those who try to change them. They've been forced to change in the past by both China and Russia over the years, and they're sick of it. They might smile and agree with you, but their hearts are contrary. God gives us the courage to take the Word to the people—but use your head. Show these people you're not afraid to learn from them and they won't be afraid to learn from you."

Though we'd spent an hour together, it was too brief. We both had places to be, so we went our separate ways, but Jim and I parted friends as well as prayer partners.

I peddled east and south through that day and into the night. Near midnight, I stopped between towns and pulled off the highway a good distance to set up a tent-less camp. It was nearly July and the weather was favorable, praise God, because a rain shower would've decimated my gear. My funds were too limited to rent shelter. That first night on foreign soil, I ate canned food and slept under the stars. Wild beasts prowled on the rocky, grassy steppes nearby, but I only smiled with my eyes closed. The God I served was Lord over even the beasts of the field.

In the morning, I wasn't on the road an hour before a trucker stopped to give me a ride. After he admired my bike for a moment, we strapped it onto the back of his truck, along with my trailer, and I stowed my duffle bag and backpack with me in the cab. The trucker spoke only Turkic, so our communication was limited. From a picture, I learned he was a proud father of a newborn baby girl, and husband of a smiling wife as plump as a cherry.

That evening, he offered the driver's seat to me, but I flat refused. He was too drowsy to continue driving and I hadn't driven since the last car I'd stolen at age sixteen. So he pulled onto the shoulder and we both slept in the cab until morning. I won't dwell on the lack of comfort through that night, but I was happy to be back on the road once daybreak came.

The Turk stopped at the next town and I continued on my bike. It was like this for three more days. Half the time I peddled, my legs growing stronger as the soreness faded; and half the time I was a passenger—thankful for every mile I could rest. A couple of the last drivers who picked me up spoke English, and God steered the conversations in a way that I could share my testimony and purpose in Asia. Seeds were planted, and Lord willing, there will be increase.

When I finally reached the US Air Force base in Incirlik, I was weary and barely able to speak. I merely showed my passport like a backstage pass, and collapsed inside a barracks on the first bunk I noticed. It must've been someone else's bunk because in the night, men roughly moved me down a row and covered me with a blanket.

The next morning, I was as giddy as a schoolboy as I ran about the base, searching for a free ride farther east. I was willing to set down anywhere inside Mongolia. The country was three times the size of France, but I'd get to Randy eventually in the far eastern side of the country on the Kerulen River. That's what my bike was for. Anywhere there weren't roads, there were game trails, since animals outnumbered humans several times over in Mongolia. But regardless of all the sorties being flown by the Air Force, no one was flying that far east. Most were headed south to Iraq, or southeast to Afghanistan.

At the end of the day, I found myself seated on a spare tire staring at the nearest runway. I wasn't defeated, only postponed.

"Lord," I prayed aloud, "I'm certain the answer is here. You've kept me safe thus far. Please, show me what to do next."

"Who you talkin' to, boy?" a man asked.

Jumping to my feet, I turned to see a man who could've been my equal as an oiler in the belly of a Russian ship. He was in his mid-fifties with white hair totally askew and a beer belly so large, it gave me flashbacks of one of my foster parents.

"I was praying."

He eyed the sky cautiously, maybe half-expecting lightning to flash down from the overcast heavens.

"Prayin' for what?"

"A pilot."

"What kinda pilot?"

"Any kind, as long as he's headed east. Are you a mechanic?"

"Among other things. I'm a base bum. Private." He shot his thumb at the military personnel hangers. "They don't touch my plane and I don't touch theirs. Where east you goin'?"

"Mongolia."

Again, he glanced at the sky.

"And this is somethin' you prayed for? A pilot goin' to Mongolia?"

"That's right."

"How often do you get what you pray for?"

"Well . . ." I shrugged. "As long as I'm in God's will, I pray for God's will to happen, so you could say, I receive everything I pray for."

He threw his head back and laughed. I chuckled with uncertainty until he suddenly became silent.

"I suuuurely wasn't expectin' you. Come on. I've got to pick up a thousand pounds of marmot furs in Havsgol." He turned and headed away. "First time I ever been a godsend!"

But I was motionless when I shouldn't have been so faithless.

"Hovsgol! Hovsgol, Mongolia?" I yelled after him.

"None other I know of!"

His name was Rex and he was a base bum. That was about all I got out of him before he introduced me to Tiffany. Tiffany was his plane, a 1936 PBY Catalina, silver in color, and in rusty condition. Two huge propellers were mounted on the over-wing assembly with internally braced cantilever wing and retractable wingtip floats.

"She's an amphibian hack-job that doubles as a small cargo and transport plane, but she hasn't dumped me yet."

The machine was a barrel of bolts with wings, no doubt about it, but I boarded this answer to prayer with my luggage as Rex ran a flight check. When he finally started the engines, the plane viabrated so badly, I put my seatbelt on before we'd even moved. I shook my head and laughed at the way God found ways to use anybody and anything— for His purpose.

"She sound a little off to you?" Rex asked me over the noise. "I jus' tuned 'er up. Them Kurds work for pennies!"

I shrugged. If the plane's prop engines weren't tuned properly, I wasn't one to know since I'd never flown in any type of aircraft before Tiffany. Remarkably, Rex didn't radio for any type of clearance from the tower before he taxied out onto one of the airstrips and pointed that blunt nose down the runway. He flipped a number of switches and levers, and I licked my smiling lips. Sometimes I smile when I'm nervous. Or maybe I simply didn't want to die frowning. Rex throttled us forward with a lurch. We spun sideways, backfired, then straightened out.

"Yee-haw!" Rex screamed as we flew down the tarmac and soared smoothly into the sky.

I sighed with relief and said a prayer of thanks. It was easy to trust God, but not so easy to trust God's tools—in this case, Rex and his flying boat.

...✝...

CHAPTER THREE

Pilot Rex pointed to a headset tangled in cable at my feet. I put it on to speak to him through his headset.

"You know, I'm flyin' at night for a reason," he said.

"I hadn't considered it."

Gazing out the cockpit windows, I saw looming clouds rapidly approaching, and the sky was growing dark.

"China has airspace issues right now," Rex said. "As if they've got anything we want! Ha! To be safe, we'll swing north into Kazakhstan and squeak across the border with Russia."

I nodded my approval, though I could say nothing anyway. My mouth was dry as a mental picture of Mongolia's bordering countries came into mind. Deep in the Altay Mountains, snow-capped year-round, Russia and China pressed against one another, as if the land itself were trapping Mongolia from escaping their clutches. It was impossible to access Mongolia without crossing into China or Russia first—Russian Siberia on one side, Communist China on the other. But I favored neither and prayed for Mongolian soil.

The drive of the vibrating propellers was strangely hypnotizing, and I must've dozed off because I awoke to a black sky and Rex yelling into my ear through the headset.

"Cursed Kurds!" he swore. "Not now!"

Something was wrong. I checked my watch to find I'd

slept for a couple hours. Rex punched one of the many dials on the dashboard until the glass broke and his hand was cut. He sucked the blood off his knuckle and growled audibly.

"What's happening?"

"My tanks didn't get topped off! My cursed needle was stuck on full. Everybody knows you gotta tap the thing!"

"So, we're low on fuel? Talk to me, Rex."

"We're almost to Kazakhstan's eastern border. We don't have enough fuel to make Bulgan or even Dund-Us. It's just a question of where we want to crash."

I acknowledged the compass heading, east-by-northeast.

"What if we shoot straight east and go for Mongolia?"

"Beats goin' down in Russia with no purpose at all, but we still have to cross Chinese air space." He nodded at me confidently. "I'm game if you're game, but you better start prayin'. We still have to get over those mountains."

I faced the darkness and felt the fear press on my chest. *All this way to die in a plane wreck?*

"Father in heaven," I prayed aloud.

"Me, too, Father!" Rex said.

"Lord, we come before you at a time of crisis."

"We're crossin' into China right now . . ."

"We need just a little extra fuel, Lord God, and You can drop us into Mongolia."

"Fine by me!" Rex said.

"You know our hearts, Lord. You know our past. We seek Your help in this most desperate of circumstances. Lord, I've spent years preparing for this mission. If it's Your will to take us down in China, then so be it. But Rex here, he could probably use some of Your saving grace right now, Lord. It seems he's not lived too godly a life."

"No, Sir, I haven't."

"And if we get shot down in Chinese air space, or fall to the ground from lack of fuel . . ." I glanced at Rex and our eyes met. He swallowed hard and gestured for me to continue, "then we want to die in Your good graces, in Your forgiving arms."

"Yeah." Rex nodded, his face full of worry.

"Your Son died on the cross and brought us near to You by His blood. And You conquered sin by raising Him up on the third day. Rex, do you believe?"

"I do right now!"

"Live or die, five minutes or thirty years left on our lives, do you take Christ Jesus into your heart by the power of His Spirit?"

"I . . . That's a mouthful, Andy!"

"Then say *no!*"

"Yes! All right, I'll take it. Live or die. Five minutes or thirty years, I'll straighten up."

"There it is, Lord," I said. "Your will be done. Put us where You want us. In Jesus' name, amen."

"Amen. And I'm sorry for cussin', too."

"That's between you and Him," I said. "Now, fly this baby, Rex!"

The engine sputtered. One prop went silent, then the other. A flash of light flew past the windshield. I blinked at the startling silence.

"Tracer fire," Rex whispered. Only the hiss of wind outside reached our ears. "It's the Chinese border. They're—"

Ping-ping-ping!

Bullets the diameter of nickels pierced the cockpit floor and passed clean through the ceiling. Glass shattered and sparks snapped as the windows and electrical circuits were decimated. Between my feet, I saw a new hole in the floor. Rex fought the controls as more ground fire whipped around the cockpit. Behind us in the cabin, bullets tore through my gear and ricocheted off a pulley system Rex had suspended from the cargo hold ceiling.

"We're almost to the Mongol border!" Rex yelled. "I'm losing control!"

"Are we high enough? Will we clear the mountains?"

He answered but I didn't hear him over the fresh volley of bullets. We were dropping in altitude, and I could now hear the thunder of the anti-aircraft weapons below.

"God, help us!" Rex shouted.

I glanced at him then followed his gaze through the broken windshield. The air was icy cold and stung my eyes, but in the darkness I saw the shadowy form of a giant snow-capped peak in front of us. The gunfire ceased below as we glided along. The night was strangely peaceful again. Rex banked our gliding boat to the right just a little to turn away from the looming mountain, but our decent was so rapid, we were falling from the sky more than gliding.

"Hold on!"

The Catalina's left wing scraped through ice and snow on the mountainside and pivoted us sideways. I gripped the edges of my seat. We flew toward a rocky ridge. I felt the belly of the plane tear apart. Rex still fought the controls, but it was no use now. My brow slammed against the side of the cockpit as the rear section of the plane was torn off. Bouncing off a glacier, we soared silently once again.

"This is it!" Rex stated as he braced himself.

We nose-dived into another vast field of white. Snow and rocks peppered my face, stinging me blind. The seat to which I was fastened ripped from its bolts and my head crashed against the ceiling, nearly breaking my neck. After being thrown onto my side, I unbuckled my seat straps and scrambled from the cockpit toward my gear with the thought that it could cushion the collision. We were still going over one hundred miles an hour, bouncing off boulders and snow, airborne for mere seconds, then slamming into the downhill slope once again.

I never reached my gear. The nose of the plane hit solid rock and upended in a front flip. Like a catapult, I felt myself rising through the plane fuselage, then flung through the opening where the tail was once attached. My arms and legs flailed wildly through the air. For a time, I was high above the plane as its own speed crushed itself against the side of a gorge. I was flying, and then I blacked out.

With a numbing shiver, I awoke. The sun was in my eyes and my skull ached. It took me three tries to sit upright. My whole body hurt. Dried blood caked my brow.

Shakily, I stood up on a glacier slope and acknowledged Tiffany's crumpled mass below me. Its nose was smashed halfway back to the cross-section of the wings—what was left of the wings, anyway.

We were in the bottom of a deep mountain gorge, ridges on two sides. Rocks were exposed through the snow in patches.

Running, I staggered down the glacier toward the plane. Debris was strewn in the Catalina's wake down the opposite glacier slope. My gear was sure to be among it all, but Rex was my first priority. Ducking low, I passed through the squished fuselage and crept into the upside down craft. I knelt before the compacted structure that had once been the cockpit. With a hand I covered my mouth. Rex had been cut nearly in half by the very controls he still gripped, his seatbelt holding him securely to his death. If I would've stayed in the cockpit, I would've also been crushed and killed.

I stumbled back out of the plane and searched the sky for an answer from God. *Had I made a mistake? Was I not supposed to be a missionary to Mongolia after all?* Angry tears rolled down my cheeks, and I screamed at the silent, blue sky that didn't answer back. My screams echoed up the gorge walls, then all was quiet again.

But I was alive, somehow, and I had to recognize that miracle. Yet, a mess of uncertainties flooded my mind. Had God saved me to send me a message that I wasn't to be here, or was the devil merely making things difficult? These were things I considered as I climbed the southern slope to retrieve items I recognized strewn across the snow. Ignoring the plane insulation and other construction materials, I picked up my duffle bag. The bottom was torn wide open and I shook it to loose a pair of pants and a broken flashlight. Though the flashlight was cracked, I took the batteries, then tossed the rest aside.

It was like this for two hours as I hiked to the south along the path the plane had left. I chased a curious squirrel from a pair of socks and retrieved my thirty-below sleeping bag. Most of my clothes were salvaged, but without the duffle, I was left with only a heaping pile of possessions. My backpack was thankfully without damage, and I found most of my canned food lodged amongst the shale. Discouraged, I shook my head at the sight of my broken uni-haul trailer; I should've had its welds reinforced as I had on the bicycle. The bike was in good shape, apparently sucked out of the tail end along with me.

Back at the plane, I studied the pile of belongings I needed to now fit into my backpack. Even if I found a way to repair my duffle bag, I had no way to transport it across the country since my trailer was a total loss.

The country! I suddenly dashed up the northern glacier. Using my hands, I clawed up the snow where it was steepest at the top of the ridge. As my head crested the top, I sighed through my panting. The most rugged land spanned far away from my elevated position. A formidable landmark was to the northwest, and at that instant, I knew where I was. It was the highest peak in Mongolia—Tavan Bogd Uul—where the borders of Mongolia, Russia, and China met.

Since I was southeast of the peak, I knew I was well inside Mongolia's Altay Mountain Range, specifically the Gobi Altays that tapered off into the Gobi Desert to the east and south. Then, I faced southwest. China. If we would've crashed closer to the border, I would've already been a prisoner of the Chinese. *Thank You, Lord.* I was exactly where I had asked to be—Mongolia.

So, facing east, I took a deep breath of the air I had

longed to breathe for many years, and felt a strange comfort at having arrived—even under those circumstances. God had brought me here, I was sure of it now. The crash was possibly for Rex's sake, which was an odd way of looking at it all, but Rex had been as terrified as me the previous night in the sky. I didn't know Rex's heart or how serious his belief was before he died. Five minutes or thirty years, he'd said, then asked for God's saving grace. It was a strange rationalization, but it put the entire crash into perspective for me. Maybe God took Rex home after his urgent prayer, and deposited me on the western edge of Mongolia, exactly as I had prayed for—and that was that.

It wasn't my place to question God, I decided, and stood up straighter and braced myself mentally for whatever might come next. A thousand miles to the east was Randy Erickson. I surely wouldn't reach Ondorhaan any time soon. Between where I stood and Randy were very few towns and plenty of rocky, low-lying mountains, rolling grasslands, sand dunes, and flat barren expanses. If the bitter cold didn't kill me, the land or its wildlife might.

Mongolia's geographic features were pretty simple— mountains to the west and north, desert to the east and south. And there was a vast river valley in the north-central region, where the capital and most of the country's population resided. But I was in the mountains, with forest below me. Then came the grassy steppes that rolled east, and very few people, which were mostly herdsmen, nomads, and farmers.

In the west and south was where I felt God had wanted me to minister, but not before I stayed with Randy in the distant city for a few months. But here I was. And it was with this understanding that I turned and descended the ridge back to the plane. I was a missionary now—alone, conflicted, haggard, and ill-supplied, but blessed in all relative aspects. Only a true Christian can know this feeling of peace, I believe, when everything else is in disarray. To God, there is no disarray. The devil may run rampant seeking whom he may devour, but this is still God's creation—though the devil's playground. Sometimes all we can do is trust God, and then we realize that's all He wants from us.

With a wary eye, I approached my gear, as if it were an adversary to further discourage me. However, I applied myself and picked out priority items that had to fit in my backpack or on my person. It was mid-morning by the time I had sorted through everything. On the ground, I made two piles—the abandon pile and the packing pile. I rubbed my hands together as I worked. The air was chilly, but warming by the minute as the summer sun rose above me.

After repacking my backpack three times, I finally had it all reduced to a manageable lot—a pocketknife, towel, ten cans of food, and my Bible. I had $200 in American cash, which was like gold in Mongolia, and a rubber band around a thin stack of stamped envelopes. Two changes of warm clothes, a sleeping bag, a lighter, and water tablets to help purify the water supply. Only thirty percent of Mongolia's rural citizens have safe drinking water. The most common beverage was fermented mare's milk across the steppes, called *airag* in Khalkha Mongol.

I had a bag of chewing gum for public relations

purposes, binoculars, hair-cutting scissors, and a sewing kit. Also, paperclips and twisty-ties, batteries, and an illustrated version of *Pilgrim's Progress*. Other things I kept were a single bar of antibacterial soap, a reduced first-aid kit, one roll of toilet paper, a toothbrush, a small tarp, a map of the world, a scarf, and a flare gun with three flares I took from the plane. Inside my coat I would keep my Bible and the journal, and I had a trenching shovel with an adjustable head and a two foot handle. That type of shovel was made famous in several wars, and I had figured it was an essential in this remote land. On my wrist, I wore a simple watch; on my head, a dark ski cap; and on my back, a warm coat. My three shirts were wool; my thermals were cotton and polyester. Army surplus combat boots would protect my feet from terrain and weather.

With almost everything set for my departure, I gorged myself on two cans of cold stew I was otherwise abandoning. Then, inside the plane, I used some of the extra clothes I wasn't taking to wrap around Rex's body. Though he was awkward and heavy, I pulled Rex out and buried him directly behind the plane under a pile of rocks the plane had already knocked free from the frozen ground. For a few moments, I stood before the humble grave, my cap removed.

"Lord, I didn't know Rex too long. I hope he's in Your presence now. Maybe in his panic last night, he spoke from a sincere heart. Please show me how to grow from this event, and give me Your strength to triumph through the next. I praise You for Your protective hand over my life. Guard me against doubting that Your hand is on everything.

Lastly, and maybe I should've thought of this sooner, Lord, but please make my feet swift before a Chinese patrol investigates their target from last night. In Jesus' name, amen."

With a sniff, I donned my cap, and with a permanent marker from the broken cockpit, I dated and wrote in Cyrillic on the outside of the fuselage: "Here lies American base bum Rex. Though he mistook a mountain for a runway, he seemed like an adequate pilot. I will send word to the embassy when able. Scavenge what you please. I can carry no more. Survivor Andrew Foworthy."

I thrust the marker into a pocket, then shouldered my backpack, the sleeping bag attached to the underside. Lastly, I fit the trenching shovel into one shoulder strap and picked up my bike.

"Rest in peace, Tiffany," I mumbled, and started up the slope.

When I crested the ridge again, the sun was directly overhead. Below me lay more rocky terrain where it ended in a thick stand of cedar timber far away. I would have to carry my bike until I was through the forest that girdled the mountain range like a mile-wide belt. Memorizing the terrain beyond the belt, I saw the mountains fading into green and brown rolling hills as far as my eyes could see. In survivalist training, I'd read that survivors were to remain with the downed aircraft until rescuers came onto the scene. But I wasn't lost. And I wasn't waiting for the Chinese military to find me. The Mongolian armed forces and border patrol was so limited in number that I didn't expect them to happen upon the crash site before winter.

Mongolia is called the Land of Blue Sky with an average of 257 blue-sky days a year, yet the cold was still deadly, especially at higher elevations. I needed to get down into the steppes where livestock and game had made trails across the land on which I could use my bike. On a smooth trail or road, I calculated I could make nearly one hundred miles a day with the bike, and that was taking it easy, when a normal mountain bike could cruise along at seventeen miles per hour on a good path.

I started down the mountain in a south-eastern direction. If I would've known how many eyes were watching me as I approached the forest, I may have stopped before ever reaching the trees. But ignorance is bliss, and in my ignorance, God watched over me as I trekked directly into danger.

...✝...

CHAPTER FOUR

When it came to living in the outdoors, I had experienced much less than what I actually knew. Book smarts can take a fella only so far, so I was trusting God to transfer my head knowledge of Mongolia to the center of my survival instincts. Eventually, I wanted to live naturally in this land, with my labors focused on sharing the Word of God. When I was growing up in New York, I'd spent many nights in the city's thousand-plus city parks—like Pelham Bay Park and Van Cortlandt Park in the Bronx. Though the parks have their wild sides, they're still set in urban surroundings. In Mongolia, winter temperatures range from five to twenty below—average. In New York City, the Atlantic Ocean tends to moderate weather extremes, and there's always an all-night laundry or donut shop to escape to, under the most dire of circumstances. In Mongolia, outside of the few and far-between towns, there's simply . . . wasteland. Yet, I had a strange peace as I hiked down the mountain range into the cedar forest. With a determined smile on my face, I conversed with my Lord on this beautiful day—perhaps my last—and saw no obstacle too great for my God.

As I stepped into the forest belt along the mountain range, I paused in the choking darkness and listened to the sounds around me. Here, I was familiar with the sounds of wind blowing through the branches and the constant chatter of squirrels. Pine, spruce, and white birch were before me, all but dwarfed by cedar trees with bases nine feet in diameter. *Nine feet!* This was virgin timber, never touched by man, though surely managed by God's system, including wildfire from time to time. There was an eeriness to it all, though, and I sensed I was being watched even then. I'd read that in the dense dampness under the boughs there were moose, giant brown bears, wolves, lynx, sable, and even reindeer. Many other species of animals were indigenous to the steppes where the rangeland spanned endlessly on the other side of the forest.

Creeping between the massive trunks, I felt truly small among the wooden monsters that reached from frozen ground to crisp sky. Patches of glacier and shale were nonexistent in the forest, but the air was still chilled. My breath vaporized in front of my face, though every step brought me to lower elevations where it would be more comfortable on this beautiful summer day.

Suddenly, I stopped and peered into the shadows on my left. Something large had moved twenty yards away, beyond a giant shrub that looked like solid fungus. There were endangered plants in this land of indefinite cold, but I wasn't interested in rare vegetation. I continued, my feet and heart both pacing a little faster.

Five steps later, I heard a whisper of movement behind me and to my right, then again to my left. Though I wanted to turn around and run back up the mountain to the wide open elevation where I could see what lurked around me, I had to travel through the tiaga forest sooner or later. It might as well be now, I figured. Stopping or running would've been a mistake, because I had a suspicion of what was out there. In prison, there were riots and frightening moments when my life had been in peril. At those times, I had simply put my back to the wall and begun to pray. There was no wall in the forest, but I could still pray.

"*Make me know Your ways, O Lord,*" I shouted in English at the trees. "*Teach me Your paths. Lead me in Your truth and teach me, for You are the God of my salvation! For You I wait all the day!*"

For an hour, I repeated those two verses from Psalm 25 as I marched through the forest. When I heard a scamper of feet nearby, I raised my voice to cover the sounds of stalking predators. Once, I paused long enough to pick up a gnarled branch that I could use as a walking stick—or a club if need be. I kept the stick in my right hand and pushed my bike along with my left, gripping it by the steering bar juncture.

A gray wolf with a slender muzzle and eyes like marbles crossed in front of me. It stopped to study me, then slipped away.

"*. . . for You are the God of my salvation!*" I repeated as another circled bravely into sight. There was nothing else I could do as they closed in around me.

My fear lessened as I realized I would have no chance of fighting off the wolves if they attacked. These creatures would have sensed my fear, anyway. Even if I used the 12-guage flare pistol, I had only three shots. I counted close to ten wolves. But as I prayed and yelled, my senses came to me as my adrenalin lessened. Hungry wolves would've attacked already, I reasoned. The land was plentiful with prey for the predators. They didn't need to eat me. They were curious. I hoped. Only curious. So, with nothing else to do but trust the Lord, I sang praises to the Creator of the highest cedar, for the same God who managed the timber also harnessed the carnivorous wildlife.

The forest began to thin, and I hastened without running to see what lay ahead. Emerging from the trees, I stopped in awe. I'd seen this from the mountain ridge, but now, I was here! At the base of the Gobi Altay Mountains, the desolate land sprawled before me like a sea frozen in its waves of grass and scattered bushes. The hills rolled high with a gentle grade, then sloped down into greener bowls where the ground was closer to the water table. I felt the ground tremble and a flock of vultures at the edge of the forest took flight. Two wolves not a stone's throw away howled mournfully as the earthquake lasted nearly a minute. Smiling, I raised my hands to the sky, tears of happiness in my eyes for being so transplanted from prison into the middle of God's creation. Behind me, and to the north and south, the Altay range was seismically active. Though I'd seen no steam yet, I had read there were also hot springs along the fault line.

A wolf padded out of the forest nearby. Lowering his head, he laid down on the coarse grass to watch me. He was a timber wolf, gray and black, with a sleek frame and jaws stained from recent kills. I imitated a canine whine at him and he barked back. Though I hadn't seen them, I knew the country had thousands of stray dogs that mingled with the wildlife, often breeding and intermixing with the wolves.

"Don't mind me," I said to him. He tilted his head. "I'll

be out of your territory in the morning."

The night was closing quickly, the moon already looming. On the open steppe, the bitter wind barreled down from the north with nothing to hinder its path. I made camp against the trees where the forest could give me some shelter from the weather and I could find fuel for a fire. Using twigs and fallen branches from the forest floor, I built a grand fire then sat with my back against a gigantic cedar to enjoy the flame's warmth. I could see the light reflecting in the eyes of the wolves as they drifted past my fire, their bodies not quite visible. And by the light of my blaze, under the starry sky, with a can of clam chowder warming next to the coals, I wrote this first journal entry:

"Gino, my first day here has been touched by both death and life. Without the patience of your teaching and challenging, I fear I would've faltered. By God's grace, I'm held upright through these struggles, and I thank Him with my every breath that He and you and others didn't give up on me so long ago."

I stopped writing for a moment. To the south, I listened to the wolves fight over a recent kill, snapping at each other for a piece of the carcass. For a moment, I recalled a night in my youth that I'd spent with an angry dog after I'd run away from my foster parents. God had been watching over me then, and He was watching over me now.

"The wilderness around me, and the savagery, is unlike the States, but it's strangely familiar as well. As wild beasts tear at each other selfishly for a morsel of food nearby, I'm reminded that such violence wouldn't even exist if it weren't for mankind bringing it into the world through sin.

Man sought selfishly for a morsel of food—the forbidden fruit. How simply and naively we destroy ourselves when there could've been infinite peace and harmony in God's perfect love.

"I trust you are well and safe, you and your family, and your congregation. I have prayed for your spiritual growth and well-being every day as I know you pray for mine. The journey across the Atlantic and through the Mediterranean was magnificent! My Russian hosts were both accommodating and demanding, as was the work . . ."

Writing into the night, I paused often to gaze up at the stars which I could see twenty times clearer without the smog and lights of civilization. *Mongolia!* And with this remarkable land came a remarkable people with whom I prayed I could share the Gospel.

...✝...

In the morning, the beginning of my second day in Mongolia, I saw no trace of the wolves except their numerous tracks around my camp. I had slept restfully, waking only twice to stoke the fire beside me. The vultures had claimed the carcass from the night before. They circled and squawked over what bones and flesh the wolves had left behind. For breakfast, I sloshed water around in my clam chowder can from the previous night, heated it to a boil, and drank it down. Since I hadn't expected to be stranded in the barren land, my food had to be carefully rationed. There were nine cans of food remaining. It was enough, I calculated, to last me four days. But my water would run out before that, even though I had filled my metal canteen with snow run-off the night before. Mongolia had its share of rivers in the central region, but they were scarce in the west and south. Water itself wasn't scarce; one only had to dig for it. If I could locate a region frequented by nomads, I would also find wells that were fashioned with nineteenth-century hand pumps if not a bucket and lever system.

Anxious to be on my way, I stomped out the coals, packed my gear, and climbed onto my bike. I slid my walking stick into place next to the shovel handle and started southeast. Until I found a trail, I had to ride and steer through the bumpy range land, which took some skill with my shoulders and wrists absorbing the pounding from the front wheel. Though it was a rolling landscape, it was mostly downhill as I headed away from the mountains.

After an hour, I stopped. My buttocks were already bruised and sore from the jarring, rough ride. I had expected to have my trailer to burden my gear, but now, the weight rested on my back, and subsequently, my rear end took a beating on the thinly padded seat. For a few miles, I walked and pushed my bike alongside, then paused once again at the top of the last significant hill. Behind me, the forest was a stand of green midway up the mountains. Though the trees provided some comforts of fire fuel and shelter, a sign of man is what I needed most.

I climbed onto my bike and coasted down the great hill. At the bottom was a dirt trail and I examined it for sign. Horse hoof prints were heading somewhat in my intended direction, but I was no expert at tracking; the prints may have been weeks old. Horse sign didn't necessarily mean people were nearby, though. The *aduu*, Mongolia's domesticated horse, made famous by the conquest of

Genghis Khan, ruled the steppes here. Though domesticated, when they weren't being ridden, they were loosed by their owners to forage. Oftentimes, they returned to the wild, needing to be broke again for riding. The animals wandered at will, from watering hole to graze land.

Peddling down this dusty, vague trail, I hoped to find a more developed trail, especially since it meant smoother riding for my troubled bones. All that day I traveled, walking up the steeper inclines, using my binoculars to scope ahead when reaching small rises. I watched for herdsmen, caravans, or even a road traversing the range, but there was nothing in sight.

Near sundown, my simple trail came upon a very small bog where mud had puddled to provide wild animals an inch of water. I'd received all my shots before leaving the States, but I had no interest in tempting some parasite against my healthy insides.

Weary to the core, I moved a distance away from the bog and made camp. I broke my stick over my knee until I could break it no more, and used it for firewood. It was a small fire, only large enough to warm my hands as I heated a can of stew. One can had been my lunch, which left seven in my stock. My coals glowed red for a while, and I read the Word, prayed, and wrote in my journal until my eyes would stay open no longer.

The next two days were the same, as I moved deeper into Mongolia's vastness. Twice, I came upon larger water sources, but I didn't pollute my canteen with the liquid—no matter how much it looked like healthy water. My canteen was still a quarter full, and though I had water purifying tablets, I wouldn't feel completely safe until I could boil the questionable, animal-trampled water. With no more fuel for fire, there would be no boiling.

But the next day, my water was gone before noon. All morning, I placed this concern before God, and near one o'clock, I found crystal clear water trickling out of a hillside into a wooden trough fashioned by human hands. I filled my canteen, dropped two water tablets inside to quench my paranoia, then quenched my thirst.

For an hour I remained at the trough, bathing and eating a can of food. Every few minutes, I felt the devil put fear in my head—fear that my food would soon be gone and I would starve to death. And about water—what if this was the last water hole for a week? Then what? But I had to shake my head and pray for God's help. He knew.

"I'm on the Lord's business," I'd say aloud. Then I'd look at the sky—which I have a habit of doing when I pray, though I know God is with us and not only above—and I'd say, "You know my provisions, Lord. I know You'll take care of all my needs."

Though I was still a baby missionary, I was quickly learning that the mission field is touch-and-go sometimes. Provisions and safety are so uncertain, one can only turn to God for the things that are otherwise out of man's control. I remembered the Israelites in the wilderness, Elijah, John the Baptist, and many others who weren't always certain how or what they would eat that day. But they depended on God, and He was worthy of such dependence. In a way, I was forced to trust Him.

...✝...

CHAPTER FIVE

That night, I ate my last can of food with a measure of excitement to see how God would provide for the next day. I didn't *feel* He would provide; I *knew* He would.

Since thunderclouds were rolling in from the northwest, I unfolded my thin, twelve-by-twelve tarp and covered my belongings as well as myself inside my sleeping bag. With nothing edible except gum in my backpack, it was unnatural that I slept so soundly. If it rained or sprinkled, I didn't hear it. The next thing I knew, daylight was shining through my tarp, and I could feel the early morning chill on my cheeks. Praying for strength, I drifted in and out of sleep, and welcomed the day with anticipation.

A critter wrestled with the edge of my tarp to my right. It could've been any number of little varmints. Maybe it was a curious bird or a—

It suddenly poked me in the cheek and I flinched with fright, but I couldn't move much since I was encased up to my neck in the sleeping bag. I stared wide-eyed at the critter that had poked me. But it wasn't a critter at all. It was a boy no older than three years old! He'd crawled under the tarp to see what stranger slept there. And then he poked me again! He was motionless, his eyes as wide as mine, his mouth open in the shape of an *O,* as if he were stuck between a question and an exclamation, the same as I was. I

44

finally gained my wits and grinned broadly.

"I thought you were a squirrel!" I said in Mongolian.

He giggled, then retreated on hands and knees from under my cover. I uncinched my sleeping bag and threw back the tarp. After tugging on my boots, I stood to stare after the boy as he ran east. Squirrel was all baby fat, and his three layers of skin and hide clothing wasn't helping his fleeing feet, but they cushioned his falls every ten or so steps. His clothing wasn't modern like that of a Mongolian citizen from a town. That meant he was from a nomadic clan, probably a Kazakh in this region. But I didn't care what kind of people they were; they were near! The boy disappeared over the top of a nearby hill.

After folding my tarp, I rolled up my sleeping bag in seconds. With my pack on my back, I was peddling after the boy in less than two minutes. Cresting the hill over which Squirrel had vanished, I climbed off my bike to admire the valley filled with life below me. Horses and camels mingled as they were herded together across the valley by herdsmen and women. Cattle were to the south, and sheep and goats were nearer to me. I didn't see any dogs, which I thought strange since I knew the Kazakhs prided themselves in their hunting and herding dogs—as well as eagles, their birds of prey.

Squirrel waddled and tripped through the sheep and goats as they parted for him. In the middle of all the livestock were ten huts, or *gers*, as they're called in Mongolia. A *ger* is a portable, round tent, too low to stand up inside, covered in thick felt in the winter and a lighter canvas in the summer—all over a wooden frame that was assembled or disassembled by the nomads at each campsite. Judging by the ten *gers*, I guessed five or six families lived in this clan, and other tents were used for storing provisions. And I believed this was a wealthy clan by Mongolian standards. So much livestock! Herding was still the principle occupation in the country. Even those who lived in the towns depended on these rural societies that were so isolated in the steppes, some of them sold stock only once a year at the markets.

Before me lay the heart of Mongolian life, and it was this heart I eagerly stepped off the hill to meet.

From Squirrel's alerting cries, a number of people emerged from the *gers* and herds. People already outside shielded their eyes from the morning brightness to see me. Squirrel ran up to a bulk of a man and hugged his legs. The man wore a long, drooping mustache that mingled with a goatee. His black shoulder-length hair was held out of his face by a fur hat. He rested his hands on his hips as I approached, the goats and sheep scattering before me. I could see this man had a presence about him that demanded respect. He looked to be in his fifties, and though I was a few inches taller than him, he outweighed me by fifty pounds. His torso and shoulders were massive. But his eyes showed curiosity, so it was this openness that I was drawn to.

Two other men stopped their camp work to stand behind their chief. One resembled the first, but was taller, broader, and younger. The other was short with broad shoulders, about my age, and seemed to prefer the bowl cut when it came to haircuts. His face was challenging, doubled by the fact that he firmly gripped a Russian AK-47 assault rifle across his barrel chest. At a glance, I counted nearly thirty people, mostly women and children, as they stood watching. Though Squirrel was dressed in the clothing of his ancestors, the adults wore coats unzipped down the front, and sweaters, as if from a Sears catalog. Their pants were wool and a few wore hide leggings. They also wore winter boots, which I knew they wore year-round.

I dropped my bike to one side, then raised my hand and smiled as I stopped five paces from the foremost man.

"Hello!" I said in Mongolian and bowed slightly. "I came alone from the mountains five days ago. It is sure good to see people!"

All raised their eyebrows, surely at unexpectedly hearing their own language from the mouth of a foreigner. They looked from my bicycle to what they could see of my backpack, and back to my face. As Jim Beckley had warned, these were a cautious, skeptical people. The books I'd read said they were quick to welcome strangers, but this small clan I'd stumbled upon was the exception since they seemed to be more isolated than most.

"You are . . . Russian?" the leader asked with a frown.

"No, I'm American, a traveler from the United States."

"Is America still at war with the Russians?"

"Um, we are often rivals," I answered carefully.

An uncomfortable silent moment passed. The one with the rifle shifted his feet impatiently.

"Ha-ha!" the leader suddenly blurted and raised his hands. "Then you are welcome in my camp! Any enemy of Russia is a friend of mine!" He held up a finger. "Unless you are Chinese or a Kazakh! I hate them, too!"

I chuckled nervously. So, he definitely wasn't a Kazakh. This was a Mongolian clan in Kazakh country, though.

"Very well. My name is—"

"Ah!" the man said. "I learned an English word from when I was last time in Dund-Us! Your hair—it is pond!"

Touching my head, I pulled off my hat.

"My hair? Oh, you mean *blond*."

"Yes! *Pond*. See?" He grinned proudly at his companions. "I am Gan-gaad. This is my clan. My brother Luyant." He nodded at the over-sized version of himself, then at the younger man with the challenging face and rifle. "And Dusbhan, my nephew. Come, Pond, you are weary. Dusbhan, take his pack. This is a remarkable bicycle!"

I stepped aside before I was trampled as Gan-gaad approached my bike. He stood it upright and swung a leg over the seat as if it were a horse. The seat was too far from the pedals for his short legs, and he couldn't quite take his feet off the ground to balance himself.

"Luyant! Push me! I haven't ridden one since childhood!"

The large brother moved behind the bike and pushed Gan-gaad into the sheep and goats. They bleated excitedly as Gan-gaad bellowed with laughter.

"Your pack, American," the younger nephew offered.

"Oh! Thank you." I slid my gear off my sore shoulders. With ease, he hefted the pack onto one shoulder, and cradled the rifle in the other arm. Since I'd grown up with guns on the streets of New York, and lived under them in prison, I gestured knowingly at his AK-47. "That's a fine rifle. I can see you take good care of it."

"It's for wolves," he said, then added, "but not only for wolves."

He gave me a threatening glare, then turned away. Perhaps to intimidate me more, he dropped my pack roughly on the grass next to the nearest *ger* and stalked out of sight amongst the herd of horses. That was when I noticed the spring bubbling out of the ground between the *gers* and sheep. It puddled in a six-foot-diameter area, churning sand from the depths of the earth, then snaked obscurely down the valley to the south in a narrow streambed.

"Move, Pond!"

I leapt aside as Luyant gave Gan-gaad a final push. He nearly collided with me, then crashed on the ground in a rolling heap. Gan-gaad caught his breath from laughter and found his feet. Leaving the bike where it was, he approached me.

"Forgive my brother." He nodded at big Luyant who stood nearby watching and listening. "His tongue is not all that is clumsy. He's an oaf! Look at him, a beautiful Mongolian specimen. Not an ounce of Kazakh in him, but he's never spoken a word. He just stands there, Pond. But he knows the camels. Yes, he knows the camels. Go on, Luyant. See to the herds."

Obediently, the big man hung his head and stomped through camp away from us. He was obviously not stupid, only mute. I watched him depart and wondered what had caused his condition.

"Is America really over those mountains now, Pond?"

Gan-gaad asked. "I'd heard they were conquerors, but have they grown so large?"

"No, nothing like that, though they are involved in a number of military conflicts," I said. "I crossed the Atlantic Ocean, and the Mediterranean Sea, then all of Turkey and Kazakhstan to arrive here. My plane crashed in the mountains about there, killing my pilot and sending me to you."

I pointed at a mountain to the far northwest.

"Huh," he grunted. "You were sent to me? You speak as a man who believes in providence from the gods. Did you see the wolves?"

"Yes, but they seemed preoccupied with other game. Had they been hungrier, I would've been a meal instead of only an object of curiosity."

Gan-gaad laughed and clapped me too hard on the back, making me stumble.

"You have a poet's tongue, Pond!" Then he became stiffly serious. "You know, we despise foreigners, especially me."

He watched me carefully to see how I might respond. I tried to match his hard eyes that were surrounded by skin as tough as leather from fifty of the harshest winters on earth. He had said I was a friend if I wasn't Russian, Chinese, or Kazakh.

"For many years, I've lived and dreamed of being in Mongolia. All alone, I learned the language. I'm not a foreigner as much as you'd think, not at heart."

"Perhaps . . ." He stepped beside me and pointed left and right. "Luyant cares for the camels. They are disgusting animals, but he loves them. My nephew, Dusbhan—you met him—has the highest honor: the horses. They are in excellent condition. Look at them! All fat! And there, my other clansmen watch over the cattle, sheep, and goats. The cattle are prized, but the sheep and goats—they are for scoundrels. I would never allow family to care for sheep or goats. There is my *ger* in the center. Luyant and his family are over there. He has only one wife. I have three, but two are growing old and one has no teeth. Dusbhan's *ger* is there, on the other side of mine. He has only one wife, but he is young. See? I am surrounded by relatives. How many wives do you have in America, Pond?"

"I am not yet married, Gan-gaad," I said. "In America, a man usually has one wife, but some want more."

"But you have none? You are poor?"

"When I find the right one, I will know. I'm patient about this matter. Tell me: don't you wish you were more patient with your choices?"

"Ah . . . I see." He nodded. "Patient for the best stock."

"Men like you who have experience have advised me to be patient, to find one with which I'm happiest and make her my first and last wife."

"But all the chores, Pond!" He pointed at the goats. "Look. All afternoon the wives milk the goats and mares. Then, there are other chores. Who mends your clothing?"

"I mend my own. Or I buy new ones."

"Bah! It's women's work!"

Most of the people had gone back to their chores, but some of the children studied me shyly from afar. I offered a teenager a pack of gum and she quickly took it and ran away, the others after her. A tall woman about my age stood amongst the sheep with a pair of shears in her hand. She didn't look my way but I could see her features.

"Ah, you see Zima already, yes?" He spat on the ground. "A Russian and Kazakh whore! My brother adopted her as a child for payment. She shames my clan. Tall as a man. It isn't natural, Pond. And skin like a Kazakh. But she is my brother's, so I can only spit at her."

But Zima, in all honesty, was beautiful. Her face wasn't small and round like the Mongolians, but more Caucasian with dark, straight hair. She resembled the Native Americans I'd seen in the States. But since she was a disgrace to Gan-gaad, I said nothing.

"Will you stay the day, Pond, or must you travel on your bicycle?"

"I've run out of food, Gan-gaad. It seems I must find employment to earn my keep for a time."

"Hmmm." Gan-gaad scratched his shaggy head. "I don't need another hand. Nor another mouth to feed. You have no money?"

"What's your offer? I do have a little money."

"You could buy some stock from me so I could buy supplies in Bulgan next week. It's southeast of us."

"I would need a *ger* as well—but not a whole one; I only need half a *ger*," I said. "Just a place to lay my head since I have only a small amount of gear and I have no wives."

"Half a *ger* will be a lonely place with no wife during the long winter," Gan-gaad said. "But we could move provisions from one into another to make space. It would be an odd thing for you to be in my clan. Others will think you are Russian. And they know I hate Russians."

"Perhaps you're a man who sees wisdom in a transaction," I said. "In time, the towns we come to will know I'm American. How much for a *ger* and . . . what livestock will you sell me?"

"I will sell one *ger*, but half will be for fodder storage, and five head of every animal is all I can spare. At the market, you pick which five, but otherwise, you help where help is needed, no matter which animal. Are you too proud to work with goats?"

"No, I have a close companion who is a shepherd and must often deal with goats." I said, considering the Good Shepherd. "How much?"

"Ten thousand *tugriks*." He watched my face as I contemplated the price. "You have this much?"

Quickly, I computed the currency equivalence. Eleven hundred *tugriks* equaled one US dollar. At ten thousand *tugriks*, he was offering me a poor man's fortune worth of livestock for less than ten dollars. In the city, an upper-middle-class family would earn no more than $2,000 a year. Here, though, cash was something of a rarity.

"It's a good price," I finally agreed. He sighed and smiled. "But I have only US currency, which comes to less than ten dollars."

"American currency? I will take it," he said without hesitation. "The men in Bulgan will think it's worth much more. Let me see it."

I dug through my backpack for a Velcro pouch containing two hundred dollars and my passport. Hastily, I counted out ten dollar bills and gave them to him. He held them up to the sun to study them, turning them this way and that, then flipped them all over.

"It's real money in America?"

"Yes, it's real. Some selfish men live and die by it."

"What will these buy in America? These . . . ten?"

"Any number of treasures." I shrugged, not wanting to discredit his livestock price, nor did I want to be dishonest. "When I was young, I had a friend who bought an automobile for one dollar from his father as a favor."

"A whole automobile? Was it a good automobile?"

"Not really." I chuckled at the memory. "It was called a Falcon, an old automobile that required more than one mechanic before it could be driven."

Gan-gaad folded up the money and shoved it under his shirt.

"I've never been in an automobile. There are many things I wish to know about America, but later." He took me by the arm and led me toward the cattle. "These animals are all we have, Pond. I hate them. They stink and are dumb, but I love them, too. Do you understand?"

"They are a necessity," I said, nodding.

"Yes. The Navi-hasgovi Clan wishes to ruin me by stealing my livestock and ruining our grazing land. We fight always. They have twice the men I have and many more livestock. Every year, we go to market in Dund-Us in the north. Navi-hasgovi is always there at the same time. But he is slower because his animals are greater in number. Now, we each race for the grazing land in the south on the edge of the Gobi before the winter kills the grass. Always, Navi-hasgovi is near. But today, we're ahead of him, and it's a good day. In a week, we'll be in Bulgan. After that, Hasagt. You know these places?"

"Only as names on a map."

"Map." He laughed. "I've seen maps and books. They don't do justice to life. I'm a socialist at heart, you know. I hate the *perestroika*. You know what that is?"

"Russia's restructuring." I nodded, familiar with the mid-90's movement away from communism—which Gan-gaad apparently disliked.

"I'm glad you know. I hate Russia. They ruined my family, but we fought them and kept our commune. Still, I fight the *perestroika* because they tell my workers they may privatize and take my livestock. You work for me now. I'll protect you from the *perestroika*. If you work, you receive an equal share. If you don't work, you receive nothing."

"Just tell me what to do." I nodded. Communism was apparently alive and well in parts of Mongolia. I had my work cut out for me.

"Go ask Luyant." He gestured toward the camels. "He'll tell you what you'll do besides standing guard."

He turned away, signaling that the conversation was over. I stared across the small valley at the huge man tending to the camels. Luyant didn't speak, so how would he tell me what to do?

Luyant wasn't like his communist brother whatsoever. Though Luyant was larger, he was younger than Gan-gaad, and that explained the hierarchy. With gestures and by example, Luyant patiently explained to me what I was to do. He gave me a tool with a moon-shaped blade and showed me how to clean each of the five different animals' hooves.

There were thirty head of horses that needed the least care, since they grazed where they pleased. I realized right away I'd need to learn to ride a horse. Sooner or later, I'd probably be climbing onto one of the twenty drooling, mangy camels as well. Above all, I wanted to prove to the chief clansman that I could and would handle anything he threw at me. It helped that I was coordinated, strong, and willing. Though it was too early to share my faith openly, there was no reason why I couldn't show it by my willingness to help.

..**✝**..

CHAPTER SIX

By noon that first day, I was standing alone on top of the hill crest to the northwest of the valley. My responsibilities seemed simple, but they weren't. I was to keep the animals grouped together while they grazed and let none stray too far from the others. The herd of goats had the greatest number of animals: close to eighty. The sheep numbered near fifty and the cattle, forty.

The difficult part would come when nighttime fell. I imagined the worst scenario: the wolves and bears would belly-crawl up to the camp perimeter from a down-wind direction. The animals would spook and crowd away from the predators, but in the morning, one or two would be missing, and I would be to blame.

The cattle could tend to themselves. The horses, especially the ones that remembered the days before domestication, would be safe since they'd lived on the open steppe before man. The camels had hooves that were deadly to any predator. So, the sheep and goats were my concern. They wanted to run around everywhere—in camp, out of camp, between the camels' legs, and out of sight on the range. I grouped them the best I could, but that first day, I wasn't much of a shepherd at all. Eventually, I found myself laughing at two kid goats who took turns head-butting one of the cow bulls. The bull, seemingly familiar with the game, kept his head lowered as the kids rammed him on his broad skull until they were thoroughly dizzy. Then, after shaking their heads, with their big ears flopping, they charged elsewhere. The bull acknowledged me as if to say, *"We do this daily. When their headaches wane, they'll be back for more. And I'll be here for them because it's all I have to do."*

Near sundown, my stomach was beyond growling. I was starving, and I won't deny the fact that I ate some grass since the animals made it look so appetizing. As a guest of Gan-gaad's, I half-expected more consideration. But then I remembered his words: food was earned. And I was being proven. Besides, I wasn't the only one standing around the perimeter. Luyant was still beyond the camels, and another man rode an *aduu* around and around the entire camp. The rider looked funny, I thought, since his horse's legs were so short and the man's longer legs often dragged through the grass. His saddle was hand-made completely of rawhide, worn but practical for the job.

The day closed, and I watched the clan crowd around their *ger* fires to serve portions from an assortment of blackened cookware. The smell reached my senses, and I fought to think of something else. My mind naturally drifted to my unfinished responsibilities that day. I'd spent no time in the Word and hadn't paused to pray much at all.

I lifted my eyes to the star-studded heavens. There were no clouds like the night before. It was a beautiful, crisp night. Though it had been almost sixty degrees all afternoon, the temperature had dropped quickly with the setting sun. If there was more precipitation to retain the heat, it would've been warmer, but it rarely rained there, and large bodies of water were scarce.

"Father God in heaven," I prayed aloud in English, "today, I find myself as a shepherd when I know more about being one of Your sheep. Give me the wisdom to approach this job wisely, and the strength to complete every step. And Lord, please open the hearts of these people to Your Word. I came so far to share so much, I don't know how long I can keep it in. Show me when it's time to open my mouth." Jogging down the ridge of the hill, I chased a ewe back into the herd. Then, I returned to my elevated place, checking the shadowy landscape behind me for prowlers every few minutes. "Lord, I've already sensed tension within the clan, and I pray You would open my eyes so I can stay alert for the doors You alone must open for me to minister."

"Is that English?" a woman's voice asked in Mongolian.

Startled, I turned to my left as Zima, the young outcast owned by Luyant, climbed up the hill with a bowl and pitcher. She handed me the meal.

"Yes, it is." I sniffed the food. Since I couldn't see it in the darkness, I asked myself if I really cared what it was. And I didn't. With two fingers, I scooped into pudding that smelled like spoiled venison. Ashamedly, I gulped half of it down ravenously before I remembered my manners. "Thank you. Your name is Zima?"

"Yes. And you are Pond."

She offered me the pitcher and I guzzled a thick, sour froth that burned all the way down to my gut. I knew what it was, but I hoped my stomach could handle it. It was *airag*, fermented mare's milk—this batch being a little more fermented than the casual beverage, I guessed.

Zima watched me eat and I suddenly stopped with a chill of suspicion moving up my spine. Everyone down in camp was eating, even those at the other perimeter posts.

"Have you eaten?" I asked.

"There . . . isn't enough," she answered hesitantly, lowering her eyes shamefully. "Gan-gaad said to bring this to you. You worked harder than me."

Just like that, I lost my appetite, and offered her my bowl.

"Here, take it."

"I can't!"

"Go ahead. Finish it," I said. "It's strange food to me, anyway. You must eat something."

She needed no more convincing and Zima scooped into the pudding with four fingers. Only on the Mongolian range could a woman eat like that and still be considered a lady. As far as Gan-gaad was concerned, though, she wasn't even human. It was my fault she wasn't being given her portion. Gan-gaad had said he didn't need another mouth to feed.

My eyes blurred suddenly, and I wavered on my feet, my head spinning. I sniffed the contents of the pitcher. The *airag* was quite a bit more potent than I'd suspected. Then, I dropped the pitcher. That was odd, I thought as I peered at my feet. There was no pitcher on the ground. But then I noticed Zima had taken the milk from me; I hadn't dropped it after all. She guzzled it dry and wiped her mouth with the back of her hand. Though I shook my head, the two Zimas I saw weren't blending into one. She giggled and waved her hand in front of my face.

"I think I'm drunk," I said, whether in English or

Mongolian, I don't recall, because I fell asleep at that instant. And I don't even remember hitting the ground.

...✝...

Since I hadn't been drunk in many years, and because it wasn't intentional, I believe God spared me the agony of a hangover. I awoke before sunrise and noticed someone had kindly thrown me and my gear into one of the *gers* packed with saddles and riding blankets. My feet had lain outside the door all night and my toes were freezing. After crawling outside, I stomped my feet to get the circulation going.

I wasn't the only one awake, though. Later, I found out that Luyant had thrown me in the *ger* and had pulled the early morning watch while it was still dark. But when I stepped from my *ger*, he wasn't watching the stock at all. He'd propped my bike up with a stick for a kick-stand and was kneeled beside it, studying the gear mechanics. Before he realized I'd approached, I crouched beside him.

"Fascinating, isn't it?" I admired with him. He glanced at me curiously, and nodded. "Sometimes the chain comes off the track when I switch gears without peddling. That's the trick: when you switch gears, you have to be peddling."

He stood and continued to nod, gently patting my shoulder as if to say he understood.

"Something needs to be done about Zima not receiving a meal because of my extra mouth to feed," I said.

Luyant's face hardened and he crossed his arms over his massive chest.

"Zima's like a daughter to you, right? She's your property?"

He hit me so hard, my feet came off the ground before I

landed six feet away on my back. I was so angry, embarrassed, and surprised that I sprang back to my feet like a cat. In prison, I'd fought for months, though it was years earlier. With the best of them, I could take a punch as well as sling them. He'd hit me on the cheekbone, which isn't a vital bone to knock someone silly; it only makes them mad. As a reflex, I swung an uppercut into his chin that nearly broke my hand. Luyant weighed one hundred pounds more than I, but a solid punch to the chin will drop just about anyone. His knees wobbled and he sat down with a dazed look on his face.

I stood over him, feeling pained in my heart, then unclenched my throbbing fist. *What had I done? What kind of missionary was I?* Slowly, as if stunned myself, I sat down next to the big man.

"Luyant, I'm sorry." He looked at me, but I couldn't meet his eyes. "I used to be a violent man but I thought that part of me was dead. I shouldn't be telling you how to handle your family. I should've trusted you to do the right thing yourself. I questioned your honor and I'm sorry."

Discouraged and disgusted with myself, I stood and walked back to my *ger*.

"Lord, what have I done?" I pled aloud. "I'm such a failure!"

Dragging my pack out, I hefted it onto my shoulders. There was no point in sticking around the clan. Barely a day had passed and I was completely destroying the testimony I'd sought to share of a peaceful and loving God. Angrily, I cinched tight my chest strap and turned to fetch my bike. Though I had no food, I didn't deserve any, preferring rather to starve to death on the steppe than pollute Christ's name in front of strangers any longer.

But when I moved for my bike, Luyant stood in front of me with a stubborn look on his face.

"I'm not going to fight you, Luyant. Just let me get my bicycle and I will leave. You'll never have to see me again."

Big Luyant stepped toward me. I could just feel my bones breaking already. Closing my eyes, I prayed it passed quickly, but not too quickly, because I deserved every blow. Instead, Luyant loosened my chest strap, lifted the pack off my shoulders, and set it on the ground. He set hands the size of frying pans on my shoulders as he stood in front of me and shook his big head sadly. Gan-gaad emerged from his *ger* just then and groaned through a stretch. Luyant ruffled my blond head and walked away.

"Pond!" Gan-gaad called as the whole camp awoke. "Get the packs from your *ger* and dismantle the camp! We move south today!"

Crawling into my *ger* while still reeling from the morning's drama, I pulled out three riding blankets and a number of animal packs, which I guessed were for the camels. People swarmed around me like bees to pollen until all but three dusty saddles had been snatched away. Two of the men produced wagons and an additional cart to which they harnessed two teams of horses. The other *gers* were nearly dismantled as I contemplated where to start on my own. The canvas covering the poles seemed like the right place, but they were tied down so the wind couldn't blow them askew. Maybe the poles were—

"Has a serpent bitten you?" Zima asked slyly as she

whipped a cord knot free on my *ger*.

I touched my bruised and swollen cheekbone, and smiled sheepishly.

"The biggest serpent I've ever seen . . ."

Luyant heard me and I saw him smile before he turned away with an armful of camel gear. Zima dragged the cord over my *ger,* taking the canvas with it. She threw me a corner and I helped her fold then roll it up into a tight bundle—¹all in one piece. Gan-gaad yelled for the camp to move out while I was still scratching my head about dismantling the rest of my *ger*.

"Pick up here," Zima instructed as she hurriedly pointed at the first exposed pole to the right of the door. She picked up the left. "Lift up, then push all the way around."

The poles were light-weight and bound in the middle and top of the *ger*. I lifted the first one and walked into the next. Like an accordion, the poles collapsed together toward the back, hinged on top, until Zima shoved all six spider legs into my arms. It was a seventy-pound burden I dragged across the trampled ground to a wagon where other *ger* poles were stacked. The second I had the poles in place, Dusbhan, the armed nephew, whipped at the two teams of horses and the wagon began rolling.

Zima ran by me, her heavy skirt threatening to trip her, and thrust my backpack into my hands. She climbed onto an *aduu*, used a short whip on her horse, and galloped to catch up to the others.

I turned in a slow circle. A couple fires still smoldered. The stream had been trampled by a hundred hooves. And my bike stood on its stick where Luyant had propped it.

Otherwise, the small valley was deserted.

Climbing onto my bike, I watched as the last of the camels disappeared to the southeast over a small rise. Two riders rode the flanks. Everyone else either rode their horses in the front, or climbed onto the wagons. The animals knew their salvation relied on the clanspeople, and they hustled to keep up with the parade. The riderless horses were the most independent, drifting along at their own pace, some of them two hundred yards away.

Starting forward, I stopped again, then set my bike aside and sat cross-legged on the grass. They wouldn't get so far ahead that I couldn't catch them. From my coat, I pulled my Bible and journal.

"Lord God," I prayed, "I feel overwhelmed by this disastrous start as a messenger of Your Word. I've struck a man and didn't use caution when drinking last night. Thank You for Your patience, Lord. Please give me wisdom. Give me the perseverance to continue, despite myself, the obstacles, and the trials. You know I'm just a man, Lord, so give me the discipline to keep my thoughts shameless when I'm close to Zima. I know I didn't come all the way around the world to lust after a pagan woman, so please keep me in check. As for Gan-gaad, Lord, if it's Your will, open his heart to my words. Thank You for Luyant's patience and not cracking my skull today. Oddly, Lord, even after our little fight, he and I seem to have a connection. Perhaps that's something I can develop since he's not kicking me out of the clan for striking him. You know I could use a friend or two in this world, even here . . ."

When I'd finished praying, I read through First Peter, an

applicable passage for those enduring the difficulties of the ministry, especially persecutions. And I wrote two pages to Gino, confessing my shortcomings to my brother in the Lord, as James instructs us, so Gino would know more how to pray for my specific needs on this side of the world.

My stomach was empty, so I filled it with water and hopped onto my bike. It took thirty minutes to catch up to the clan but no one seemed to notice I'd been missing. I set my backpack on the back of one of the wagons and peddled my bike with ease without the extra weight.

Zima kicked her horse over to me.

"Set your bike on the wagon, too." She held out her hand. "Ride up here with me. See? I have breakfast."

"Maybe tomorrow I'll ride my own horse," I stated, obviously disappointing her. She tossed me a twisted, dried stick of tasteless venison and rode ahead.

I'd never ridden a horse, but I knew the basics after I'd drilled an old cowboy in prison for information. He'd worked on a horse ranch down in Virginia years ago.

"It's easy, even for a city-slicker," he'd said, scoffing. "Rein to the right to go to the right. Left to go left. Back to stop. Heels to the ribs to get 'em goin'—but not behind the ribs! That'll get you bucked off in a hurry. Voice commands never hurt, either, and some horses are neck-reined and don't even need a bit at all. Where'd you say you were goin' again?"

Maybe it seems odd that I received my missionary training in prison, but you would be surprised how much knowledge and how many survival skills can be gained behind those bars.

I nibbled on my breakfast venison and admired the caravan around me. After Genghis Khan's empire had fallen apart, Outer Mongolia, the Mongolia of today, had become a province of China. The overthrow of the Qing Dynasty in 1911 separated them, and they became their own communist country by 1924. They developed as a nation with tsarist Russia encouraging it along and kicking the Chinese out permanently. When the USSR crumbled in the 1990s, Mongolia was essentially left to stand alone. The Mongolian People's Revolutionary Party (MPRP) was defeated as another political party arose, but the communist MPRP couldn't remain idle after so many active years. They won elections in 2001 and had been striving for exclusive power ever since.

When I studied Gan-gaad, I saw a product of all his country's conflicting movements. He claimed to be a communist, but he hated Russia and China, which had pushed Mongolia onto that track. Russia was a democracy now, and China seemed to be making similar steps, regardless of the recent rumors of military domination on several fronts.

Gan-gaad and his clan were rare, I decided. Even in the clan leader's lifetime, his country had grown and modernized in the eastern cities and towns, where there were even one hundred television sets for every thousand people. The world was privatized. The free press printed newspapers for citizens in Ulaanbaatar, the country's capital. They were combatted by communist propaganda, but the country was evolving.

And here . . . Gan-gaad ran his clan like a small dictator

runs a country. He owned all the livestock. Some of his customs weren't even found in the history books I'd read as he'd evolved on his own over the years, maintaining some traditions and disregarding others.

But the Gospel of Jesus' death, burial, and resurrection was for him, too. I'd come for the Gan-gaads as much as for the Squirrels of this ancient region.

"Pond!" Gan-gaad shouted from his horse not far ahead. "How fast is your bike?"

"Very fast, Gan-gaad."

"As fast as a horse?"

"Nothing's as fast as a horse," Dusbhan said from my right.

"Over a great distance, yes," I said.

"Then let us save the horses. Ride your bike to the north and see how far back Navi-hasgovi is behind us."

"Yes, Gan-gaad," I said, turning my bike around.

"I'll go with him!" Zima said.

"No! See to the children, Zima!"

Zima rode up to me as I zipped up my coat to keep my Bible, journal, and binoculars safe so I could travel at high speeds. My canteen was secure on the back of my belt.

"I must always care for the children." She dropped a pouch of more venison into my hands. "Everyone is talking about how you hurt Luyant this morning."

"Oh, I didn't know anyone saw." I frowned. "I was a fool."

"No, it was good. Luyant has said he will give me a portion every night. That was your doing."

"Luyant speaks to you?"

"Of course not. He writes. I taught him. And I teach the children now."

"Do you teach Mongol script or Cyrillic?"

"Both," she said.

"Could you teach me to read Mongol better?" I asked. "I only learned to write Cyrillic."

"If you teach me English."

"Maybe we should ask Luyant first," I said.

"As long as we teach everyone, he won't care."

"I should still speak to him about it," I said, pulling my cap down over my ears.

She pouted stubbornly, but I wouldn't discuss it further. I stood up to peddle to gain my speed away from the caravan, then settled into a brisk pace on the trail north. Switching to a higher gear, I felt the rush of speed as I cruised along faster than I'd ever taken the bike. Free of my pack, I felt light as a feather, floating over the hills and flying down them.

...✝...

CHAPTER SEVEN

I suspected I'd been sent on this errand so the clan could speak about me more openly. For all I knew, Gan-gaad could've been holding a tribunal for my demise at that very moment. But I welcomed the opportunity to stretch my legs now and feel the wind in my face—and to talk to my God. He was my only refuge in the world. Regardless of my errors, I needed to remain repentant and close to Him as I was His son and servant first.

When I passed our previous camp, I maintained my speed up through the hills that continued to increase in size as I got closer to the northern and western mountains.

By noon, traveling at a comfortable, average speed of about fifteen miles per hour, I'd put seventy miles behind me. My thighs were cramping so I stopped to guzzle some water to wash the acids from my muscles. Sighing tiredly, I tried not to think of the long trek back to the clan. Fortunately, they were moving only a couple miles an hour away from me.

I pushed my bike for a mile up a rocky slope that leveled off on a wide plateau. Finally, I saw dust in the distance. Through my binoculars, I studied what was known as the Navi-hasgovi Clan.

Gan-gaad was right to say they were a larger clan. I counted fifty men and women and hardly any children. They had twice as many men as Gan-gaad and three times as many wagons to carry their gear and feed for the coming winter.

But Gan-gaad was wrong when he said they were traveling slower. The Navi-hasgovi Clan had no sheep or goats, and they were moving swiftly across the plateau with only the larger livestock.

They were still a couple miles away when I turned back to the south and rode away.

...✝...

I stumbled into Gan-gaad's camp an hour after dark. Two men were on the perimeter watching the animals as they bedded down for the night. Exhausted, I dropped my bike against my northern-most *ger*, and noticed how everything else in the camp was set up exactly the same as the last time.

As I passed Dusbhan's *ger*, I heard a portable radio playing brass jazz from the 1950s, and an infant crying in another *ger*. Luyant strummed a horsehead-shaped, two-stringed instrument at a fire with Gan-gaad and a dozen others. When Zima saw me, she jumped to her feet and offered me a bowl of pudding, the same meal as the night before. These were the evening activities that I'd slept through the previous night.

Luyant stopped playing his *morin-khuur*, as the two-stringed lute was called, and all eyes turned to me for my report. I positioned my toes in front of the fire, which burned smoke-choking coal and horse manure. After I'd eaten three mouthfuls of pudding, Zima offered me a pitcher of *airag*, but I declined and drank from my canteen instead.

"They're gaining on us," I said between bites. "Maybe at

one time, they were a slower clan, but not anymore. True, they have more gear, but they also have more wagons to carry it and more cattle to harness. And they have no goats or sheep."

"How soon until they catch us?" Gan-gaad asked. One of his three wives at his side refilled his pitcher.

"We'll reach Bulgan before them," I said. "But they'll arrive the next day, by my calculations. They're two days back right now. After Bulgan, they'll be ahead."

"*Two days back!*" Gan-gaad said. "You rode that far?"

"Yes." I nodded. "I passed two of your campsites before I saw them at a distance."

"It's not so far. I could've ridden that far on horseback," Dusbhan said, boasting from behind me, having emerged from his *ger*.

"Two days there and two days back?" Gan-gaad laughed at his nephew. "You couldn't travel four days in one without eight horses to relay every hour! *Great Zanabazar!* That's far!"

"And now I feel pain in every joint." I grinned. "But I enjoyed the challenge."

Gan-gaad, quite drunk from his over-fermented mare's milk, burst into laughter and clapped his hands. Luyant continued to play his *morin-khuur*, and Zima moved closer to me. Dusbhan stewed a moment longer, then returned to his radio.

"I set your pack in your *ger*," Zima said quietly in my ear.

One of Gan-gaad's wives began to sing a *tatlaga*, a melodic, rhythmic song that told a story, usually sung by men, but in this clan, anything could happen. She sang about the earth and the sun and the marriage of the two with a band of clouds. This was yet another strange quality of Gan-gaad's socialism. He allowed songs of the gods of the traditional Tibetan Buddhism, also known as Lamaism. There were numerous religious symbols and designs carved or painted into their gear. Not everything was necessarily Buddhist, though. Zima wore a bracelet with tiny bronze figurines meticulously crafted. She fingered the ornament when she saw me studying it.

"It's all I have from my mother," she said. "My parents were killed in Dalandzadgad when I was young. The Russians' fault during the *perestroika*."

"I'm an orphan as well, but God gives us strength to continue, doesn't He?" Glancing at Gan-gaad, I saw he was drunkenly consumed with the music.

"Which god gives you strength?" she asked.

"I believe in only one God. He wasn't so weak that He could create only the sun or the trees or only the water. He created it all. He's the God who gives me strength."

She touched her lips to signal silence.

"Gan-gaad was afraid you brought your religion. You mustn't speak of it openly." She waited to continue as Luyant stopped then started playing a new song. "But you'll tell me, won't you? My father was Russian, you know. And my mother was a Kazakh. They used to argue because my father swore there was only one God."

"Tell me about this," I asked, pointing to her bracelet.

Zima touched a dangling bronze sun.

"This is my favorite—the sun god. He made the gods

that move in the day, I think. And this is the god of the moon. He made the night gods, like the owl and bat gods. You really think one God made it all?"

"I know it," I said. "He spoke with the first man and woman, and through time, to others. He helped them write a book of it all, from the beginning to what He'll do in the end."

"Oh! The Bible!" She checked her voice. "It's the Bible, yes?"

"That's right. You've heard of it?"

"Only because I'm Russian. Gan-gaad won't let me go into the towns any longer because I'm too curious." She giggled at the charge. "But I have spoken to foreigners before. I have government books only, but I once saw a library in Dund-Us at market. Gan-gaad curses me and says I'm smart enough to destroy him, but I don't know what he means. Then, he curses Luyant because Luyant allows me to learn and teach the others."

"I have a Bible," I whispered.

"You must teach me English so I can read it! Please, Pond!"

"It's in Cyrillic." I chuckled at her excitement for knowledge. "Every morning, I read about God and what He wants us to do. Then I pray and ask for His strength to live better for Him."

"And what do the words tell you to do?"

"To trust Him." I was about to explain more, but her face seemed so illuminated by the simplicity of this godly desire.

"To trust Him," she repeated, staring into the fire. "Trust that He made all things?"

"Yes, and that He loves us and gave Himself as a sacrifice so those who believe in Him don't die in anguish for the bad things they do. God is forgiving, but we must approach Him for that forgiveness."

"By praying," she said with understanding. "Every morning you pray?"

"I try to."

"When the clan leaves, you will stay behind to pray?"

Of course, she'd noticed my absence that morning when few others may have.

"Yes, I'll do that."

"Can I listen?" She raised her eyebrows in hope. "If I don't interrupt?"

I considered this. Were her intentions God-centered, or Pond-centered? Her request seemed innocent enough, and she was the only one who seemed open to new things.

"Okay, but we must be careful," I said.

"And you teach English this winter to everyone."

"This winter?" Remembering what I'd read about the long winter months, I knew they were spent in the *gers* since it was too cold to stay outside any longer than a few minutes. "We shall see," I said, holding my hands toward the flame. "I still must speak to Luyant about it."

In the morning, I was awakened by Gan-gaad's call for everyone to move out. I crawled out of my sleeping bag feeling more weary than the previous night. It wasn't even light outside! But it was my own doing for not going to sleep sooner. Pulling on my boots, I knew why we were getting on the trail so early: Gan-gaad was making sure we remained ahead of the trailing clan.

Zima was there to help me tear down my *ger* since she and Luyant's wife had already put theirs on the wagon. She must've been up early, because I noticed two horses picketed off to one side as the clan headed out—and my bike was in the wagon, too. No one glanced back at the camp as I stood there on the trampled ground. As soon as they were out of sight over a knoll, Zima leapt at me and wrung her hands.

"Let me see it!"

That morning, I gave my first Mongolian Bible lesson. I trembled excitedly as I introduced Zima to the basics of how we received God's Word, then set my Bible in her lap.

"We'll start at the beginning," I said, "by reading the history of God's people."

"There are so many pages!" she said with admiration. "Have you read it all?"

"Several times. Start here. And stop when you have a question."

"Me? Read? Aloud?" Her face lit up as the sun peeked over the eastern hills. "*In the beginning . . .*"

As she read, I opened my journal and wrote a page to Gino to share the news of some initial interest, even if it was only from a young lady in her late twenties. And if I taught English to the whole clan that winter, there were certain to be other hearts open to deeper questions about my beliefs.

Zima stopped often, even in the first chapter, to clarify little things like the singular-plurality of God in verse twenty-six. She read to the end of chapter three, then we both agreed it was time to leave. I tucked my Bible and journal into my coat.

"Now, I pray," I said, and folded my hands traditionally. She nodded and copied me sincerely. "Some people, when they pray to God, they bow their heads, and some close their eyes so they're not distracted. Some kneel, as if before a mighty king. Through the Bible, we see God as the One and Only Almighty God—but He's also our Father. The closer you grow to Him, the more you'll know how to address Him." I cleared my throat. "With you, I think I'll close my eyes."

"Okay. I'll watch," she said.

After bowing my head, I tried to concentrate. Thinking back, I felt like most of what I said were just words that first time. But she was curious and I wanted to show her how to pray.

"Dear Lord God in heaven, we come before You now in this vast land, Zima and I, Your servants. We thank You for Your forgiveness for the many wrongs we've committed in our lives, and we know that we need Your strength to live as we ought to. Thank You for what we've learned today from Your Living Word. Continue to teach us how to love and forgive others as You love and forgave us. In Jesus' name, amen." I looked up slowly. "At the end, many say, 'amen,' which means, 'let it be so.'"

"Amen," Zima repeated. "Your God does all of this?"

I rose to my feet and pulled her up with me. We were suddenly standing too close and I took a step back.

"He does it all and more. In the Book of Jeremiah in the middle of the Bible, it says He makes the sun, moon, and the stars shine. Also, He knows the number of hairs on your head. Nothing is too big or too small for Him."

She kept me talking, which may have been an intentional distraction, because before I knew it, she'd led me over to my horse. I mounted and took the reins in my hands.

"I'll race you!" she yelled.

Jumping onto her horse, Zima dug her heels in, and took off with a lunge. My own horse pranced sideways, anxious for the signal to go. I squeezed my legs around her thick torso, trying to figure out how to not fall off and break my neck. But the short *aduu* took that squeeze as the signal. The mare bounded forward after Zima as I tumbled off the back of the horse.

Landing on my face, I looked up in time to see Zima push her horse faster as she probably heard the hooves rushing up behind her. My mare, of course, hadn't come back for me. Picking up my tired body, I brushed off my clothes and started walking. It was destined, though, as I needed some one-on-one time with God. Around Zima, it didn't take much to have a one-track mind—she was so beautiful!

...✝...

CHAPTER EIGHT

For several days, our mornings began like this, though I fell off my mount less and less. We'd read for an hour, then race to catch up to the clan. Once caught up, I would see to the stray animals in case some had wandered off for a nibble of grass, but I otherwise rode toward the rear alone. Dusbhan kept his AK-47 handy and in sight at all times, and constantly cast me scowls, though I knew not why. He certainly didn't seem like a happy young man.

Two days outside the town of Bulgan, I saw Luyant alone and rode out to him on the right flank. My riding was improving, but anything faster than a trot, I still bounced all over the back of my beast like a rag doll. I needed a lot of practice.

Since Luyant was mute, we had a muted conversation. I had a pen and paper ready for this opportunity. Riding abreast of him as he admired the sky and landscape, I wrote my message.

"Do you object if I teach those who want to know how to read, write, and speak English?"

Passing it to him, I waited ten minutes for his response while he considered it.

"I don't object, but keep your culture to yourself unless you want Gan-gaad to break your neck. He hates foreigners. What have you been teaching Zima?"

As to the first part of his response, I understood—enough of the Mongolian culture had been lost to outside forms of collectivization and communism. But what could I say to his question? With Luyant, I decided the truth was the best route.

"I've been explaining to Zima the ways of the God of her father."

Luyant reined in sharply and scribbled hastily.

"That's worst of all! The Russian Orthodox Church killed her father! Whipped to death! You must stop this immediately!"

Instead of riding away, he seemed to sense I would respond, so he lingered next to me.

"God is a God of love. How can you inhibit knowledge of the truth because the Russians greatly mistreated and abused their authority?"

After reading this, he glared at me as if he wanted to punch me again. Perhaps God was using my mistakes for good, because Luyant's eyes drifted down to my hands and he winced, maybe in remembrance of the blow that had dropped him to his seat.

"Fine, but only Zima, since she's like you—and only in secret! If Gan-gaad finds out, I will swear I never knew."

"Thank you, Luyant," I said aloud. "I'll pray that you'll have an interest in the Lord God someday as well."

Before he could respond, I wheeled my mare around on her back legs and raced across the plain to the rear of the procession. Laughing, I bounced along with little control, and the whole clan surely thought I'd gone crazy. I pulled up next to Zima as she handed out that day's food rations.

"It's wonderful, isn't it?" I asked after she'd read our conversation.

"This is so important to you?"

My countenance dimmed. I'd expected her to share my joy.

"Pond!" Gan-gaad shouted. "Get the bike and spy on Navi-hasgovi! We are less than two days ride from Bulgan."

I parted with a wave from Zima and turned my mare over to one of the men's wives. Pulling my bike from the wagon, I zipped up my coat, and took off to the northwest. No farther than a mile out, I noticed vultures circling ahead. My heart skipped a beat as I knew what it meant—something was about to become vulture food. Changing gears, I sped faster.

Hitting my brake two miles later, I dove off my bike, relieved to see it was just an animal.

"Get!" I waved my arms at the bald-headed birds. "Shoo, get out of here!"

But the carnivores sensed death and hopped only a few yards away. When those circling above saw that I was harmless, they landed nearby as well.

I knelt next to a black and white kid goat that wasn't yet a year old. It craned its neck and cried up at me. He tried to stand, but one of his front legs dangled limply, broken. Opening my coat, I pulled him into the warmth of my chest as he shivered. With disgust, I kicked at the birds and returned to my bike. There, I examined the kid's leg more closely. It was a bad break. Gan-gaad would toast to goat meat that night, but until then, the kid was safe. For now, I zipped him up in my coat with his little head and floppy ears poking out just under my chin.

Continuing north, I reflected on the Scriptures. Much of the Old Testament involved people who were nomads, to some extent. I wondered if King David, when he was a shepherd boy, had found any of his sheep with broken legs. What had he done? Though I was a man who'd lived a hard life, my heart still lamented my little passenger's fate.

For two and a half hours, I rode hard before I quite suddenly came upon the Navi-hasgovi Clan. They appeared over a hilltop as I was just ascending it. Two men on horseback whipped their mounts after me. I turned and peddled like lightning.

"Get him!" one yelled.

If the distance had been greater, I could've worn their horses weary. But as I was only a hundred feet ahead when they charged, their mounts caught me easily. I braked to a halt as they headed me off, then others from their clan joined around on all sides. They appeared to be much the same as my clan when it came to clothing, but their faces were coarser, harder, and I sensed a whipping of some kind was coming. Their whips were short, held in their teeth or on their wrists by the loop at the leather end.

No one said anything, and I wondered why they waited, but then a Kazakh man on a dark *aduu* rode up from the approaching clan. The others parted for him and I faced him while still astride my bike. There was a time when I would've glared hatefully at those hard men around me, but I was no longer that man. I pet my passenger's head and ears, whispering comfort.

"We have seen these bike tracks before," the one on the

dark horse stated. He wasn't too tall, but had bold features. "You are with the Gan-gaad Clan?"

"I am. He's been a gracious host since I joined him a week ago."

"Your accent . . . You are Russian?"

"American."

"Really?" The bold man seemed shocked. "And Gan-gaad hasn't given you your own funeral yet?"

"He's a man of prejudice, but he's restrained himself from murder thus far."

"I am Navi-hasgovi. He speaks of me?"

"Yes, he does."

"Three head of livestock I have lost because of his carelessness just this week."

"How?" I asked.

"You don't know? Hmmm. I suppose you wouldn't. We push our stock hard all day. When we come to water, we find the pools trampled by Gan-gaad's cursed animals. My stock falls dead as they wait for us to dam the streams again. Gan-gaad does it intentionally."

I considered this, thinking back. The trickling streams had been rather destroyed in our wake.

"Warn him if he does it again," Navi-hasgovi said, "my men will leave our own stock to the wild and attack him. Rest assured, we won't stop until he replaces every head we have lost this year!"

"Okay, I understand." I nodded. "I'll tell him, and even if he won't listen, I'll remain behind next time and salvage the stream."

Navi-hasgovi raised his head.

"You ride your bike with a kid in your coat?"

"He broke his leg. In a few hours, I'm sure he'll become stew."

"You may go," he said, nodding at me. "We often winter near Gan-gaad. Perhaps I will hear your story in the coming months."

"I'd like that. My name is Andy, but I'm called Pond by the clan."

The hard-faced horsemen parted for me and I rode away.

...✝...

Again, it was dark by the time I reached my clan's camp, but I wasn't too weary since I was growing accustomed to the grueling days of riding. And that night, I was to stand watch over the herds and flocks—circling my mare around camp until I was to wake Dusbhan for his shift four hours before sunrise. Only one herdsman was needed at night with the principle male animals picketed to keep the others near. It generally worked without a problem. But some still wandered off as if sleep-walking, and there was the ever-present threat of a predator stalking nearby.

With reluctance, I gave my kid goat to Dusbhan after he volunteered to slaughter it, and he disappeared into the darkness. The women had made a stack of cakes to eat with the venison pudding that night, and I found it much more appetizing. There was a joke amongst them that I couldn't drink the strong mare's milk. Gan-gaad brewed it himself and made it strong on purpose. It was said he enjoyed more than a small buzz before he passed out in his *ger* every night. But my mind was settled contentedly on drinking only water or fresh mare's milk. The lactating mares were milked every two hours during the day.

Zima and I sat together as was becoming customary, and since she was often finished eating before me, she seemed to take pleasure in holding my water bottle or bread cakes as I ate. We were growing closer, which was inevitable with as much time as we spent together. I prayed for God's guidance in dealing with her.

"They've lost some time," I explained as I finished my food. "The Navi-hasgovi Clan is at least a day behind from livestock exhaustion."

"How so?" Gan-gaad asked.

"When we leave a watering hole, we're destroying the streams so the pools are ruined for those who follow."

"Hah-hah!" Gan-gaad belched and slapped one of his wife's knees. "And it has slowed him? Wonderful!"

"He requested that we leave the dams intact and the streams as we found them," I said. "Under threat of him attacking us, as well as realizing what's honorable, I assured him we would be more civil."

"Bah!" Gan-gaad laughed, then realized I was serious. "No! Who are you to speak for me? Pond, it would take too long to repair our sites. It's out of the question. Let his stock die. He would do the same if he were ahead of us."

"You know I'm an American," I said.

"Of course, Pond. A fine representative, too!"

"And I'm ignorant of many Mongolian practices."

"You'll learn our ways." He shrugged. "In time, you will learn."

"Wouldn't it be proper to show courtesy to your neighbor, regardless of his intentions?" I asked. "Let your neighbor's guilt be on his own head. Why don't we do the honorable thing?"

Gan-gaad stood abruptly, knocking his bowl and one wife to the ground. He glared at me with fiery contempt. Luyant, on my right, rose slowly. As a more cautious man, he glanced from his brother to me. I knew where his loyalties lay, but I wondered if he knew what was right.

However, I remained seated, feeling no need to stand and fight physically with the clan leader. Or his larger brother again.

"You're right, American!" he blurted, pointing a thick finger at me. "You know not our practices!"

"Then I will assume you have a plan for when he attacks us in full force," I said slyly, "all his men thundering down on us over a few head of cattle." I clucked my tongue. "I admire your courage, Gan-gaad. A lesser man would stand down in the face of sure defeat, but not you." Slowly, thoughtfully, he eased back down to his seat. "No, not you. This is why I ride with you, Gan-gaad. We ride to the death, the death of us all."

I raised my canteen to salute him. In his semi-drunken state, he probably wasn't sure if I was mocking him or actually sincere. Zima had started to squeeze my arm, but she relaxed as the tension passed.

"He wouldn't leave his herds to attack," Gan-gaad said.

"But he swore he would," I said, "and he wouldn't leave us until all his stock was replaced by our own."

"Let them come!" Dusbhan said daringly from the darkness behind me. The hammer slid back on his rifle. "I'm not afraid of them!"

Zima appeared as if she wanted to speak, but she wasn't allowed to be involved in the matters of men, and she held her tongue. Perhaps in a more modern clan than Gan-gaad's, her opinion mattered, but not here.

"To avoid a range war, I could stay behind every morning," I said, "and fix our sites while the clan moves on. I have a good shovel and I enjoy healthy labor toward a peaceful resolution."

Gan-gaad played with his mustache and Zima fingered her bracelet nervously. Luyant was still on his feet as if he were prepared to separate two lions. However, a dozen verses from the Bible were drifting through my thick head. *Be humble. Be gentle. Love never fails* . . .

"You don't know Navi-hasgovi like I do," Gan-gaad said with slurred words. "Last year he did the same thing to me all the way to Hasagt!"

"Even in the face of injustice, an honorable man maintains honor. If the whole matter is a bother, give it to me and think no more of it. You have enough to worry about."

"Yes, I do! Fine, Pond, you deal with the remains of our sites after we leave. Your reasoning is not realistic, but it is sound. Just be sure it doesn't interfere with your other duties. I'm going to sleep now." His wives helped him to his feet. "Wake me at the end of your watch, Pond. We'll leave then so we can reach Bulgan before sunset."

Dusbhan went to his *ger* as Gan-gaad and his wives went to theirs. A stone's throw away was the fire where Gan-gaad's other three men and their families gathered. There seemed an immense gap between the two groups, as if a caste system existed that I hadn't noticed until then. Rarely did the three other men even speak to Gan-gaad. Dusbhan was the one who gave them their few orders. The clan had been doing this for so long, their motions could be done in their sleep—their hearts had been that cold for so long.

"No one speaks to Gan-gaad the way you do." Zima said, beaming.

"It's only counsel." I shrugged. "Nothing more than what Luyant would offer if he chose to. Right, Luyant?"

Luyant stared into the fire, then glanced at me to nod once. He rose with his wife and left me and Zima alone. I stood and stretched with a yawn.

"I'd better get to the beasts of the field," I said. "No one's watching over them right now."

"You know, Gan-gaad won't allow the women to enter the town tomorrow," Zima said. "He says we come back to the clan too worldly."

"It could be true. Much of the West is coming through Mongolia's borders now. Not all of it is good."

"But you'll be going into Bulgan, won't you?"

"Yes, I have matters to address for myself as well as whatever Gan-gaad has for me to do."

"Would you bring me something?" She blushed in the firelight.

"Like what?"

"I don't care. Last week, I became twenty-eight, the day we met. Do you give gifts in America for celebrations?"

"Yes. I'll find you something." I smiled and put an arm around her shoulder. "A present, a surprise."

"Do you want me to stay up with you tonight? You

won't get any sleep if we leave at the end of your watch as Gan-gaad intends."

"No, you sleep. There's no point in both of us sleeping in the saddle tomorrow."

The rest of the clan went to their *gers* as I climbed onto the back of my mare and rode around the flocks and herds. I remembered reading in the Bible how Christ's sheep know His voice, so I softly sang several old hymns to comfort the animals—as well as to worship my God. It was a cold night, but I was happy to be involved in the well-being of the clan.

...✝...

CHAPTER NINE

It was an hour past midnight during my watch when my mare snorted and shied away from the western plain. My eyes were already adjusted to the darkness, but I still had trouble spotting the sulking creatures out in the grass. Sulking because it seemed the wolves were ashamed of their stealthy instincts and prowling in the night. To me, it was appropriate they seemed ashamed; there was plenty of game to attack, but here they were after my animals.

Several of the animals on the edge of camp had sensed the predators as well. I continued singing, regardless of the danger, and rode back to my *ger*. At the top of my pack was Rex's flare gun from the plane. Taking the gun and all three cartridges, I rode back to the western perimeter. When I'd loaded the flare gun, I climbed off my mare, selected a handful of hand-sized stones, and stepped into the grass.

I wasn't afraid. The wolves wanted a tender leg of lamb, not my unbathed flesh. Laughing inside, I made a mental note to bathe the next time I was sent alone on an errand. Gan-gaad and Luyant smelled worse than the camels, so apparently no one really cared.

Raising the flare gun, I fired into the sky. A loud bang pierced the night. The clan's animals flinched and tensed as a shimmering ball of fire glowed eerily from above. The crouching wolves were caught in a state of shock—exposed by the light.

"Get outta here!" I whipped my rocks at them with brutal force.

After half a minute, the flare burned itself out in the sky, but the wolves had scattered. I looked back at the *gers*. Only Luyant had been startled. From across the flocks in the moonlight, I raised my arm to assure him all was well. He returned the gesture and went back into his *ger*.

Comforting my spooked mare, I climbed back onto her.

"'*I am the Good Shepherd,*'" I recited from John 10. "'*The Good Shepherd lays down His life for His sheep. He who is a hired hand, and not a shepherd, sees the wolf coming, and leaves the sheep and flees.*'" The animals in camp settled back to rest, moving close to one another for warmth on the cold night. "'*And the wolf snatches them and scatters them. He flees because he is a hired hand and is not concerned about the sheep. I am the Good Shepherd, and I know My own. My own know Me, even as the Father knows Me and I know the Father; and I lay down My life for the sheep. I have other sheep which are not of this fold; I must bring them also, and they will hear My voice; and they will become one flock with one Shepherd.*'"

"Only a fool would lay his life down for a sheep," a quiet though challenging voice said.

I reined up as Dusbhan strode toward me, cradling his AK-47 in his arm, as always. He smoked a cigarette, then flicked the butt at a ewe as he drew closer.

"If the Shepherd truly loves His sheep, He will die to save them," I said.

"Once he's dead, the wolf will still get the sheep."

"The wolf dies with the Shepherd," I insisted, "then the

Shepherd comes back to life to care for His sheep."

Dusbhan passed me, cruelly slapping the nose of my mare. He lit another cigarette as he eyed the darkness for more wolves.

"So, the Shepherd comes back to life and there are more wolves." Dusbhan continued to challenge.

"The wolf that died with the Shepherd was the father of all wolves. He represents evil," I explained. "The Good Shepherd destroyed the father of evil."

"And what do the sheep represent?"

"People who need a Shepherd."

He puffed on his tobacco and looked up at me.

"Where did you get this story?"

"It's from an ancient text that describes the heart of man and other mysteries."

"I don't like it." Dusbhan cast me a glance. "Besides, I don't need a shepherd."

"Have you never felt insignificant in this amazing world?" I asked with a sigh. "I'm not a great man, but I have met a few. The best of them admit they are lonely in this world, small and powerless to sickness, death, and the elements of the wild. So they depend on something greater than themselves."

"What is greater than man?"

"The sun is greater than man," I said. "Some worship the sun. But the sun cannot care for us or love us or correct us. So I look higher."

"Higher than the sun?" Dusbhan admired the sky. "You worship the stars?"

"The stars cannot love me, either. At times, all of

creation may seem against me. Logic tells me to worship the Creator, not the creation."

"There is nothing that is not created. How do you worship?"

"Through admiration. Through obedience to ancient texts of men who've learned what the Creator desires of His simple sheep. And by loving and caring for other sheep around me."

Dusbhan flicked his cigarette butt at the grass and blew smoke at the stars.

"You're a foreigner. What can you know about life here?" He looked at me again. "Every day is the same. There's no end. Someday, I'll lead the clan. That will be nice for a while, but then I'll be like Gan-gaad. And the days will be the same again. I'll always need something more."

"Yes, perhaps." I nodded. "Unless you had a purpose to pursue. Something to seek while you live this simple life. When I was growing up, I lived in a huge city. The buildings were ten times taller than the tallest cedar you've ever seen. A man, even a proud man, begins to feel small there. Everyone eventually attaches themselves to something they feel completes them, or makes them feel more important or useful. Some choose money, but they can never get enough money to feel happy or fulfilled. Some choose women or drugs. All of those have their limitations. It seems wisest to choose a Being that has no limits."

"You're talking about your Good Shepherd again," he said with understanding. "It seems too simple."

"The decision to follow Him is simple. I've never

regretted it. But others are selfish and eventually die for no purpose. Something to consider," I suggested. "Something to think about on all the days that seem the same."

I urged my mare farther around the perimeter and left Dusbhan standing there. Having given him plenty to consider, I didn't want to push him. Besides, it wasn't me who would change his heart, but the Holy Spirit who had to work in him. It was my job to plant a seed. From a distance, I watched him. For a long time, he stared at the sky, smoking. As I made my rounds, I prayed for him aloud in English.

At three in the morning, I woke Gan-gaad as he'd asked. Though I'd had a long day and night and needed sleep, it would have to wait. The camp rose, dismantled the *gers*, and trampled the landscape in its departure. Zima and I remained behind as always, but with a chore to do before we sat down to read and pray. By the light of the moon, we used our hands and my trenching shovel to rebuild the dam so the stream could pool for Navi-hasgovi and others who would follow. I made the pool deep with the dam half-constructed by rock so it was stronger and more likely to be noticed by the coming hooved creatures. What small wonder I could've fashioned with a little cement!

In the glow of a single piece of coal in the early morning darkness, we poured over the Scriptures. I wrote Gino of the possible breakthrough with Dusbhan. A seed had been planted, and I asked Gino and his small congregation to pray for him.

"I don't understand why Joseph didn't punish his brothers," Zima said as we climbed onto our mounts to pursue the clan. We'd just finished Genesis. "He had the power and they were certainly in the wrong."

"Well, I believe he set for us an example to be loving and forgiving," I said. "Above all, God guided his heart to save his entire family who would become a great nation. It's a lesson that is stressed many times in the Bible: '*Love covers a multitude of sins.*'"

Instead of racing back to the clan as we normally did, we reviewed Genesis, and it was noon before we reached the clan at a wide creek that traversed the steppes from the mountains. Though there hadn't been one previously, Zima and I built a dam above the trail. Then, we raced to catch up to the clan again, where I loosed my mare and climbed into the back of a crowded wagon to finally sleep.

"Pond! Pond!" a voice boomed.

Waking with a start, I tumbled out of the back of the wagon. Zima and several of the youngest children were there to laugh at me. She tossed me a stick of venison and a wild potato she'd recently unearthed. Her sparkling eyes held my gaze, and I became more fully aware of her intentions toward me through that one look.

"Pond!" Gan-gaad yelled as he galloped his horse back to me. Worry creased his face. "My son is ill. Do you know medicine?"

I looked to the front of the caravan where Squirrel usually rode in the back of another wagon with his sisters.

"Some," I answered. "Take me to him."

Jogging, I went ahead with Gan-gaad as Dusbhan rode in from the left flank to see what was happening. The cart, driven by Gan-gaad's second wife, didn't stop rolling as I climbed into it. The four other children moved away from Squirrel who lay on his back. He'd messed his drawers and vomited since he was in too much pain to climb out of the cart to do so. After checking a few of the obvious vital signs, I found he was running a fever and delirious.

"Has he eaten anything strange lately?" I asked the eldest of his sisters, Chita.

Chita shook her head. In the week that I'd been with the clan, the children hadn't spoken to me. They'd been so warned of evil foreigners, they only stared and hid from me, but perhaps were hoping for more gum. Squirrel was the exception. He was so mischievous, just as he'd been from the first moment I'd met him when he'd poked my cheek.

I tenderly touched Squirrel's abdomen. It wasn't until I pressed on his right side below the ribs that he yelped and began to cry.

"His appendix has burst," I told Gan-gaad. "How long has he been like this?"

"Since yesterday. Is it serious?"

"He will die very soon without a doctor's care. How far are we from Bulgan?"

"Still five or six hours. You know his illness. You can cure him."

"No. He requires a minor surgery. Any doctor can perform it, but he'll need antibiotics. Medicine."

"I'll take him and ride ahead," Dusbhan said. "Give him to me. I have the fastest horses."

"No," Gan-gaad said. "Pond is faster on his bike."

Dusbhan scowled as his hopes to save his cousin were dashed.

"Let Dusbhan take him." I said, not waiting for Gan-gaad's approval. "I'll ride ahead and find a doctor and have him waiting and ready by the time you get there, Dusbhan."

Picking up Squirrel, I held him out to Dusbhan who rode alongside. He pulled him close and cradled him much better than I ever could while riding my bike. Without a parting word, Dusbhan urged his horse into a run to the south. I leapt off the cart to find my bike.

"Pond, watch the doctor!" Gan-gaad ordered. "Stay with him as he cares for Marbin! The doctor may be Russian or Chinese!"

"We'll make sure he's safe, Gan-gaad."

I sped away on my bike. The trail had turned into a packed, centuries-old path as we drew closer to the town. Dusbhan's horse had settled into a steady canter by the time I caught him.

"Find the largest hospital in town!" I instructed. "I'll be there to meet you."

"All right, American." Dusbhan carried Squirrel stiffly in one arm as if he were unaccustomed to children.

Peddling ahead vigorously, I was so focused on the glimmer of the town ahead that I didn't acknowledge the sound of tires on pavement until a semi-truck and trailer roared past me! Astonished, I steered to my left, rode down then up a ditch, and onto a well-paved highway. The highway was in good condition, so I put my head down and pumped ahead. Cars and trucks occasionally passed me as I rode on the shoulder. Praying for speed and safety, I reached the town in less than thirty minutes.

...✝...

Once or twice in our lives, God allows us to experience an event that forces us to contemplate our mortality. That was the look of concern I saw on Dusbhan's face as he watched through the small window in the door of the clinic's operating room. As Gan-gaad had feared, the physician was Russian. After only a couple questions, though, I realized the man was as competent as anyone I'd go to in New York City.

"He'll be well now, Dusbhan," I told him. "You got him here in time."

"I had a sister once, you know." His eyes didn't leave the operating room window. "She wasn't much older than Marbin when she fell ill. Luyant didn't know what to do. He didn't trust the doctors. So she died and Luyant never spoke again." Our eyes met. "The world is changing. Gan-gaad and Father are afraid, but they let us bring Marbin here. Now he doesn't have to die."

"It could be their hearts are changing, too," I said.

"That is your doing, Pond. I listen to my radio and know more than Gan-gaad and Father. The Good Shepherd is your God. You have brought Him here."

"God is everywhere. He listens to the prayers of His humble people. But He won't force Himself into our hearts. That's a decision for each man and woman—to follow Him."

"And your ancient text is the Bible, isn't it?"

"It is."

"The Russian Bible people killed my grandfather. Gan-gaad—"

"Gan-gaad can't stop the power of God," I said.

"Already, Luyant knows I have a Bible. He knows the Russian religious leaders who killed his father weren't loving men who honestly represented what is really written in the Bible about the Good Shepherd. In just the short time I've been with your clan, I've learned that Mongolia is hungry for the truth the rest of the world has already taken the opportunity to accept or reject. Mongolia and people like your father and uncle, they can't keep God out any longer. It's the reason I came."

"Luyant knows you follow your God so devoutly?"

"He knows, but he is wary."

"But this . . . Good Shepherd, He's more powerful than Buddha?"

"Buddha was a wise but worldly teacher—and he was just a man. I've studied much of Lamaism," I said. "Buddha didn't wish to be made into a center of worship like a god. He wanted others to reach true enlightenment. From what I've read, Buddha sought the Good Shepherd, where all wisdom originates, all enlightenment, but Buddha didn't know how to find Him because no one told him about the true God, or he chose a different path. And he fashioned a form of worship as he tried to understand the purpose of life. Then he died and left behind followers who shared his pursuit for purity and perfection. God holds the answer to all of these vain pursuits—the pursuits of man to save himself. Buddhism has become a tradition and source for spiritual meaning, but God—the Good Shepherd—*is* truth. Only He fulfills and quenches that thirst and saves us from ourselves."

"No, I don't want to hear any more!" Dusbhan said

harshly. "I want to read of it myself. If He is all you say He is, then I won't be left wanting if I seek the truth, right?"

"Truer words have never been spoken. I'll find you a Bible of your own. You'll stay here while I run some errands?"

"Gan-gaad and Marbin's mother will be here soon."

I left the clinic to see more of the town I'd ventured into. Here was a civilization trapped between two ages: the ancient that still herded animals on the open steppes, and the modern world of technology and advanced enterprise. A small section at the western end of town had been purposely left behind in the town's modernization to accommodate the nomads when they came to town with their stock. Gan-gaad had made camp outside of town, and since he'd already taken his stock to market that spring in Dund-Us, his business in Bulgan was confined to purchasing supplies for the coming winter.

The few people on the modern streets reminded me of pictures I'd seen of Native American reservations from the 1980s. They wore jeans, sweaters or long-sleeved wool, and light coats or jackets since it was a summer night. I blended into the town nicely. By my blond hair, I would be characterized as a Russian descendant, so I kept my cap on. But Gan-gaad, with his hide leggings and ungroomed exterior, would announce his status as a nomad. His place was at the western edge of town.

Thinking of grooming, I touched my cheeks and chin to find almost three weeks of thick growth. I hadn't shaved since Istanbul, nor bathed in over a week.

It was after eleven at night by the time I located an inn. I paid in US cash. The next day, I'd have to convert what I had into *tugriks*. It cost me another two hundred *tugriks* to use the inn's lobby phone. The clerk listened as I connected through two different switchboards to reach Ondorhaan. But the clerk seemed disappointed when I began speaking English.

"Randy!" I exclaimed. "So good to hear your voice!"

"Andy?" he asked sleepily. I was calling very late.

"Yeah, it's me."

"Wow. It's great to hear your voice. Everyone thinks you're dead. Praise God, you're not!"

"My plane went down southwest of Tavan Bogd Uul. And my pilot was killed, an American named Rex, but I escaped without injury. I'm mailing you a package tomorrow with details to get to the embassy in Ulaanbaatar."

"Okay, I'll take care of it. How are you? Where are you?"

"I'm in Bulgan now. And I'm doing okay, living with a nomadic clan. You can pray for me, because it's not without its difficulties, but I'm reaching the people with the Gospel and finding a small life in which I can be used."

"Oh, that's wonderful! So are you even going to come east?"

"Maybe next spring," I said. "Listen, I'll be in Hasagt in two weeks. Is it possible to send me a package of Bibles?"

"Absolutely. We just got some in from Irkutsk. It helps to have the only international railroad nearby. How many do you need?"

"Can you spare five?"

"I'll have them waiting at Hasagt station. Anything to pass on to Gino? He emails me twice a day for news on you."

"Tell him I'm well. God is gracious. And I'm mailing you letters for him in your package tomorrow."

"If you're ready for Bibles, does that mean you're already breaking down the Lamaism barrier?"

"Not without tension, Randy. How are things there?"

"We have two congregations, but they seem stagnant. I was really looking forward to your arrival to shake things up. There's also been some refugees pouring in off the railroad from China. Things are getting pretty hostile in the south, Andy. '*Wars and rumors of wars*,' as the Bible says."

"'*Watch and be ready*,'" I reminded us from Scripture. "Maybe I can come after winter, if the Lord wills. I'd leave now, but I'm neck-deep in sharing with these hungry souls."

"That's great, Andy. I'll spread the word that you're alive and we'll wait for your package."

"I may not be able to reach you again until May."

"May?"

"Unless it's by letter. I'll do my best to set up a mailbox in Hasagt. How's that?"

"Yes, do that! We'll help you with costs, just let us know. You need to stay in touch. No telling when you'll need a few more Bibles."

"All right, Randy. Say hello to the family. Sorry I couldn't make it out there."

"Hey, you're preaching the Word where you are, so don't even apologize. God bless, Andy. We'll be praying."

"You as well. Bye."

When I hung up, I sighed aloud as if a huge weight had been lifted from my shoulders. There's a certain comfort in the fact that the people you care about, who also care about you, know your condition. Perhaps that's a superficial identification, but I was once again connected with the outside world. They couldn't do much for me in many respects. But Bibles and prayer? That was a priceless connection!

My rented room was actually heated! The bathroom was a community situation down the hall, and though I was bone-tired, I showered in hot water. I redressed in my dirty clothes since my pack and belongings were with the clan. Before I bothered hunting down a razor, I decided to let my beard grow to protect my otherwise tender skin since winter was fast approaching. On a spring mattress, I fell asleep, my Bible on my chest, its pages open to Psalm thirty-four. There was certainly joy in serving the Lord.

In the morning, I took advantage of my late checkout and lay in bed until mid-morning. I knew it would be one of the last times for many months that I'd be able to relax in relative quiet. Besides, the clan wouldn't move on for a few days, not until Squirrel was free of IVs. My few responsibilities with the clan did call at me, though, and I hastened to plan my errands after another hot shower. Lastly, I wrote a final note for Gino, then one to Randy.

At the Hasagt Bank of Commerce, I exchanged the remainder of my funds for *tugriks*. I was left with over a hundred thousand *tugriks*, a small fortune by nomadic standards.

At the post office, I packaged up pages of my journal

and my letters into a secure envelope and sent them on their way. I had included approximate coordinates of my downed plane for the embassy to recover Rex's body. Chances were that Rex would stay where he lay since the area was both remote and soon to be under several feet of snow at that elevation. For loved ones whom Rex may have left behind, I made certain it was known that he'd called upon God in his final moments of life. Surely, some would be comforted by that news. Others would be angry, but I couldn't stress over things in God's able hands.

I was one errand short of returning to the clan, and I found myself in a delicate situation. Zima couldn't come into town herself, so I'd agreed to select a present for her. But Zima and I both knew it was more than just a gift I'd be delivering. In truth, it was an item of courtship, which made me uneasy since Zima wasn't a follower of Christ, yet there was some escalating romance.

Now, I had learned to take II Corinthians 6:14 literally. So, being yoked to a nonbeliever would be a recipe for a life of sin for me. The flesh would always chase sin, so Christians must live by the Spirit. We see that fact over and over in the Old Testament when God instructed His people not to intermarry with pagans. But the Israelites didn't listen and often fell for their wives' gods.

Also in my mind were Paul's words in Corinthians as he reasoned for the single man or woman. There were advantages within the ministry for staying single. Thus, I had decided long before if I were to marry, she would first be a believer and like-minded with me, and second, she would be a mutual helpmate in our efforts to spread the

Gospel. The gifts and the calling of God are irrevocable, and I couldn't allow anything or anyone to come before my work for the Lord.

So, why was I picking out a gift for Zima? I prayed my intentions were pure.

I bought her a mirror twice the size of my hand, rimmed with flowery decorations. It was made of flexible plastic, making it safe for travel, but it reflected as well as glass. And as for the rest of the clan, I purchased South Korean chocolates. Though Gan-gaad hated foreigners, I hadn't heard him mention the Koreans directly, so I hoped I wasn't overstepping my generosity.

...✝...

CHAPTER TEN

As I rode my bike west out of town into the countryside with the Gobi Altays rising up around me, all thoughts of what I'd bought for the clan were forgotten. The Gan-gaad Clan, minus Gan-gaad, if he was still in town, was sprawled out in its usual fashion. A water pump was in the middle of the camp, the flocks and herds opposite the *gers*. But what caused my mouth to go dry was that Navi-hasgovi and his clan had arrived that morning after pushing through the night, and his herds needed water badly.

The men of both clans faced-off. Dusbhan spoke for the Gan-gaad Clan, while his mute father, Luyant, stood at his side. And Navi-hasgovi shouted for fairness amongst his men. A war was brewing. Worse yet, since Mongolians don't usually use branding, the women of both clans were running frantically about to keep the mingling animals separated. Some of the stock desperately wanted water, while others simply wanted to wander curiously through the other clan's herds. The Gan-gaad Clan was outnumbered two-to-one. I arrived with the intention of taking no one's side. Words from Romans came to mind as I dropped my bike and ran between the two companies: "*If possible, so far as it depends on you, be at peace with all men.*"

I pulled off my hat to show my blond distinction amongst them, and as one of the tallest present, I found

CALLED TO GOBI | 107

some barbaric rational to settle them to silence.

"This cannot be sorted out by yelling or fighting!" I said strongly. "The matter is simple, especially between two peoples who live off the same land!"

"He's Kazakh, Pond!" Dusbhan said with hatred. "Gan-gaad would never—"

"Quiet! Gan-gaad isn't here, and if he were, he'd want to keep his camp separate whether he wanted to assist Navi-hasgovi or not. Now, Gan-gaad's clan will move twenty meters to the south of the well. Navi-hasgovi, you take the north by twenty meters. That should—"

"Everyone knows it's colder in the north!" Navi-hasgovi argued. "We want the south!"

"It's twenty meters, forty combined!" I said in disbelief. "The temperature isn't—"

"Who put you in charge?" a Navi-hasgovi man demanded, then shoved me into Luyant.

Somehow I kept my balance. But Luyant shoved me away from him back into Navi-hasgovi. The yelling began again and the bodies pressed closer. The brawl started as most do, I suspect. Someone shook a fist and another misinterpreted the gesture. Someone punched me from behind as I faced Luyant, and Dusbhan pushed me aside to wrap his hands around Navi-hasgovi's neck. The only pleasing thing to see was that of the few guns and many knife blades possessed by the two clans, none were brandished.

I was knocked to the ground and stepped on. A heel stomped my fingers and I felt my blood begin to boil. In all my years on the street, and during my rashest days in prison, I had welcomed a good rumble now and then. But around me was chaos with no sense of remedy whatsoever. And in the melee, there seemed only one way to communicate.

Wading through elbows and fists, I found Luyant. I dragged two men off of him using a choke hold, not hurting them at all as I rendered them unconscious on the trampled grass. When I gripped Luyant by the collar, he swung at me, his eyes not quite focused from the whipping he was both giving and receiving. Ducking under his blow, I punched him in the gut to steal his wind and his fight for twenty seconds.

"Help me stop this before we lose everything!" I ordered Luyant.

Once he gained his senses, he nodded, and we stepped together into the brawl—which, I should add, was more wrestling than actually fist-fighting. Mongolians love horse racing, but they love wrestling more. Luyant and I double-teamed our own clansmen to drag them away from the others. As soon as Navi-hasgovi realized our intentions, his men backed off under his direction. Dusbhan was the last to be hauled away by the seat of his pants by his own father. Luyant deposited him at the edge of the scuffle.

Everyone stood or sat panting for a couple minutes, grass and grime in our hair and ears, our noses bloody, and plenty of hateful glares cast both ways.

"That's it!" I waved my arm. "Navi-hasgovi, give us a few minutes to back away to the west and you may have the east!"

"But—" someone from my clan began.

"I know they're closer to town, but someone has to concede somewhere! It may as well be us since we're the ones who'll lose altogether if we keep fighting! Navi-hasgovi, can you share the water pump with us?"

"If you take the west, yes."

"And we can share the pump?" I checked again. "The animals as well?"

"We can if you can."

"Luyant, your word is law in Gan-gaad's absence. Will our clan peacefully share the pump?"

Huffing like the bull he was, Luyant nodded hesitantly.

It took thirty minutes to sort out the livestock and move them and the *gers* twenty paces west of the pump. The few mischievous goats that had wandered into Navi-hasgovi's herds were quickly identified and caught since the wealthy Kazakh had no such flocks. His stock was watered in turn, then his *gers* were erected beginning twenty paces east of the pump. Their watering took the better part of four hours as the camels alone could hold twenty-five gallons apiece and hadn't been watered in over a week on the fierce march south.

Meanwhile, the wives saw to my clan's wounds, and Zima saw to my broken fingers with a heel print still showing below the knuckles.

"Gan-gaad will be furious you didn't beat them all and take their herds when you had the chance," Zima said as I grit my teeth at the pain while she set my fingers one at a time. "Do you have any idea how much he hates Navi-hasgovi?"

I winced as she straightened and braced the last finger.

"Then I'm glad he wasn't here today. A little blood is better than a lot of lives."

When she was finished, she held my wounded hand and pet my fingers. I can't say her touch was unwanted. That would be a lie.

A shadow loomed over me then.

"I will tell Gan-gaad all you've done here, American!" Dusbhan stated hatefully. "All of it! I will counsel him and my father will rid you of our clan!"

Rising to my feet, my mouth had a dozen things to bark at this youth, but I swallowed my pride, barely.

"If Gan-gaad wants me gone, I'll go, but I'll miss you all."

"Well, if he leaves, I leave!" declared Zima boldly as she rose to her feet.

Dusbhan cocked his arm to slap Zima, but I saw it coming and reached across to catch his wrist. He struggled against my stronger grip, even with damaged fingers.

"You aren't yet this clan's leader," I stated softly, our faces inches apart. "Someday, you may be. Leave nothing behind you that will darken your heart too deeply with regret. It will cloud your choices in the future."

I let him wrench his wrist free, then he stomped away. The whole clan was watching us, and I felt foolish for drawing so much attention with so little resolve. Zima clung to my left arm. She moved behind me as if in hiding from her own clan. Luyant cast us both a warning stare that gave me a chill.

"You could've been a warlord!" Zima whispered in my ear. "Your words alone defeat them all!"

Shocked, I turned to meet her gaze.

"*A warlord?* Haven't you learned anything?" I asked. "I desire peace, as God desires peace. And I certainly don't desire followers. Violence makes me sick and pride brings out the worst in all of us, especially me! The lack of compassion I find in this clan disgusts me!"

Pulling away from her, I climbed into my *ger* to escape it all. For a moment, I was disappointed I'd bought the mirror and chocolates. Everything was a mess now. In my frustration, I refused to communicate with God and I flopped onto my back to pout.

As I reflect now upon those first days in Mongolia, I see myself as a child. I was a child of God, yes, but I was also an immature believer, unstable in the gifts that were necessary to adequately fill the position of a missionary. When I finally came around to humbling myself before the Lord, as I did that night, He took on the burdens of my inadequacies and imperfections, and renewed in me a pure heart. After I wept in my *ger* that evening, I sought the Lord's strength and patience to continue. I emerged from my *ger* with the armor of God, ready in meekness to approach the next challenge. One of the first was to approach the clan.

I found Zima at the evening campfire with Dusbhan, Luyant, and their wives. Two of Gan-gaad's wives were also there with their children, but the clan leader and Squirrel's mother were residing in the town while the boy recovered. Multiple children from the combined families sat or played nearby.

Zima and the others were halfway through their meal

when I sat down next to her. She handed me a bowl she'd prepared. By now, no one ever offered me fermented mare's milk. They knew I drank only water or fresh milk from the goats or mares.

Before I took a bite, while all eyes were still on me for arriving late, I cleared my throat.

"I apologize for losing my temper this morning," I stated. "My actions were like a spoiled child when things don't go my way. This is something I need to work on in my life. You have all been kind to me. I consider you all to be companions and friends, and I will try to be a better companion and friend in return."

"Apology not accepted," Dusbhan said quickly. "Even if I hate you for it, you're the only sane one here. Without you today, Gan-gaad would've had no flocks or herds or even a clan to return to. That's what Luyant says, and I must agree. Eat your food, American."

Raising my eyebrows in surprise, I smiled and took a bite. *What a turn of events!* With relief, I saw the same message on Zima and Luyant's faces, and I put my arm around her shoulder in a half-hug. She patted my leg in understood affection, and we ate the remainder of our meal in silence. After the meal as the animals settled for the night, the camp's children ran off to play before they were rounded up for bed. Luyant played his *morin-khuur* and Dusbhan went to his radio.

When we were alone, I drew Zima toward my *ger* and handed her half the chocolates I'd bought in Bulgan. I took the wrapper off one and popped it into her mouth. She gave a melting expression.

"I've never tasted anything so good!" she said. "Maybe raspberries, but it was so long ago."

"Take your half and help me pass them out to everyone."

And we did just that. Little to the mothers' knowledge, the chocolate had the children awake until midnight, but the clan wasn't traveling, so it was more amusing than it was troublesome.

I also went to the other fire where Gan-gaad's sheep and goat families ate their meal. They all received a chocolate, though some tried to refuse out of humility. However, I insisted, and I foresaw a time when I could introduce them to a greater Gift—the Gift of love through Christ's sacrifice.

While the children once again left their beds to run about the camp, I approached Luyant and Dusbhan with my extra chocolates. There were only four left and I gave two to each of them.

"What do you suppose we should do with these left-over chocolates?" I let them think about that for a moment, each one starving selfishly for the candies. "Perhaps . . . give them to someone who hasn't been given one?"

But everyone in the clan had received one, except for Squirrel, and I had his safely stored in my *ger*. Dusbhan chuckled quietly as he understood my intentions.

"You don't expect us to . . ." Dusbhan shook his head and looked toward the large camp of Navi-hasgovi.

What I suggested, or implied, was truly absurd in their minds, but I could see them considering an avenue of kindness they'd never before considered toward a rival.

"The chocolates are yours to do with as you wish." I shrugged. "I expect nothing of you."

Praying they did the right thing, I sat down next to Zima at the fire as she braided a horsehair bridle. The other women saw to the cookery—having given up on recapturing the children. I watched Dusbhan reason in whispers with his silent father as to what they should do with the four chocolates. Excess was foreign to the clan, as were simple delicacies. They'd been given a difficult responsibility, one they took as seriously as if I'd given them four camels to do with as they wished.

"I wish Gan-gaad were here to see how happy you've made everyone," Zima commented.

"It's okay that he's not," I said. "The chocolates are from a foreign country."

We laughed the tense day away, along with its misgivings and violence, and I felt closer to her than before having experienced it all with her.

Dusbhan and Luyant seemed to have decided upon some course of action and left the campfire, walking to the east. For a moment, I thought they might only be going to the water pump, but they passed it and called out to those in the Navi-hasgovi camp. Navi-hasgovi came forward, as did several other men. Though I couldn't hear what was said, I was pleased they weren't wrestling again! After a few minutes, Luyant and his son returned to the campfire, each with a grin they couldn't hide. As he passed me on the way to his *ger,* Dusbhan gave my shoulder a friendly punch. All animosity between us had vanished. I knew it had less to do with the chocolates than the lessons we'd learned that day.

"Praise the Lord," I said in English.

Zima glanced at me.

"You just spoke English. What did you say?"

"'Praise the Lord,'" I said, repeating in Mongolian. "It's a reference of reverence, not to a lord of war or a lord of a fortress or a land, but to the Lord God of creation, of the world and of life."

"And why do you praise Him right now?"

"I should praise Him with every breath. I try to. His hand works so many wonders. This morning, I was certain I would be chased from the clan. I saw no remedy to the rift between me and Dusbhan. But God pulls the strings to every man's heart. What seems so difficult to us is simple to God. We must only trust Him."

"Trust Him like Abraham did?"

"Yes." I smiled proudly that she remembered. "Trust Him like Abraham to provide."

"And trust Him like Noah did to save his family." She beamed at the look of pleasant surprise on my face. "Yes, I'm learning. It's easier to see what wrong things men and women do when I read it from the Bible. But they do right things, too, and I see how your God blesses His people for their obedience. What do you think His voice sounds like?"

"Later in the Bible, you'll read how God's voice is heard. Sometimes it's a still, small voice. Then, it may be a loud, authoritative voice. Or, God may speak through someone else who is close to Him, or through our circumstances."

"Does God speak to you? Do you hear Him besides what He tells you in the Bible?"

"I hear Him, but not in words like those men in the Bible did. Once the Bible was completed with all of God's

intentions for mankind, and the instruction He wanted us to
have, there hasn't been a need for Him to speak audibly to
us as He once did. The Bible is complete and can prove
itself. We don't require additional signs when we're to trust
by faith and not by sight or other senses. God speaks to His
children through His Word, in the minds of those who have
Him living inside their hearts. It's something more profound
than a mere conscience. He gives us gifts of peace, joy,
love, and other things—as He gives us a new heart once we
fully decide to follow and live for Him. When the whole
world is upset around me, that's when I hear God the most,
when I rely on Him the most. This is a state of fellowship
with God that everyone should try to seek all the time, but
we're often distracted by our own pursuits, which are only
temporary satisfactions at best."

Realizing how quiet the camp had become, I looked up
from the coal fire at which I'd been staring while speaking.
The children still dashed about, but the wives and Luyant
and Zima had been listening to my every word, words I'd
intended for only Zima's ears as she seemed to be my only
pupil. But God has a way of bringing His message to more
than just intended ears.

"How is it that you speak so boldly," Tzegabor, Gan-
gaad's first and eldest wife asked, "when such things are
forbidden?"

"Especially by Gan-gaad!" another added.

Normally, they wouldn't speak in front of other men, but
I was a foreigner and Luyant was a mute—and they were
curious. Besides, Luyant seemed just as interested.

"Many years ago, during the years that introduced

perestroika to Mongolia, your government also made many social reforms, allowing the citizens the freedom to choose between faiths, occupations, and other pursuits. Though the great restructuring, the *perestroika*, has been difficult on Mongolia after so many other forced changes from the past, the *perestroika* was meant for good, to rid the land of fear and forced socialism.

"You ask why I speak so boldly. But I ask why we don't all speak and live boldly? The government allows us to express ourselves openly and boldly now, though there are remnants of the old authority still seeking the old ways of absolute control. That generation will pass—and is passing—Gan-gaad's generation. But with the new openness comes evil as well as good. It's the evil I believe Gan-gaad and the others fear most from the *perestroika*."

I paused before the next part and peered into their eager faces. What I'd said was essentially forbidden in this clan, but I couldn't stop now.

"It's not so much a battle between good and evil as it is a spiritual war between the One and Only God and the demon angel, Satan. And as in any war, we must choose a side. If we don't choose, we automatically stand with Satan, because if we don't live as a servant of God, then we only serve Satan's worldly purposes in our flesh. There are only two ways. One is right and difficult, though fulfilling. The other is wrong and tempting, though ultimately destructive."

"But we have our gods," Tzegabor said. "Why would we need another?"

"There is only one God," Zima said. "All the others we sing in *tatlagas* about are made from the minds of our ancestors. Pond's God made everything, even our imaginations, but we still dishonor Him by admiring false and imaginary gods."

"Who are you to speak, Zima?" Tzegabor frowned. "What do you wear on your wrist?"

Zima held up the bracelet of gods molded in such detail, the only remnant of the memory of her mother. With a mighty yank, she tore the strand of leather off her wrist. She stood and violently cast the bracelet into the fire.

"There should be no confusion in what I believe now!" Zima stated.

And that concluded the conversation, punctuated by Luyant rising to his bulky height and walking to his *ger*. That was everyone's cue to disperse. Luyant's wife extinguished the fire and the others began to catch the children as they ran past.

Zima and I rose to our feet. She started toward Luyant's *ger* when I took her hand to stop her. We were familiar with the other's casual touch, and even the time we'd spent alone wasn't sparked with tension. But in that moment, I felt butterflies in my chest, and her hand felt softer than it had before. I was falling for this beautiful Russian-Kazakh.

"I know you wanted me to pick up something for you from Bulgan, something special, besides all the chocolates."

"It's okay." She smiled, and tenderly touched my bearded cheek. "We all loved the candies, and I'm sure they weren't cheap."

"But I bought you something, anyway." I grinned.

"You did? What is it?"

I led her to my *ger* and left her standing outside as I

crawled in and wrapped the mirror in the scarf I'd brought from New York. Under the half-moon, I stood and gave her the small bundle. With girlish excitement, she unwound the scarf.

"It's a neck scarf from America made from fine cotton."

"Oh, it's so soft!" She draped the scarf over her shoulder when she found the mirror inside. The reflection of the moon lit her smiling face as her fingers traced the ornate frame. "I love it. It's the first mirror I've seen in many years."

"And it's plastic, too, so you don't have to worry about it breaking so easily."

"You think of everything."

"Well—"

"Don't you need the scarf? It'll be cold this winter."

I swallowed nervously.

"What I feel in my heart right now will keep me warm through ten winters."

We gazed into each other's eyes for a long while, and I thought for sure she was going to plant one on me.

"Thank you, Pond," she whispered, looked around, then wrapped her arms around my neck.

When I thought the embrace was finished, I realized she was crying softly against my neck. I didn't know why she was crying, but I hoped it was from happiness. Gently, I held her until she was quiet, then she pulled away. The cold air was giving us both a chill. Without a second glance, she stepped around me and slipped over to Luyant's *ger*. My heart did flip-flops as she disappeared inside. *How could I sleep now? How could I ever sleep again?* What a day!

"She loves you, American," Dusbhan said from an opening in his *ger* hide-covered doorway. I didn't know he'd been watching. "No one else would ever touch her because she's Russian and Kazakh. But both of you, your hearts aren't your own. They belong to each other now."

He climbed out of his *ger* and stood beside me as we admired the starry sky. When he offered me a puff on his cigarette, I accepted as is customary, and passed it back. It was a gesture of the peace between us.

"Dusbhan, I didn't know you were a romantic."

"I listen to the radio with my wife." He shrugged. "We listen to people who call on telephones to talk to experts about marriage."

"And what have you learned?"

He flicked his cigarette butt into the frozen dirt. Across camp, one of the clan men in charge of goats was riding his horse on watch.

"That it's easy to be a man. Not so easy to be a husband. But if there is love, hard and easy don't matter. You know my wife is pregnant?"

"Really?" I rested a hand on his sturdy shoulder. "Congratulations."

"Not so easy to be a father, either, I think," he said. "But I think love makes it easier. Do you think?"

"You'll make a good father, Dusbhan," I said. "And you'll have much to share with him as he grows."

"Yes, I think so." He nodded and ducked back into his *ger*.

I lay down in my own shelter with a smile on my face, and fell asleep with a prayer of praise on my lips.

...†...

CHAPTER ELEVEN

In the morning, it was as if I'd awoken with a completely different clan. Since we weren't traveling, the women were seeing to the laundry at the water pump. I stared at them for several minutes to ensure my eyes weren't deceiving me—because I saw the women of Navi-hasgovi's clan washing their laundry as well—with my clan's women! And even more, they were clucking away like old hens, gossiping and sharing grievances of their travels and struggles over their obtuse husbands.

It was truly a sight of wonder, and I wasn't the only one admiring the compatibility. The Navi-hasgovi men who'd been left behind as the others went to town for supplies watched from the midst of their herds while their wives and older daughters chatted with our women. Dusbhan sat backwards on his *aduu* and watched his wife. Luyant sat at a small fire stringing a pair of snowshoes. Every few seconds, he looked up at the gathering at the water pump. I sat down next to him and watched him work.

"There isn't much snow in the south where we're going, is there?"

He strained as he stretched one last withered length of sinew around the wooden frame, then handed it to me for inspection. Of course, I knew the purpose for snowshoes, but I'd never held any in my hands. What was I to inspect? I checked the tightness of the sinew, as well as the heel and

118

toe straps that would fasten a boot in place. Finally, I passed it back to Luyant.

"They look good," I told him, nodding.

Picking up a pencil and tablet, he wrote me a message and handed it to me.

"When the mountains receive their first big snow, Dusbhan and I will go west to hunt. The snow will push the game down into the steppe, but sometimes we must still walk into the snow. You may come if Gan-gaad approves."

"I'd like that," I said. *A real Mongolian hunt?* How could I say no to that? In the books I'd read, the hunts were usually accompanied by hunting eagles and dogs, but this wasn't a normal clan. What opportunities and doors God was giving me!

Suddenly, I jumped to my feet. My heart skipped a beat. I looked from the women at the pump to the approaching bulk of Gan-gaad on his horse.

"Luyant, is this going to be a problem?"

Slowly, Luyant stood and dropped his snowshoe materials in front of the fire. Gan-gaad was riding alone, most-likely checking on us since Squirrel wasn't yet ready to leave the clinic. Dusbhan slid off the rump of his horse and crushed out his smoke. He caught at Gan-gaad's bridle as the clan leader stepped off his *aduu*.

Gan-gaad was fuming mad. There's no other way to describe him. He pointed at the water pump and stepped toe-to-toe with Dusbhan. Dusbhan moved back, but his uncle kept coming.

"What is this? Now we are happy neighbors with the Kazakhs?"

"But . . . the women must see to the clothes while we aren't—"

The clan leader back-handed Dusbhan and sent his nephew sprawling onto the cold ground. Dusbhan tried to scramble away, but Gan-gaad booted him in the ribs.

"How long have you betrayed me? My own blood! Did you not even watch them in the night as they steal our stock? Or have you given them free rein to come and go from your fire?"

"Uncle, please!"

Gan-gaad continued to curse and kick at the young man as he backed into the filth of the livestock. Sensing the scene was escalating, all the women at the pump withdrew to their clans for fear of more retaliation against them for what Gan-gaad saw only as betrayal. Zima ran to my side holding a pair of still dripping wet riding pants.

"I turn my back, you traitor!" Gan-gaad spat. "And you make alliances with the enemy!"

But Luyant wasn't standing aside this time. He stalked over to Gan-gaad and shoved his smaller brother away from his son. Luyant tried to use sign language to explain the situation, but Gan-gaad only pushed him back.

"How could you let this happen? My own brother! Sleeping with the Kazakh dogs!"

Having seen enough of Gan-gaad's outburst, Luyant picked up his brother by the collar of his coat. With strength I've rarely witnessed before or after that eventful day, Luyant lifted him two feet off the ground at arm's length. He then twisted him sideways and slammed him hard onto the ground. Gan-gaad lay motionless on his back, with his eyes wide and staring, the wind surely knocked out of him.

Luyant didn't seem willing to take any chances, though. He rolled his brother onto his belly and put a sturdy knee on his back to hold him in place. Dusbhan, having recovered slightly, tripped and bolted toward his *ger*. Luyant waved me over to them and signaled for me to talk to Gan-gaad, to explain things. And with such an audience! Besides our own, Navi-hasgovi's clan was watching intently, too.

"Lord, give me wisdom here," I prayed under my breath.

I crouched down in front of Gan-gaad to see his face when he lifted his head.

"You! I should've known you were behind—"

Luyant pushed Gan-gaad's face into the ground, filling his foul mouth with grass and soil. Gan-gaad spat and coughed and cursed.

"He wants you to listen to me for a few minutes, then he'll let you up," I said. "Um, yesterday, we had a big fight with the other clan. That's why our faces are still red and swollen. Since Navi-hasgovi has more men, we fought hard because we tried to keep the water pump for ourselves, but we were losing horribly. They were about to stomp us into the earth and take all of our stock, so we had to make a truce. One on this side, and one on that side of the pump. In your absence, it seemed the best solution to save your stock while we must all coexist here for a few days." I glanced at Luyant. *Was that enough?* He urged me to continue. "Uh, no one's betraying you, Gan-gaad. All of us bear the wounds of the fight yesterday; we all shed blood while defending the clan. You're missing no stock. No loyalty has been lost. We're still your clan."

Nodding, Luyant slowly eased off Gan-gaad. I stepped away to give the man space.

Gan-gaad's face was graven, his eyes downcast in humiliation. He rose to his knees, paused to look around, then lifted his bulk to his feet. Ignoring me and Luyant, he stomped away toward his *ger*. Those in his path quickly leapt aside. But when he reached his *ger*, he snatched Tzegabor by the wrist and threw her into the *ger*. She yelped out in pain from the force as he disappeared into the *ger* after her.

Then, one of the most horrifying times of my life took place. Even after my violent and careless upbringing, I still grimace when I recall that morning.

Inside his *ger*, Gan-gaad began beating his first wife. I knew well the sound of fists. But at her whimpers of pain, my soul ached for her. In the five minutes that it lasted, I turned numb and felt sickly. Twice, I moved to halt the beating, but Luyant gripped my arm firmly and shook his head as if to say, "*It's his wife and not your affair.*"

But I felt it was our affair. It had been a mutual agreement among us all to make peace with the Navi-hasgovi Clan. If anyone was to be beaten, it should've been me.

Our clan stood in shock through those long minutes. I tried not to hate as I prayed for us all, including Gan-gaad, and especially Tzegabor. Toward the end, I fell to my knees, a tear rolling down my cheek. *How could anyone be so brutal?*

Zima ran to me and fell beside me, weeping for Tzegabor.

"Can no one . . . do anything?"

When it finally stopped, I sighed with relief. Even the livestock were still, not even grazing, seeming to sense the horror in the air.

Gan-gaad emerged from his doorway, his knuckles stained crimson. In places, I saw he'd torn the flesh of his own skin, exposing bone. We all held our breath. Zima squeezed my cold hand. The clan leader walked over to the deserted water pump and washed his hands. No one moved toward his *ger*. Then, he walked past us, climbed onto his horse, and galloped into town, whipping the *aduu* the whole way.

I took a deep breath and rose to my feet. Luyant moved up beside me as Zima clung to my left.

"It's bad, Luyant," I said softly in warning. "I know what men's fists can do. She can't be a sight for the women to see."

Together, Luyant and I walked to the *ger*. I knelt and crawled in first as Luyant held the flap open for the light. Gently, I touched Tzegabor's bare leg. I reached up farther toward what was once her hardened but motherly face, and searched her neck for a pulse. My hand was wet with blood. Choking on my own breath, I prayed away the vomit rising in my throat. Withdrawing my hand, I shook my head at Luyant. He nodded in understanding, then made a rolling gesture with his hands.

"All right. Just keep everyone back," I said, "and find my shovel."

In numbing sorrow, I took care in wrapping Tzegabor's body in two blood-soaked blankets. There was more blood and splatter, but the other wives could tend to that. Her body was no heavier than one hundred pounds as I handed her out to Luyant's able arms. He cradled her against his chest as a wail from the other women erupted. Zima's jaw trembled as she brought me my trenching shovel.

Luyant walked slowly out of camp to the west and we followed. Only the three herdsmen stayed behind to watch the camp. The women and children fell in step behind me and Zima as we walked arm-in-arm behind Luyant. Dusbhan, carrying his AK-47, rode his horse far to our right about two hundred yards. I was thankful he'd not had the weapon when Gan-gaad had stormed into camp. That may be an odd thing for me to say, but I didn't wish for Dusbhan to kill his uncle. In prison, I'd known many different kinds of killers. Death seems to stay with a man. Dusbhan didn't need that burden.

Silence followed us as we climbed the hill still covered with grass in its final season before the landscape became desolate from the below-zero temperatures. At the crest of the hill, Luyant stopped, and I began to flatten an area with my shovel. The clan gathered around, but Dusbhan sat on his horse at a distance. I didn't dig quickly, but it didn't take long to have a four-by-six area prepared for their customary sky burial where the body would be left to scavengers. Luyant still held Tzegabor, a frown on his face, but I saw no tears. He laid her gently on the plot of dirt, and I stepped back as the women came up one at a time to place food or blue stones around their clan mother's body. Zima had brought a piece of white canvas and placed it over Tzegabor's face.

That day, I didn't even feel led to speak, only to watch and listen. Sometimes, there are no appropriate words to say. One can only feel the loss of life deep inside the heart. With my shovel over my shoulder, we all turned sadly and walked back to camp.

The next few days were difficult for the clan. No one made eye contact. Dusbhan rode his horse around the camp in an endless circle during the days and some nights. He slept like that more than a few times, his head bowed while astride his horse. Luyant continued to string his snowshoes and we all took care of the livestock, though with few words and no conversation.

"I feel I'll never smile again," Zima confessed to me on the third day after Tzegabor's death.

She lay her head on my shoulder, and I read from the Psalms at the dinner fire. Luyant and the others listened and stared into the flames. But Dusbhan sulked in the darkness behind me at the edge of the firelight.

On the fourth day, Navi-hasgovi and his clan packed up and started south. They didn't offer us any parting words.

There was no government investigator who would look into Tzegabor's murder. Very few people care what happens out there in the remote wilderness. For a time, I struggled with the lack of justice that would be dealt Gan-gaad. But God knew what had happened, and every man is held accountable for his actions, eventually, whether good or bad. I shared this with Dusbhan during the night watch after the fourth day.

"Tzegabor was like a mother to me," he mumbled in response, "a second mother. That's why Gan-gaad killed her. And he never loved her at all."

"Dusbhan, look at me. Try not to hate. Hate injures your soul. The pain is deep, I know. I lost my own mother and father."

"How did you continue to live?"

"I hated everyone," I said. "That's how I know hate isn't the answer. Eventually, I gave the burden to God, the Good Shepherd. The sorrow is still there, but the pain is less. And I don't hate. God saved me from that destructive path."

"Then what am I to do?"

"Let me tell you a story, and you'll understand. A long time ago, southwest of where we stand, Romans ruled what they knew to be the world at that time. Then God came to earth as a Man, pure and perfect. His name was Jesus. As a Man Himself, He became an example for mankind, but He was also fully God, called the Son. He taught in many towns and performed miracles that healed the blind and lame. But the religious leaders hated the things He taught and did because it took the peoples' attention and money off their traditional ways.

"So, the religious leaders plotted to kill Jesus. They found a man to betray Him, a close friend of Jesus, and they found Him in a garden with a few of His followers. They bound Him, beat Him, and spat on Him."

"On the God-Man?"

"Yes, and He deserved none of it. He'd created the whole world, and loved the whole world and every man and woman in it, which is why He didn't destroy them all with a single word. That's true love. But they tortured Him, and as they were killing Him, during His final hours, you know what they recorded Him as saying?"

"What?"

"He said, '*Forgive them, for they know not what they do.*'"

"Forgive them? Forgive the religious leaders?"

"The religious leaders, His followers, everyone and anyone who had allowed Him to be killed."

"And He died? God died?"

"He died, but because He was God, death couldn't hold Him. He rose from the dead, from the tomb where they laid Him, thereby conquering death. This is why we depend on God to save us from all evil, because Jesus conquered it all."

"And the wolf was destroyed." Dusbhan understood. "He really forgave them?"

"Yes, He did," I answered, then I went into my *ger* to sleep.

In the morning, I climbed Tzegabor's hill with my Bible and journal. I prayed and read from Hebrews chapter four. The passage about rest was comforting to my soul, reminding me not to design my own comfort, but to trust God through all hardships. When I finished writing Gino my thoughts, I looked up to see two riders approaching the camp from town. It was Gan-gaad with Squirrel's mother holding the boy in the saddle.

"Lord, open this man's heart and change his ways," I prayed. "Meanwhile, protect us all from his anger."

Those in camp saw him coming, too, and stood tensed for his arrival. Zima, however, bridled her horse and rode out to join me to escape any of Gan-gaad's left-over frustrations. She dropped to the ground next to me, leaving her horse to wander and munch the dying grass close by.

"Pond, have you seen? He's back."

"Yes, I've seen."

"What will happen?"

"We'll go south to the Gobi. Gan-gaad will lead us, and we'll follow. And slowly, we'll live again beyond this difficult time."

"Are things always so easy for you?" she asked.

I studied her face. It was so full of fear and sincerity. Life had been hard on her, but she could've done worse than having Luyant for an adopted father, even if he saw her as a creature below the horses that his brother, Gan-gaad, owned.

"No, things aren't easy for me, Zima. Sometimes, I try to force things to happen instead of submitting to God's direction of events around me. We live in a complicated world, but everything is easier to handle when God is foremost in our thoughts."

"The snake from the Garden ruins so much." She sighed. The clan began to dismantle the camp and move the animals south for a two-week ride to the next and last town. "We'd better go help. Gan-gaad will want to leave this place behind." She faced Tzegabor's site. "Sleep softly, Sweet Mother. I will miss you."

...✝...

CHAPTER TWELVE

With Navi-hasgovi ahead of us, Gan-gaad saw no need to hurry along that first day. We moved at a steady pace, Zima and I riding our horses in the rear, occasionally rounding up strays that wandered from the caravan. Everyone kept their distance from Gan-gaad, yet many doted over Squirrel with the fresh scar on his belly. I'd already been elected to remove the seven stitches from the boy's abdomen, and I'd assured Gan-gaad I could do it without trouble.

Riding alone, Zima and I read the Gospel of John a chapter at a time and then discussed it. We were also still working our way through the tutor of the Old Testament, and God was truly giving her the understanding to move swiftly through the complex issues. I've found that when a man or woman learns in isolation, he or she learns quicker and retains more than those not isolated. Since Zima was my only steady pupil, and an avid learner at that, we didn't linger over issues that most American Christians seem to argue about when the Word is so plain. The world was created in six days. The Jews are God's Chosen People. Jesus really would return for His believers in the near future. I taught her the historical, literal method of interpreting Scripture, as I was taught—God's Word says what He means it to say.

In the late afternoon, Dusbhan rode back and joined us.

He saw my Bible on Zima's lap. She knew she didn't need to hide it from him.

"Will you still give me one of those so I can read it for myself?" he asked me.

"I have one waiting for you in Hasagt."

"You have friends there?"

"No, but I have mail there. My friends are in Ondorhaan."

"Someday, I'll go there," he said. "I'll travel many places. I've decided I don't want to be a clan leader. Maybe your God has another place for me."

"I'm sure He has a plan for you. And perhaps it's time to call Him your God as well."

"Perhaps," he said, avoiding my eyes, then he changed the subject. "I rode ahead. Navi-hasgovi destroyed the next spring, knowing we were soon to follow. He's a day ahead of us, maybe more."

"Gan-gaad will be furious about the spring," I said. "We'd better go fix it before we all get there."

"You and Zima are best at that," Dusbhan said. "May I read your Book while you go ahead? I'll keep it hidden."

"Yes, you may."

Zima gave him the Bible and he nodded his thanks. He was the type of man who had to sort out the Bible for himself, no matter how long it took. So, I gave him no recommended passages as I would have done for a person with less ambition for the truth.

The two of us rode ahead with my shovel. When we arrived, we were only thirty minutes ahead of the clan. The spring was in worse shape than I'd imagined, as if Navi-hasgovi had thrown a stick of dynamite into the spring mouth. It had only been a trickle to begin with, I was told, but Navi-hasgovi had left it dry. Zima set about constructing a dam to pool the water while I climbed into the trough and cleaned out the mud. I tried not to think about the type of man who would do this intentionally to his neighbor and his neighbor's stock. Gan-gaad and Navi-hasgovi weren't that different. Both were stuck in a bitter world, a selfish existence.

Finally, I cleared away sludge to permit a gurgle, then a bubbling, then a small geyser of water. In truth, I believe the spring had never flowed so well, even before it had been ruined by the preceding clan. The pool was filled and the mud began to settle as the first horses trotted up to quench their thirst. I was covered in mud from head to toe, but I was happy to defuse the bomb that could've blown.

That night, Gan-gaad was drunk well before the meal was served, and surprisingly, his words became slurred and so misunderstood that he began to sob in frustration. Luyant, who hadn't touched his two-stringed lute yet, helped his brother to his *ger* and into bed, his wives and children with him.

Dusbhan emerged from his *ger* with my Bible to read silently to himself by the firelight. Luyant didn't seem to approve with Gan-gaad so near, but he didn't communicate to his son to do otherwise. Instead, Luyant began to play his lute, and his wife chanted a quiet *urtyn duu*, occasionally smiling at her husband who smiled back at the words of their song. The song was about a grain of sand that came from the sky in a snowflake. It was blown across the Gobi in a sandstorm into a clansman's eye. The clansman washed the grain of sand from his eye and a fish swallowed it. A bear ate the fish, digesting the sand as well. The clansman killed the bear, ate the meat and the sand grain, but it got stuck in his tooth. He lost his tooth and the sand with it and—

Mutely, Luyant cried for mercy as he stopped playing and covered his wife's mouth in fun.

"It's a tale that goes on forever," his wife told me with a giggle. Her name was Skaamaan. She was plump, but lovable and loyal to her husband, who asked for very little on paper and nothing by word. "Do you know any songs, Pond?"

All eyes were on me.

"I know some, but they're all in English. Let me think."

I flipped through a mental list of songs, mostly religious, and realized I'd have to translate them on paper into Mongolian to see if they worked with the tune since Mongolian words are generally much longer than English words. But I did sing for them a halting version of "Amazing Grace," in Mongolian. They loved it anyway, and I urged them to continue because I wanted to learn their much more sophisticated vocal skills. Like the couple we'd become, Zima and I held hands and listened—until she leaned close and whispered into my ear.

"I know what Nicodemus didn't understand."

"Yeah?" I asked, startled.

"Born again," she said. "It's starting fresh, like a baby."

Her words seemed to wipe away the recent sorrows from my soul. I grinned. God opens hearts in His time, not ours.

"That's right. Just like a baby."

"You were born again?"

"Yes, I was. About seven years ago."

"Can I be born again tomorrow? Can God do that?"

"Oh, yes, Zima. God can do that. I can't think of a better way to begin the day. Afterward, you'll be a child of God."

"A child of God?" She watched the coals glow. "A child of God . . ."

...✝...

As you can imagine, I didn't sleep much that night. In II Timothy, chapter four, we're told to be ready in season and out of season to preach the Gospel. To make sure I was ready, I studied up on verses for a new believer to understand the steps toward salvation. There are many verses that explain these born again truths—with only one way to get there. I generally used five steps to clarify that a person understood exactly what he or she was asking of God.

First, it must be understood that everyone is a sinner and is separated from God. Second, God loved us so much that He gave His Son to die for our sins. Third, dying in our sin means separation forever from God, while eternal life comes by trusting Jesus Christ. Fourth, in order to begin a new life in Christ, to be saved, one must believe that Jesus died for their sins, then declare that Jesus is the Savior. Lastly, Romans 10:13 gives us that simple and eternal promise: if you call on Jesus, He will save you for eternity.

It seemed I'd just fallen asleep when Gan-gaad's voice shattered the morning air barely after daybreak. Time to move out. I'd already learned to pack the night before, except for final necessities. Hastily, I rolled up my sleeping bag and set my pack outside the *ger*. Since I shared my living space with a pile of riding blankets and saddles, I was often caught by surprise by any number of visitors while I was dressing or sleeping. But in a land of necessity where one can't even answer nature's call in much privacy, I was getting somewhat used to the lack thereof. Prison hadn't been much different.

So, while I was getting dressed or putting on my boots, the gear from my *ger,* and the *ger* itself, always seemed to be hauled away before I was completely prepared. Why we had to leave within five minutes instead of ten, I shall never know. But I was adjusting to the lifestyle, even if I didn't fully understand it.

In minutes, Zima and I stood alone on the trodden ground, waving at Squirrel with his sisters in the back of the cart as the clan moved off in the distance.

We sat beside the small spring, which would again need some engineering after being trampled, and we opened the Bible. That morning, I did most of the talking. Even though she'd read John's account of being born again, and understood what Nicodemus couldn't, I still reviewed the steps through John and Romans. I didn't want her rushing into the greatest choice one can make.

Much of what I explained to Zima that morning was what I'd witnessed in my own life. A Christian, if he or she is living right, is the best testimony that exists, outside of the Word. Before we prayed, she heard the brief story of my life—my rebellion on the streets of New York City, my years in prison, which became my turning point, and my pursuit of being a servant of the Most High.

Initially, I felt it was possible that Zima's desire to commit her life to Christ was based largely on her affection for me, rather than from a sincere heart. However, I'd witnessed the general and specific revelation of Jesus Christ manifested in her over those first weeks. Also, I'd seen her throw her pagan bracelet, a family heirloom, into the fire and defend God as the Only God. Genuine faith will always be proven by genuine works. And if she was honestly seeking God's direction in her life because of me, then I was humbly honored to be used by my Lord. She recognized the Bible as the Truth. Only the Spirit can open the eyes to see that!

"Are you ready?" I asked.

Sensing we were about to pray, she folded her hands and nodded. She was ready.

"Pray from your heart," I said, "and speak to God as your Lord. Tell Him what you desire."

Already, tears were welling in her eyes.

"Dear God, I know I have sinned and I want to thank You for Your forgiveness." She spoke in a clear, soft voice. "I believe Jesus died for my sins. I now receive Your offer of eternal life. I will follow Jesus as my Savior and try to obey Him in all I do. Thank You for my new life. In the name of Jesus, amen."

Barely had she closed her prayer than she threw her arms around my neck and cried. This was such a big step in her life, a step of freedom from the penalty of sin, and a future of security. But in that land, being a Christian could make one an outsider. I'd recently read how Christians in China had died for the Gospel. Zima knew the risks, though—the risks from possibly even her own adopted uncle, Gan-gaad, if he should find out. But she also knew the risks were worth the choice. The cost of following Christ is never truly loss.

I rubbed her back and mumbled reassurances until she finally pulled away

"Are you okay?" I asked.

She nodded and wiped her nose with a sleeve.

"But I feel selfish," she said.

"Selfish? How so?"

"I have found what I know so many want. Tzegabor didn't believe in Jesus, and now she's dead. The kids in the clan . . . How can I not tell them, Pond?"

"You can tell them, Zima. The Bible commands us to tell them. We simply must be wise and careful when dealing with Gan-gaad and maybe a couple of the others. But because of you, there are twice as many believers in the clan now. I have no doubt there'll be more soon. Two is just the beginning. Speaking of the clan, we'd better repair the spring and catch up with them!"

Those days before we reached Hasagt blended together with activity as had the days before reaching the previous town of Bulgan. Except, instead of trying to stay in front of Navi-hasgovi's clan, we were a day behind him. This created more problems than just the destroyed watering hole nearly every night. Grazing land became an issue as well. Navi-hasgovi's livestock nibbled everything edible nearly to the roots for a mile in every direction around the night's water source. This meant we had to set up camp, then drive the animals in another direction to graze for a few hours. This made for longer days, because the stock had to be driven back to relative safety in the camp vicinity where they could bed down for the night, rather than leave them to spend the night on the dangerous, open steppe with no water.

With concern, Luyant noticed that all the animals were losing weight from the extra strain. On paper, we discussed the best remedy, and we brought Dusbhan into our considerations for a solution. I suggested we linger for a week and allow Navi-hasgovi to get far enough ahead so when we came upon his week-old camp sites, the grass would've regrown some. This was quickly dismissed, however, for Gan-gaad would never linger longer than we had to. Besides, the farther south we traveled, the slower the grass would grow since there was less moisture.

We were already behind schedule that season because of Squirrel's appendicitis. Normally, Dusbhan explained, the clan was a week or two ahead of Navi-hasgovi, closer to the edge of the Gobi before the winter fell upon them.

Luyant suggested we graze the animals midday, let them rest, then continue in the afternoon to the intended water source where they could graze more if they wanted to. He wasn't worried about longer nights or lack of sleep, only the condition of his stock before the harsh winter set in.

When we presented our options to Gan-gaad, he was greatly troubled and admitted he'd noticed the fatness of the animals diminishing as well. The answer, he believed, was to overrun Navi-hasgovi once and for all at Hasagt. He decided to ration out the grain stores to build the animals' layers of fat back up, and replace the used grain in Hasagt using the money I'd paid him for my stock. Agreeing with Gan-gaad's solution, we pressed toward Hasagt and even threatened to overtake Navi-hasgovi on the second week out of Bulgan.

During the days, Dusbhan borrowed my Bible more often. He would ride his horse sitting backwards so he could use the *aduu's* broad rump as a table for the Book. He usually rode on either the left or right flank where no one bothered him during his studying. And his horse plodded along parallel with the clan without further guidance.

Without a Bible to read during the long rides, Zima and I lapsed into stories of our childhoods. She spoke of hers as if it were a bad dream nearly forgotten. Though she'd not been abused, she'd been neglected and forced to fend for herself since she was of Russian descent. Her parents had died in Dalandzadgad, a town in the heart of the Gobi, isolated from towns by hundreds of miles of sand and rock. She felt certain the communist MPRP party had killed her parents in the misguided retaliation of Russia's press for Mongolia's independence movement and the privatization of its markets. Orphaned, Zima had been passed from relative to relative and then to a neighbor of a distant acquaintance. One of her guardians saw her value and gave her to Luyant to pay his debt owed. That was nearly twenty years before I'd met the clan.

When Zima had joined the clan, Dusbhan was two years older at the age of eleven. At his uncle's encouragement, Dusbhan tormented Zima nearly every day. He cut her hair, stole her food and blankets, and knocked her off her horse.

That lasted until Zima had her growth spurt, before Dusbhan's voice had changed. She'd been a skinny girl, but she was strong and almost as tall as Luyant. She caught Dusbhan one day and whipped him black and blue. He had welts all over his body, and she'd promised him it would be worse next time if he told. And if he told and Gan-gaad beat her, she'd still come for him sooner or later, she'd threatened. But they'd been children then. By the time the young man had grown in size and was strong enough to whip Zima in return, he'd lost interest. Having heard her story, I better understood Dusbhan's reserved personality, at least in part.

The years after that were consumed with labor. Luyant never hit her, but Gan-gaad had a few times. And when Dusbhan moved out of Luyant's *ger*, Zima was left alone with Luyant and his wife. As his only other child, though adopted, Zima liked being alone. Luyant's wife was kind and Luyant was silent. With Dusbhan in his own *ger* with his own wife, Zima had more space and finally found peace for herself in the clan. Because of pressure from Gan-gaad, Luyant never gave her enough affection for her to feel like an actual daughter, but she accepted her place in the clan under his wing.

Zima sympathized with my years of foster homes. I told her of my crimes and my prison term—and all that God had saved me from, though I still had to pay my debt in jail.

The two of us still remained behind after every camp to repair the watering holes and read the Bible each morning. And in the afternoons, we rode ahead to see the damage Navi-hasgovi had left us.

CHAPTER THIRTEEN

When we were two nights out from Hasagt, Zima and I rode up to a small lake that Navi-hasgovi couldn't destroy, though he may have wanted to. It was half the size of a football field and even had fish in it! That was the first real body of water I'd seen in Mongolia. While I was happy we didn't have to rebuild a dam that evening, Zima was enthused for another reason.

"I'll ride back to the clan and you can bathe!" she ordered rather than suggested. "Tomorrow, you ride ahead and I'll stay back and bathe."

Lifting my arm, I sniffed.

"Am I really that smelly? I've smelled Luyant. He smells like a camel!"

"That's the point, Pond!" She laughed. "You're starting to smell like Luyant!"

As she rode away, I stripped down and waded into the icy—*and I mean icy*—water. It was the first I'd seen anyone in the clan show any concern for personal hygiene. I'd noticed everyone else living like cavemen, so I'd joined them! The women no doubt sponge-bathed with heated water in their *gers*, but I knew Luyant and Gan-gaad hadn't washed in months. Now Zima had actually told me to bathe!

Shivering and turning purple, I dressed as the clan arrived and the animals trotted forward for a place on the shore. Feeling self-conscious now, I changed my clothes and washed my dirty ones in the lake, vowing to do my laundry more often. The issue had so bothered me that during my night watch when starry darkness covered the steppe, I waded back into the pool, this time with my bar of soap from my pack. At that point, I realized it didn't hurt to practice a few American customs—like cleanliness.

The next day, after our reading and my journal writing, it was Zima's turn to bathe. Since she hadn't seen or smelled scented soap in years, I let her use my bar. Riding ahead, I joined the clan. Dusbhan noticed my arrival and asked for my Bible.

I rode alone in the rear for a while until I was joined by Uhaat. Uhaat was a fifteen-year-old boy who'd been encouraged by Gan-gaad to take up the responsibilities of a man. He was Gan-gaad's firstborn by Tzegabor, who was now buried. The next oldest was Chita, Squirrel's older sister of twelve. Before that day, Uhaat, who was small for his age and a little slow, had avoided me as the rest of the youngsters had. But on this day, instead of playing riding games with the younger children, Uhaat had been coaxed into riding horseback all day along with the adults.

"What kind of name is 'Pond' in America?" he asked.

"It's like a small lake, but that's not really my name," I said. "Your father mispronounces the word 'blond,' which refers to my hair color. My real name is Andy."

"Andy. So what should I call you?"

"Pond is fine. I believe a man's name isn't as important as how a man makes a difference for the better in the lives around him."

"You buried my mother," he stated. "Were you sad?"

"Very sad, Uhaat. That was a difficult time for all of us."

"I don't think Gan-gaad likes me as much as Marbin. He's the one you call 'Squirrel.' Do you think Gan-gaad will kill me like he killed my mother?"

Gasping, I tried not to show my shock. He was a maturing youth with many concerns. But no question was too trivial.

"No, I don't believe he'll kill you, Uhaat. I think he's ashamed for what he did to your mother, and when he looks at you, he may be reminded of that sad day when his anger overwhelmed him. Squirrel is special to him, but don't doubt his love for you. Men like Gan-gaad oftentimes don't know how to show love to the ones they love most because they're so busy acting strong for the whole clan.

"Look at Luyant, your uncle. Much larger than your father, he's like a small giant. Luyant doesn't speak, and most of the time, he lumbers about like a great big bear. But at night, he plays his *morin-khuur*, right? For his wife, he plays love songs, tunes with silly lyrics, and music with no words. He doesn't have to speak to show his love, but you still have to pay attention to notice how he expresses his love.

"Gan-gaad seems like a tough wolf sometimes, so you may have to look for the special and different ways he shows love to those around him. Maybe love doesn't come out of Gan-gaad like it does from his brother, but he expresses himself in other ways. He makes sure we're all fed every night. He tries to find good locations for our *gers* so we don't have far to travel for water. These are small ways that he shows he loves you. I'm sure if you considered it more, you could think of other ways, too."

He nodded and seemed to consider that for a long time. We both turned around at the sound of Zima's horse trotting up the trail. The reins were dragging along the ground and its back was bare except for the saddle. No Zima.

I stopped my horse and wheeled to the north.

"If anyone asks where I am, Uhaat, tell them I went to look for Zima. Something's happened to her."

"Can I take your place here at the rear?" he asked with hopefulness.

"Yes!" I yelled over my shoulder, and heeled my *aduu* into a run.

Trying not to panic, I knew there were any number of possible reasons why Zima's horse was riderless. It could've wandered away while she was bathing. Or other herdsmen from the eastern plains had ventured to the pond and found a beautiful woman, spooked her horse, and—

Topping a rise with a prayer in my throat, I saw Zima afar off, alone, walking on the path. As I slowed my horse and trotted up to her, I noticed she held her left arm with her right hand.

"I was thrown." Her face, still rimmed with wet hair, displayed worry. "I think it's broken, Pond."

"We can deal with a broken arm." I climbed off my horse and rolled up her sleeve gently. "If it was a leg, your head, or your spine, those would be a challenge—or a sprained finger. That would be the worst. I'd probably faint at the sight of a sprained finger!"

She tried to chuckle, but she was in too much pain. Indeed, her arm was broken—and not just slightly. Below the elbow, her ulna bone protruded through the skin. Swelling had begun around the rupture. I wasn't worried as much about the pending deformity as I was about the threatened nerves or marrow poisoning. Nerve damage from such a break could render the rest of the arm and hand useless.

"It . . . hurts to move, Pond, even to walk." She looked pale.

"Can you wiggle your fingers?"

"I can't even feel them. Satan is trying to discourage me, I think."

"Let's get you up on my horse, all right?"

She hadn't taken a step before her knees buckled. I caught her halfway to the ground. My mare sensed something amiss, and she shied away, but I held the reins tightly in one fist. Lifting Zima into my arms, I drew my mare closer.

"Zima? Can you help me out here?"

But she was out. Loudly, I scolded the nervous, prancing *aduu* as I tried to heft Zima onto the mare's back. After a couple minutes, I managed, then tried to mount behind her while holding Zima from falling off. Finally, my mare steadied for a few seconds, and I vaulted upward. I landed behind Zima as she sat side-saddle limply in front of me, her head against my chest. She was breathing steadily, but I checked to make sure her throat hadn't swelled from shock, though I don't know what I would've done if I'd found swelling.

We started off at a walk. Staying on the horse by myself was something I'd barely managed to do. Now, I had to keep two of us up there. It certainly wasn't easy.

My mare knew we were headed back to the clan and the other animals, so she began to hasten her pace. I loosed the reins and she sped into a jolting trot that made Zima moan in anguish, though she wasn't fully conscious. At last we were moving fast enough to catch the clan.

It was noon before the clan came into sight. They'd paused on the trail to milk the mares, and to pass out food rations. Gan-gaad saw me coming and shook his head. But Luyant and Dusbhan rode their mounts toward me. Luyant's wife, Skaamaan, who drove the wagon with most of the children, left her station and ran to inspect Zima. Luyant relieved my tired arms as he and his wife lowered Zima to the ground.

"Her arm is badly broken," I said. "I have to get her to the medical clinic in Hasagt. She'll lose the arm otherwise."

Luyant pointed to the cart in which two children rode with some fodder and supplies. It was drawn by two cattle and driven by Gan-gaad's second wife.

"Yeah." I nodded. "That's the only way to go."

Dusbhan turned his horse away.

"I'll harness a fresh pair," he said.

"Husband?" Skaamaan asked Luyant. Her face was full of worry for her adopted daughter. "May I go? One of the others can drive the wagon. This is . . . Zima."

Luyant looked at me. I nodded. It would help to have another person, especially a woman, caring for Zima. Thankfully, Luyant shrugged, which Skaamaan took as a nod. She hugged him briefly, then knelt over Zima again.

I ran to help Dusbhan with the cart. We loaded the

supplies and fodder into the other two wagons. While I was tying my own mare to the back of the cart, a rough hand grabbed my shoulder and spun me around. Gan-gaad's eyes were full of fury.

"What do you think you're doing, Pond? You can't take my cart!"

"Luyant offered it." At this moment, I barely held my own frustrations in check with him. "I have to get her to Hasagt before it's too late!"

"Strap her onto her horse since she can't stay on it!" he bellowed. "I'll not have you or her holding up the entire clan by taking one of my vehicles!"

I was about to bark back at him when Luyant set a heavy hand on Gan-gaad's shoulder. Luyant nodded at me to continue preparing the cart. But Gan-gaad had to have the last word.

"You do this to me, Pond, and you are part of this clan no longer! You or your cursed Kazakh!"

My eyes locked with his, but I didn't respond. If that was the case, so be it. I marched over to the wagon that carried my gear and grabbed my pack. Wasting no time, I set the pack in the cart with Skaamaan and Zima, then climbed onto the driver's seat, which consisted of a plank nailed to the front. The cart was only two-wheeled, but its bed was as long as a wagon. As it was nearly empty now, the fresh horses Dusbhan had harnessed in place of the others could pull the cart easily. Though I'd never driven a cart before, I'd been watching for some weeks. Taking the reins in my fingers, I gave the horses a snap on the rump and we started forward.

"We'll see you at Hasagt," I said to Luyant and Dusbhan.

They waved at me and Skaamaan as we pulled ahead of the clan. Behind us, I heard Gan-gaad's boisterous yell to get the clan moving—and that the kids on foot had better not become a hindrance or cousin Dusbhan would shoot them with his gun! Dusbhan growled playfully with the children as they squealed and dashed around the wagons. But part of me felt Gan-gaad was serious. Perhaps Uhaat was right and there was little or no love in Gan-gaad after all. Thinking of Uhaat, I twisted around and peered back at the clan. There was Uhaat watching us go. He was squinting his eyes and craning his neck to see who I was looking back for. But I pointed at him and waved. Uhaat grinned and waved back wildly, then we passed from sight over a hill.

"Oh, Skaamaan?" I asked her nervously. "Exactly how far is it to Hasagt?"

"If we hurry all night, we can be there by mid-morning."

Suddenly, all the necessary items we would need for such a journey came to mind. But a look in the back told me that Skaamaan hadn't forgotten to come prepared. She'd packed food and there was a water skin in the front of the cart. Relieved, I focused on the pace of the wagon—not too slow, but not so fast as to weary the horses, either. And if necessity demanded, my mare—tied onto the back, trotting happily and burden-free—could spell one of the horses.

Finally, I had a few minutes to think. I considered Zima's broken arm and all it entailed. She would have a cast for the first few weeks of winter. That would cut back on her usefulness and slow her down during chores, especially the milking. Perhaps I could do the milking when I wasn't on watch at the campsites. That was . . . if I'd be allowed into camp again. Gan-gaad was such a rash man and his brother too mute to reason with him for me. No one else was bold enough to face the brute. If Zima and I were really outcasts, I decided then and there I would buy a second bicycle in Hasagt. Once Zima was able to move about, we'd start for Randy's in Ondorhaan several hundred miles away.

But no, that wouldn't work, either, I realized, with bitter winter approaching. I wasn't about to get caught in the Selenge Basin on a rural highway on our bikes when the wintertime high temperature was seven degrees below zero! We'd have to stay in Hasagt for the winter, which would drain me of my finances. Then, we could buy a vehicle somehow to drive east, or convince Gan-gaad to take us back into the clan.

I felt the inside pockets of my coat. My journal was where I always kept it, but no Bible. Dusbhan had borrowed it! But I wasn't too disheartened. How could I be? Dusbhan, by God's grace, would discover all the truth he needed to. The Bible was in good hands. In Hasagt, Randy would have five more Bibles waiting for me. How exciting! Zima could have her own, and Dusbhan his. I would certainly need mine back from him. That would leave three available to give away or share.

These were things I pondered for an hour as we traveled until I reined in sharply, causing Skaamaan to fall against the buckboard.

"Sorry about that." I pointed ahead. "Look."

Skaamaan gazed around me. Before us, Navi-hasgovi

occupied the next watering hole. His livestock were grazing in every direction.

"He's supposed to be a day ahead of us!" Skaamaan whispered fearfully. "Gan-gaad will be here by nightfall!"

"Navi-hasgovi must've had problems if he had to stay here two nights in a row." I rubbed my brow, a headache beginning to throb. "This is going to get ugly for both clans, but we have to take Zima to Hasagt."

"No, Pond, you must stay behind. There's no one else to keep the peace, otherwise—as you did for us in Bulgan."

My heart groaned. If that was peace, then what was war? Staying and dealing with more clan disputes was not what I wanted to do! I wanted to go to Hasagt, take care of Zima, pick up the Bibles, and send word to Randy and Gino that I was still alive.

"You're right, Skaamaan." I sighed and tore a page from my journal to write instructions. Gan-gaad didn't normally allow Skaamaan or the other women in the clan to venture into any towns. "Take Zima to the largest clinic or hospital you can find. Locate a doctor or a nurse, and give him or her this note that I'm writing in both English and Cyrillic. Though you don't have any money, most doctors vow to care for the sick and injured no matter what. If it helps, tell them I'm an American and I expect Zima to be cared for before I arrive. And I have money. They'll use a machine to x-ray her arm to look at the bones, then they'll straighten the bones. I'm telling you so you know what to expect, okay? I'll join you in Hasagt as soon as possible. Zima considers you her mother, so I'm sure you're worried about your daughter."

"And will I stay with her all the time?"

"Much of the time, yes. At some point, they may ask you to wait in another room, but it will be brief as they operate on her arm. Then, they'll put her in a room or ward where you can sit with her while she lays in bed and rests."

"What do I do with the cart and horses?"

"Oh. I don't know, Skaamaan. I hadn't thought of that. You may have to abandon them outside. But they should be safe. I trust your judgement. If anything happens to the cart or horses, don't concern yourself with them. When I arrive, I'll figure something out. We just need to focus on Zima."

"Maybe I should wait and . . . my son can go with me."

"Zima needs help now, Skaamaan. Dusbhan is miles behind us. Go. I'm sure you'll do wonderfully well. Drive the cart right into town down the street and ask for directions to the hospital. And I'll see you sometime tomorrow."

"Okay, Pond. I'll do what you say."

"I'll be praying. God will watch over you."

She nodded.

Untying my horse, I took my gear from the cart and touched Zima's cheek as she slept.

"She's Your child, Lord. Speed them along safely."

Skaamaan slapped the reins and was off. Right away, she left the path and made a wide arc around Navi-hasgovi's herds. I watched her go at a trot, then beyond the herds, she returned to the trail, which angled southeast.

Now, I had to focus on the problem before me. Navi-hasgovi had probably done this on purpose, knowing he could play the bully since he had more men than Gan-gaad.

That's why he'd continued destroying waterholes, I assumed. But there wasn't another watering hole for perhaps twenty or thirty miles.

"Lord," I prayed, staring at the rolling, dry landscape, "tell me what I should—"

And then, it came to me—just like that.

Turning my horse away from Navi-hasgovi's clan, I started up the trail back to the north until I could no longer see his herds. Then, in a shallow bowl where thick, green grass grew, I dismounted. The green grass meant water was close to the surface. My mare began to graze as I adjusted the head of my shovel at a ninety degree angle. The clan would arrive in about three hours. Three hours to find water or there'd be a war. Fortunately, my hands were already calloused from the hard work, and my back and arms were strong. It had already been a taxing day emotionally, but I wasted no time digging into the ground and uprooting the green grass.

As I chopped at the soil, I turned in a circle about the size of a *ger*. Once that layer of ground was loose, I adjusted my shovel head and scooped the dirt out of my circle, throwing it off as far as I could.

After an hour, I shed two layers of clothing. I hadn't worked this hard since joining the clan. Finally, I was down to just my white t-shirt. My horse had wandered a good distance away toward Navi-hasgovi's herds, but I didn't have time to get her. She was thirsty, no doubt, and smelled the water down the plain.

The hole was finally waist deep, but there was still no sign of even a little mud. But I was hopeful that I wasn't much higher than the water table. By the second hour, my depth hadn't quite doubled. I was laboring more to heave the dirt out of the hole instead of simply throwing it aside.

Suddenly, I dropped to my knees and dug my fingers into darker soil. It was wet and sticky.

"Thank You, Lord!" I praised the One who was watching over me.

Steadily now, I carved away the steep edges of my water hole so the animals could approach it easier. It would still be crowded, but with a little patience, they'd have water. After the sides sloped at an agreeable angle, which had required moving more than a couple of tons of dirt, I dug fervently where the dirt was darkest and heaviest.

I'd only shoveled another foot deeper when muddy water seeped around my shovel blade. Widening the area, I tossed sloppy mud out of the new cistern. Rolling up my pant legs, I took off my shoes and socks to wade in the deepening hole.

As I was working on the approach again, I was nudged aside by my thirsty *aduu* and she stepped into the hole I'd dug. Where there'd been no water, now there was. She sniffed the muddy liquid. I continued to spread the displaced soil around as the mud settled and my horse filled her belly.

The sun was just setting when the first of the clan's horses trotted up to my watering hole. I picked up my boots and gear and moved a distance away to collapse on the ground.

Gan-gaad was still scratching his head, not quite remembering this watering hole, when the clan began to set up the *gers*. Dusbhan rode up to me as I tugged on my boots.

"What happened? Where's my mother and Zima?"

"They had to go ahead. Navi-hasgovi's at the next water hole just over that rise," I said. "I knew there'd be problems if I didn't find us water."

Dusbhan slowly acknowledged with a smile.

"You . . . dug a new well?"

"I didn't see any other way. It'll work, I hope."

"It's small, but it'll work. Zima and my mother are alone then?"

"Your mother's a strong herdswoman," I said. "She can fend for herself for a day or two. I gave her written instructions for when she reaches town. Zima's life depended on me sending them ahead. There are blood clots to consider, not to mention a fever and shock and—"

"Are you going ahead to Hasagt?"

"As soon as I can get something in my belly."

"I'm going with you. I'll get more horses."

In minutes, Dusbhan had gathered two fresh mounts for each of us to relay while riding through the night. He explained his intentions to Luyant, ignored Gan-gaad, and came back to me with a brick of goat cheese and a stick of dried meat.

"We'll change horses every hour," he said as he swung onto his horse. "They have three or four hours on us, but we should gain on them at such a pace. Can you do it?"

"I can do it." I tied my pack securely onto my spare *aduu*.

"You love her, don't you?"

Nearly ready to mount my horse, I froze. *Love? In a romantic way? Had we come that far already?* Dusbhan was grinning and wasn't moving until I answered.

"I look forward to every minute I can spend with her. Her touch warms my heart and melts my knees to jelly. I hope that's not love, Dusbhan."

"That's love, Pond!" He laughed with a wild cheer, took the lead rope of his spare *aduu*, and galloped away.

Glancing back at the clan, I saw Gan-gaad watching us with his hands on his hips. His frown gave me a chill. No one had told him what was happening, and we were riding away with four of his horses. For argument's sake, however, I did own five head of each herd and flock, so it wasn't stealing.

My two horses turned and we dashed after Dusbhan. It would be a long night.

...†...

CHAPTER FOURTEEN

The town of Hasagt was the end of the line in two ways. First, it was the most southwestern remnant of civilization worth calling a town just inside the Gobi Altay Mountains. When travelers are heading into the massive territory of Xinjiang Uygur Province in northwest China, they pass through Hasagt. Anywhere to the north or south, the journey would end through impassable mountain ranges or the seemingly endless Gobi Desert.

Hasagt was also the end of the line as it was the last hint of notable civilization before passing through fragmented foothills of the Gobi Altay into the Gobi itself. The highway that connected Dund-Us to Bulgan and Hasagt did continue toward the desert region, yet no one traveled it. It was hundreds of miles to Dalandzadgad with few fueling stations, no shopping markets, and certainly no above-ground moisture. So why would anyone travel down there? There was no reason unless a man knew where to find the underground rivers that ran beneath the wells and the water holes, which were more often seasonal than not.

And because Hasagt was the end of the line, few found it necessary to visit its humble streets and twentieth century buildings. It was an outpost, the residents more or less ambassadors in businesses of furs and flocks rather than residents by choice. Pride in their universal monarch, Genghis Khan, lived on, but most of the country's citizens were too poor to tour the west where the conqueror had marched his forces—and was rumored to be buried. These were citizens from necessity, and in many ways they were a second generation remnant stationed at the outpost by a government that had once demanded more than it offered. While technology was booming in the eastern cities, it was barely trickling to the forgotten Mongolian west.

It was into this Hasagt that we rode, admiring the hustle and bustle as clansmen from other clans also gathered their winter stores and supplies. Many of them would graze their livestock somewhere to the east, closer to the Selenge River Basin, and closer to such towns as Tsetserleg and even Ulaanbaatar, the Red Hero City Capital. And while eastern herdsmen were more inclined to settle vast ranches than to follow nomadic herds, smaller clans, like Navi-hasgovi and Gan-gaad's, remained in the west to serve the needs of the Gobi Altay Range. In the spring, the ewes and mares and other animals would bear lambs and foals, and the trek back to Dund-Us would complete the yearly migration to off-load livestock at the markets.

Dusbhan and I found the hospital without much trouble. We arrived before noon, not far behind Skaamaan, after relaying our horses through the night to preserve them. And what a grueling night! I couldn't tell which looked more haggard—us or the horses.

As expected, Skaamaan's cart was outside the hospital entrance. The two horses, still in their harness, had collapsed in exhaustion, but their necks were extended as they nibbled at a stand of decorative bushes growing against the hospital wall. Two old men stood nearby admiring the

weary animals. Most clan animals were picketed or stabled
at the edge of town, so our arrival brought much curiosity.
We dismounted next to the cart, and I volunteered to tend to
the six animals while Dusbhan ran inside to locate a hose
and bucket to haul water to our animals before they dropped
dead. The two old men scratched their heads, and I knew
they were wondering about my blond hair and thick beard,
but they preferred to mumble between themselves rather
than quench their curiosity by questioning me.

After taking care of the animals, I figured they'd be safe
from thieves, so I trudged into the infirmary to locate my
friends. It was a smaller building than the Bulgan hospital
where we'd taken Squirrel, but I hoped size didn't matter
when it came to quality care. I hadn't gotten beyond the
administration desk and intersecting halls before I was
drawn to the nurses' desk by a barrage of English.

"Oh, this is no good, darling!" a man said in a British
accent. He checked a watch on his wrist. "In three hours, I'll
be as good as dead in a coma with the word 'insulin' still on
my lips!"

He was a backpacker, I guessed at first glance, though
trimmed and so manicured I could tell he hadn't been in the
country long. His wife or companion bit her nails nervously.

"Try pantomime again, love," she suggested. "They have
to understand!"

I stepped up to the high counter as the gentleman acted
out the motions of giving himself a shot. The two nurses
who watched shook their heads and diverted their eyes
every time the backpacker lifted his shirt and pinched his
skin. When they all noticed me looking on, their confusion

was put on hold for a few breaths. My blond hair was acknowledged, as was my rugged, herdsman appearance and smell.

"Please tell me you speak English!" the man said to me, pleading.

His girlfriend touched her nose with a grimace. I couldn't have smelled that bad; I'd bathed only a couple days earlier.

"Oh, I don't think so, love," she said. "He's Caucasian, but probably Russian. They have blonds, too, you know."

"What's with these two?" I asked the nurses in Mongolian.

"Foreigners," the eldest nurse said, accepting me the instant I spoke their language. "They want syringes for their drugs. Western capitalists! I'll not give them any sort of needle!"

"We're pretending we don't understand they're asking for syringes," the other nurse added proudly. "Soon, they'll give up and go away."

I chuckled, perhaps inappropriately, but it was quite silly.

"They think you want drugs," I mused in English to the Brits.

"Drugs?" The man gasped, then noticed the obvious. "You speak English! Oh, thank heavens!"

"What happened to your insulin?" I asked.

"We rode the rail from Beijing to Buyant-Uhaan. I had two syringes on me, but one case must've been left aside at the customs desk. The other one broke on the train here."

"Maybe we can track down the other case this

afternoon," the woman said. Both of them appeared to be in their mid-thirties. "But first things first, right? He hasn't had a shot in nearly twelve hours!"

"You two on your honeymoon?" I asked.

"Here? Never! We're seismologists." He pointed at the nurses. "Would you be a pal, please, before I lapse into a coma?"

I leaned over the desk, trying to keep a straight face.

"They're not drug users," I relayed in Mongolian. "They're scientists. This one . . . he has a condition known as diabetes."

"Yes, we know what diabetes is, but—" The older nurse caught herself as it all became apparent. "He wants insulin! We have that."

"Not all foreigners are evil and corrupt," I reassured them. "Could you tell me where the woman with the broken arm might be?"

"Down the hall and to the right, but she's not yet conscious."

"Did you tell them, mate?" the Brit asked. "Do they have any?"

"She'll take care of you," I said. "Hope you two know where you're going. It's pretty rugged territory along the northwest fault line, not to mention winter comes early here."

"Well, I'd rather be eaten by wolves than get blown up in Beijing!" the man said. "Wouldn't you? That's all we have to fear out in the snow, right? Just wolves?"

"Blown up in Beijing?" I asked. "What're you talking about?"

"He doesn't know, love!" The woman covered her mouth. "I guess he's been away from the telly. Are you American, sir?"

"Yes . . ." I answered hesitantly. "What's happened?"

"The Chinese have bombed Washington!" she exclaimed.

"They're not certain it was the Chinese, darling," the Brit said. "Truth is, they're not certain of a whole lot, mate. Half the satellites in space were given a good electromagnetic shock and have malfunctioned. Our handheld picked up the BBC in Beijing. We figured it was time to leave, being foreigners and all. The best place to be is anywhere but America's first target for retaliation—if it was China."

Swallowing hard, I took a step back. My palms were sweating.

"The bomb . . . How big was it?"

"I don't know the kiloton, friend. Nobody's certain, you see. Millions dead, though. The whole eastern seaboard, they say. Maybe multiple bombs, is my guess. The fallout isn't a handsome thought, though, with Britain just over the pond!"

"It's World War III." The woman shrugged casually. "Everyone knew it would happen, just not when."

"You don't look so well, friend," the Brit said to me. "Maybe you should find a seat while I get my insulin. Darling? Stay with him, won't you?"

Nearly collapsing against the wall behind me, I slid down until I sat on the floor. My eyes were sightless, my body numb. *A bomb? I was just there! How could this be?*

Flashes of the weather channel for New England's states came to my mind. Living in New York my whole life, I knew the storm patterns. Anything that ever hit D.C. always blew northeast. New Jersey and New York would be wiped out, poisoned by nuclear fallout. Hundreds would be killed while fleeing the panic. Gino, his family, the few Christian brothers and sisters I knew . . . *Millions . . . gone . . .*

Finally, I felt the English woman's hand brush my hair out of my eyes as she felt my forehead. Gathering my legs under me, I rose to my feet. She was talking to me, but I wasn't listening. I trudged back down the hall to the entrance. Once outside, I walked past our horses and past the two old men until I was away from the building to stare up at the clear, blue sky.

As if in a trance, I searched the sky for some meaning to the news I'd just heard. Tears streamed down my cheeks. I had no family in the world, but my heart ached over the pain I knew was being experienced on a massive scale. The sky in Mongolia was blue, but far away, it was ashen gray. People were gasping for breath and dying. And it was just the beginning.

"'*You will be hearing of wars and rumors of wars,*'" I said, quoting from Matthew. "'*See that you are not frightened, for those things must take place, but that is not yet the end. For nation will rise against nation, and kingdom against kingdom, and in various places there will be famine and earthquakes. But all these things are merely the beginning of birth pangs.*'"

"What are you talking about?" the English woman asked me, glancing from the sky to my face. I didn't know she'd followed me outside. "Did you see something?"

I looked into her eyes.

"Jesus is the only One who can deliver us from the wrath to come," I stated, reflecting on Thessalonians. Sighing, I wiped my eyes. "It's just the beginning. People need to recognize Jesus Christ or perish in their sins."

"Oh, you're one of those." She dismissed me with a wave of her hand. "No wonder you're way out here in the middle of nothing. I see your kind on the telly all the time. Is that why you're here? Because of conspiracy theories?"

"I'm a missionary, sharing God's love."

"And these people actually listen to you?"

"Haven't you ever wondered what your purpose was on this earth?" I asked, ignoring her sarcasm.

"Sure." She laughed uncomfortably. "Nothing that a visit to the pub won't cure, love. Just be glad you're safe and don't over-think it all, okay? I'm going to find Willie. You'll be okay. Thanks for your help."

She patted me on the arm and left. I took a deep breath. As a man who takes the Bible literally, I knew the Rapture was coming soon. All the prophecies, the degree of sin, and the many false teachers . . . Everything was falling into place for Christ's return.

"Give me strength, Lord, to do Your will in these Last Days."

Inside the infirmary, I found Skaamaan and Dusbhan sitting beside Zima while she slept peacefully, buried under a small mountain of cotton blankets. Her arm was encased in a white plastic and Velcro brace from elbow to fingertips. Sitting on the edge of her bed, I watched her face. She was beautiful. I was happy that at least she, out of the whole clan, was going to be saved from the wrath to come. Perhaps that was a selfish thing to think. But I still needed to reach the others with the Truth as well—Luyant, Skaamaan, and yes, even Gan-gaad.

"The doctor said to wear the brace for six weeks." Skaamaan held Zima's good hand on the bed. "Is that right, Pond? So long?"

"It sounds right." I nodded. "How long until she'll be able to move about?"

"Two days. He gave me these for her, too."

Skaamaan handed me a baggie with two kinds of pills. One was an antibiotic in case of infection. The other was for pain.

"Gan-gaad won't be patient with her, Pond," Dusbhan said.

"He's already threatened to dismiss me from the clan," I said. "Maybe I can convince him to take us back."

"Perhaps Father will take half the clan and part from Gan-gaad once and for all," Dusbhan said. "Gan-gaad needs us more than we need him. Maybe that would teach him a lesson."

Skaamaan frowned at her son, but she didn't say anything in front of me.

"You two had better rest and then meet up with the clan," I suggested. "They should be here tonight, right?"

"Will you stay with Zima?" Skaamaan asked. "You may be left behind if Gan-gaad wants to keep ahead of Navi-hasgovi after he gets supplies for the winter."

"Just leave us two horses. We'll catch up to you. I don't

think we'll be more than a week behind. Thank you both for your help."

After a while, they left with four of the horses and the cart to find a place to rest near the stables. I remained with Zima's silence and my racing thoughts. Though I was bone-tired, I couldn't sleep, and it was just as well since I had things to tend to. Using a notepad, I wrote Zima a message in case she woke in my absence.

Then, I arranged with the nurse to use a phone. It rang twelve times before Randy answered.

"Oh, I was just thinking about you," he said wearily. "Have you heard the news?"

"Yes." I sighed. "What are your thoughts, Randy?"

He didn't speak for a few moments, but I could hear him weeping. The image in my mind of this God-fearing man crying brought tears to my own eyes.

"Andy, I've been up for two days. It hasn't been easy contacting the States with the time difference and all. I believe we've seen the last of the United States of America. This event may be why there's not more than a hint of America in Scripture's future prophecies."

"It's really that bad, then, isn't it?"

"China may be able to lose a million or two in a war," Randy said, "but the US . . . ? We're looking at close to forty million dead. A couple more million will die in the next couple weeks and months from exposure alone. As of yet, the military is stretched too thin between Homeland Security and overseas operations to organize any kind of offensive. No one's claiming responsibility, either, but China seems to be the culprit. I think it's safe to say, Andy, that we're cut off from what was once our home country. And as much as my family and I would love to be rescued from the coming havoc, I feel a last minute passion to reach out to a few more souls. The Church as a whole will be spared the wrath to come, Andy, but we may have tough times, nevertheless, with what time we have remaining."

"Yeah, that's what I was thinking."

"Did you get the Bibles in Hasagt?"

"That's where I am now, so I'll be picking them up in a few minutes. But I won't be near a town for months, Randy. We'll be wintering in the south, out of contact. I'm not sure I can stand not knowing what's going on."

"None of the world matters, Andy. We'll both finish this race doing what we've been sent to do. Do you remember what Peter wrote?"

"*In this you greatly rejoice, even though now for a little while, if necessary, you have been distressed by various trials.*"

"That's right. Go get your Bibles, Andy. See to the people you're with, and after the winter, Lord willing, I'll speak to you again. Otherwise, my brother, we'll rejoice together in a place that isn't on this earth."

"All right. I'm with you."

"Yes, I know you are. You didn't come all this way for nothing."

"Oh, I led a woman to the Lord a few days ago."

"Andy, that's great!"

"I'll write you all about it before I leave town. I'm swimming through obstacles, but the blessings and fruit are obvious. How're things there?"

"They're disappointing. The more modernized these eastern towns become, the less the people listen to me about their need for a Savior. Simple commerce and technology seems to tend to all their needs, so they ignore the needs of their souls."

We each prayed on the phone. The events so far away in the world gave us a sense that this was the last time we'd be talking together—in this age, anyway. When I hung up, I did feel encouraged. Yes, the end was near. But God was my strength. Those were the only two things I needed to remember as I continued my ministry.

I found a small warehouse on the east side of town that served as the postal service. The clerk watched me with an odd look on his face when I opened the box of Bibles in front of him while trying to hold back tears. There was a letter from Randy, signed by the few believers in his small church. Then, there was an email from Gino, and my knees nearly gave way as I began to read. Gino had no doubt perished by now—or was soon to be gone. With such disrupted communication across the Atlantic, there was no way to know for sure.

Dear Andy,

I'm praising God about the progress of your work there that Randy passed on to us. I've read your letters to the congregation as well. God is doing mighty things through you. We can't wait to hear from you again. You remember Travis and Samantha? They used to always sit in the front pew. They're almost done with language school, enough so they can join Jim Beckley by Christmas in Turkey. And I passed your letters on to a sister church in Boston. They want to support you! Even though you're so independent, their help will be needed in the purchase of more Bibles and other materials you may need. I have enclosed a traveler's check. I know it's not much, but it's from our church here in Ridgewood. We hope to do more for you next month. May God keep you safe and use you mightily—continually!

In Christ, Gino and Family

Closing my eyes, I said a short, quiet prayer for those special people. Their status was unknown, whether they were living or dead, but God knew. What a man of God Gino was! And I could think of no greater honor or compliment given by men than to call another a man of God.

Packaging what pages I had filled in my journal, I sent them to Randy. They were written for Gino, but Randy was my accountability partner now, I figured. Randy had graciously converted Gino's traveler's check into *tugriks* already, so that saved me a hassle. It was the equivalent of about one hundred dollars, which would last me a long time in western Mongolia.

While whispering a prayer, I walked back to the hospital, then to the stable area with the two horses that Dusbhan had left me. I paid the keeper for three days, and returned to the infirmary without looking around to find Dusbhan and his mother. Zima hadn't moved since I'd left. Exhausted, I slumped into the chair against the wall. As I sat there staring at Zima's peaceful, silent face, sleep gradually overtook me. My head bowed over my weary body, and I slept.

CHAPTER FIFTEEN

We spent four days at Hasagt. By the time we departed, Zima was moving around well enough to ride a horse. I'd been instructed by the physician to make sure she kept the plastic brace on her arm, even though it could easily be removed. For the time being, her arm was cradled in a sling, but as the pain subsided, she would lose the sling and begin to use her fingers that protruded past the end of the plastic.

While still at the hospital, I didn't tell Zima about the war and devastation. We were happy together, alone from the rest of the clan. She was grateful for my help, and we spent hours talking between her naps. It wasn't right for me to withhold the state of the world from her, yet I wasn't sure she could fully understand the level of destruction one bomb could do—the sheer impact of lives lost was staggering. Her world had been small and sheltered within the confines of Gan-gaad's own sense of preservation. She seemed to sense my hidden grief, though not the source, but she didn't ask me to explain my countenance. So, I didn't yet share my burden of sorrow.

During those days in Hasagt, I anticipated the long winter that was approaching, so I purchased supplies of my own. I bought more bars of soap and winter clothing. From the stables, I bought a third *aduu* to carry my additional gear and backpack. We weren't a day's ride out of Hasagt to the south when we noticed a clan far to the east. It was several times larger than even Navi-hasgovi's clan, and I pointed it out to Zima.

"It's a Kazakh clan," she said. "There are many clans in this region. They may be close to the mountains preparing for the early winter hunts."

I watched the clan move parallel to us all that day. Unlike Gan-gaad's Mongol clan that had evolved with its own traditions and customs, what I saw of the Kazakh migrators reminded me of the texts I'd read of the truest and most widely known western Mongolian nomads.

In the mid-nineteenth century, the Russian Empire troops had pushed Kazakhs into neighboring countries. The Dzuuz Clan, specifically, had fled into Mongolia and were allowed to settle in the Bayan Ulgii area. For over two hundred years, their isolation preserved their traditions. They became the Mongolian Kazakhs. Even after Kazakhstan's president promised money and livelihoods to the Kazakhs to move back to their homeland in the 1990s, many remained in Mongolia. Those who returned to Kazakhstan were valued for their knowledge of the old customs since they'd not been so polluted by Russian influence. It was this remnant that stayed in Mongolia, and other clans like it, that I observed to the east.

As the first night gradually closed upon us, we left the trail and rode across the steppe toward the Kazakh clan. Gan-gaad would've been furious that we intended to mingle with another clan, but Gan-gaad wasn't the one whom I obeyed. God had sent me to Mongolia to reach out to everyone from any clan or nationality, even if it was Gan-gaad's despised foes, the Kazakhs. They weren't my foes.

"When we're close, we must yell out our arrival," Zima said. "If we don't, their hunting and herd dogs may attack us since we're strangers with a strange scent."

"Herd dogs!" I exclaimed. "Of course! Why doesn't Gan-gaad have them?"

"Navi-hasgovi has no dogs, either, but for good reason. Both clans' stubbornness is to blame. About eight years ago, when Navi-hasgovi and Gan-gaad began to use the same migration lands, they started killing each other's dogs. Dusbhan was involved. Killing dogs was once against the law in Mongolia, but now it's not so condemned since there are so many strays. No one knows for sure, but I believe Gan-gaad started the war to cripple Navi-hasgovi's travels since he was a superior clan. Both men are so arrogant and determined to outdistance the other that they haven't taken the time to buy new pups to train. Every time Navi-hasgovi buys pups, Gan-gaad finds ways to bait them from camp and kill them. The last couple of years, both clans seem to have settled into a routine of life without dogs, though they forget how much better life was with them."

Even as half-Kazakh herself, Zima had never lived with her own people. However, her Russian blood was rich, and her features alone would separate her from either culture, as would mine, though I was often assumed to be Russian. It was these people—the Mongolian Kazakhs—whom I'd come to reach specifically, but God had led me to Gan-gaad for a reason—so Dusbhan and Zima could be reached with the Gospel, but the others were on my heart as well.

I peered through my binoculars to the far south, seeking

a flicker of distant firelight. Gan-gaad was at least a day's ride ahead of us. How serious was he about kicking me out of the clan permanently? He was a stubborn man, but even he couldn't resist the working of the Holy Spirit.

A low, deep growl, then barking brought me back to the present. I stowed my binoculars in a pocket.

"Hello!" I yelled at the Kazakh camp. "Two riders from Hasagt!"

Unlike Gan-gaad's camps, the Kazakh's burned their fires mostly inside their *gers*. Even more amazing was the size of these *gers*! They were twice as wide as the other clans' *gers*, and tall enough for a short man to stand up inside. The *gers* used for supplies and gear were smaller, though.

A number of men walked toward us. Dogs were roaming all around the camp. There seemed to be about forty *gers* interspersed across the hillside with livestock—mostly sheep. Like Gan-gaad, all the *ger* openings faced south since the cold northeast winds were increasing.

Three of the closer dogs stopped barking as their masters approached, but they continued to pace slowly to and fro before us. With eyes that seemed almost human-like, they studied me and Zima cautiously. Their thickening winter coats were mostly black with golden spots above the eyes, which meant they were purely bred. Off to my left were three wooden plates on the ground that were sure to be the dogs' feeding dishes. I wondered if we should have approached from a different direction, but the dogs were everywhere.

"Lion! Shepherd! Lucky Hunter!" one of the men yelled

at the dogs. The dogs instantly acknowledged him, ready to obey. He pointed at the flocks drifting on the graze land. "See to the sheep!"

The dogs turned and trotted away to shepherd the flocks. The man stepped close to me and gripped my horse bridle to see me better in the fading light. He and his men all wore *dels*, the ankle-length felt coat I'd seen in books. This man had gentle eyes, though, unlike his dogs, and regardless of the loose-fitting *del*, I could see he was lean and powerful. Though in his early forties, he had barely a wisp of a mustache.

The clan men behind him, however, were all larger and fiercer-looking. They searched beyond me and Zima for any companions or aggressors. It was then that I realized two of the five men in the background carried rifles slung over their shoulders. Farther into the clan's camp, others paused in their duties to study us as well.

"Where is your clan?" the man asked. "Neither of you are Mongolian, yet you have nomadic belongings."

"We're from the Clan of Gan-gaad," I said. By the name itself, he knew it wasn't a Kazakh clan. "He's one day ahead of us and we have no shelter for the night."

"You know of Gan-gaad?" the man asked another.

"Small Altay herder," the man responded with a shrug.

"I am Lugsalkhaan," the man greeted with a sudden smile. "Come, both of you. I hope you bring news of the war."

"What war?" Zima asked me with a frown, but I gestured to her that now wasn't the time.

We were welcomed with open arms and a warmth that I

would expect from a clan of Buddhist shamans. We were whisked off our horses and our animals were taken away for water and pasture. One clansman with a tradesman's eye inspected the stitching on my American-made backpack. In minutes, we were surrounded by dozens of curious Kazakhs ranging in all ages, even women and girls. Lugsalkhaan grabbed my arm and led me through the throng with Zima at my side.

"Zima, I'm sorry, I should've told you about the war," I managed to say along the way. "America was bombed. I found out in Hasagt and didn't want to worry you."

Looking behind us, I noticed several young men admiring the supplies I'd bought in Hasagt. They sniffed the bars of soap approvingly. With their curiosity quenched, they closed up my packs and carried them after me. Everywhere I looked, I saw smiles and excitement. Even the dogs near the sheep crept closer in interest, daring reprimands from their masters.

There was a much different atmosphere here than with the previous clan. Instead of a shy people raked by fear, here were joyful families glowing with life itself.

We reached one of the middle *gers* and I glanced through its doorway. Three wood-framed, short-legged beds—*actual beds*—lined the circular dwelling. A metal stove stood in the middle, the pipe rising to the *toono*—the small hole in the ceiling to expel smoke and allow sun and air into the shelter.

"You have a Russian look to you," Lugsalkhaan observed as he studied Zima's face.

Zima, shocked that she, being a woman, was being

addressed so openly, could only nod in speechless astonishment. The clansman turned to me.

"But you . . . English?"

"American," I said. "How'd you know I wasn't Russian?"

"Ah. I must admit, I saw the patch on your backpack. It is in English, no?"

"It is. You have a good eye."

"I'm Russian-Kazakh," Zima finally said.

"My brother-in-law is half-Russian. He lives . . . there!" He pointed at a group of four *gers* with a flock of sheep and dogs nearby. "Everyone will want to speak to you both, but I will be first, yes?"

"Of course." I glanced at Zima. She shrugged her approval. "Will you be continuing south?"

"Yes, to the edge of the Gobi, I fear," the man said with a frown. "Other clans press us from the east, and we must move into other ranges now as well. All around the Hangayn Mountains, there is development. It's sad to see the old ways pass away. We run, but they follow."

He led us into the *ger*, and others crowded around to sit with us on the soft beds. The children—all of them belonging to Lugsalkhaan—reached out to touch Zima's arm brace in open curiosity.

"Do you know the clansmen we will live near this winter?" he asked me. "We wish to keep peace if possible. Since we are the largest clan in this region, we may make the winter easier for others. But before we continue, spare me the embarrassment of calling you 'American.' What are your names?"

"I'm Andy, and this is Zima."

"You are man and wife?"

"No, only . . ." I said, pausing. *What were we?* "We're close friends right now."

"Ah, I see," Lugsalkhaan stated skeptically. His knowing eyes had surely noticed how Zima's right hand was never far from my left. "And the clans?"

"I'm recently from America, still learning your ways, but Zima has lived here for many years."

"Many of the clans are small," Zima said. "There are more in the mountain valleys to the west and even into Xinjiang Uygur Province, but you won't be going that far west, will you?"

"No, no. The farthest we'll hunt is to the mountains to the southwest. I'm not excited about grazing my stock on the thin grass and thorns of the *sha-mo*, but graze land will be difficult for everyone this winter. The weather experts from Ulaanbaatar say it will be a difficult season."

Since I didn't know otherwise, I only nodded. His use of the Chinese word "*sha-mo*" I knew referred to the Gobi as the sand desert, which told me that the clan wasn't as isolated traditionally as I'd first thought. The fact that his brother-in-law was half-Russian spoke volumes as well. The Russians had oppressed the Kazakhs in time past, especially during the Bolshevik era.

"Tell me, Andy, the war. What do you know?"

When I took a breath, many leaned forward to hear my words.

"I know it's just the beginning. What has happened in America—though it has impacted America greatly—will escalate to great wars around the world. The millions who have died in America will be followed by many more in Asia, Europe, and Africa."

"It's God's judgement," Zima said. "Paul told us this would all happen, didn't he, Andy?"

Her openness to share the Gospel shocked me for a moment. Of course, she was right to speak so freely! As a child of God, she was led by the Holy Spirit, even if she didn't understand everything. She had a hunger to learn and share that I couldn't and shouldn't hinder.

"Who is this Paul?" Lugsalkhaan asked for everyone. "He's an official?"

Zima nudged me to expound. All eyes were on me.

"He wrote of many things to come in the Last Days before mankind is to be judged as individuals before God Almighty. Only those who accept His gift of life will be spared. Some writings were penned by Paul, and many others—Daniel, Isaiah, John, and Jeremiah—penned truths as well. Most of all, Jesus, the Son of God, fulfills all truth."

"It's all in the Bible," Zima added. She wasn't often such a focal-point of attention. Here, she was regarded as an equal. "The Bible is more profound and truer than the texts we have from India and Tibet—which aren't even complete. The Dalai Lama may have been enlightened by men's standards, but Jesus was truly God Himself."

Again, she looked to me to complete her words. We were like a spontaneous relay team. If Lugsalkhaan had heard of the Bible, he gave no contrary indication. They were all listening intently. Very rarely did outsiders come to bring them news of the outside.

"Yes, it's true. The Bible explains the origin of man as well as God's wisdom to man. He is the One and Only God who possesses wisdom and knowledge from eternity past, long before Buddha himself walked the earth."

"Like you," Zima said with empathy, "I was raised to learn and practice Lamaism. But when I took time to study the Bible and its complete text, I understood the world better. I became one with the Creator through belief that His hand guides all things by love and justice. And in here," she placed her hand over her heart, "I'm a better person, free from the judgement that will soon come on all people. If a bomb lost its way today and landed right here instead of in Urumqu because of a war with America, I know in my heart that I'll immediately be with my great God and Savior who loves me.

"We won't be reborn as animals, my new friends, or as other people. That is an old belief from men's minds when they tried to grasp understanding of the afterlife. The truth is, we will be judged for the good and bad that we do." She pointed to a young boy on the floor at our feet. "When you fight with your sister, you know it's wrong. That feeling of knowing wrong—where does it come from? God made us to know right and wrong. Pond, tell them the true story of the beginning of the world and languages!"

Her enthusiasm was contagious and not merely to the young minds present. Several men and women stood at the door listening to our words with great interest.

I began to tell the story, my hands motioning wildly and excitedly as I spoke. Zima's memory of Genesis and our talks were like crystal cutting through stone as she added details and more graphic vocabulary where appropriate. At one point in the middle of the origin of the rainbow, several clanswomen brought us meat and bread on plates, but hardly anyone noticed. They were too spellbound by the story of the righteous few delivered from a flood. While I ate, Zima spoke, and I was in awe at the way we were being used as true mouthpieces for God that night.

Here were answers to prayer. Here were people whose hearts had been prepared for our words of hope long before we ever arrived. Here were people hungry for something beyond their ancient traditionalism. It was late into the night when I concluded at the end of the dispersion of people at Nimrod's tower.

"The lesson being," I said, "that even when many people get together to do great things to lift up their own names, they will only be humbled as God corrects their proud hearts. We should live our lives for God, assuming every day may be our last, lest we are punished as the nations are beginning to be punished right now for their godless ways—punished by the ugliness of war and death."

The youngest children were tugged from our midst by their mothers as Lugsalkhaan clarified several points about creation and how sin entered the world. He was an observant man—so much so that he asked questions he seemed to understand himself, but he wanted the other men and women present to see the finer points as well. On that first night, I believe many in that *ger* listened for mere entertainment, out of interest or even politeness. But some listened because they needed to. And the seeds of truth were planted.

"I never want to leave these people!" Zima whispered to me as Lugsalkhaan discussed with his people where Zima and I would sleep while we were with them. "I feel alive around them, Pond. They deserve to know the truth. I don't want to go back to Gan-gaad!"

...✝...

CHAPTER SIXTEEN

That first night with the large clan, Zima slept in a *ger* with several of the unattended wives and, quite literally, concubines, while I slept in Lugsalkhaan's *ger* with his latest wife and children. Adultery was rampant throughout all the clans, and I prayed for wisdom in dealing with such ungodly customs.

As I lay on my dog-hair mattress on the wood-framed bed, I should've fallen asleep in an instant, yet I felt the pressures of the age crashing down around me. I had the strongest temptation to just enjoy the time I had remaining in this world, to relax and let my guard down—to be comfortable. None too successfully, I fought these thoughts until I finally rose and exited the spacious *ger*.

Outside, I was greeted by one of the dogs they'd called Lucky Hunter. The dogs were the only tame animals in a clan that were given a name, as if they were part of the family. Lucky Hunter sniffed me warily, then wandered away to lie down. The other two dogs had herded the sheep in close to camp for the night, and were curled up near their feed plates. Since I'd already undergone their inspection, I was able to pass the other two without receiving much regard. I pulled my coat tightly around me and sat down on the edge of a low hill overlooking the wealth of the clan. For these people, not much had changed since the days of Abraham. Wealth was measured by their livestock. They made their own clothing, their *gers*, their food, and even their socks, by hand.

Many in the civilized world believed there would be less sin if there was less technology, or less exposure to sin. But sin lives in the heart of the lost. Without God, even the peaceful Tibetan Buddhists practiced immorality that was quite shocking when compared to biblical marriage principles. Reforming the Mongolians wasn't my primary objective, though. My goal was to see them saved from sin and eternal death.

Marriage. Paul's words to the Corinthian church came to my mind. *How could I think of marriage at a time like this?* The Tribulation years were on the horizon . . . The world was beginning to experience signs of things to come . . . And the Rapture was ever closer . . .

Zima was an amazing woman. And what a mind! If it weren't for her, I would've spent the night talking about America and warming up to the clan. Yet Zima hadn't hesitated to jump in with both feet and talk of nothing but God's original dealings with men!

She didn't want to go back to Gan-gaad. I could understand that, but she had to leave his clan with his blessing, or Luyant's blessing in the least. But as I was still reeling from that thought, Matthew chapter twenty-eight hit my conscience like a brick. "*Go therefore and make disciples.*" Though the passage continued, there were only those five words for me that night. It was as if God were trying to make it simpler for me since I was making it difficult for myself. "*Just go . . . and make!*" My calling wasn't to solve every moral dilemma in the country. No, my job was to share the Word, plant the seed, make disciples. God would work out the rest.

All my worries vanished as I gave them to the Lord to be burdened by his broad shoulders. I was so preoccupied with praising Him for His help that I didn't notice the chubby little man ascending the hill from the camp until he was standing next to me. Hastily, I climbed to my feet. The man reminded me more of a giant ball than a human, but it may have been partly from all the layers of clothing he wore that cold night. Standing, I offered my hand.

"Hello. I don't think we've met. I'm Andy."

He gripped my hand roughly and pumped it so hard my shoulder nearly dislocated. There was power under all that fat! On his head he wore a snow leopard hat, though yellowed from years of use.

"Duulgii!" he declared. I knew from his features that he was probably Lugsalkhaan's half-Russian brother-in-law. He nodded at the stars. "I see I'm not the only one who seeks wisdom from the sky."

"I seek wisdom from the Maker of the sky," I said. "It's a beautiful night."

"In Semey, my home in Kazakhstan, I know Christians, but you aren't like them," he said. "You have no candles and you don't ask for money." He laughed heartily. "I think that makes you a good man."

"When I came here from Turkey," I said, smiling at his joke, "I flew over Kazakhstan in a plane. But it was nighttime. I regret not seeing the country in the daytime."

"You missed very little, Andy." He grunted. "I have traded one lonely country for another—except there is pride here. Do you know of the *touman?*"

"Genghis Khan's forces? Yes, I've read of them."

"Formations of ten thousand horsemen in each wave, Andy. Imagine such soldiers riding across this plain. They conquered everyone—the whole world—from Korea to Germany. Ah! In my next life, perhaps I will be born a true Mongol!"

We stood together for a while. Lion, one of the dogs, trotted around Lugsalkhaan's flocks, separating those belonging to other clansmen.

"I think he counts them," Duulgii joked, nodding at Lion. "He doesn't have much of a nose for hunting, but he knows his sheep. You have no dogs?"

"No. Someday I may buy one, though."

"One of my dogs will have pups any day. There are three others before you, but you may have fourth choice."

"That's gracious of you, but I may not be ready to raise a Manchurian."

"But mine aren't Manchurians. They are sure to be Mongolian Mastiffs, the largest of the mastiff breeds. Do you have any stock?"

"A small number."

"Then it's settled. You will have a dog—my gift to you to make your herding days easier."

"Thank you, Duulgii, but I don't have anything to trade of equal value."

"Bah! It is a gift, Andy! Only . . . you will have to stay with the clan until the birth and weaning. That is the charge for the pup, perhaps, and the stories you tell, yes?"

"Yes," I said with a chuckle. "I do have more stories."

"Good. The children love the stories. I missed them tonight, but my wife told me some. I won't miss them tomorrow night, though. Can you tell them at my camp?"

"If Lugsalkhaan approves. I'm his guest."

"He's not a selfish man. I'll ask him. Do you know any stories about soldiers? I want to hear stories about soldiers."

"Oh, yes," I said, "some of the best soldier stories ever told. Great battles and strategies."

"I want to hear those. Of course, the characters won't be as mighty as Mongol soldiers. And dog stories. Do you have any of those?"

"Dogs? Hmmm. I'm afraid I don't know any specific dog stories, though some of the people I'll tell you about had dogs to watch their flocks as you do, as they did thousands of years ago."

"Yes, a dog has such wisdom—but not all of them. You must choose your mastiff carefully, Andy, and that won't be easy since you have fourth pick of the litter. Always consult with a monk if you are able, before you choose. I already know it is a favorable year, but there is the day and hour to bring the puppy into your *ger* that must be considered as well. But you don't believe in such superstitions, do you?"

"No, but I'm sure there are other ways to choose a good puppy."

"Of course. You pick it up by the tail or leg. If it arches its back and doesn't cry, it will be a good, strong dog. The last born is the best preference, but you won't get that one. A heart-shaped spot on its chest is a sign of bravery and loyalty. Red in the eyes means the dog will fight enemies even when outnumbered. White spots near the claws could mean wealth, but white on the tail or feet means it will be lazy and steal food. But those are more superstitions. Even I know that. Just look for short, soft hair, flexible skin, a wide chest, and a small back. That's all you must do."

"That's good advice." I nodded.

"And when you bring it home, you whisper its name into its ear. They never forget them after that. You could be poor with no flocks to herd, and the Khaan himself could pass by, but your dog won't leave you for another."

Duulgii eventually asked about my childhood in America, and I was able to share my testimony with him, of the life of bondage God had saved me from through the gift of Jesus. We talked until sunup, and I knew I would regret it later that day, but we enjoyed ourselves.

The large Kazakh clan wasn't in such a hurry to leave as Gan-gaad was every morning. This clan had more to pack and larger herds to move. It was nearly an hour before we departed after a horn was blown. Zima and I moved among them, assisting where we were needed. Almost naturally, we waited behind as the great caravan started to the southeast. Smiling at one another, we sat down on the grass still wet from morning dew. She opened her new Bible, one of the five I'd picked up in Hasagt, and I opened one of the others, my original somewhere to the south with Dusbhan. We read and prayed together, and talked about the Holy Spirit's effectiveness the night before. Already, we anticipated the coming evening's story time.

Once we were back on our horses, we planned which stories we'd tell that night in Duulgii's camp.

"Since I'm Russian and Duulgii is Russian," Zima said,

"he told me he and I should marry, but I told him you and I have hearts for one another, so he left me alone."

Riding beside me, she watched my reaction carefully until I could stand it no longer and I burst out laughing.

"What's funny, Pond?" She pouted. "It's not true? Don't you love me?"

"This is one of the things I was praying about last night," I said. "It seems we'd best find an adequate minister after we discuss the matter with Luyant."

"Do we have to?"

"Zima, you know we do. You're still in his care, and I must offer an acceptable dowry on top of any blessing he gives you to leave the clan."

"I never imagined I would marry." She beamed and sighed. "We'll need our own *ger* and flocks. Do you have money for all of this?"

"Yes, I believe so."

"And we can live with the Kazakhs afterward?"

"That's something we need to ask God about," I said. "As my wife, you'll be under my protection, so there'll be no need to fear Gan-gaad if we should live with his clan again. We need to go where God leads us, not necessarily where we're most comfortable. The best place to be is in God's will."

"Yes, you're right," she said with another sigh, then grinned broadly. "But I will be your wife and you will be my husband!"

"It's starting to look that way," I said with a chuckle.

"We'll be happy together, won't we, Pond? Until Jesus comes?"

I gazed into the sky. *What a day that will be!* But at that instant, far to the south, I saw a small formation of Chinese fighter jets. They were on a northwesterly heading. However, as dreadful as their presence might've been, I felt a strange calm—that peace that passes all understanding.

"Yes, Zima, we'll be happy together."

...✝...

That day, the clan stopped before dark to set up camp. We'd traveled no more than twenty miles, and I realized with some concern that Gan-gaad was becoming more separated from us. While I helped set up the *gers* that evening, I resolved to go ahead and catch up to him before the distance became even greater between him and the slower-moving Lugsalkhaan Clan. So Zima and I could make plans regarding our future together, her adoptive parents needed to be consulted, and perhaps even given a dowry—of which I knew very little.

As the cook stoves fired up and the evening meal was prepared, I wandered amongst the *gers* in search of Lugsalkhaan to convey my decision. I was stopped often by different families, asked questions of my origin, and complimented on my grasp of their language. Here, I found children with books, their parents or other tutors prohibiting them from running off to play until their studies were completed. It's true that Mongolian literacy rate is at ninety-percent, even amongst nomadic clans, though one wouldn't know it by observing Gan-gaad's clan.

Since I hadn't found Lugsalkhaan, I backtracked toward his dwelling when a giant shadow loomed from the sky over my shoulder. I flinched and dove to the ground where I found myself half-covered in mud from a wash pot. Laughter erupted around me. I rose and sheepishly brushed off my clothes. As I stood, the settling flap of wings on Duulgii's outstretched arm alerted my curiosity. And then I found the source of my fear: a giant golden eagle with a wing-span of eight feet perched on Duulgii's arm. The bird was gripping a marmot, pierced through with the black, curled talons.

Duulgii took the marmot from his eagle and gave the hunter a sliver of venison as a reward.

"No need to fear my raptor, Andy!" Duulgii laughed with the others. "Unless you're a fox with a nice winter coat! Come, touch her. She brings in more food in a day than I could with the dogs in a week."

The brown and seemingly frazzle-feathered hunter eyed my approach. Her head twisted this way and that every few seconds, as if ready to be off to hunt for more prey. I stroked her soft neck feathers and noticed some of the other Kazakh men had eagles as well. All were fully grown eagles, and I said as much to Duulgii.

"They were born in the early summer. This one is twelve years old, the best hunter we have. Already, even the young chicks we stole from the nest earlier this year are trained to hunt."

"But not just for marmots?" I asked. "You said foxes, too?"

"Raptor here has killed a couple foxes and even small wolves," Duulgii boasted. "She knows her limitations— which are cattle, I suppose!"

We all laughed.

"How does she kill a wolf?" I asked.

"She dives onto its back, breaking its spine. When I see her dive and then not return to the sky right away, I know she's captured something too large to carry. I find her by her cries and oftentimes by a cloud of dust as she continues to fight and hold on to the wounded animal. She shows no mercy, Andy, especially this one, which is why we send them to hunt at different times. The eagles will kill each other over a carcass."

"And she's the oldest here? Only twelve years old? I thought eagles lived to be about fifty."

"They do. We normally release them back to the wild after a decade, but this raptor refused to be loosed."

I shook my head. *Amazing!* The more I thought about it, the more I recalled having seen the carnivores in the sky the last couple days, but I hadn't thought about them being birds of prey belonging to falconers!

"We can't all eat this marmot, Duulgii," I joked. "Let her hunt more! I'd love to see this."

"It's another bird's turn now. My raptor would hunt all day if—"

The raptor suddenly took flight as if startled. I ducked with the others as all the eagles flapped their giant wings and soared into the sky. Their masters were momentarily speechless. They'd given no command to fly. It made no sense! Beside me, Duulgii and the others yelled at their eagles to return. But the birds didn't heed the men or boys running after them.

Curiously, I stepped away from the yelling and put an ear to the wind. There was a noise in the air, something foreign. Whatever it was, it had spooked the eagles. I continued to the west up a small hill above the expanse of *gers*. Around me, the flocks of sheep stopped grazing and became suddenly alert as well—but not because of me.

Now, I wasn't the only one to hear it. Even the falconers had ceased their calls skyward to glance about the campfires for the source of the disturbance.

Something was wrong. *Very wrong.* No one moved within the clan, not even the animals. I gazed over the tops of the *gers* and found Zima on the opposite eastern side of the camp. She held an infant on her lap. Her eyes likewise were scanning the camp for me. Since I was taller than everyone with my blond head, she quickly located me on the hillside above the camps with the livestock. Like the others, she surely wanted to know what the distant noise was.

It was a motor, I decided. An engine. More than one, though. And a rumble, like machinery, to the southeast of us. But the small bowl in which we'd camped around a spring caused the sound to be distorted and echoed around us. As I was higher, I could hear better. I glanced into the sky where the eagles drifted on warm air currents. They could see what we couldn't.

Trying to swallow, I sensed grave danger. My mind compiled everything in an instant. China had bombed the American coastline and the US capital. The fighter jets I'd seen that morning had been flying over Mongolian airspace. Mongolia had no national guard, only about six thousand border guards, an army of about eight thousand, and a police force. And now, the rumble of heavy machinery that shook the ground. Machines where there were no roads or fuel depots or—

I was running before they came into sight, leaving the sheep behind. Leaping over a campfire, I fell against a *ger*, breaking some of its wooden framework, but I couldn't stop then.

"Get the horses!" I shouted accidentally in English, then corrected and repeated myself in Mongolian. "Pick up everything you can carry! Get the kids!"

A few people began to move as I dashed past them. Most stared at the near horizon, watching the animals' reactions, waiting for more sign of danger. Zima, too far away to hear me, saw me running toward her. I prayed she saw the fear on my face.

"Get the horses and run!" I yelled to everyone I passed.

Zima kept the infant on her hip, but reached down and shouldered my backpack. That was good. I kept it stocked and ready to go. She knew what was necessary and seemed to ignore the brace on her arm and the pain within.

A crack of thunder sounded over my left shoulder. I stopped and turned in time to see one of the clan's few cattle shiver violently, stumble forward, then collapse dead. At that instant, a green, all-terrain vehicle seating three men skidded to a halt on the southwest perimeter of the camp. A man in black jumped out of the back of the vehicle with an assault rifle. He aimed and fired again. Another head of stock slumped to the ground. He aimed at another, fired, then another.

The men were Chinese.

CHAPTER SEVENTEEN

The camp erupted in utter confusion and screams around me. Horses and sheep stampeded through the camp away from the gunfire. Still, I stood my ground and watched a second vehicle appear. This one was an oversized armored personnel carrier with eight wheels. It was big enough to carry twenty men in is belly, but I saw only three men emerge and begin to quarter the dead animals. A fourth man on top of the carrier manned a mounted machine gun. He held his fire, though he swept it over the clan threateningly.

I'd seen enough. It could only get worse now. Grabbing at an *aduu* as it ran by me, I caught its halter, and was dragged beside it until I could settle it down enough to mount. Though I had no reins or lead rope, I'd seen the Mongols ride their horses bareback without reins as the animals were neck reined and even partially voice-trained.

It took all of my strength to control the frightened animal as it high-stepped in a panic through the camp. I heard more gunshots. My horse danced in a circle around a boiling tub of stew, spilled it, and then bucked me off. I landed on my back, the wind forced from my lungs. Another horse was coming toward me at a full run. When I tried to sit up or roll away, I found I couldn't breathe. At the last instant, I raised one arm, praying the beast wasn't scared blind. It vaulted over me, its hooves clearing me by an inch.

195

A clansman paused over me. With one hand, he yanked me to my feet. In his other hand he held a Russian assault rifle. He held it against his shoulder and fired at the Chinese. The gunshot made my ears ring. I saw one of the Chinese soldiers clutch his belly, and another leveled his machine gun at us. Gasping, I dove to the ground yet again, this time into the stew. The clansman fell on top of me then rolled away, his head half-missing from a small artillery round.

Machine gunfire swept across the camp, tearing chunks out of *gers* and flesh alike. A dog ran past me and snapped at my hand. I scrambled to my feet as more gunfire churned dirt to my left where another clansman returned fire. People were screaming. Animals were crying. Dogs yelped and growled, fleeing in terror in every direction.

I skidded to a halt in front of Zima. With seemingly more calm than I felt, she held in her braced arm the reins of two horses as they pranced excitedly about. In her other arm, she still held the infant. Taking the reins from her, I grabbed my backpack, slung it over a shoulder, and then cupped my hand to launch her onto the horse. Turning, I ran and ducked into a *ger* where I surveyed my wealth of gear I didn't want to leave behind.

Food and shelter was all I could think about. I snatched up a bundle of blankets I'd bought in Hasagt and a saddlebag of dried beef. My extra Bibles were tucked into the bundle of blankets, and . . . water! But my canteen was full inside the backpack already on my back.

"Hurry, Pond!"

Crawling out of the *ger*, I draped the saddlebags over the

horse's withers and jumped onto its back, holding the blankets in one arm. If Zima could cradle an infant and ride with a brace, I could hold the bundle of blankets. She tossed me the reins to my horse and whipped her own into a run to the west. My *aduu* spun in a circle once, enough for me to see dozens of dead Kazakhs, several *gers* on fire, and more Chinese vehicles arriving on the hill to the south.

A five-year-old boy screamed with tears streaming as he knelt over a beloved dog now dead—trampled or shot, I couldn't tell. I heeled my horse up next to him, reached down, and grasped him by the back of his fur coat. Frantically, I yanked him upward to sit in front of me, straddling the horse's neck, then shoved the blankets into his arms.

"Hold these!"

I wrapped my arm around his midsection and my horse started away with a lunge. Ten steps later, we were flying across the steppe toward the mountains after Zima. She was two hundred yards ahead of me with a small pack on her back. How much had she been able to get? She must've jumped into action the second our eyes had met across the camp.

There was no need to look back as more machine gunfire steadily raked the Kazakh camp. Then I could hear no more crying, no more screams.

After a mile, I slowed my winded horse to a walk. To my right and left, other Kazakhs who'd managed to find mounts and escape were riding into the foothills of the Gobi Altay Mountain range. Zima was waiting for me at the top of a ridge. I reined up and turned to follow her gaze. Far away, the camp appeared to be a total loss. Fires and the endless column of military vehicles were destroying the camp as they drove straight through it, over the dead, wounded, and felt-covered *gers*. The convoy stretched as far as my eyes could see to the southeast. The initial recon vehicles had loaded up the carcasses from their kills and moved to the front of the column again.

"Butchers!" Zima said in disgust. "Why Mongolia? We have nothing!"

"It's not about Mongolia," I said. "It's about Russia. They're probably attacking Novosibirsk and other Russian military installations. Along this side of the mountains, they have a clean run right into Western Tava. There are roads most of the way, once they reach Hasagt. If the satellites really are no longer working, nobody will see them coming, and nobody would expect them to attack from Mongolia over the mountains, either."

Two men rode toward us along the ridgeline. One was Duulgii, but I didn't know the other. Duulgii still wore his falconer's sleeve, and he'd managed to grab a hefty pack, which he'd strapped to his *aduu's* rump.

"How many do you count, Andy?" Duulgii asked, his mount moving alongside mine. "How many escaped?"

"Perhaps twenty. Maybe less."

"Anyone who didn't get away quickly on horseback was killed," Zima said, her jaw clenched in anger.

"Have you seen Lugsalkhaan?"

"Not yet." I shook my head, then pointed to a number of moving dots on the opposite side of the camp. "But he might be among those who fled to the east."

"There's nothing to the east, only desert." Duulgii said. "They'll die there without shelter. And it looks like it'll be some time before this convoy thins enough to go back and salvage what's left of the camp. Look there. The sheep go east as well. In a week, they'll be dead by wolves or thirst."

I watched the land below us, but I was also thinking of Duulgii and his companion. Both had time to pack gear, but neither had bothered to bring family members in their escape. They'd been behind us with more than a few women and children still in the camp. This wasn't a healthy thought to dwell upon, so I sighed it away from my mind. Fear and self-preservation are a nasty mix. But what was done, was done.

"What do you suggest we do, Duulgii?" I asked.

He shot a thumb toward the west where the sun had set. It was near dark.

"The mountain woods are our only chance. It's a bad time of year to have nothing. In a few days, we'll return to the camp for *ger* felt to build new shelters, but it would be pointless to continue the southern migration with no livestock or supplies. From here, we're only a few days out of Hasagt, but that may not be safe now, either."

After one last look at the plain below, Zima and I turned our horses around, and we headed toward the snow-capped mountains. I remembered one Scripture passage in Judges at that moment that seemed fitting, though it didn't necessarily apply to us. *"The sons of Israel made for themselves the dens which were in the mountains and the caves and the strongholds."* Though we weren't the children of Israel whom God saved from the Midianites, I was certain God heard my pleas for protection that night. Only He could give the helpless so much hope.

"Are you doing okay, Little Man?" I asked the boy sitting in front of me.

He looked up at me with big, brown eyes.

"My toes are cold."

"Try to wiggle them," I suggested. "Keep them moving. It won't be long until we stop and start a fire."

But the temperature was dropping rapidly, and few of those who had escaped had adequate clothing as I did for winter weather.

As we approached the mountains and the dark green belt of forest that girded them, I noticed a pack of wolves in the gathering darkness. They trotted toward us, but when our horses didn't shy away, I realized they were five clan dogs. Romping and chasing one another around us as we trekked, they seemed to have forgotten the evening's terrors, their herding duties now interrupted.

When we reached the timber line, it was below freezing. Our horses' heads drooped wearily, the duty demanded of them reaching its limit after the full day's journey.

I led the way weaving through cedar and larch trees. The canopy above was so dense, the moon and stars were blotted out. A little later, I found what I sought—a fallen cedar tree—and I helped my passenger slide to the ground. We listened to the wind in the trees, but above the sound of the wind was the sound of water. A brook was trickling over rocks not far away.

"It's a good place," Duulgii said.

Behind Duulgii were four more riders, one of them a

woman. A couple of them carried children as well—but their faces communicated their grief. Many children had been lost.

"Set up camp here," Duulgii instructed. "I'm going to ride south to see who else escaped."

He and his riding partner departed when we needed them most. I tied my horse to a sapling and knelt in front of the boy I'd brought with me.

"How are your toes doing?"

"Cold. And I'm hungry."

I gave him a stick of meat from my saddlebags.

"What's your name?"

"Manai."

"Well, Manai, my name is Andy. The woman over there is Zima." Zima stood next to the fallen log holding the baby. "You did a good job hanging onto these blankets for us. We'll need them tonight when we sleep. But before we sleep, we need to build a shelter and a fire. While you eat your meat, I need you to collect all the sticks and branches you can find, okay? Moving around will keep you warmer."

The boy marched off, accustomed to small chores, and I unwrapped my bundle of blankets. I positioned them in a sort of nest fashion for Zima to lay the infant to free her helpful hands. Already, the four other adults were also gathering wood. They'd brought next to nothing besides the clothes on their backs. Between Zima and me, this camp was sure to be doing better than most of the others who were probably banding together up and down the belt of forest.

Holding hands, Zima and I knelt against the fallen tree.

"Lord God, we trust You in this difficult time. Give us wisdom to do what must be done and the strength to do it. And please give us the words to share with these others about Your love, which doesn't wane through stormy weather. In Jesus' name, amen."

The first thing I did was test to see how rotten the log was. The top seemed to have weathered better than the moldy bottom. Using my trenching shovel, I easily battered away the bottom of the log to make a sort of cutaway underneath it. The tree itself was three feet wide and would work nicely for what I had in mind. I gave Zima my lighter as I continued to excavate beneath the log. The ground was soft and I piled the earth aside. Under the log and extending on both sides, I dug a hole about two feet deep and nine feet square. This took a half-hour, by which time the others had a nice blaze burning. The tarp from my pack was ten feet square and I draped it over the log evenly on both sides. I anchored down the tarp ends in the piles of dirt I'd dug up, so even if it rained, the hole would stay dry. If we squeezed in, all of the adults could sleep five side by side, and the fifth at the head or foot. The three children could pile between us without much trouble. It would be tight either way, but we'd be warm and dry for the night. Perhaps the next day, I would think of some improvements.

At the fire, everyone had their knives out working on chunks of wood. I didn't interrupt to ask questions, only watched as they began to fashion crude bowls and plates. Zima walked out of the woods and up to me. She held her braced arm with pain on her face. It was clear she'd been straining the healing bone too much.

"There's a stream to the west that runs from the glacier," she said. "It'll be frozen in a couple weeks, but we can always melt the snow. It's about a hundred paces that way. As soon as they have a bowl ready, I'll milk the mares. The baby needs to be fed, too."

Approving, I nodded, and she continued about her work. I hadn't used everything in my backpack since my arrival to Mongolia, so I dug through it to find what else we could use. There were my two changes of clothes and the sewing kit that would come into play at some point. None of us had been wounded, so I left the first aid kit in the pack. Sitting at the fire with the sewing kit, I took the blankets in my lap, along with the baby, and began to sew the blankets together in pairs. In the bundle from Hasagt, there were six blankets, making three sets. It was better than handing out one blanket for each adult. Everyone would have three layers of covering, though shared, then I'd sleep at the foot in my sleeping bag in front of the shelter's opening, which faced south.

All of this would be adequate for now, but it would need to be reinforced eventually—and preferably before the ground froze.

One of the clansmen sat next to me as he carved expertly at his wood. I knew him to be Sembuuk, someone Lugsalkhaan had said was a skilled hunter. He was built like me, though a little shorter and older. In the light of the fire, his face appeared as the others: weary and grieved.

"You have lived in the woods before, Andy?"

"As a youngster, I slept in tents in forests quite often. I know how to care for myself just fine. But out here, with six adults, three children, and a baby?"

"The forest has everything we need. We'll be okay."

He noticed that I was looking at his falconer's sleeve.

"I have a young eagle," he said. "Tomorrow, I'll ride out into the steppe. If she's near, she'll find me. With her hunting for us, a group this small can survive the winter."

"And we have the mares' milk," I added.

"Yes, but we may need to kill a couple of the old and dry ones for meat and skins. I've heard it may be a long winter."

Nodding, I noticed Zima and the other woman, a plump mother of about thirty-five, milking the mares. Zima could only use one hand, but she was helping.

"We need to watch the convoy as well," Sembuuk said. "As soon as it breaks its long procession, we need to go down and find grain for the horses, lattice from the *gers* to improve our shelter, and any tools."

"I've been thinking," I said quieter for only his ears, "that the convoy probably won't cease." Sembuuk looked up from his wood crafting. "As long as there are Chinese troops in the north, there will be constant traffic back and forth through the steppe. That's armed traffic, Sembuuk, with escorts. They'll be worried about any rebel bands disrupting their supply train."

"Then they'll shoot us if we draw near." He continued carving.

"And any livestock they see, they'll continue to take it to feed the troops. You already witnessed that. They knew they didn't need to bring much food because they could pick it up as they went along."

"It's very wicked, but you're right." He scowled. "You

were in the military in America?"

"No, but I've read a lot of books about the military and wars. I was just a shameful criminal in America, but God saved me from that life."

"Your God is more helpful than my gods, then."

"My God has promised to work all situations toward a good result for those who love Him, Sembuuk. As difficult as that may be for you to believe, it even includes this situation."

We talked about what it meant to love God as the women chilled the milk with snow from the glacier and split the meat from my saddle bag. Manai climbed onto my knee, perhaps as he would've done with his own father.

I blessed the food aloud before we ate. They seemed to think it odd that a man would thank a God at a time like that, but they were polite. In minutes, we had bellies full of milk and dried beef. Yawns soon followed. It was well after midnight, but no one wanted to leave the warmth of the fire. Taking leadership, I announced the sleeping arrangements, then encouraged everyone to get some sleep. We would have a busy day ahead of us.

...✝...

CHAPTER EIGHTEEN

It seemed natural for me to take command of our small camp, and no one objected since I'd brought most of the supplies. Sembuuk surely knew more about living off the land than me, but I had a better overview of our entire situation.

The sleeping arrangements inside the lean-to were simple. The two horse blankets made of felt were lain on the ground under the sleepers for padding and some warmth, and when the three layers of blankets were added, everyone sighed with relief that there was in fact escape from the cold.

The two men without wives were on the one side. The man and wife were in the middle, and since Zima told me she didn't want to sleep next to a man unless it was me, she slept on the other side next to the wife. The children lay among the adults, the baby between the women. I slept at their feet across the entrance in my sleeping bag. If any animal were to attack us, it would have to confront me first. As there were many wolves in the woods, no one asked for the doorway position in my stead. Unfortunately, none of the dogs had stuck around and had instead romped off with Duulgii. We had to make do with what we had.

In moments, the feet in my face stopped wiggling and their breathing became regular. Snug in my sleeping bag, I watched the fire light flicker on the tarp roof.

"Thank You, Lord, for keeping me safe today. You obviously have more for me to do."

Though I remember only closing my eyes, it was suddenly morning. I awoke to Sembuuk climbing over me to exit the lean-to. With the birds chirping noisily, it was certainly time for me to rise as well.

Sembuuk and I took the horses to water, then returned with wood to stock the coals from the night before. The other two men emerged sleepily and sat with us, heating water in the primitive bowls.

"Today, we need to scavenge for food," Sembuuk said. "Andy and I will check the convoy. If it has thinned or is gone, we'll all go down to pillage our camp. Andy?"

"We need to locate other clan members, too." I gestured at Kandal, an elderly Kazakh, and the other unmarried man. "There are survivors out there. Families should be together. Can you make contact?"

Kandal nodded.

The men agreed on our individual duties. When the two women awoke, their hands would be full with caring for the children and their own chores, none of which I needed to address.

Mounted our horses, Sembuuk and I rode to the east. Ten minutes through the forest was all it took to emerge onto the open plain. These were the last trees for a thousand miles, maybe more. The belt of trees was strangely even on our left and right, as if they'd grown at the last possible altitude along the mountains. We were a lot higher than I'd thought we were.

Adjusting my binoculars, I spied on the caravan of

military vehicles far below, still streaming along steadily.
But I did notice some gaps at certain intervals. The trail on
which they drove was a well-defined dirt road now, one
section passing through the clan's old camp where a vehicle
stopped as we watched and two soldiers picked through the
debris. All of this I reported to Sembuuk, then passed him
my glasses. Instead of focusing on the carnage, which may
have been too painful to see, he trained his view at the sky.

"There." He pointed. "My raptor." He handed me the
binoculars. "She can spot a squirrel a mile away. I know
she's already seen us."

"Look." I gestured down the forest edge to the south.

Two other riders stood with their horses as we were,
watching the convoy roll along from horizon to horizon.
Beyond them some distance was yet another rider. These
riders represented remnant camps, I guessed, and we rode
toward them. We were the most northern. When we met,
Sembuuk knew them all, and they each announced who they
had in their camps. As presumed, ours was the largest. The
middle camp had six adults with two children, and the
southern camp had four adults and one child. No one had
seen Duulgii and his riding partner, which I thought was
odd since they'd departed from our camp the night before to
search for others. I suggested it might mean a fourth camp
was somewhere nearby.

"If there are any more gaps in the convoy by nightfall,"
one man said, "we might sneak down and get some gear."

"There's no room for error," Sembuuk said in warning.
"If we're a crowd, we'll be spotted. Their vehicles have
lights. We already know they'll shoot anyone they see,

though we're too far away from them up here. Tonight, two men should go down and find everything for all three of our camps. I have no wife or family left, so I will go. Who else will go with me?"

It was an unattractive offer and a potentially deadly mission, so no one spoke up.

"I'll go," I finally said. "But I suggest we leave the horses well out of sight."

"We'll walk the last distance in the dark." Sembuuk pointed at one man. "You hold our horses and pack up the gear we bring back. To make that easier, we'll get saddles first."

"How about a wagon or a cart?" I asked.

"No, we'd need a horse to draw it," Sembuuk said. "Besides, it would leave more noticeable tracks." He climbed off his horse and tossed me his reins. After a few seconds, he'd arranged three fist-sized rocks on the ground in a triangle. "This is Three Rocks. Every morning, we have *khuruldai* here—a meeting. Three rocks for three camps. As time goes on, we'll meet once a week. We'll send you two people from our camp to make us equal in number. More survivors may show up, and we'll distribute them evenly. Keep the camps separate for now, and small—to draw less attention from these Chinese murderers."

"And don't engage the Chinese," I added strongly. "We can't win against so many guns. If we antagonize them, they'll take the time to hunt us down in the woods. They know some of us escaped. Since they haven't come after us, they probably believe we won't cause any problems, and we need to hold ourselves to that."

"At dawn, we'll split what Andy and I are able to retrieve from the camp. Our grandfathers started over time and again. We will, too."

The men nodded, though gloomily, and we parted ways. We would meet again at Three Rocks at dusk.

Sembuuk and I rode north again, then watched the convoy and studied the terrain below. Gradually, we put together a plan for that night. For smaller items, we would act as a relay team, and work together for heavier things. We also discussed a list of gear we wanted to find—if it wasn't too damaged by fire, gunfire, or vehicle tires.

"If we find only one axe, then we draw straws for the axe," Sembuuk decided. "And that camp must chop wood for all three camps for one week. Then we'll rotate. If we find two axes, then two camps split wood and share with the third camp. This rule should apply for all gear."

Leaving him there to call for his eagle, I started into the woods toward our camp. One hundred feet later, I heard a soft whine to my right—a dog's whine. Right away, I recognized Lucky Hunter, Lugsalkhaan's dog, and climbed off my mount.

"Easy, boy. What do you have there?"

At first, I thought it was a wild animal carcass that Lucky Hunter was guarding, but then I realized it was a human. I knelt on one side of the body, opposite the dog. Lucky Hunter, silent now, watched me with those patient, cautious eyes. He wouldn't leave his master. Lugsalkhaan lay before me. He was shot through the side by a bullet. A lung had probably been punctured and he'd slowly suffocated there through the night. It was impressive that he'd made it as far as he had before falling.

"Come here, boy," I called.

The dog hopped over his master and sniffed my hands. He was hungry and smelled meat or milk on my fingers. We needed the dog desperately, and though I could've used the food myself, I tore my last stick of meat into pieces and fed Lucky Hunter from my hand a piece at a time. Gobbling it up greedily, he then sniffed at my clothes for more. It was all I had, and I hoped it was enough to draw him away.

A few minutes later, I rode into camp with Lucky Hunter trotting alongside. The dog was welcomed with hugs from everyone, as if he were a long-lost relative, and Zima was wise enough to bait him into staying with a small bowl of mare's milk.

Quietly, I told Zima of Lugsalkhaan's fate. Also, I informed the husband and wife and their son from our camp that they were going to another camp at dusk. They weren't very happy to leave our developing camp until I told them someone had saved one of their other children at the southernmost camp. That would leave seven at our camp: Zima, the baby, Manai, Sembuuk, Kandal, and the last adult, Bolor, the father of the other child, his seven-year-old daughter, Beveg. It was still several to look after, but more manageable.

Kandal was nearly seventy, and when it came to the skills required to make wooden tools, or knowledge of vegetation, he knew more than all of us. When Lucky Hunter lost the camp's attention, Kandal explained to the three children the kind of edible plant he wanted them to find. Lucky Hunter bounded along after them as they entered the forest. With the children on their quest, Kandal explained to the others, for my sake mostly, how to make a small *ger*. We needed birch saplings and willow lengths and many leather strips. Since I was to bring us the felt and canvas that night, Kandal wanted to have a frame for a small *ger* ready as soon as possible. He said I could sleep under my tree, but he was going to live in a civilized shelter. Even though the husband and wife were leaving that night, they helped collect the items Kandal needed to construct the first of several *gers*.

While everyone was busy, I walked back through the woods with my shovel and found Lugsalkhaan's body. The adults in all three camps anticipated seeing the great clan leader alive, and that gave them hope, so I buried him in secret in a deep grave with a cross engraved in the tree at his head. I stood there for a while, my hands folded, not sure of what to say. Already, I had buried more people than any man ever should.

"Who died, Andy?" Sembuuk asked. I hadn't heard him approach. He led his horse as his eagle perched attentively on his arm. "One of us?"

"Lugsalkhaan," I said. "A bullet through the chest."

"Does anyone know?"

"Only Zima."

"You're wise to keep this quiet. His legend will go on, and he will live forever."

"And we adopted Lucky Hunter."

"Then we are doing better than the other camps. None of them have birds. They have dogs, but too many dogs become unruly. There's already talk of killing the dogs for food and fur. Their winter coats are in season. But if we have only one dog, it's perfect to keep our camp clean and guarded, especially by Lucky Hunter. He's known to be dependable. The wolves know our giant herd dogs as well. They've killed wolves before to protect the herds, and the wild cats will stay away. Look." He held up a small rabbit. "We'll eat well tonight. Has Kandal found his tongue yet? He's wise in the things we must do now before winter."

"He has the kids running around for herbs and the others are building a *ger*."

Sembuuk laughed and his eagle screeched.

"All is well, then. I can already tell that the other camps will want our Kandal on loan. We may need to hunt for them, too, which my raptor prefers. They hunt best in their own territories rather than taking turns with competitive raptors."

We returned to the camp and worked on an assortment of tasks. I even went to the stream and built a large pool in front of a log jam. With the others, I helped peel the bark from the saplings so they'd dry faster, and then dragged logs in for firewood. With Sembuuk's help, we enclosed the camp with a fence of woven branches, then an adjoining corral for the horses. The horses couldn't be allowed to range freely as they were used to since the Chinese would shoot them for food if seen on the plain. In a few hours, the camp became a large courtyard, with several large cedar trees standing tall in our midst. We plotted out spots for four *gers* at ten paces from each other, with a central fire—three *gers* to live in, and one for supplies.

In the afternoon, I took a nap as Bolor, Zima, and the

kids went with Sembuuk to graze the horses on the plain. There didn't seem to be much of a threat from the Chinese as long as we didn't approach them.

I awoke to Lucky Hunter's wet nose on mine, but Zima's smiling face pushed the dog aside.

"Did you sleep well?" she asked.

"Um . . . yes."

It couldn't have been a bad sleep; I had draped all six blankets over me.

"Are we engaged, Pond?" she asked, smiling. I blinked several times, and she had to repeat herself. "Are we engaged?"

"To be married? I . . . Yes? Um. I thought we agreed on it, right?"

"Then why do you wish to make me a widow before we even have the wedding?" Her smile had faded.

"A widow? I don't—"

"You're going into the Kazakh camp tonight."

"Oh. Yes. I am."

"Do you think that's wise?"

She didn't ask if it was safe, only wise. But it seemed like a trick question.

"We need the winter supplies."

"Let someone else go. You do everything."

"No one else wanted to go."

"Well, I don't want you to go. I don't want you to be shot."

"Zima, it's—"

"I won't let you."

"Zima, I'm listening to what you are saying, and I

believe it's wise to be concerned, but I must do this. The others may be too afraid to go, and fear causes people to make mistakes."

"You're not afraid?"

"A little, but not much, because Sembuuk and I have a good plan."

"And your plan stops bullets?"

"Zima, you have to understand that all three camps need this gear right away. Do you remember I was a criminal for many years in America?"

"Yes."

"As a criminal, I did many dangerous things, especially during the night. What I did back then was wrong, but tonight, God is allowing me to use those old experiences to do something good. I know how to move in the darkness, and how blind the Chinese will be from their own lights. And I know how to avoid looking into their headlights so I can keep my night-eyes. Other things, too."

She sighed, then kissed me slowly.

"How can you do that, Pond?"

"Do what?"

"Turn all the bad into good?"

"The good is already there, Zima. We just have to look for it."

"When will we marry?"

"I have an idea. When we're all ready for winter, we'll invite the other camps to celebrate the autumn season and have our wedding. At Three Rocks tonight, I'll make the announcement."

"May I come?"

"If you want. There'll be a lot of waiting. What about the baby?"

"Sembuuk says a woman in middle camp lost her baby that was still nursing."

With my fingertips, I touched her face. I knew she'd grown attached to the infant, but the new arrangement would be for the best.

"You'll be giving them the baby?"

"I'm not a mother, Pond. Maybe this will help her pain."

"How do you do that?"

"Do what?" She frowned.

"Make everything so beautiful?"

"You think I'm beautiful?" She smiled.

"Oh, yes."

"The Mongols believe I'm ugly."

"They have to say that."

"Why?"

"Because they are bitterly jealous."

"What about Gan-gaad and Luyant? I worry about Skaamaan and the children."

"After our wedding, perhaps we can take a trip down south if there's no snow yet. It shouldn't be too hard to find where they're camped. Unless they're hiding in the mountains from the Chinese as well."

"I think Gan-gaad would fight the Chinese."

We talked some more, then read the Psalms and prayed for our safety as well as the safety of the others. It was a glorious afternoon.

$$...\dagger...$$

When it was dark, ten of us gathered at Three Rocks, some from each camp. Still, we didn't hear from Duulgii, but no one could look for him. We had to fend for ourselves.

The convoy five miles below us was thinning out. Yet in its scarcity, there was an additional danger. Occasional vehicles were now passing from the north and going back into China. Some looked like ambulances, probably carrying wounded from whatever battle raged in the north, and some were official vehicles, with emblems on the doors, likely carrying ambassadors and officers. But then, between the traffic, there were gaps of five or ten minutes, but no more. Only after these observations did we depart with ten horses—Sembuuk, me, and one other man, Jugder, to hold the horses and do the packing. Jugder was a large Kazakh with only two fingers on his right hand. Regardless of his handicap, those from Middle Camp claimed he was their most able and leading man.

The moon had set early that night, so it was unusually dark on the open plain. Sembuuk was in the lead and Jugder brought up the rear with his train of pack horses. Jugder wasn't much for words, which was especially handy on such an operation.

About two hundred yards from the destroyed camp, Sembuuk and I dismounted and gave our mounts to Jugder so we could continue on foot. Prowling now, the two of us moved ahead only when there were no headlights in sight. When we reached the edge of the camp debris, we lay on our bellies as a truck bounced toward the south going far too fast on the dirt road. After it passed, Sembuuk rose and ran into camp. Halfway through, he crossed the road, and located something of value.

There was a growl and a bark no more than a stone's throw away to my left. Whether they were wolves or dogs, I didn't know, but they were carnivores tearing at one of the many dead animal or human bodies. As long as they stayed away from us, we'd be fine. We certainly weren't going to fight them for their food. If they came toward me, I'd hiss at them like a snow leopard. For an emergency, I'd brought my flare gun. I had two more flares left, but I prayed I wouldn't need them as it would only draw attention.

Sembuuk dove to my side and lay as still as a rock along with me as a tank rumbled past at forty miles per hour, then a Jeep not far behind it.

"Two saddles," Sembuuk whispered.

As soon as it was clear, I dashed away with my two burdens and Sembuuk ran away to find more treasures. I reached Jugder and handed off the two saddles. The seven-fingered man had staked each *aduu* side-by-side but spread apart enough for him to fit between. It was a smart way to move amongst them while he packed our goods onto their backs.

I ran back in time to retrieve three more saddles. Sembuuk had found a stash.

It continued like this for some time. Sometimes we were

resting with our faces to the ground, and other times we were madly dashing with burdens too heavy to carry except for the rush of adrenalin that pushed us onward.

When we had twelve saddles—four for each camp—the canvas and felt for the *gers* was our next important need. He found bundles of these, and others he dragged off collapsed *ger* frames, wrapping them hastily for our transport back to camp. Some were torn or partially burned, but anything and everything would be used.

Next came food—human food. Like the Mongols, the Kazakhs had smoked and dried much meat. There was also flour, a half-trampled bag of potatoes, wild radishes, and turnips.

Then came the horses' grain. This was mandatory to supplement the horses' diets since they weren't going to be eating much during the winter.

Sembuuk located and brought me tools—axes, shovels, saws, wood-carving tools, blades, two picks, and a dozen axe heads. All this he brought in a single trip that was so heavy, I had to half-drag the bundle back to Jugder's station.

At this point, it was two in the morning. My elbows, knees, and chin were skinned and bleeding from diving to the ground so often, and my legs were cramping every time I rested when there were passing vehicles. The cold night air has a way of tearing and breaking a man down, in time, to a trembling heap. I hadn't run and darted this much since I was twenty-two when police were chasing me through the Bronx.

"How's Jugder doing?" Sembuuk asked me as we

huddled together. A train of five tractor-trailers filled with machine parts drove past. "Can he take more?"

Our cheeks were to the ground as we hid our faces, our heads only inches apart as we spoke. At a glance, we probably appeared as some of the many dead scattered around the camp since our bodies were motionless.

"Yeah, we can go till daylight if we have to," I said, "but we'll be walking back. There'll be no room to ride. How are you doing? The dead . . . I mean, you knew these people."

"I try not to look, Andy. I lost a child a few years ago. It was a hard time. But this? There are no words for it. They are all gone now. You are lucky to have Zima still."

"I'm sorry I didn't know your family."

He said nothing for a few moments, then lifted his head.

"We have to get the wood stoves together," he said. "I've already taken off the chimney pipes so we can pick up the stoves."

"What about the pipes?"

"They're too awkward. We'll have to get them another night or make our own back at camp. If there's time, maybe we can get them last."

"We'll need about nine stoves," I said, calculating. "A stove per *ger*."

"I think I only found six. The others are too damaged or crushed."

"Crushed is okay. If it eats wood, heat is all that matters."

"Fine." He chuckled. "You and Zima get a crushed stove in your wedding *ger*."

Jumping up, we ran together to the nearest stove. The

stoves were two-by-two-by-three, a little large for the *gers* Kandal was fabricating, but I'd trade space for heat any night! The stoves weren't too heavy for two of us to carry, just awkward. We reached Jugder five minutes later with the first stove. Jugder began to strap the stove onto one of the horses, then stopped and dropped the stove on the ground. He opened the hinged door and dumped out five pounds of ash.

"How often do you guys clean those out?" I gasped. "Listen, we're running out of time. We need to each put a stove on our shoulders, then get back. Either that, or we relay like we've done with everything else. They're not too heavy if we pour out the ash first. Going together like this, we're wasting too much time."

"Fine," Sembuuk said. "We'll both carry one."

Dashing back, we found two more stoves, made sure the ashes were discarded this time, then I hefted one onto his shoulder. I'd managed to get one onto my shoulder, but gestured him closer.

"I can take another one on this shoulder, too. Go ahead."

Shaking his head, he set his stove on my other shoulder, my head sandwiched between the two. He found one for himself and we ran—though I was a little slower. Halfway back to Jugder, my shoulders felt so bruised, I was nearly in tears. I rolled them onto the ground with a wince. Sembuuk noticed and slapped me on the back.

"Two at a time, huh?" he said, laughing. "I think you should carry three!"

"I got greedy," I said, rubbing my shoulders.

We went back and forth two more times, finding

222 | D.I. TELBAT

ourselves with a total of eight.

"That's all I can pack on here," Jugder said. "Anything more and I'll have to strap it between the horses' legs."

"Just one more," I pleaded.

"One more and you carry it!" the seven fingered man declared.

"I can carry it." I nodded. "We're walking back, anyway."

Sembuuk plopped down on the ground at Jugder's feet. I rested my hands on my hips. Every muscle in my body hurt.

"Come on, Sembuuk. One more trip."

"You can manage. Let me rest before we go back."

Turning, I walked back to the damaged camp. At the edge, I hid as a half-dozen all-terrain vehicles zipped past. *Chinese soldiers on four-wheelers?* When I started to climb to my feet, a burst of gunfire made me sprawl flat. A dog or wolf yelped to my left. Another burst silenced it. Breathlessly, I opened one eye. While I'd been watching the ATVs approach and pass, I hadn't seen a Jeep with a trailer coming from the north. The driver of the Jeep—holding a Chinese SKS at the ready—stood on his seat and watched as his passenger, an officer in uniform, picked through the camp debris. The same assault rifles were in New York City, and with the glow appearing on the horizon, there was no mistaking the long banana clip. The officer was armed as well, with a pistol on his hip, and he worked his way through the deserted camp, picking up objects and throwing others aside. He seemed set on finding something valuable in the mess.

Praying in silence, I squeezed my eyes shut. It was

growing lighter by the minute as the sun rose. A careful look to the west and I could see ten horses burdened with goods. They would never outrun the Jeep if a chase ensued, but I hoped they were obscured enough by the dim morning light.

The officer stepped in my direction and kicked a cooking pot so hard, it soared over my head. It landed behind me. He spoke Chinese to the driver and the driver laughed. The man picked up a sack of dog hair and shook it out all over the ground. His voice sounded cruel, like he was ridiculing the primitive culture. Then he spotted me. I shut my eyes and didn't move. My breath came in shallow half-breaths from my stomach—indiscernible breaths, I hoped.

He kicked me lightly in the ribs. My eyelids fluttered, but the lighting seemed too weak for him to see the slight movement. The officer spoke again to his driver, another joke the driver didn't seem to find too humorous.

I could smell whatever stench his boots had stepped in, and even his aftershave.

The officer nudged my feet, then stooped down to untie my laces. *My boots?* He tugged at my left boot, but it wouldn't come off. They were tight on my feet and usually took much of my own effort to pull them off. But because they were the most modern and most expensive item he'd probably seen this side of China, he wanted them. Fortunately, I couldn't see what he was about to do next or I would've flinched away.

Since he couldn't get the first boot off, he gave up trying. Instead, he drew his sidearm and pulled the trigger. My whole body jerked. My eyes bulged, but then I quickly closed them again. *Lord, please help me!*

He loosened my laces more, and when he tugged again, the boot came off smoothly. The officer held my boot up to his own foot, which I wish he'd done at the beginning. My boot was two inches too long for his small feet. Cursing, he threw the boot into the air and shot at it again and again as it landed on the ground. The man emptied his pistol at the boot a dozen paces away from me.

Frustrated, he stomped back to the Jeep. When I opened one eye to see if he was departing, I wished instantly that I would've kept my eye closed. The officer ripped the driver's machine gun from his hands, chambered a round for good measure, and pulled the trigger. Bullets snapped at the ground all around me, battering the debris on all sides like hail from a horror film. I was too frightened to move. Deep down, I wanted to run, but I believe God kept me still, protecting me as well as those not far away on the plain who were watching everything unfold.

The gunfire lasted five seconds—until his fifty-round clip was smoking and exhausted.

The driver started the Jeep and drove to the south with the officer mumbling, probably about the boots being too large, or his feet being too small. A tanker truck nearly collided with the Jeep as they zoomed away. Both vehicles honked, swerved, and continued on their way.

I listened to the dawn breeze through the ringing in my ears. Full daylight wasn't far away now, so I wasn't hasty to jump up. It was bright enough that I could see my boot. *Was it safe to move? Maybe . . .* Jumping to my feet, I limped to the boot. *Had the man been shooting blanks? There wasn't a hole in my boot!* Only when I tugged it on did I feel wetness in my sock. Pulling up my pant leg, I saw that when he'd shot point-blank at my calf, the bullet had grazed me—enough so I knew they weren't blanks he'd been firing!

"Lord, I don't even know what to say right now," I said as I tied my boot. "I should be dead, but I'm humbled at Your protective hand."

In thirty seconds, I found a stove, though a crushed one. A horse hoof had caved it in on one side, but it would prop upright adequately. After dumping out the ashes, I checked for vehicles, then shouldered the stove. I jogged all the way back to Sembuuk and Jugder.

"How are you still alive?" Sembuuk exclaimed in awe. He patted my shoulders and head as he walked in a circle around me. Jugder stood silent, his eyes narrowly judging my condition. "If I wouldn't have seen it myself, I would never—"

"It's his God," Jugder said. "Isn't it, Andy? The God that saved those people in the boat with the animals from the flood. It's the same thing."

Jugder turned and led the horses up the mountain at a fast pace while we followed after.

"If your God is this powerful, Andy, why were you even playing dead?" Sembuuk asked.

"Because nobody, not even God, likes a show-off."

Sembuuk laughed and slapped his leg as we walked back to camp.

...✝...

CHAPTER TWENTY

At Three Rocks, there was a mighty cheer for the three of us as we arrived mostly unscathed. A few more from the other camps had gathered since the day had fully dawned. Sembuuk supervised the separation of the gear as Zima inspected me from head to toe. Using my binoculars, she and the others had observed much from afar and couldn't believe what they'd seen. Finally, she found the entry and exit hole in my pant leg, with my light wound beneath.

"You did get hurt!" she shouted.

"He was shooting at me, Zima. I'm not invincible."

"But God was protecting you, wasn't He?"

"Of course! See? I'm alive. That's just a scratch to remind me it was Him doing the saving." I pointed at the sky. "And it was Him telling me I'm still human."

"I told you not to go, Pond!" she said, fuming, and kicked me square on the shin.

The following days were spent incorporating all the gear Sembuuk and I had found. Everyone's spirits were high as we realized we could actually survive the winter now.

While Sembuuk hunted with his eagle, Bolor and I took the axes and a saw north of our camp to cut firewood. Since winters are nearly nine months long in Mongolia, there was an amazing amount of wood to be cut, split, and stacked for our small camp. There was little need to actually chop any trees down since the virgin timber had plenty of blow-down. Splitting the wood into sizeable pieces for the stoves was a chore that would extend well into the winter. Normally, on the steppe, the stoves burned only horse dung.

Kandal and the two kids still in our camp—Manai and Beveg, Bolor's daughter—made good time with the *ger* frames. Sembuuk had gathered nearly twenty felt covers and canvas pieces, but three were so badly damaged, they needed to be cut and patched to make one. As it was, every camp received their issue of four covers, and all accepted their allotment without complaint. One camp might have had more of one item than the other two, but there was a compromise to off-set with an extra tool or blanket.

South Camp had already slaughtered and butchered one of their aged mares and was putting its hide and organs to use. Sembuuk brought in a number of little critters every day, and at morning *khuruldai*, when at least one person from each camp met at Three Rocks, an exchange of items was made. However, there was no doubt in my mind that our camp was doing better with provisions than the others, so the three of us able men—Sembuuk, Bolor, and I—made a point to chop extra wood and provide extra meat for the other two camps.

Though it was a sad time of loss for everyone, the level of companionship was astounding. No one argued. No one had a dispute. Everyone knew what needed to be done, and if they didn't, Kandal or Zima would set them straight. If I saw something to address, I addressed it. One such example concerned the stove pipes.

Even though every *ger* being fashioned in every camp

had a hole in its roof—a *toono*—the *gers* were still as smoky as a brush fire. The answer to this discomfort was to have stove pipes. But getting the stove pipes meant someone had to go back to the plain and find them. The military traffic on the road below was just as constant after a week as it was the night Sembuuk and I had prowled about. But I was the one who had to go.

Late one night after the evening meal, I claimed I was going for a ride, which was no lie, though it wasn't the full truth. Saddling one *aduu*, I grabbed a good amount of extra rope, and rode out to the plain. The vehicle headlights crisscrossed the plain, showing me where each vehicle was, so I rode down to within two hundred feet of the road. There, I staked my horse and jogged into the old camp. I was very cautious and made only three trips back and forth. The wolves were back, tearing at the rotting bodies, but they left me alone.

Back at my *aduu*, I tied down fourteen stove pipes. Nearly every pipe was dented and cracked, but the tin was thin enough to straighten out by hand.

I rode first to South Camp and called out as I approached so their dogs didn't attack. Most of the camp was asleep, but not for long. They were thankful for the pipes and I received many embraces. Middle Camp was the same, though seven-fingered Jugder pulled me aside and chastised me for not taking him along. The chastisement he gave me was nothing compared to the lashing I was certain to receive once I rode into my own camp and Zima saw what I'd done. It was late now, and she alone was awake at the central fire. Joking with her, I said I'd sent the *aduu* into the old camp alone to retrieve the pipes, but that didn't help matters. Though I feared she would kick me in the shin again, she was only quiet for a spell. Finally, she wrapped her arms around my neck and kissed me.

"Is this going to be a habit of yours?" she asked.

"Which part?"

"The part where you run all the dangerous errands that no one else wants to do."

"Only if they have to be done. I have no intention of making you a widow, Zima, even after we're married."

She nodded.

"I know there's no stopping you, Pond, but don't sneak off next time. That hurts me. At least let me say good-bye."

"You're right, Zima. I'm sorry."

"The *gers* are almost finished."

"Yes, I see that. Everything is coming along nicely."

"Tomorrow, I'm going to Middle Camp. South Camp gave them their horse hide so one of the women can make me a new *del*. It'll be their wedding present. I've never worn a new *del*. I used to always receive Skaamaan's old clothes."

"That's nice of the other camps to do that for you. You deserve it—with all the extra work you do for them even with your arm bound up." I looked into the fire and counted the days. "The last *ger* should be finished in three days. Today's Thursday. Pass the word that we'll have a wedding and Autumn Festival on Sunday night."

"Can we start at noon?" She grinned. "That way we can play *kekbar* until dark, then have a *dostarkhan*. Everyone can toast us!"

I'd heard of *kekbar*, a wild form of polo, except played with a dead goat instead of a ball. We didn't have a goat, but I knew we'd improvise.

"We have a lot to do before then."

And we did. The *gers* had to be finished and more wood needed to be stacked inside our fenced courtyard. Zima was busy making cheese and Sembuuk was off hunting much of the time. I'd been working on writing up the wedding ceremony for Kandal to read and perform for us. Though I'd considered accepting the Mongolian marriage ceremony, it was so Buddhist and spiritually pagan that I declined. Kandal, the eldest of all three camps, decided a nontraditional wedding was acceptable since Zima and I were both essentially foreigners. So that was resolved, but the next problem was that I'd never been to a wedding in my life. All I had to work with were the few I'd seen on television while in prison, so I figured I knew the basics— that it was to be done before God and witnesses. The rest, I guessed at. Zima was drafting her vows separately, which I couldn't wait to hear.

But, I was nervous. *Me? Married?* I'd been praying non-stop for God's will on the matter, and every day I received confirmations that Zima would be helping and not hindering my first objective in life: my ministry for Christ. She'd already enhanced my endeavors to share the Gospel, and was constantly teaching the two children stories from the Bible and lessons to be learned. Kandal didn't like the seeming intrusion into Kazakh tradition, but he didn't speak much about it. In some ways, the old man was like Gangaad who'd seen the negative effects of the Russian

Orthodox priests long ago. But he knew I wasn't the same, nor was I teaching such bondage. Since no one told us to be quiet, we shared about Jesus' gift of salvation every chance we could.

Knowing the end was near, kept us striving fervently forward. Besides spending time with the others, Zima and I fellowshipped with one another as well. And when we were apart in the mornings doing our chores, I often noticed her pausing to read her Bible. She loved the Book of Psalms. And when she was finished, she would tuck the Bible under her ragged overcoat to carry it always with her like I did mine. From some of the things she'd said, I knew she assumed all Christians carried their Bibles and praised Christ as much as we did. I didn't have the heart to tell her that professing Christians didn't always carry their Bibles on them wherever they went. She would've been surprised to hear that many people who claimed to be Christians didn't even read their Bibles every day. And even worse, that many who called themselves Christians in America seemed to live their lives no differently than the rest of the world.

Though I told her none of this, she could easily conclude from the Word that the world would grow worse and worse, not better, until Jesus Christ came to save humanity and the world from itself, and to judge the wicked. And with this conclusion, she pressed forward with our mutual ministry amongst the Kazakhs. Her desire to serve her new God encouraged me to do the same. She recommended that immediately after our wedding and subsequent "honeymoon" to the south to find Gan-gaad's clan, we should start a church in the three camps. A church, she insisted, was all that was missing from the peaceful Gobi Altay forest.

Sunday morning, the day of our wedding, I rose early and hiked to the west. I left the dimness of the belt of larch and cedar, and climbed the steep, rocky slope of the nearest mountain. After crossing the expanse of a glacier, I pressed myself until I was panting for air in the high altitude. The peak I reached wasn't too high. It wasn't even snow-capped yet like those to the north and west. But I was high enough to see fifty miles of steppes to the east. As I watched the sun rise, tears came to my eyes in that rugged, forgotten land.

Too few ever leave the comfort of their lives to seek out their purpose in the world. I knew that morning without a doubt that I was where God wanted me to be. My regret was that I hadn't gotten there sooner.

When the orb of the sun was above the horizon, I sighed and smiled in my contentment, and read Revelation 3:8. Though I'd never led a church before, I knew the components that the Body of Christ required. Knowing didn't mean it was going to be easy to raise up believers around me, especially in those Last Days when Satan seemed to be fighting to claim every soul for himself. And that's why I needed to be praying and arming myself for the work ahead—that I, with the church we would found, could have a little strength, keep the Word of God, and not deny His name. *To the end.*

Revelation 3:8 became my mission statement, and I determined not to stray from it through whatever came next.

Before I left my mountain, I prayed for two things

specifically. I prayed for the church, even if only Zima and I remained its only members. And then I prayed for my bond with Zima to be Christ-centered and Christ-purposed, until whatever end God destined for us.

With those two exciting thoughts, I tucked my journal and Bible into my coat and dashed down the mountain.

I wasn't the only one who was excited about the day. When I strode into camp, guests from South and Middle Camp were already arriving. They turned their horses into our corral and their dogs tested Lucky Hunter's well-marked boundaries. Zima had departed for Middle Camp, from where I guessed she would arrive when the time was right. Since I was the only one who had a watch, I often kept it in my backpack to keep it safe. The time was of no concern to the Kazakhs—during the night, we slept, and during the day, we worked. Except on this day. No one seemed to pay any mind to our previous arrangement to begin the celebration at noon. As soon as each camp's chores were completed, it was simply time to start the ceremony. That was that. Thus, I had to sneak away into the woods for an hour to finish my wedding gift for Zima.

Watching the others carve the plates and cooking bowls had given me the idea for my gift. When I'd been splitting wood, a cracked piece of larch wood had rolled against my foot. For the last few days, I'd been hollowing out the bottom of the block to form a box. And the cracked part had a gnarled knot in its top that made a natural handle for the lid. The box itself was no larger than my hand. For the lid, I'd fashioned it to fit snugly on the box, and then I'd carved Zima's name in Mongolian Cyrillic and English. The lettering was decorative around the lid's handle. Now, I'm not a stylish man, nor am I one who's skilled to decorate objects in this world, but I must say, the box looked quite sharp, especially considering I had no sandpaper. For sandpaper, I ground fine sand from the stream against the wood with a stone until the wood became smooth.

With my box complete, I hid it under my clothes and returned to North Camp, which was as lively as I'd ever seen it. The men stood around the edges of the courtyard smoking handmade pipes and sipping quarts of *airag* prepared for the event. While they drank, the women hustled about with bowls of cheese, unleavened bread, meat stews, and puddings and—I'm not sure what it all was, but they went all out.

Until Sembuuk rode into camp and threw a small fox onto the ground at our feet, I hadn't noticed he'd been missing. His eagle sat proudly on his arm, glancing this way and that as Sembuuk told of the fox hunt. The children from all the camps actually stopped darting about to listen to his tale. Like American fishermen, I have no doubt Sembuuk embellished the story somewhat—which he made sound like a battle.

When Zima arrived with a couple other women, my heart did flip-flops. She had bathed and her hair was rimmed with white flowers. *Flowers!* When I approached her—both of us with nothing but smiles for one another—I noticed they weren't flowers at all since it was too late in the year. They were feathers from one of the doves the eagle had killed. The feathers were knotted and twisted and then woven into her dark hair to look like daisies.

"I've read stories of princesses and beautiful maidens," I whispered in her ear as she giggled, "but they all wither before you, Zima."

She pulled a feathery flower from her hair and tucked it into the collar of my coat.

"I trust you'll bathe before our wedding . . ."

Teasing me, she flicked me on the ear, then moved away to mingle with the women.

"Well, I was going to," I fumbled after her. "After the . . . the game we're, um . . ."

Giving up, I marched into the woods. Where no one could see me, I sniffed at my armpits and breath. Yes, I needed a bit of scrubbing, but there was no point in bathing before the game of *kekbar* when we'd be handling the dead fox carcass and riding our horses to a lather. I'd bathe later, but I'd wash up a bit in the stream so I'd be more presentable before our many guests.

Back in camp, we nibbled on meat and cheese and congregated for an hour. The men admired our courtyard fence and made suggestions about how to weave it so tight that it would keep the mice out of the camp. But Sembuuk declared that mice weren't a problem in our camp while his raptor could still spread her wings. The women doted over Zima, and the kids wrestled with the dogs. Altogether, we numbered sixteen adults, six children, and the one infant that Zima had saved. None of the children of the clan were older than Bolor's daughter, Beveg, who was seven.

Manai was still attached to me. I was honored to have his little arms wrap around my neck as he jabbered about a squirrel he and Lucky Hunter almost caught, or a fish he thought he saw in the stream. Even while playing with the other children, he often paused to search the camp for my face as if he were afraid I would disappear. And after he'd locate me, he'd smile and dart away. Since I'd saved him, he was my responsibility. It was the closest I'd been to being a father in my life, and it seemed an unspoken obligation that I was to adopt him. Zima already mothered the boy.

When it came time for *kekbar*, I was anything but aware of such games and their ramifications. I followed Sembuuk's lead and saddled a horse. Everyone began migrating toward the open plain as the women closed up our camp edibles inside the *gers*—though only to avoid attracting the wild animals of the forest. The camp dogs, though rowdy, had been taught since pups to never steal food. They were to eat only what they caught themselves or were offered in their individual plates. Even a morsel of food that had fallen on the ground had to be coaxed into the animals' mouths.

On the plain, Sembuuk designated the teams as Kandal explained the game's basic concept to me. The skin of a goat—in this case a tan fox—was the object of attention. One team tried to throw the skin across the opposing team's territorial zone. Different cultures have different versions of this game, some using hoops. I knew I wasn't good enough to play even before we started. Nevertheless, Sembuuk drew me, Bolor, and a South Camp man of thirty named Olz, to play with him against the other six men. Bolor warned that Jugder from Middle Camp wasn't to be underestimated.

My team, which mostly comprised of North Camp men,

though Kandal was sitting out, started with the fox skin. We faced the opposing six riders and I suddenly realized the Kazakhs took the game of *kekbar* very seriously. Except for the cheering and jeering women and children on the forest edge, none of the men were smiling as they generally did during joyous occasions. The horses seemed to know what was happening, too, as if they'd been born for this game where they could prove their superiority through competition along with the men.

Sembuuk held the fox overhead as we started down the playing field, which Kandal was still defining with the heel of his boot. The other team charged us with barred teeth. At the last instant, before two riders collided with Sembuuk, he hurled the fox at me. Snatching the dead thing expertly from the air, I wrapped it around my arm. But while I was still reveling over my catch and the women's cheers, Jugder slammed his mare into the side of mine and sent us both flying. Diving clear, I thought my *aduu* was about to fall on me. I landed on the near frozen ground on my shoulder and head. My horse somehow kept her footing and, just shy of trampling me, pranced around my head. A rider leaned down, ripped the fox from my arm, then galloped away, the others in chase. The cheerleaders taunted me until I found my feet. My mare knew vengeance was in order as soon as I was mounted again, and she tore back into the game without much direction from me.

Kekbar is rough. I was knocked from my saddle and bounced off the hard ground ten times in the first hour. About the time my mare was ready to play without me, I started to figure out she knew what to do better than I did.

All I had to do was stay on her back and catch the fox when it was thrown to me. Sure enough, when the press of horses loomed against me, I gave her the reins and she twisted about to face our attacker breast to breast. This worked better than me trying to steer her, and us both getting confused in the process.

Using my arm length and strength, I started to steal the fox from the opposing team more often, and after two hours, we were starting to pull ahead of the other team. I was glad when Jugder called for a water break, but it was really a strategy session to assign a double guard of riders on me.

...✝...

CHAPTER TWENTY-ONE

During the break from playing *kekbar*, Zima gave water to me and my horse, and Manai told me to throw the fox to my mates more often. He said it was funny when the fox landed on someone's head unexpectedly.

But the excited chatter suddenly vanished. The horses tensed and the dogs growled.

"Pond. Look."

I followed Zima's gaze to the east where five Chinese vehicles had driven to within two hundred paces of our *kekbar* field. They were sitting on their hoods or standing around their escort vehicles with machine guns cradled in their arms. One man was on crutches and another wore a bandage around his head. It seemed these soldiers were from the north, returning to China under guard, most of them wounded.

If it were anyone but the Chinese watching us play, we would've welcomed them to come closer. But as it was, our small clan could only stare with sad eyes, eyes that had seen them kill dozens of clanspeople without mercy. The Kazakhs would've sold livestock to the Chinese for a few *tugriks* or ammunition so they could've hunted wild game for themselves.

Gino had taught me years before to listen to the small, quiet voice of the Holy Spirit at all times. He'd told me not to be driven or swayed by the faultiness of feelings and emotions, but to be a man sure of God's directing—even when I didn't feel like doing something. And in that moment, the Holy Spirit brought a Scripture to mind that may as well have been a trumpet in my head. It was Romans 12:21: *"Do not be overcome by evil, but overcome evil with good."*

This time, I didn't want to listen to the Holy Spirit, but I raised my hand in greeting, anyway. Zima's mouth dropped.

"What are you doing?" She gasped. "They're at war with America and Russia. You and I are both those nationalities!"

The Chinese soldiers waved back enthusiastically.

"We have to be bold in our God," I said under my breath, "to speak to the lost even in much conflict."

"Pond! Did you hear me?"

I kicked my mare forward. Alone, we trotted away from the others. The Kazakhs watched fearfully, probably wishing they could pull me back with an invisible rope.

"Pond!" Zima hissed hoarsely.

But I was too far now to turn back. Several of the Chinese straightened up and cocked their rifles. They glanced at their commander, a sergeant, who stepped from the cab of his transporter. He snapped orders at a couple of the men who weren't injured, and they spread out in a firing line to defend themselves from me.

Slowing my mount to a walk, I stopped ten paces from the officer. A thin smile touched his lips, then his eyes drifted down to my feet hanging nearly down to the ground. He seemed to recognize me—and my boots—and I recognized him.

"My Mongolian is not too good," he stated haltingly, "but not many have those boots in this land."

"I'm fortunate your aim is as good as your Mongolian," I said with a smile. "If they fit you, I'd give them to you."

He dismissed the thought with a wave.

"Ah, I was drunk that morning. Or was it night? I don't remember, but I remember you. You are not dead? Not even injured? I shot at you a number of times."

"Just a scratch." I shrugged. "God was looking out for me."

His eyes narrowed.

"You know, we war with Russia. If I shoot you now, I get a promotion."

"Oh, I'm not Russian, but you could still shoot me. I knew that when I came over here."

"What are you? European? French? German?"

"I'm an American."

"American!" He exclaimed with widening eyes. He looked past me at the Kazakhs. When he spoke again, his English was nearly perfect. "I speak better English than my own Chinese. I went to Princeton, can you believe that?"

"It's a good school. I grew up in New York City."

"Ah." He nodded, his face lost in memories of a better time and happier place. "Why're you here with these Mongolians?"

"Sharing God's love with a hungry people."

"A missionary. What faith?"

"The only faith. I'm sharing Christ's forgiveness."

"Ah, yes. The blood, the cross, I know it all. Do they listen?"

"Some. They're rooted in tradition and old gods," I said, "but you know tradition is only so fulfilling."

He ordered his men in Chinese to stand down. They relaxed their trigger fingers and rifles, for which I was thankful.

"So what were you doing the other night in the old garbage camp?"

"Winter is coming and we didn't have much when we fled." I peered east, down the slope. "I'd returned for supplies."

"And now you play horse games?"

"A wedding celebration mixed with a final farewell to summer days."

"They were not saddened by so many of their people dying? I saw the wolves tearing at their loved ones' remains."

I stared at the ground for a few breaths before answering.

"These are a close people, but strong as well. It hasn't been easy, but with the few things we've salvaged, they're learning to live again, even to laugh again."

"What's your name?"

"Andy. And yours?"

"Sergeant Xing. I must be honest with you, Andy. I was drawn by your horseback game, but there are rumors of sabotage and spies in your midst."

"Among these people?" Frowning, I turned in the saddle to study my companions. They were far away, but I knew them all by name now. "I don't believe it," I said, looking back at Xing. "Now I'm a leader among them, and no one has time for any of that. Besides, we all agreed to stay away from you. And none of us has weapons."

"I'm not talking about weapons. It takes little effort and time to turn on a radio and report troop movements across the plain, Andy. If it persists, we'll see if the forest can burn in extremely cold weather. Understand?"

A radio? I swallowed hard. He wasn't bluffing, but he was warning me. The soldier knew something I didn't. Maybe he was testing me as well.

"Are you fighting America?" I asked. "I haven't heard any news for some time."

"The US is too unstable to fight now. The bombing of Washington crumbled morale. Be glad you're not in New York, huh?"

"In the name of Jesus, I'll pray for us all, Sergeant Xing, that our souls aren't lost with the evil of this age. May God save us."

"Maybe we'll meet again, Andy from New York. Your friends wait for you. I'll tell the supply officers not to shoot at the clansmen here, but still be careful. No one listens much to a mere sergeant anymore."

"Thank you, Sergeant. God's peace to you."

With an expressionless face, he grunted as I turned my horse and trotted back to the playing field. Behind me, the engines started and their vehicles bounced to the south.

"What did he say?" Sembuuk asked for everyone.

"He's the one who shot at me the other morning. He went to school in America not far from my hometown."

"Was he among those who killed our families?" Kandal growled.

"I think not. He said he would instruct the others to leave

us alone, but he's not sure they'll listen. We must be careful still. But I know his name now, and though he's a lowly officer, if we have any problems with them, I may be able to reach him one way or another. It seems he frequents this area now.

Zima rested her hand on my leg and shook her head as she looked up at me.

"You made my heart nearly stop beating, Pond, when you went to them. Why do you do these things?"

"My God puts it on my mind to love my enemies," I said for the others to hear as well as her. "The Chinese are certainly our enemies. God knows we are hurt and angry, but you are a strong people. I believe we met this sergeant by God's will. He's a soldier at heart, I think, but he can feel a little compassion for your losses. That's why we must pity and pray for him rather than hate him. Only God can change his heart. We can talk of him more later. The sun is wasting. What's the score?"

...✝...

As fun as my first experience of *kekbar* was, I wasn't too discouraged when Jugder said we should conclude the event. Both men and horses were exhausted, and I'd fallen off my *aduu* more than anyone else. I was pretty sure I'd cracked a couple ribs when a hoof had come down on me while I was on the ground. It hurt like fire to breathe, but it was all worth it.

To conclude the event, the winning team was to take the fox skin and throw it into the *ger* of the family who would host the after-game celebration. This was called *dostarkhan*. But since North Camp was already hosting the party and wedding, there was quite a roar as Sembuuk led the march back to camp and Manai helped him throw it into his own *ger*. But *dostarkhan* itself was still put on hold since the next event in that late afternoon was the wedding. Hastily, I slipped out of camp to the pool I'd built and quickly bathed. After washing, I trimmed my hair and beard, then dressed in a clean set of clothes. I was interrupted by Bolor and a few other men as they watered the horses. They laughed as I shivered and turned blue from the icy water.

What can be said of a wedding in such a setting? Dusty rays of the sun peered through the green heights of larch and cedar trees. Sembuuk was my best man, and Bolor stood beside him. Kandal ushered Zima through the throng of standing observers. Zima had chosen two maids of honor, and Beveg was the flower girl, though she had only green leaves to sprinkle on the ground. None of this was Kazakh tradition, but they all loved the ceremony, anyway. It was a flavor of my country as well as Zima's heritage, though she'd never seen this part of her Russian culture.

Zima and I stood together as Kandal slowly read the script I'd prepared for him. As we stated our vows, Zima and I held hands, neither of us needing to read our pledges since we'd both memorized exactly what we wanted to say.

"Though our lives have been full of turmoil, I have never known such peace." Her eyes brimmed with tears. "I believe God sent you into my life for two reasons, Pond. First, to show me the true God, my Savior. And second, to hold my hand. I love you and exist as yours entirely."

How could I match such words? I took a deep breath.

"I was born thousands of miles away in a country of

people who've never heard the Mongolian language spoken. But God put it in my heart to sail a ship across a sea and fly a plane over mountains and deserts to come here, to see the passionate people of this wild land, to feel your pain, and to laugh with you. I will always be an ambassador of my Lord, with you serving beside me, and I will hereafter also be your loving husband, through good days and bad, through laughter and through crying. And if the water's not too cold, I promise to bathe at least once a week."

Everyone howled with laughter. Even the dogs barked.

"I now pronounce you man and wife," Kandal said. "Andy, you may now kiss your bride."

And I did.

Jugder presented Kandal with a repaired *morin-khuur*, and we all knew he'd snuck into the plain to get it. Kandal began to pluck away as two other men sang in turn, and I joined in with the others in dance. Since I didn't know the steps, I drew more laughs than I'd heard in a while.

As darkness settled, the central fire was lit and stoked. We crowded around to hear Kandal sing in his ancestors' Turkic, then the hunting stories began. Around the circle we went, each man telling a tale—true or not, no one cared—always working in a toast to Zima and I and our happiness.

When it came time for my story, I admitted I'd never actually been hunting before, but I knew a hunter's story. I told them the whole story of Samson, the foxes, the lion, even Samson's fall and death. It was a hunting story only as far as the Philistines had hunted Samson all his days. Then I raised my cup and toasted to a woman—my woman—and to companions who were a hundred times better than

Samson had. Most everyone would've been drunk by now, but the *airag* hadn't fermented much.

The night was drawing to an end and our guests slowly left in small parties. Manai stubbornly agreed to sleep in Kandal and Bolor's *ger* instead of mine, and Zima and I cuddled together under the felt covers as the first great freeze of the year fell upon the forest.

"I have something for you," I said, and produced the box I'd carved.

She traced her fingers over the letters fashioned into the lid.

"Oh, Pond, I like it. I'll keep the sewing kit you gave me inside it. And I have something for you, too." From her Bible, she unfolded two pieces of paper and handed them to me. "One's for you, and one's for me. We'll keep them in our Bibles, okay? They'll be our symbol of this day since we have no rings."

I read the papers. Both were identical. It was a marriage certificate written in Zima's flowing script, then signed by every adult from all three camps as witnesses. She'd secretly gathered them all sometime before the wedding, though I'd never suspected it.

The certificates would be legal in any court on earth. We were truly married. I had a wife. And with Manai, we were a family.

CHAPTER TWENTY-TWO

"What I'm about to tell you doesn't leave this camp," I instructed the adults in North Camp. Beveg and Manai were still asleep. I'd decided to tell Bolor, Sembuuk, Kandal, and Zima the rest of Sergeants Xing's words. The coals from the previous night's celebration still smoked in the bitterly cold morning. Though we had our chores to do, I'd called the camp meeting before anything else.

Briefly, I explained Sergeant Xing's warning, that the saboteur among us must cease his efforts or we'd all suffer.

"Now, I know it's none of us five," I said, "but I don't know all of what the other two camps do. We know that Jugder snuck down and got that *morin-khuur* and who knows what else from the camp. That's his business. If someone feels they must covertly fight the Chinese down there, that's not my business, either. What is my business, though, is that those actions endanger the ones I love. We made an agreement, I thought, to stay clear of the Chinese. Am I wrong?"

"You're sure it wasn't a general warning not to interfere?" Sembuuk asked.

"I don't think it was general," Kandal answered for me. "According to Andy, he made specific mention of a radio. That's unexpected. They know someone is broadcasting their troop movements—broadcasting among us or near us."

248

"That's true," I said. "Frequencies can be traced with the right equipment."

Studying Kandal's face, I saw he knew more than he was saying. I didn't know these people as well as I thought I did; they were keeping secrets.

"I'm not a violent man," Bolor stated, "but I will tear the man to pieces if it brings harm to my Beveg."

"It must be someone in one of the other camps," I said. "We'll identify him, then decide what to do. Any objections to that?"

"Oh, I'll tell you what I'd like to do to him," Sembuuk said.

"Don't talk that way," Zima said. She would've never corrected a man in her old clan. "We can't say what we'd do when we don't even know who it is yet." She stood behind me, her hands on my shoulders. "I move more often among the camps than you. I'll notice anyone acting suspicious."

"But you and Andy are traveling south, aren't you?" Sembuuk asked. "My raptor and I will watch for tracks leading off in a strange direction. If someone has a radio, they may be hiding it outside camp so others don't find it."

"Zima and I will be back in about a week," I said, "but all of us should pay more attention until the person is identified."

I looked into each of their faces. Kandal still evaded me, though. He knew something that I felt I should know. Had I missed something? Perhaps I'd overlooked someone's deception? And what would we do to such a person who endangered the others? Reporting troop movements of the

Chinese would profit the Kazakhs little, but something was certainly amiss.

Since we were in fact leaving on our "honeymoon" the following morning, Zima and I busied ourselves by preparing North Camp to make do in our absence. Seven-year-old Beveg was an avid milker and could cover for Zima. Bolor and I had stacked a wall of firewood against the courtyard's northern fence. It was due to snow any time, but the dense tree cover overhead would protect us from all but a few white flakes. Sembuuk provided us with a week's-worth of meat and assured us we weren't taking too much from their own mouths. Since the winter cold was pushing more game into our forest for his eagle to hunt, the meat supply would be better than when he'd lived on the steppe. However, he tried not to hunt too near the camp so game would be plentiful nearby when the temperatures made traveling far more difficult.

That afternoon, I climbed the mountain with Lucky Hunter, but only high enough to see over the tallest of the trees. Hidden in the forest below me were the three camps living off the land that God gave us. Beyond the forest was the rolling plain where the Chinese vehicle tires dug ever deeper ruts into the near-barren ground.

I sat on a boulder as Lucky Hunter dug at a ground squirrel hole nearby. From the Word, I read and prayed, then opened my journal. Since I wouldn't be near a post office anytime soon to mail letters to Randy, my journal had taken a new route. I began to write a book—a story of my life and my calling to the Gobi region of Mongolia. It is this journal from which you read now. If it somehow happens

CALLED TO GOBI | 251

into your hands, I pray you sense even a fraction of my passion that I have for this land and its special people.

A tumble of pebbles drew Lucky Hunter's attention, and then mine, then we watched Manai make his way up the slope toward me. He was alone, which meant he'd followed me out of camp, but he must've gotten lost in the forest along the way because I'd been on my boulder for an hour. Nevertheless, he was rosy-cheeked and grinning when he finally reached me.

"Hi, Andy!" he said and climbed onto the boulder with my help. Lucky Hunter went back to his ground squirrel. "Can I go with you tomorrow?"

"Not this time, Manai. Zima and I need to find some of our friends from the last clan we lived with before we met yours."

"Why did you leave them?"

"Because Zima broke her arm and we stayed behind at the town hospital for her treatment." I tucked my Bible and journal into my coat. "You'll be okay with Bolor, won't you? Sembuuk might even take you hunting."

"Oh, yeah! Whoosh! Ah!" His hands acted out a dramatic eagle hunt and an unfortunate rabbit's demise. "Could I have my own eagle someday? This spring there'll be chicks born. We can go find their nests up in the cliffs!"

"Having an eagle is a big responsibility. If you feel you could care for it as Sembuuk does, the clan could certainly use another mighty hunter."

"Zima said she's going to teach me to read this winter, then I can read that history book you're always reading with her."

"That'd be wonderful," I said, "but I have a book you can read just from its pictures."

"A picture book?"

"Pages and pages of pictures that tell a very exciting story."

He climbed onto my back and I carried him down the slope. Lucky Hunter nipped at his dangling heels and Manai squealed with laughter, urging me faster.

Back at camp, about a ten minute hike from the western forest edge, I dug through my backpack to find John Bunyan's *Pilgrim's Progress* in illustrated form. I presented it to Manai whose eyes bulged at the front cover where Christian wielded a sword of light and fought a foe of darkness. On each page, he fingered through illustrations that came alive with comic book color. The captions to the illustrations were in English, but once Manai knew the story, he could simply look at the pictures and the characters would come to life.

Beveg sat on my right and Manai on my left at the central fire while I told them the story I knew by heart. In America's frontier days, *Pilgrim's Progress* had been second in print only to the Bible, and both had seen many trails in saddlebags into the West.

Kandal listened from across the fire for an hour as we worked through the exciting story. Zima prepared a thick venison stew, and eventually we were all gathered around the fire.

"It's like a life story," Beveg said with understanding.

"That's true, Beveg. Some people don't understand the deeper lessons. This book takes important lessons from the

Bible and draws them into a man's journey. It's not more important than the Bible, but we can learn a lot from it."

"How can you be so certain, Andy, that your Bible speaks the truth?" Kandal asked. "Why not Buddhism and our ancient texts from Tibet?"

"Buddhism is full of philosophy, Kandal," I explained. "At the heart of its philosophy is the remedy for all of my problems: myself. But every man knows, no matter how wise or loving or enlightened he may become, he's still powerless over his own life and death. The remedy, so to speak, must be greater than mere man. The answer is God, Kandal, a loving God with open arms. He's heartbroken that we worship His creation more than we worship Him."

Kandal scratched his head. Everyone waited for him to respond to me.

"If you compliment the *ger* I made for you," he said in argument, "then it pleases me, even if you don't praise me directly."

"True," I agreed, "but I don't praise the *ger* for making itself presentable, nor do I expect the *ger* to help me become a better person because I admire it."

"I see . . ." He nodded, narrowed his eyes, and stared thoughtfully at the trees on the edge of our camp. "You're talking about the Source of it all, even of wisdom and philosophy."

"The Source, that's right." *Finally, the eyes of this aged man were opening!* I pressed on. "We're men who recognize the need to make tools and felt and *dels* as well as we can. And we make these things for ourselves, our children, and our clan. Why then, would we choose to worship something less than the best available?"

"Your God?" he asked.

I nodded.

"And all of this is in your Bible? All that you speak of—the stories, the history, and the end of days?"

"It's all there."

"Can you leave one of your Bibles behind when you leave tomorrow?"

"Of course."

"I want to read that story of Samson and the Philistines as well."

We continued to talk as we ate the evening meal, and it was a fitting end to the last night before our departure. Since we were leaving before sunrise the following morning, we said our good-byes that night. Our plan was to be gone only a week, hopefully less. But one never knew in that land, so there were tears shed, especially by Beveg as she was sure she'd never see Zima again, of whom she'd grown quite fond.

In southwestern Mongolia, all you have to do to see a spectacular sunrise is gaze to the east. The Gobi is mostly sand, especially the eastern section, one thousand miles across. The sky is usually cloudless, but the sand in the air gives the sun a shimmering, red haze that you can stare directly at before it rises far above the eastern horizon.

It was this sunrise that greeted us an hour after Zima and I left North Camp. Riding along the tree line with the plain to our left, we stayed within a few feet of forest cover in case the Chinese vehicles came threateningly toward us. We rode two horses and had another two to carry our gear.

Since the temperature was too bitter to sleep exposed, we'd packed one *ger*, minus the stove. Taking four horses with us would've set North Camp back if they were traveling, but they weren't, so we'd chosen either young males mostly too rowdy for their own good, or mares too old to milk. The clan would miss them little.

Every couple hours we stopped to scout the land ahead with my binoculars, and we took our time to enjoy each other's company. We missed our morning rides together when we could talk alone. Oddly, we were planning very little for our future as a family. Our time on earth as man and wife was limited, we understood, as the Rapture was drawing ever nearer. I suspected that every other honest believer around the world was feeling the same urgency to finish their work in this realm and get ready to go home. In light of Mark 12:25, Zima and I felt blessed to have found each other when we did. Similarly, in John chapter 14, another quote from Jesus was ever-present in our minds: "*I will come again and receive you to Myself, that where I am, there you may be also.*"

That first day, I paused often, sitting tall in my saddle with my binoculars pressed to my brow to study the plain for sign of Gan-gaad's clan. I knew they couldn't have been more than three days ahead of us when we were initially attacked. But if they'd escaped the murderous advance of the Chinese troops, then they'd be well to the southeast at the edge of the Gobi already. But the chances of that were slim since the Chinese had intentionally traveled the nomadic migration route to secure meat for the troops' winter stores.

However, throughout that day, we saw no sign of another clan or camp slaughter. We made camp early with plenty of daylight available to set up our *ger*, so we moved deep into the mountain forest to find shelter from the wind.

In under an hour, we'd erected our humble *ger*. We built a large fire with little concern for drawing curious visitors since the tree branches overhead dispersed the smoke adequately.

We sat in front of the fire, my arm around Zima's shoulders and our backs against a log, and read the Word. As we prayed, we focused on safety for the two clans we knew, and for Kandal who was so interested in the Bible that he'd asked for one of ours. When our fire had dwindled, we crawled into our *ger* and whispered to each other as the silence of the forest closed in around us. Slowly, Zima drifted off to sleep, and I listened to her breathe for a while since it was too dark to see her. I'd given up all prospects in America to come here to serve my Lord, and He'd still given me more than I expected.

I don't remember falling asleep, but when I was startled awake, it was still dark. Perhaps I'd only been asleep for a moment. Yes, that was all; the fire's embers were still popping, though their glow was long gone. But what had startled me awake?

Quietly, I sat up. The horses were loosely picketed a stone's throw from our *ger*. One of them snorted at being disturbed and shifted its feet.

Leaning over Zima, I put my hand on her shoulder and my mouth brushed her ear. She stirred at my touch.

"Zima, wake up. Quiet. Get dressed. Put your coat on."

"It's just an animal," she whispered, but I urged her again, as I quickly dressed.

Our *ger* door was covered by a felt flap, which I crawled halfway through and froze, listening. It was much too dark to see anything. The tree cover was too dense and the moon had set already, but I heard voices. Though it was nothing discernible, the noise was close enough to give me chills. A friendly visitor announces himself from afar when advancing on a camp. A foe prowls around, unannounced.

I reached into the *ger* and pulled Zima out next to me where she indicated she heard the voices as well. Then they were suddenly quiet. She pushed me ahead to lead the way, and I crawled forward. Moving along behind me, she lay her hand on my shoulder as I placed both hands and knees carefully on the ground. Closing my eyes, I tried to mentally picture our simple camp—surrounding shrubs here, a stand of young cedars over there, a dragged log from—

Automatic gunfire suddenly split the night. Eerie flashes of gnarled trees and shadows danced around us, lit by just a few muzzles flashes.

Fit and strong from weeks of cutting wood and other chores, I rose to my feet, whipped Zima into my arms, then threw her like a man throws a sack of flour. In strobes, I could see our surroundings, and she landed behind a fallen birch tree that still bore its branches. Diving, I leapt on top of her to pin her down and hold her ears. But the gunfire lasted only five seconds. Then darkness settled on us again.

"Don't . . . move," I mouthed into her ear.

She panted fearfully beneath me, but my breath was a little steadier. Calculating the odds always calms me, and while Zima was praying that we wouldn't be found, I wondered how we could safely get farther into the forest. In mere seconds, the assailants would find the *ger* empty and begin to search for us.

A flashlight flicked on, then another. The now familiar sharpness of Chinese words drifted to our ears. One of our horses whinnied, and a man laughed. They were ten yards away. I counted three distinct speakers. As yet, they hadn't reloaded their weapons. We could run, but they'd give chase. Maybe we could circle back for our horses, but if not, then what? The chill of the air was below freezing, but we had grabbed our coats. As cold as it was here, it would be even colder on the plain where the wind blew.

Someone lifted back the *ger* flap. A fourth voice shouted an alarm. Now, they reloaded their weapons. This was our chance. I started to rise when gunfire from the trees behind the horses spat in our direction. Again, I held Zima down.

A man screamed. The flashlight beams drifted across the trees around us. Someone stumbled, then fell and sighed his last.

"What's happen—"

I clamped my hand over Zima's mouth to silence her question. How would I answer her, anyway? What were the chances of two opposing parties attacking us on the same night? Maybe the large fire hadn't been such a good idea after all. The Chinese were possibly starving. Maybe they had seen us during the day on the plain, and were now fighting each other for our horses. That would mean someone had been watching us talk at the fire, waiting in the darkness for us to go to sleep. It was a violating thought.

"You can come out," a voice called in Mongolian. "They're all dead."

We didn't move right away, though I knew that voice. It was someone from my past—our past. I peered over our birch tree, but I couldn't see anything, not even shapes.

"*Dusbhan?*" I whispered, then ducked back down, fully expecting a barrage of bullets to impact our hiding place.

Even though I'd whispered, he heard me clearly, for not even the night creatures were stirring after all the noise.

"Yes. It's me and Uncle Gan-gaad. Do you have any food?"

I pulled Zima with me as we found our feet and crept back into camp. It took me a few seconds to find my lighter and start a fire. Zima huddled close to me. When the flames leapt high enough, I grimaced at the sight of our two old clansmen. Both were filthy and shivering, their coats in tatters, and their fingers clinging like claws to two foreign-made rifles. My foot bumped something and I glance down to see a dead man in uniform staring up at me. It was a Chinese soldier, and he wasn't the only one.

Dusbhan kicked at another body on his side of the fire.

"This one said something about a radio. My Chinese isn't good, but I believe they wanted to see if you had a radio to transmit something."

Zima and I exchanged glances. The Red Army was beginning to hunt the woods for the spy and radio that was making troop reports. Unless winter itself froze the soldiers in place, they would reach South Camp within a couple weeks as they searched the woods. But I said nothing of this at that time. I studied Gan-gaad who hadn't spoken yet. He held his bare hands to the fire. His cheeks were sunken, as were Dusbhan's, and I knew they hadn't eaten well in days.

"What of the clan?" Zima asked Dusbhan. She unwrapped a frozen block of cheese and meat.

"Gone. The Chinese . . ." Dusbhan shook his head and shivered.

"It's okay," Zima said. "You don't have to say any more."

"And we wouldn't be alive, either, if we hadn't gone to the forest to hunt," Dusbhan said. "We left the clan on the plain. The Chinese saw us awhile later, but they ignored me and Uncle, even after they'd butchered and left the clan like that. And the livestock, they . . . Luyant must've gone crazy. When we returned to camp, we could read all the sign. Luyant killed ten of them, I think, before he was gunned down."

"Sit down." I rolled up a couple logs. Zima gave them food and a wooden bowl of milk to share. "We were coming to find you, hoping you were far to the south along the Gobi already."

Without speaking, they gobbled the food. Gan-gaad stared into the flames, too stricken, it seemed, to respond any other way. Once, these two men were fierce and courageous, but now they seemed like frightened children trembling in shock at what they'd witnessed.

"They need rest," Zima said to me. "Perhaps they should sleep in the *ger,* and you and I—"

"No," Gan-gaad stated, but his eyes remained on the flames. "We'll sleep here by the fire where it's warmest." He pulled his rifle close. "I won't inconvenience you."

Zima raised her eyebrows. Here was a truly beaten man. He'd once had everything, commanded men and beasts alike. Now, he begged for food and slept in the dirt. Compared to what these men now possessed, Zima and I seemed wealthy.

From the *ger*, Zima pulled two felt blankets and draped one over each man's back. I stepped around the bodies behind us and fetched one of their flashlights.

"What of the bodies, Pond?" Zima asked.

I studied the four deceased. Even though many in America taught that killing was justified under certain circumstances, I felt it was wrong for any reason. But we were a long way from American justifications, and I was left with quite a predicament. We would've been dead for certain if Gan-gaad and Dusbhan hadn't killed them. Our *ger* alone looked like a noodle strainer, the canvas dome speckled by a hundred holes.

"The ground is too hard and frozen to bury them," I said, "but if we're found with them, we'll be executed for sure."

"They must've come in a vehicle," Zima said.

"It's in the plain partially concealed against the woods," Dusbhan said. "When we saw it, we followed them in. We knew they were up to no good."

"I'll get started," I said and kissed Zima's forehead, then went to saddle the horses I'd need. Pausing, I pointed at the two men at our fire. "Zima, I know these two. Don't let them eat too much. We don't know how long it'll take us to get back to camp since we're one horse shy due to our load of gear."

Loading the four dead men onto the horses was

distasteful, messy, and an endeavor I hope to never have to do again. Zima held two flashlights to give me light as I hefted the bloody corpses onto the horses' backs. I was sure the animals were not too thrilled, either, about the night's bone-chilling venture with the smell of death in the air.

When I left, I took no flashlight with me, though I was tempted. Hiking, I led the horses west rather than east to the soldiers' vehicle. The forest thinned, and the stars came into sight as I emerged from the trees that rimmed the range. From the stars, I could see the shape of the mountain and its precarious curves and shadows above me. The horses' sight was better than mine, but I left nothing to chance. Rather than attack the mountain straight up, I led them on a traversing route with quick switchbacks. Up and up we climbed until I could see over the trees into the plain below where even Siberian timber wolves shivered in the northeasterly wind, and where the Chinese traffic still crisscrossed the country. But I saw no other lights or headlights near the forest, and I prayed the four I had on horseback were the only radio hunters that night. Most likely, they were killing anyone they found in the woods, hoping to silence the secret operator along the way.

I reached a rocky ridge rimmed with fresh snow, and sunk up to my knees in the drift as I continued leading the horses through a narrow gorge with steep, vertical walls. The pass ended abruptly at a landslide of rocks and ice. Overhead, I glimpsed terrifying boulders that could crash down on me at the slightest tremor of seismic activity. But this place would serve its purpose, if I wasn't crushed first.

Hastily, I dropped the four bodies to the ground and

dragged them over against the gorge wall so they were in a seated position. Then, I led the burden-free horses out of the narrow pass, and picketed the lead *aduu* at the snowline where they could nip at the snow.

From there, I climbed the mountain, but this time, I worked my way above the gorge on the high northern wall. After testing my footing before applying my body weight, I found the ledge above the four bodies. Stabilizing myself, I pushed my shovel into an icy crack a foot from the ledge. To gather all my strength, I took a deep breath, but the shale had already begun to give way beneath my feet. Dropping my shovel, I twisted around to dive for safety. My feet kicked wildly in midair. Weakly, I clawed at the wall of rock as it crumbled around me, before me, and under me. A shrill gasp escaped my throat and I felt my death very near. I'd never survive a fall to the floor of the gorge—especially not with boulders hailing down upon me.

With one last desperate effort, I threw my right arm toward the ledge. My fingers caught at jagged ice. I hung there for two breaths, but my hand was already slipping inside my dog hair gloves.

"Lord, I—"

My hand slipped from the ledge. My other hand reached up to replace it on the falling rock, but it was no use. I only slapped the rock face.

Suddenly, a firm hand clasped around my left wrist. For a moment, I dangled there, too tired to even kick or flail. I breathed a sigh of relief as I was pulled upward. My feet walked up the sheer wall, trying to find footing to help my rescuer.

"Thank God! I was hoping one of you might've followed me out of camp!" The hand let go of my wrist and I steadied my quivering nerves on my hands and knees before standing. "My shovel was lost, but I—"

My eyes narrowed as they swept the quiet mountainside. Behind me, a few pebbles continued tumbling into the deep ravine. The horses chomped thirstily at snow a hundred yards below me. The wind whistled through a crevice to my left.

I forced an acknowledging swallow through my dry throat.

No one was there. I was alone.

What can one say at a moment such as that? What words can express the joy and relief, yet not without some tingling fear?

Before they turned to ice, I wiped away my tears.

"*Thank You, Lord.*" I breathed it in a whisper, but He heard me. He hadn't left me alone.

I descended the mountain with my horses.

CHAPTER TWENTY-THREE

Back in camp, Zima rolled two more logs onto the roaring fire in front of Gan-gaad and Dusbhan. Gan-gaad had turned sideways in his sleep, his head against his nephew's shoulder.

"I'll see to the horses," she offered, and took the reins.

After warming myself at the fire for a few minutes, I strode out of camp again, this time to the east. It took me twenty minutes to find their Chinese-made SUV. After finding the keys, I started the engine, laughing as I revved the gas pedal and turned the heater on high. The fuel was at half. Plenty for what I had in mind.

In the back of the SUV, I found a propane tank and a box of packaged troop rations—rice and chicken meals including a cookie the size of a half-dollar coin. With two extra men now, the additional food would help. I dumped the rations onto the ground outside, but left the box in the SUV. It would be a mistake to be found with anything that could link us to the missing soldiers. We could burn the packaging after we ate the food.

Munitions and radio gear were also in the back seat, but wanting none of that, I left it.

Trembling from the busy night's excitement, I climbed into the driver's seat again and turned the vehicle northward. From a bag of fatigues in the passenger seat, I drew out a nylon belt from a pair of pants. When I'd gotten the SUV up to thirty miles an hour, I tied the belt onto the steering wheel, then set the cruise control and aimed the vehicle east. I tapped the brake to decrease speed so I could easily jump out. Finally, I tightened the steering wheel's belt against the seat belt strap so the vehicle would go straight while unmanned. Opening the driver's door, I initiated the cruise control again, and hopped and skipped from the vehicle.

Alone on the plain, I knelt and listened to the SUV reach its cruising speed as it rumbled away from me. I bit my lip nervously as it bounced over the ruts of the new Chinese road. But I'd left the SUV's lights off, so it crossed the road and continued east without drawing attention from the few vehicles I could see to the north and south. Soon, the SUV was too far away for me to see. Standing, I sighed with relief. This wasn't missionary work by any means, but the deaths of those men—I couldn't have controlled that. God had saved me and Zima from death that night. His protection and safe-keeping confirmed yet again that He had more for me to do.

Arriving back at camp, I dumped the ration packets from my coat onto the ground in front of the fire. Gan-gaad and Dusbhan were still fast asleep as Zima and I heated up a couple rice and chicken meals. Zima giggled as she tasted one.

"This is pretty good!"

"Well, it's not cheese and venison," I said with a chuckle, "so it has to taste all right."

"The soldiers probably complain about this food all the time," she said with a mouthful, "but it's a banquet to us."

She suddenly stopped chewing. "What did you do with the vehicle?"

"It'll be halfway across the Gobi before it runs out of fuel." I nodded at the sleeping men. "What should we do about those two?"

"We obviously can't leave them behind, Pond. They haven't fended too well on their own. Look at them. All three camps have room for them, but Gan-gaad hates Kazakhs."

"I think he'll humble himself for the winter, at least. South Camp could use Dusbhan's knowledge of this area. He'll be back to his usual self in a few days. But we'd better take Gan-gaad into our camp, because I don't think anyone else could handle him."

"And you can?"

"As my guest, he'll mind himself and work, or he won't eat."

"That should sound familiar to him," Zima said, laughing.

"So, is that okay with you?" I asked, taking her hand in mine. "He and Sembuuk can have the third *ger* to themselves."

"Yes." She nodded. "I think Gan-gaad will learn to respect Sembuuk. He likes hunting, too. Just keep him away from me and don't let him take charge. You know he has a way of ruining morale by intimidation. Those are my only two suggestions."

I nodded in understanding.

"Right. Okay. It might just be a matter of finding something he can offer to the camps."

"Oh, he does! Gan-gaad is probably more knowledgeable than Kandal when it comes to the old ways, but he's usually too busy ordering people around to put his skills to work. I think he'll find his place."

"Or he won't eat," I said sternly.

We both laughed, but I thought, *how the proud do fall!*

"What? Where's my gun?" Gan-gaad cried as soon as he awoke the next morning. He struggled to his feet with Dusbhan next to him. "Pond! Our weapons! They're gone!"

Zima and I tightened the cinches on our saddles. We'd already packed the *ger* and gear.

"Have you seen the sky?" I looked upward. "There's no blue. It's certain to snow today."

Pouting, Gan-gaad did look toward the sky, but his eyes stopped midway up the nearest tree.

"Pond!" He pointed at their two rifles resting securely thirty feet up where I'd hurled them onto wide branches. "Our guns!" He searched the ground for something to throw and knock them down.

Dusbhan, always more level-headed and thoughtful, stepped toward me.

"We need those weapons, Pond. What if we come upon more Chinese?"

"I would say the chances of that happening are pretty good," I said almost too cheerily, "especially if we stay here."

"Where do you propose we go?"

Behind him, Gan-gaad was cursing at the tree, and throwing sticks. *Better at the tree than at me,* I thought.

"About a day's ride to the north, we have three camps. You'll both be welcome there. If we leave this place behind, we might make it through the winter."

I handed Dusbhan the reins to my horse.

"And the Chinese?" he asked.

"We'll do our best to avoid them. But, in matters I can't do anything about, I trust God. I'd say—"

"God!" Gan-gaad interrupted. "Who saved you last night? I say we stay here! We need those guns! *God?* Hah! The saints, the Bible, your God . . ." He spat on the ground. "There's your God!"

Before I could stop her, Zima moved past me and slapped Gan-gaad hard across the mouth, startling more than hurting him. He stepped back, his hand on his face, and tripped over his sitting log. The clansman stared up in shock at Zima, as if to say, *the nerve of such a woman!*

I rubbed my brow, barely withholding a smile.

"Zima," I said quietly, "that isn't helping matters."

"You heard what he said!" Pointing at him, she spat onto his legs. "That's what you are, Gan-gaad! Spittle!" She turned back to me. "I'm already tired of him, Pond! Put him where you put the soldiers last night!"

Dusbhan's mouth dropped. He didn't seem to know who to cheer for. Gan-gaad rolled to his feet, fury on his face. When he reached for Zima, I held him back easily. I'd put on a good ten pounds of muscle since he'd seen me last. Though he still outweighed me, he wasn't all muscle, by any means.

"Just a minute!" I shouted. "Zima, please. Gan-gaad, first of all, Zima and I are married now. Luyant is dead.

She's my wife. You want to touch her, you have to touch me first. Second of all, unlike you two, we have horses and gear. I'm assuming you ate your own horses long ago. These horses belong to the clan we came from. And in that clan, we have no guns because they'd only attract conflict. The Chinese know us up there as peaceable people. If you want to carry a weapon, you're welcome to stay behind and climb that tree, but you'll get none of my assistance. Thirdly, when I first came into your clan, I did as I was told, and I honored you. Because I worked, I ate, and not once have you seen me as a lazy man. Now, you've come into a new clan, my clan, so to speak, and you need my help. Gladly, I'll assist you if you follow my rules, the rules of my clan—your clan, your rules; my clan, my rules. Period!"

His chest swelled with a deep breath and clenched teeth

"For five generations," he said, "no one has ever spoken to me as—"

"Quiet!" I said. "I'm through arguing with you. You're not in charge, Gan-gaad. Fall in line or stay behind. It's your choice. But we're leaving. Zima, lead the way on the western side of the forest. I saw a trail there. We'll avoid the plain today. Dusbhan, you follow her by leading my horse, and I'll walk the first leg."

I offered Gan-gaad the reins of the final riding horse. The fourth horse was piled high with the gear that wasn't riddled with bullets. Zima and Dusbhan headed their horses west. Gan-gaad and I were alone.

"Your clan is gone, Gan-gaad," I said gentler. "Many others have died as well. I won't put up with your fury while the rest of us work together to help each other survive. If you accept this horse, you accept it as an equal to me and the others you'll be joining. Luyant whipped you a time or two, I know, and you know I whipped Luyant that first day we met. Now, I shouldn't need to threaten an older man, but I will surely take my belt and whip you like a child if you can't keep your temper in check."

He gritted his teeth and glared at me. Slowly, his demeanor softened and he reached out and took the reins.

"So, Zima is your wife now?"

"That's right."

"And you have your own clan?"

We started on foot after the others. Dusbhan led my horse with the gear heaped so high on it that I couldn't see Zima or Dusbhan.

"It's not only my clan; it's all of ours."

"How big is it?"

"About twenty people between three camps. We keep the camps small so we're more manageable and not so visible."

"And you're killing the horses to eat?"

"South Camp killed one, but we have a good hunter. We shouldn't have to kill any more, but some might think we need to."

"What's your hunter's name?"

"Sembuuk. He's a good man in our camp. You and he will share a *ger*."

"You have *gers*?"

"Oh, yes. Every camp has at least three. Dusbhan will probably go to South Camp. They need an extra hand with firewood."

After a short distance, we caught up to Dusbhan and Zima, then Gan-gaad mounted his *aduu*. Zima and I took turns explaining how the three camps were run, and the morning faded into afternoon. It had been a short honeymoon, but Zima and I were both ready to get back to camp. We'd enjoyed the previous evening in front of the fire, and that would have to be the extent of our private time for now.

...✝...

"Kazakhs?" Gan-gaad recognized the people as we rode into camp that night.

North Camp had heard us approaching, alerted by Lucky Hunter's low growls, and had run out to greet us. Gan-gaad and Dusbhan saw the style of *dels* and heard their Turkic accents, and knew immediately this was a Kazakh camp. Dusbhan turned around on his horse to see how his uncle would react. Gan-gaad was white-faced and rigid in his saddle.

"You set me up, Pond," Gan-gaad said.

"Yes, I suppose I did," I said, and patted Bolor on the back as he joined us. "But I know you'll be civil. If you want to live."

He didn't respond as Sembuuk and Kandal came alongside and escorted us into camp, helping us with our burdens and shoving wooden containers into our hands to drink.

Dusbhan and Gan-gaad were welcomed with more familiarity than they were used to. Gan-gaad smiled and shook hands uneasily. It was obvious he was Mongolian and these were Kazakhs. The two didn't normally mix, but here they were. What else could he do? He seemed to relax after a few minutes. Out of the corner of my eye, I saw the ex-clan leader shrug and pat Lucky Hunter on the head. Zima smiled at me from across camp, and I nodded and smiled back at her. I scooped Manai into my arms as he rattled off a dozen questions about our adventure.

That night, after a feast among friends, I stretched and said I was going to go water the horses. I caught Kandal's eye, the signal was passed to Sembuuk, and the three of us excused ourselves. As I was leaving camp, I glanced back to see Beveg and Manai paging through *Pilgrim's Progress* with Dusbhan. But the part that amazed me was that Gan-gaad stood over them all, his hands clasped behind his back as he looked over their shoulders at the exciting, colorful pages.

"In Your time, Lord," I said, praying for patience.

Gan-gaad was a relatively captive audience for the much more open-minded Kazakhs. But even his stubbornness wasn't impervious to their sense of togetherness.

At the pool, I broke a thin layer of ice with my boot and moved aside so the horses could drink. Kandal and Sembuuk joined me and I relayed the specifics of our trip south and the details of our confrontation with the Chinese.

"I agree," Kandal said thoughtfully. "They're scouring the forest, looking for potential rebels, killing everyone they find in the woods."

"Any chance these two new guys are the ones with the radio the Chinese are looking for?" Sembuuk asked.

"No, not these two. Gan-gaad despises all outsiders equally," I said. "He wouldn't help anyone else gain an advantage over the Chinese. Besides, neither of them have the knowledge to operate a transmitter. And the state in which they came to us—they're still half-starved." I nodded at Kandal. "Now, I think it's time you tell us what you know before the Chinese kill us all."

"Maybe," Kandal said slowly, "I know who has the radio, but only maybe. Would it matter if I knew? Will the Chinese still seek to purge the forest of rebels?"

"And what about those soldiers you buried?" Sembuuk asked. "Maybe we should all be fighting the Chinese."

Turning away from the men for a moment, I groaned and prayed under by breath. *Lord, what am I missing? I need Your help and direction here, Your wisdom.* I faced the men again.

"There was a time when I would've been the first to lead us against the invaders. If you want to fight them, I can't stop you. Zima and I see greater issues to face. As followers of Jesus Christ, we don't war against flesh and blood; we war against spiritual wickedness and the darkness of the heart. These are my priorities." Suddenly, the answer came to me. "What about Duulgii?"

Sembuuk and I studied Kandal's worried face.

"We mustn't jump to conclusions," Kandal said.

"The day of the massacre," I said, "Duulgii and one other rider escaped with us here. At the time, I thought it was strange neither man had bothered to rescue anyone else but themselves as we all ran from the camp. But they'd taken time to collect their packs."

"What kind of packs?" Sembuuk asked. "I barely had time to get a horse and the girl that's now at Middle Camp."

"Duulgii's was square-shaped." I showed the dimensions with my hands. "What could that be?"

"Too small to be a stove," Kembuuk said. "Blankets or bags of supplies wouldn't be shaped like that. But I've never seen Duulgii with a radio. He's half-Russian, though. He would have a motive to help the Russians against the Chinese."

"Kandal? What do you think?"

The old man sighed.

"I've seen the radio. Duulgii and the man you saw riding with him were both paramilitary in Kazakhstan. The other man joined us just a week before you did, Pond."

"Do you know where they are?" Sembuuk asked, impatiently. "I can't believe you would withhold this from us! This isn't something to keep secret! It endangers us all!"

"Well, I had my reasons!" Kandal shouted back. "I couldn't implicate Lugsalkhaan's brother-in-law. It wouldn't have been good for the clan. Lugsalkhaan could still be alive. He may have been among those who fled east, maybe meeting up with another clan."

"Lugsalkhaan is dead," Sembuuk mumbled. "He died that first day. Andy buried him in secret to keep his name alive."

Kandal glared at both of us in turn.

"Look who speaks of keeping things secret! How dare you speak to me as a pup, Sembuuk! I would die for this clan, and for Lugsalkhaan!" He lowered his voice. "We were like father and son. Where is he buried?"

I told him, and we were silent for a moment.

"Duulgii must be hiding nearby," I said. "You may care

for what's left of this clan, Kandal, but Duulgii doesn't. It's not his clan. He married into it. And now he's using the clan for cover to mask his mischief. If there was any honor in him, any loyalty, he wouldn't be endangering us."

"And you propose we turn him over to the Chinese?" Kandal asked. "This isn't your clan, either, Pond. What do you care?"

"If tears and sweat and blood and sleepless nights could make a man a clan member, then this is my clan as much as anyone's," I said. "As for what to do with Duulgii, we can only reason with him. Maybe he'll go north or south and not draw us into his conflict any longer."

The rumble of military jets could be heard high overhead. The war continued in the north.

"I've seen no sign on the ground of Duulgii or anyone else nearby," Sembuuk said. "Every time I hunt, I watch for sign."

"He must be in the mountains, then," I said, "somewhere to the west."

"That's difficult terrain," Kandal said. "We're people of the steppes."

"The mountains aren't strange to the Mongolians, though," I said. "Every autumn, they hunt this area as they migrate south. I know they were going into the higher elevations because they were preparing snowshoes."

"The new man?" Kandal asked. "Gan-gaad?"

"Yes," I said, nodding, "and his nephew, Dusbhan."

"But they nearly died on their own, you said," Sembuuk said.

"They were fighting the cold, looking for food and

shelter, and hunting the Chinese all at once," I said. "Anyone would work himself to death at that rate. Let me go with them into the mountains tomorrow and find Duulgii's camp. I've met him, but I know him only well enough to ask him to meet with you and some of the others. If he will, maybe you can convince him to go elsewhere. It may be time to bring this up at the Three Rocks meeting in the morning to see what the others think of it all."

"I'll go to Three Rocks tomorrow," Kandal said, "but you find Duulgii, anyway. The others will see it our way."

"And be careful," Sembuuk said. "I'm sure Duulgii will be armed."

...†...

CHAPTER TWENTY-FOUR

The next morning, there was a slight change in plans. South Camp felt they were behind in their winter fortifications, so Dusbhan went to them without delay, and I knew he wouldn't disappoint them. Dusbhan was a hard worker and stronger than most men his size. Though he'd killed the Chinese soldiers recently, I was anxious to discuss the Bible with him again as we had in the past. Looking forward to that time, I gave him another Bible to take with him to South Camp that morning, and invited him to the service that North Camp was to host on Sunday morning. Earlier, I'd spoken with the others about a meeting, and regardless of the cold, they saw it as an opportunity to congregate—and didn't seem opposed to the stories I might share during the time. But I'd planned to share with them the most important story of all—the story of Jesus' life, death, and resurrection.

So with Dusbhan off to South Camp, Bolor widening the corral, and Sembuuk hunting with Manai, Gan-gaad and I mounted up and rode west.

"I needed this escape, Pond," Gan-gaad said. "Zima has had me doing women's chores all morning. Can you imagine? Zima giving me orders!"

"She knows what needs to be done," I said. "I hope you helped."

"Yes, I did, because her arm is still in that cursed cast. I

278

hate milking mares, Pond. *Hate it!* But I knew if I didn't, since she's your wife now, she would tell you."

"You'll do well here, Gan-gaad," I said. "The beautiful thing about these people is that whatever work must be done, they do it for everyone without complaining."

"But I'm a complainer, Pond. You know that and you flatter me to say I'll do well here. Their *airag* isn't strong enough. The tea is too strong. And Sembuuk snores too loudly. I think you put me in his *ger* because no one else can sleep near him!"

"We can still hear him in the next *ger*, too, Gan-gaad," I said, laughing.

Two hours later, we dismounted our horses and crawled to the edge of the highest ridge of the mountain behind our camp. The mountains stretched out to the west—jagged peaks among rugged gorges and treacherous walls of rock. The view wasn't without its color of green, though. Large patches of forest clung to the mountainsides, obscuring hidden valleys and canyons. It took Gan-gaad a few minutes to familiarize himself with our coordinates, then he pointed out landmarks.

". . . And over there, Luyant killed a giant doe three winters back. See the white stone that looks like marble? There's a meadow there, though hardly more than a small clearing."

"I see the stone," I said, eying the landmark with my binoculars, "but no clearing."

"It's there, only obscured by trees. Look to the northwest, against the same rock face."

Focusing my glasses, I swept them slowly.

"What am I supposed to—" I stopped. "I think I barely see white smoke. It might be a hot spring. Or it could be nothing more than vapor."

"No." Gan-gaad shook his big head and took the binoculars to see for himself. "There's a spring there, but it's as cold as ice. And there's a deep cave in the rock there, too. I've been in it, seen the ancient drawings, even studied them a couple times, though I'm not a learned man. Ah, yes. It's a campfire." He gave my glasses back. "You know, they say Genghis Khan is buried in the mountains here. Somewhere in the west, but I think it was farther south, closer to where he died."

"How do we get down there?" I asked, staying focused on the mission at hand.

"This ridge forks in the north, then drops into the valley. Once we're down there, we'll follow the bottom of this mountain around . . ." He traced it with his finger. "Then we'll cross the meadow and catch them by surprise. I think we can be there by midday."

We remained kneeling so as not to give away our position with silhouettes against the horizon. When we did finally cross over the ridge, we did it quickly on horseback.

"I would much rather do this with a rifle, Pond," he said. "It makes little sense to hunt with no weapons."

"These men aren't enemies of ours. They're friends of the clan and we're only messengers to invite them to speak to Kandal and the others."

"What if they don't want to come?"

"Then I'll reason with them. I know Duulgii a little. He was going to give me a pup, once."

"You've come far, Pond, in a short time in this country." He sighed aloud. "It's unfortunate you come at a time of strife, though. Mongolia is truly the best place on this earth."

I rode on in silence. He'd never been outside Mongolia, but I agreed, the country was spectacular. For the most part, it was untouched by the direct threat of warfare. We'd merely suffered some indirect fallout from the wars around us.

The ridge from which we descended faded into the valley floor to a narrow game trail, and we took a sharp left to follow the base of the mountain in a wide arc. It was a beautiful, blue-sky day for a ride, but our every breath left a cloud of vapor lingering on the brisk air.

On our left, the mountain towered over us, looming almost threateningly, and on our right, we passed larch and cedar timber speckled over rocky outcroppings and ditches sculpted from the ancient flood itself. As we neared the meadow, we were wary and quiet, but not because we feared we would alert Duulgii of our presence directly. A meadow would be a place for deer and other animals to feed. It was them we didn't want to spook, for they would in turn alert Duulgii and his partner of approaching foreigners. And any foreigners, Duulgii was likely to consider his enemies. We didn't want to be shot accidently.

The meadow came into sight and we dismounted. I stepped over a narrow crack in the ground caused by the region's many seismic disturbances. We didn't picket our horses; we let them graze freely on the dry range grass as we walked quietly west along the edge of the meadow. Gan-gaad, an expert when it came to animal senses, hummed a quiet tune to communicate to four curious deer nearby that we were no danger to them. The deer, perhaps seeing humans for the first time, watched intently as we passed by.

We followed a vague game trail through a small stand of trees, then slowed our pace as Gan-gaad led. Regardless of his bulk, he was more naturally light-footed than me. In the plains, he'd stomped about intimidating everyone, but here, he padded on the balls of his feet, barely disturbing the ground. He was a hunter at heart, and I wouldn't want to be the man's unsuspecting prey. The very fact that he had attacked a superior Chinese patrol only a few days earlier spoke for itself. The man was a predator.

The game trail drifted down to a seasonal streambed that was now dry, but Gan-gaad waved me forward and pointed up at the sheer rock face on our left to show me where water still trickled from ice. Or was he pointing at something else? I frowned and shook my head, not understanding what he wanted me to see or do. He leaned close to my ear.

"The path. Now, you lead. You have better luck with bullets than me."

I didn't argue, but I still didn't know where to go. The trail went down, but he was motioning upward. Carefully, I studied the face of the rock. Was that another path? It led at a steep angle upward, but it was by no means a safe route. Most of it was loose gravel that had crumbled away from the rock face. But forty feet up the face, I saw an actual ledge, and I assumed that was the location of the cave.

Gan-gaad nudged me from behind and I stepped onto the path leading upward. My boot sole was steeply angled—so much so that I thought my ankle would sprain if I didn't slip off the mountain altogether. Facing the rock, I edged my way along with my back to the drop-off, my right foot leading. Ignoring the dead air at my heels, I tried to concentrate on shifting my feet forward. Glancing back at Gan-gaad, I kept my hands on the rock in front of me for balance. Again, he urged me forward, an impatient look on his face as if I were taking unnecessary precautions. But I continued no faster, even for his sake. I loved heights . . . as long as I was looking up at them from below.

Twice, I nearly lost my footing completely. If I started to fall, I planned to shove away from the rock with all my might, with the hope of breaking my fall by landing in the tree tops and branches of the trees below.

But my feet finally reached level ground on the ledge, and I breathed a prayer of thanks.

To my left, the mouth of the cave opened. It was a black hole four feet wide and almost as tall as me. Gan-gaad licked his lips, ready for confrontation, and prodded me forward yet again. With one eye, I peered into the cave mouth for two seconds, then withdrew quickly to allow the image to process in my mind. The cave floor angled downward like a low-grade ramp to a single room cavern where a small fire was burning. Glancing up, I saw wisps of smoke drift skyward. Beside the fire were two men, one with his back to me, the other, his left side to me. Both had been laboring over skins in their laps. Horse hides, I decided. They'd probably killed their horses for food and winter coats.

What concerned me most was that it was a good thirty

paces down the ramp. That was plenty of distance to get shot if I didn't reach them before they recognized me. None of this I could convey to Gan-gaad, but he'd said he'd been there before, so he knew what lay ahead.

I took a deep breath and cupped my mouth. Why startle them when I could announce our presence? We had them cornered now. They had to listen to us. Gan-gaad saw my intentions and gripped my arm like an iron vice. He shook his head as if to say, *"No warning!"*

Shoving away from the rock, I two-stepped down the ramp with barely a whisper from my boots on the pebbly floor. Gan-gaad saw we had the upper hand; we weren't being shot at right away, so he moved up beside me.

We were five paces from the man with his back to us when the other startled and spied movement at his elbow. He reached for a rifle on the rock floor, but I was already on him, and his hand overshot the weapon. I plowed into him hard and sent him tumbling with the hide still on his lap. Gan-gaad did the same to the man with his back to us. Shoving the man hard, he sent him sprawling into the fire, but he rolled out the same instant.

"Are these them?" Gan-gaad asked hungrily, his fists clenched as we stood over them. He wanted a fight.

The men were on their backs, staring up at us with looks of terror in their faces. I recognized Duulgii by his filthy snow leopard hat, but neither of the two appeared to be a fraction of the men they once were. They looked worse than Gan-gaad and Dusbhan did when I'd found them half-starved. These men had thinning hair and sunken cheeks from malnutrition.

Duulgii's fight wasn't gone, though. His hand wrapped around a piece of firewood.

"We're just here to talk, Duulgii," I said. He probably thought otherwise—me being a foreigner and Gan-gaad's accent identifying him as a Mongolian. "We jumped you because we figured you'd shoot first if given the chance."

"Just to talk?" Duulgii asked, his voice weak and scratchy. He glanced at his partner who was brushing sparks off the felt of his *del*. "I thought you were . . ."

"You thought we were the Chinese, I know." I acknowledged the radio and transmitter against the cavern wall to my right. "Just be glad I found you before they did, and believe me, they're searching high and low for you. Come on. Kandal, Jugder, and the others want to talk to you."

Gan-gaad moved around me and gathered their rifles. Both were Russian-made AK-47s.

Duulgii rose weakly to his feet, then pulled the other man upright. His partner was wounded, I noticed, but not by anything we'd done. There was dried blood caking his pants, and his thigh was bandaged.

"Who's he?" Duulgii asked, casting a glance at Gan-gaad who was inspecting the radio gear. "He looks Mongolian."

"That's right, he is. But he's with the clan now. He's friendly."

"Well, he doesn't look friendly."

"None of us are friendly," I stated harshly, "with you risking our lives like this—bringing the Chinese onto our doorstep!"

Gan-gaad snapped his head toward Duulgii.

"I'm not friendly because I hate Russians."

"Where's Lugsalkhaan? I'll only speak to my brother-in-law."

"He's dead. I buried him myself in secret so his name lives on. The others don't know."

"Who's leading the clan?"

"Kandal, Sembuuk, Jugder, and a few others."

"And you?"

"I do my part."

"You still tell your stories?"

"Every chance he gets," Gan-gaad said. "I'd gag him if the others didn't actually pretend to enjoy his adventures."

I laughed as the tension subsided.

"The Chinese are looking for me?"

"Of course." I waved at the radio equipment. "They can track all this, but only when you're transmitting. I suspect you're not on the air long, so they're having trouble narrowing the search. Right now, they're hunting the woods on the eastern slope and killing everyone they find."

"So," Duulgii said, swallowing, "Kandal is not happy that I've brought this on the clan." He shook his head sorrowfully. "I can't meet with them. Jugder will kill me, I know."

"Maybe you deserve it," Gan-gaad said. I cast him a silencing glare. He shrugged. "Maybe he does."

"What do they want to talk to me about?"

"Ceasing what you're doing. If you stop, the Chinese will stop hunting the woods."

"I can't stop." He shook his head again. "It's for my

people. They rely on this intelligence."

"Then go north or south," I said, making it sound like an order. "Anywhere that isn't endangering lives."

"Look at us. We can't travel. We're nearly out of food and it's not even truly winter, yet."

"You'll die without the clan," I said, "and the clan surely won't allow this radio business in their midst." For a moment, I let him think about that. "May I offer a word of reason?"

He nodded.

"Every time you transmit, people die. You're causing death. Sometimes it's death in Russia. Sometimes it's down here among your adopted clan. Within a month, if you continue here, you'll be dead from starvation, or from Chinese torture. If you don't quit for the sake of others' lives, then quit for your own sake. Walk away, Duulgii. Just walk away."

Duulgii's partner cleared his throat. He appeared as if he were ready to burst into tears, maybe because he was in worse shape than Duulgii. When he spoke, he spoke in Russian, but I knew enough to understand.

"Moskva is lost, comrade. I'm finished. He's right. We can't even get to the ridge to spy on the plain. Duulgii, we're dead."

"Will the clan take us back?" Duulgii asked me.

"I believe so, but I'm putting you in Jugder's camp. He can keep an eye on you two. Middle Camp needs a couple extra hands to help with firewood, anyway. Gather your things." Then, I went over to Gan-gaad. "Pack up the radio gear. I'm turning it over to my contact in the Chinese military as an act of good faith. They won't leave us alone, otherwise."

"And what of these?" He held up the rifles.

"They can be used for hunting, but they'll remain stowed in this cave, otherwise, and only we and Dusbhan knows of this cave. Hear that, you two? Don't tell anyone back in camp about this cave. It would defeat the clan's efforts of peace if someone were found with a gun among us. If one of these guns disappears, I'm holding you two responsible."

The trek back to camp was a considerable challenge. Duulgii and his Russian partner were so weak they had to ride our horses. This wouldn't have been a problem except it meant that Gan-gaad and I had to walk, and Gan-gaad wasn't up to his full strength, either. It was sunset when we arrived at camp. Nearly frozen, Duulgii and the Russian were sleeping in their saddles. Gan-gaad was shivering with such ferocity that he spilled his first cup of tea at the central fire. I was weary, but not so disabled that I couldn't assist the others.

Kandal was all for bringing the two old clan members into camp, which was voiced at the camp meeting we held right away. But Sembuuk and Bolor were openly against it. However, it was agreed by all that we couldn't send them back out into the cold. Middle Camp could use them, if they behaved. No one felt hesitant about treating the late clan leader's brother-in-law with caution, and Duulgii didn't object to any of our decisions. I guessed he felt the burden of spying finally lifted. He was now among friendly people who had nearly everything that was once available to the original clan.

So, the next morning, the two newcomers were whisked off to Middle Camp where clan elder Jugder could oversee them. However, the issue wasn't concluded. I still had their radio, and the Chinese were surely still seeking to purge the forest, slowly working their way north until they found it. They wouldn't be appeased, I decided, until they had the radio in hand. Hopefully, they would simply leave us in peace when they finally had it.

It was a nice thought. If only situations go as planned every time . . .

...✝...

CHAPTER TWENTY-FIVE

The following day, I spent time with Kandal and Sembuuk as we devised a safe way to deliver the radio to the Chinese. I was taking responsibility since I was the one who'd met Sergeant Xing on two separate occasions, and it was my idea to deliver the radio to him in the first place—rather than destroy it outright. Otherwise, we'd need to move the clan so far north and west into the depths of the Altay Mountains that no one would find us.

"That's not a bad idea," Kandal had mused as we nibbled on a midday meal near the stream. The water was frozen, so sections of ice were taken to camp for thawing—cut directly from the stream with our axes. "But we'll keep that idea as a last resort. The journey would be hard and dangerous, the cold too severe. If it was certain we'd have game along the way—and a safe route to travel—we could make the trip. Oftentimes, the weather pushes the game into the mountain valleys more than the plain."

"Maybe we should send someone ahead to scout a route." I suggested.

"You believe it will come to that? Us running from the Chinese?"

"I believe everything will continue to grow worse until the final days before Christ sets up His kingdom of peace on earth."

"Ah, you speak of the Book of Revelation again,"

Kandal said. "You were testing me. Yes, I've been reading. Will we still have the gathering tomorrow, even though you'll be tending to the radio?"

"Yes, I'll leave after the gathering."

"Someone who knows the mountains should go to the northwest," Sembuuk said.

"Dusbhan from my old clan would be a wise choice. With the right supplies on a mount, he could find the easiest route for us, perhaps avoiding the plain altogether. It would be best to stay in those mountain ranges, hunting along the way."

"Fine," Sembuuk said. "Prepare him to leave, but keep this between us. The others would lose hope if we shared such a contingency plan of departure. Returning the radio may not go as planned."

That night, I paid South Camp a friendly visit to help with their wood cutting. As soon as I had Dusbhan alone in the woods, I explained our intentions to find safe passage north for the clan if we had to flee from the Chinese soldiers. After considering the responsibility carefully, he said he knew it to be a dangerous chore alone in such weather and terrain. But he understood the precautionary measure, and accepted the task. We agreed he would take two horses with minimal supplies, and I even insisted he take my sleeping bag, which would be both warmer at night and lighter for traveling than bulky skins. For hunting purposes only, he would fetch a rifle from the cave. I didn't worry that he would venture into the plain to assault the Chinese. He wouldn't attack them alone. Since many lives depended upon a safe, unexposed escape route, I believed

Dusbhan took the assignment seriously.

"I'll leave tomorrow," he said, "and spend the night in the cave, then continue north. Using your binoculars, I can spy down on the towns of Hasagt, Bulgan, and Dund-Us on my way. If I relay my mounts, I may be gone three weeks, maybe less, but I may need to hunt, so it's wisest to assume a month. Is that too long?"

"Well, it's a long time, but hopefully we don't need to leave before that."

Looking down at the ground, he kicked at a frozen piece of wood.

"It would be wise to be accompanied by your God on this journey, wouldn't it?"

"Absolutely." His change of subject was a reminder to me that regardless of frantic events, the Holy Spirit was still working on hearts. The clan's spiritual safety was more important than their physical safety. "Do you feel God calling you?"

"Yes." He nodded. "I want what you have, but I don't know what to say or how to pray as you do."

There, in the freezing forest of the Gobi Altay Mountain region, we knelt on the hard ground and prayed together. Dusbhan wept before his Creator over his past sins, and we laughed together as brothers in the joy of the Lord as those same tears froze to his cheeks. But he prayed because he believed the Word, and this was my essential mission: to plant the seed and allow God to give the increase.

"Can I ride back to North Camp with you?" he asked. "I have to tell Zima I'm now a follower of Jesus."

"By all means! Let's go!"

...✝...

The following morning was Sunday, the day of our first service. Everyone in all three camps gathered at North Camp. I was so excited and praising God about Dusbhan's decision the night before that I was speechless when Kandal approached me before the service with a similar desire.

"My gods never do anything for me," he said, "and Buddha's wisdom seems stolen from Solomon, anyway."

This was a remarkable transformation since Kandal was an old-fashioned skeptic, one who I'd believed would rely on tradition more than the others. But man's reasoning isn't God's reasoning. His love transcends even the aggressive traditionalists and grips their stubborn hearts!

Kandal and I prayed together, then we were joined by Zima and Dusbhan as the first Christian family I'd witnessed in Mongolia.

As the service began, the glowing faces of the three converts beamed at me from different parts of the gathered clan. Everyone listened to my words, and regardless of the two most recent converts, I knew the Holy Spirit was urging us to remember that the time was indeed short. Every soul mattered—especially now since something seemed to be shimmering on the horizon.

I taught rather than preached about Israel's struggles in the wilderness. The people loved stories and I didn't disappoint them while establishing foundational concepts for relying on God as well as obeying His Word.

Our Bibles were limited, but the new Christians among the people helped them find the passages to read.

When I closed in prayer, I knelt on one knee as was

often my custom, and bowed my head. The people followed suit. By their faces, I knew many of them had been convicted by the message God had put on my heart to share with them.

"Lord God," I prayed aloud, "please work in our lives and in our hearts, and don't let us be like the stubborn Israelites. We praise You for sparing our small group from tragedy thus far, and we can only assume You've called us unto Yourself because you desire to use us. Let us meditate on these words. In Jesus' name, amen."

The children were instantly dashing about the camp, chasing the dogs, but the adults were less swift to part one another's company. They wanted more, which I assured them there would be, but we all had errands to run—especially me. In the activity, Dusbhan quietly left, heading toward the west, taking two horses with him.

Kandal patted me on the back, Zima kissed me, and Sembuuk saddled my horse. He would accompany me to Three Rocks, then I would approach the Chinese motorcade on my own.

"See you tonight," Zima stated with hope as she waved good-bye.

Only a couple of the men knew what Sembuuk and I were doing that afternoon, and he said as much as we neared Three Rocks.

"It's as if you're purposely trying to sacrifice yourself for the clan, Andy," he said. "I don't like it, even if I do sound like your wife for saying so."

I laughed.

"The Bible says the purest kind of love there is, is shown

when a man lays down his life for his friends. But don't misunderstand, Sembuuk. I'd rather live for my friends, not die for them, if I don't have to."

"Let me accompany you to meet with the Chinese, Andy. I know some Chinese, more than you do."

"That's not part of the plan," I said. "And if something happens to me, who'll go back and tell the others?"

"If we're not back by tonight, they'll know," he said. "No messenger will be needed. Let me go with you." He pointed at the sky. "Look. There's our watcher. My raptor. She won't take her eyes off us."

I admired his soaring eagle. It wasn't much reassurance, though.

"Well, I suppose we can do this together," I said. "Just don't do anything that seems threatening, and interpret everything exactly I say."

As we rode, I adjusted the pack behind me that held the oversized transmitter. Its battery was the heaviest component, but soon we'd be rid of it. I had also drafted a note in Russian Cyrillic to explain our intentions just in case our objectives were lost somewhere in translation. All our angles seemed to be covered, but to be even safer, Sembuuk and I rode a mile south of Three Rocks before we turned onto the plain to confront the Chinese vehicles and drivers.

The war must've been progressing nicely for the Chinese since the supply train flowed in a constant stream of convoys. A battalion of tanks fresh off the assembly line rumbled by, the soldiers barely glancing at us as they focused on their northern route.

When we neared the road, two armored personnel

carriers led by an ATV Jeep slowed to see what we wanted. I studied the vehicles for any sign of Sergeant Xing, but he wasn't among them. That would've been too easy, I thought. Without making any sudden gestures, I moved the radio onto my lap.

Sembuuk exchanged greetings with a lieutenant that stood in the turret. The officer scowled and rattled off a series of questions at Sembuuk. I picked up only a few words. He asked if we had any *airag*, and Sembuuk assured him we didn't. Then I lost track of the conversation and waited for some sign from Sembuuk that the greeting was over and we could discuss the radio we were turning over. But I received no signal, and Sembuuk delved into the reason we were there without checking with me.

The lieutenant cast his eyes on my Caucasian face and studied me suspiciously. Thinking this was my cue, I raised the bundled radio up off my lap. Right away, I realized that was the wrong thing to do. Apparently, Sembuuk hadn't completely relayed the matter of the object in my lap.

With bulging eyes, the lieutenant scratched for his sidearm. It seemed that, in his mind, he saw me as a potential Russian with a packaged bomb. In that split second, Sembuuk and I realized the misconception.

"No!" Sembuuk shrieked as the officer leveled his pistol at me.

I raised the radio up higher to protect myself as he fired the gun. The bullet tore into the radio. Shrapnel fragments cut into one of my hands. My *aduu* reared from the sudden explosion. Two more soldiers drew and fired at me while I was still gasping from my hand wound. A round tore through my horse's neck, spraying me with blood. A third bullet slammed into my left upper thigh and my mouth opened in a silent scream at the fire that coursed my nerves.

My *aduu* did her best to maintain her footing as I tumbled off her backwards while gripping my leg. Soldiers dragged Sembuuk off his *aduu*, beat him into submission, and searched his thick coat for a weapon. My mare screamed and thrashed as a hail of bullets cut her down once and for all. She nearly landed on top of me, as her black eyes clouded over and she breathed her last.

When the soldiers leapt on me, I thought they would kill me immediately, but they only pinned me down. Others hesitantly inspected the package and discovered it to be none other than the sought-after radio rumored to be in this area. This was almost as unfortunate as having a bomb since Sembuuk apparently hadn't completed his explanation. And now he was unconscious.

"Sembuuk!" I called, and was clubbed in the mouth with a rifle stock.

Dazed, I shook my head as my jaw sagged. A barrel pressed against my temple and I stopped struggling. The lieutenant was inches from my face, screaming an order I couldn't understand.

"English. I'm American!" I said in Mongolian and English. "My leg . . . I'm bleeding."

He must've understood because he stepped back and noticed the oozing from my thigh. Then, stooping down, he squarely punched my wound. I saw stars as if I'd been boxed on the chin. As I fought consciousness, someone fell beside me. It was Sembuuk. His eyes were closed, his brow bleeding, and he appeared to be dead.

Facing the yelling lieutenant again, I tasted blood in my mouth. *What was he saying?*

"An American," I said again. "I'm a missionary!"

When he kicked me in the side of the head, I passed out.

I awoke without immediate memory of the day's events. Or had it been two days? After blinking several times, my eyes focused on a cement wall two feet away from my head. While lying on my side, I moved my limbs slightly as my predicament with the radio came back to me. Thankfully, I wasn't bound, but from the throb in my leg, I could tell they wouldn't have to bind me; I wasn't walking anywhere soon.

With all my effort, I pushed myself into a sitting position. Someone had tied a soiled rag around my wounded thigh. Feeling the underside of my leg, I gasped in pain, but found the exit hole from the bullet. It had gone clean through, and since I wasn't already dead from blood loss, I assumed it had missed an artery. Maybe there wasn't any bone damage, either.

The chill of the air made me shiver, and I zipped up my coat. My journal and Bible were gone, though—my two most prized possessions.

"God, help me . . ." I cried as I tightened the rag around my crimson-stained pant leg.

My holding place was obviously a cell. I'd spent enough time in prison to know, though this was a cell built decades earlier and had no running water or plumbing. A drain in the concrete interrupted the middle of the floor, and a bucket for waste sat in the corner. The cement walls were cracked and molding. High up on one wall there was a vent that blew no air, nor heat. A naked light bulb, covered in grime, dimly lit my cell.

Sembuuk. Where was he? Was he alive?

I inspected my cell door from my seated position. It was steel with four massive hinges mounted halfway behind a second flange of steel. No escaping through there.

Using my arms to scoot myself, I moved to my right side and lay down with my back against the wall. They wouldn't have transported me far, I figured. Maybe I was in Hasagt, or Bulgan, at the farthest. That meant I was in one of the old Russian buildings in one of the towns the Bolsheviks had built to assist Mongolia's communist revolution. And, it probably meant the Chinese weren't merely passing through Mongolia; they were taking isolated towns along the way.

"Lord, I'm Your servant. Please, straighten this mess out."

While praying for strength and deliverance, I drifted off to sleep.

A heavy boot kicked my cell door, and I awoke with a flinch. The steel door squeaked open and two pairs of mud-crusted boots tromped into my cell. Hands grabbed my arms and dragged me upright and out the door. Breathlessly, I tried to use my wounded leg, but the muscles were too torn from the bullet. As they moved me quickly through two cold rooms, I did my best to hobble on my good leg until I was set roughly on a metal chair under a hot lamp. Thankful for the rest, I raised my face contently toward the heat. It felt so good. I couldn't resist and barely noticed as my arms were strapped to the chair's armrests at the elbow and wrist. My ankles came next, secured to the front legs of the chair.

The two who had handled me stepped back a few paces, but remained in the room. A third uniformed figure swung the hot lamp away. Almost deliriously, I watched it move, then it was replaced by a Chinese woman with cold eyes. Her face was so severely lined and wrinkled—maybe scarred—that she appeared to be sixty-years-old, but her neck and hands told me she was probably younger.

She spoke stern Russian to me. I sighed and shook my head.

"I only speak English and Mongolian fluently," I said. "Please, I'm from—"

"You lie!" she hissed in rough English and slapped me on the cheek. "No more lies!"

Her slap resurrected the pain from my previous facial wound, and I felt again the memory of the rifle stock that had crushed my lips.

"My journal . . . I'm American."

"Journal lies!" She moved to one side of me and bowed over my shoulder to speak directly into my ear. She wasn't too tall, maybe five-two or -three. "We analyze journal. Find you have hidden intention. Bible, hah! You saboteur with Mongolians! With Kazakhs! Russian spy! Say it, and you may live! Deny you are man of God. All lies! A mission of war brings you here!"

She slapped me again, though not too hard, but I felt every bit of it in my weakened state.

"Where are conspirators?"

"No conspirators. I'm a Christian . . . for Jesus," I said with emphasis.

"No Jesus! No Bible! Spy! Say Russian spy!" She

backhanded me on my ear, then changed sides. "Christians not have spy radio! You have Russian radio. You caught!"

"I was turning in the radio. I had a note for Sergeant Xing. It was in my coat. Surely, you must've gotten it!"

Again, she slapped me, and I tasted blood.

"You lie! No letter! No Christian! Where you get radio? Where other spies?"

Didn't they get the note? It must have been lost on the plain where I was shot.

"No." I shook my head. "I'm not a spy. American missionary. No spy."

She slapped me so hard, I saw her wince. Stepping back, she massaged her fingers.

"This part of Mongolia, no Christians. All Lamaists. Buddhists. Speak Russian. We hear you on radio. No lies!"

I bowed my head. Every story I'd ever heard about torture, interrogations, and pain came to mind. *How much could I take? Could they break me? Would I know it when they broke me?*

Sadly, I was in fact protecting Russian spies, but by protecting them, I was protecting the whole clan, including Zima. In my agonizing, I reasoned that Duulgii and his partner weren't spies any longer.

"There are no spies!" I said.

"Where get spy radio?" She had a short belt in her hand now, and she slapped it against the palm of her other hand. "We do this all day. No end. Every day. You talk? Pain end. You free. Where get radio? No lies!"

I tasted blood. *No lies?* I couldn't tell her the truth, not even a fraction. A crack in a dam becomes a hole, and then a hole becomes a raging flood.

"Sergeant Xing. He knows I'm no spy."

"There is no Sergeant Xing. You lie!"

"No lie. Xing knows me. He's one of your soldiers. I was bringing the radio to him so spies wouldn't be able to use it."

"What spies? Where spies?"

"There are no spies!"

With fire in her eyes, she hit me with the belt. A welt quickly blistered from my neck to the corner of my mouth, stinging like a burn. I closed my eyes. It was only pain. *Take the pain, Lord.*

"Where's my friend?" Had Sembuuk told her about Duulgii? He wasn't too fond of the man after he'd put the clan in danger. "Where's Sembuuk?"

"Friend dead. I kill him, but he talk no lies before die. He tell all. This how I know you lie!"

I shook my head. She was the one lying. Sembuuk wouldn't break. I knew he had too much pride. He wouldn't kill those left in his clan, even for Duulgii's capture and punishment. If she knew all, then why question me? They could go to the forest and search.

"No spies," I said. "I'm a Christian. I help people."

She hit me with the belt a little harder this time, but across the back of the neck.

"Where get radio? From Russians?"

"What radio?" I cried, suddenly in amusement. She wasn't listening to me, anyway. There was no harm in playing the game of circles she'd started, I figured. "I don't remember a radio!"

Her eyes narrowed hatefully—probably seeing exactly what I was doing.

"You play tricks. Russian radio. Where get?"

She hit me again on each cheek. Gasping, I fought my binds.

"Get what? I don't know what you're talking about!"

"Radio! Where spies? No lies!"

"Your English is too bad!" I shouted back. "I don't understand your speech!"

The woman frowned and I could see her reflect on her language skills—probably wondering if her vocabulary was off. Was she saying *radio* correctly?

In her pause, I continued in my mock madness.

"I want to eat a radio! Look under the spy! Radios are good to eat! Spies grow on trees!"

Crossing her arms, she studied me with a glare. I spouted nonsense for a few more minutes, then spat blood onto the floor.

"No spies, no lies," I stated softly, seemingly back in control of my senses. "Let me go. I have work to do for Jesus—unless you want me to tell you about Jesus. Otherwise, I'm wasting my time here."

She stepped over to the two guards for a moment and they conversed in Chinese. Then, she addressed me once more.

"Pretend American missionary, everyday worse and worse till no lies. You cry with hurt. Say who give you radio, where spies. You free. Talk now? No lies? Very bad pain tomorrow. Then next day. And next. No end."

I sniffed. *More pain tomorrow?* After a week of this, I

wouldn't have to pretend madness. I would be mad.

"Jesus is a spy of the heart," I said. "He's the only spy I know now. Give me food and water. I'll tell you all about Jesus, the spy."

Scoffing, she marched from the room. I was unstrapped, dragged from the chair and back to my cell. When I tried to take a step on my wounded leg, I found it was too painful to put any pressure on it at all. They threw me inside. Lying on my back, I stared at the light bulb planted in the ceiling. The guards closed the door, locked it, and stomped away down a corridor I'd only glimpsed.

"You can save me from this, Lord. I have complete faith in You." Tears rolled from my eyes. "You know my heart. This is just a test. You've saved me from a plane wreck, and bullets, and falling off that cliff the other night. This is nothing. You control the authorities, even the evil ones. You put them where You want them. You give them power and You can take it away. Please, give me strength today. Give me strength tomorrow. Lift me up, Lord, in my humble state. Tend to me, I pray . . ."

Even as I watched and prayed, the light bulb blinked off. I was surrounded in total darkness, perfect for praying.

"You are my Light, Lord Jesus. I praise You for even this moment. You have given so much for me."

And then I slept peacefully.

$$...†...$$

CHAPTER TWENTY SIX

When the light blinked on hours later, I guessed it was morning. My leg was stiff, but some of the pain was gone. I rolled up my pant leg to look at my wound. It was pink rather than red around the hole. Since I wasn't bleeding now, I left the soiled rag off. There seemed to be no infection, but if there had been, I wouldn't have been able to do anything against it.

My stomach growled. I heard doors slam once in a while and boots walk past my door.

I suddenly remembered the vent in the wall. *The vent!* Of course! During my prison years in New York, we often spoke to each other from cell to cell through the ventilation system.

Using the wall for support, I slowly stood on my good leg, and felt above my head for the vent. It was ten inches wide with mesh bars wide enough through which I could stick my fingers. Feeling vertically, I discovered the vent to be about six inches high. After fitting my fingers inside, I lifted myself up twelve inches from the ground until a faint stench drifted into my face. My muscles trembled as I held myself there and listened through the vent for voices, breathing, anything.

"Sembuuk!" I whispered forcefully, just loud enough for him to hear if he were indeed in a nearby cell.

Straining for any sound from him, I listened for five

seconds before I could no longer hold myself up. I dropped down to stand on my good leg. After gathering my strength, I pulled myself back up to the air vent to try once again.

"Sembuuk!" I called louder. "Sembuuk!"

Faintly, so very far away it seemed, I heard someone. I slid down the wall, rested for a few seconds, then went back up.

"Come to the vent!" I said, then rested long enough to give him time to get there. He was much shorter than me, but nearly as strong. The fact that he probably hadn't eaten anything since our arrival certainly didn't help matters, though.

"Andy!" he finally answered. "They beat me, but I told them nothing!"

I laughed in relief until I was nearly in tears.

"Are you okay otherwise?"

"Yes. You?" he asked.

"Well, I was shot in the leg, but it's healing. God is with us, Sembuuk! Pray to Him. He hears you."

"Like Joseph in prison," he yelled and chuckled, "but we have no butler to help with his dreams to get us out!"

We laughed together, not caring momentarily if anyone could hear what we said.

"God knows our situation, Sembuuk." I rested my arms, then went back up. "He'll give us strength to endure if we trust Him."

"Andy, I'm not afraid. We've done no wrong."

"I'll pray for us. We'll talk again soon. This is our secret. They told me you were dead, but I refused to believe it."

"Me, as well!"

"Good-bye for now, friend."

Sliding down the wall to the floor, I rested on my back. My smile couldn't be wiped away as I praised the Lord for my friend's well-being. My friend, Sembuuk the Hunter, was alive.

That afternoon as I was strapped into the interrogation chair, I eyed a table full of food and knew it would be used as a form of enticement. The smells had brought my hunger pangs to the surface before I'd even entered the room. There was wine, cheeses, smoked beef, and fresh lamb.

The guards hovered nearby and my same tormentor held her belt as she walked between me and the food. She appeared even meaner than last time.

"You see food? It make you hungry?"

"The food, yes. It looks very good. Are you having company for dinner?"

"Funny." She stopped walking. She glared at me, my eyes darting about unsure of what to expect next. Then she hit me hard, on the left side. "Funny now?"

The belt had nicked my eye and it teared in pain.

"I can't eat your food, but thank you, anyway," I said.

"Why can't eat? You are ill?"

"No, I'm fasting."

She hit me. It hurt, but I swallowed through the pain and pretended I was unfazed. Oddly, I expected a true torturer to maim me, but her treatment was nothing debilitating.

"Fasting. Funny again. No play crazy today. Confess all and eat."

"What would you like to know?"

"Who you speak to on radio?"

"The radio I was bringing to Sergeant Xing?"

"So you say."

She hit me, cutting my lip afresh.

"Who use radio?"

"I don't know any spies. I'm a Christian. I preach and teach about Jesus Christ and His love for all people, even you." She hit me, but I tried to ignore it. "I have only been in Mongolia a little while. The story is in the journal."

"Lies! Where spies?" she screamed and hit me.

"Do you know Jesus?"

Her eyes went to the guards. Neither seemed to be paying attention as they snacked on dry beef sandwiches. *Why did she look at them?* I knew they didn't speak English as we did.

"Don't say that name! You not real Christian. Real Christian not have Russian spy radio!"

"I told you, I was taking it to Sergeant Xing."

"Lies!" Whack! "There no Sergeant Xing. Who you work for?"

"Jesus."

Whack!

"Speak Russian!" she ordered. "I know you speak it!"

"I don't know it too well. How about I tell you about this one man I heard about, though?"

"Why? A spy?"

"Was he a spy?" I asked myself aloud. "No, I think he was just curious. He was a religious ruler named Nicodemus. And the first time—"

Whack!

"No Bible stories! Tell me of spies!"

Startled, I stared at her. *Had I heard her right?*

"Uh, how would you know Nicodemus was a man in the Bible? I didn't say he was."

She glanced at the guards. They weren't watching. She hit me with the belt on the side of the head where it didn't hurt much. Then, she winked at me. *Winked?* An instant later, she turned away and walked to the table. *What was happening? How many Chinese torturers knew who Nicodemus was? And what did the wink mean?*

Taunting me, she offered me a slice of beef, dangling it inches from my nose.

"Tell me answers! No lies!"

She reached out and unzipped my coat a ways, made sure the guards weren't watching, then dropped the meat inside my coat. She hit me with the belt above the ear, then zipped my coat up.

"I'm telling you . . . no lies," I stuttered. She gave me a look of warning. *Was this a game?* A thought began to take shape. "You're a . . . *believer* . . .?"

She lunged forward and violently gripped me by the throat, and though she could've choked me since I couldn't resist, the gesture seemed only for show.

"Careful what you say!" she snapped, her grip not hurting me at all. "The guards don't know English, but they know attitude."

Backing away, she hit me as her words registered. My head spun. *Was she for real?* Her face twisted ruthlessly.

"I will speak harshly, but these two will know nothing." She hit me almost too lightly. "Do you hear me?"

"Yes, I hear you. What do you want me to do?"

She circled me and gripped my hair in her stout fingers.

"To keep you alive, superiors want information. Give me something."

"I've got nothing to give you." I chuckled, wondering what this new game was about.

She shook my head by my hair.

"Make something up, idiot! Something to buy you time!" She slapped me. "Something real, but nothing that would hurt whomever you protect. Now!"

My head was spinning as she hit me again. I licked my lips and tasted blood. *Make something up?* If she was on my side, I wasn't completely convinced yet.

"South . . . southeast of Tavan Bogd Uul, we crashed our plane after China shot us down. My pilot died. I lived."

She savagely clutched my throat again.

"The plane is there?" she asked harshly. I nodded, unable to speak or breathe. "It's something I can send them to hunt and no one be hurt? Something real?" Again, I nodded. She released me. "I'll give them this. They want spy confession at head office about spy radio. They bring me from Nanjing to question you." She hit me lightly to maintain the façade. "Soon, I help you escape, but I stay here to help others after you gone." Gripping my hair, she shook my head. "The trumpet calls us soon, you know?"

"I know. I'm doing what I can."

"Good." She stepped back. "Your friend is alive. I try to help you both. Now, this one will hurt."

She cocked her arm and hit me hard across the ear with the strap, so hard my ear rang. Then she snatched up a slab of lamb and shoved it at my mouth. It was too big to get into my mouth, so I bit onto it as she ordered the guards to take me back to my cell. As they were busy unstrapping me, she nodded at me from behind them, then touched her hand to her heart briefly. I couldn't respond; I could only blink. The guards hauled me back to my cell and threw me on the floor where I wept with mixed emotions.

How grievous it was that this woman maintained such coldness when her heart was obviously loving. She gave herself to the façade in order to help others, and I knew such torment for her was a hundred times worse than any pain she could inflict on me. No doubt she'd saved others as well, by living as an undercover Christian.

I wept for myself as well—though with joy. God had brought this strange woman, this believer, hundreds of miles from Nanjing, and used her to touch my life. God was in control and had sent this Christian—our guardian—to save me and Sembuuk! Yet, at what cost? Her heart had to be torn apart every day, while she hurt people to help them.

As I ate the lamb, I prayed for my tormentor and other Christians who lived in secret throughout the world governments in those Last Days. And I prayed for the clan, that they wouldn't just be safe from those who purged the forest of rebels, but that they would grow in Christ in my absence. And I prayed for Sembuuk, for his salvation, and for Dusbhan as he explored to the west.

Climbing up the wall, I clung to my vent.

"Sembuuk!"

A few moments passed. *Was he still there?*

"Andy!" he called back only moments later.

"I have great news, Sembuuk!"

...†...

It was three days before I was taken out of my cell again. During that time, Sembuuk and I both received food and water, and I was brought meager first aid and dressing material for my gunshot wound. Unlike New York, that part of Mongolia was too cold for rats or cockroaches, so I didn't need to worry about any critters crawling or nibbling on me as I curled up on the cold floor to sleep. That's not to say I slept soundly, but it wasn't the torture we would've received if the strange woman hadn't been watching over us, making sure we received sustenance. If it were anyone else, I have no doubt we would've been stripped naked and left to freeze, and the food could've been much worse, or even nonexistent. Meat, bread, and water was more than either Sembuuk or I ever expected, so we had much for which to praise the Lord.

And I did praise Him. I remembered Peter and Silas, and though my circumstances weren't as severe as theirs, there was no reason why I couldn't lift up my voice. All I sang were old English hymns, the golden era of Gospel music being my favorite due to the passionate lyrics. My singing was discouraged, though, which I understood when my cell light was turned off for hours at a time, engulfing me in darkness. I tested this theory by singing at the top of my lungs, and concluded that a guard in the corridor could hear me and turned off my light to discourage me from singing. This information was passed to Sembuuk—that there was someone near enough to hear us if we spoke too loudly. So, we spoke low, directly into the vents, speaking only

Mongolian, which was essentially safe, and we didn't take any risks talking about the clan or their location, just in case. Cautiously, I had informed him that the torturous woman was a fellow Christian and he was to play along if he came before her again. We were careful not to discuss the issue further for her sake. With only one friend in there, we wouldn't betray her.

The same two goons took me out three days later, but the woman interrogator was joined by a Chinese captain in uniform. He wore a scowl, but as appearances go, the woman's lined face and cold eyes were still more menacing.

As they strapped me to the chair, I mentally braced myself for pain and abuse. It would be nothing that wouldn't eventually heal, I tried to tell myself.

The table was bare of food, though there was a closed briefcase on it. No doubt, the case belonged to the captain. I tried to keep my eyes from wandering by bowing my head as an obedient prisoner should. But inside my chest, my heart pounded wildly.

"Andrew Foworthy," the captain said in perfect English, "we found your plane and the message you left on the fuselage. Most importantly, we found this 'Rex,' a known smuggler of contraband over many East Asian borders. Do you deny this?"

"Since I was only his passenger, I knew nothing of his smuggling endeavors."

"I assure you, he was a smuggler. But still, I'm bringing you up on murder charges unless you tell me what he had in the plane."

"Murder charges?"

"His murder—Rex, the smuggler. Murder is a crime, you know. Is that where you got the radio? Was Rex a Russian spy? You brought the radio from the plane?"

"Rex was an American base-bum pilot. Neither of us are or ever were spies."

"We have reason to believe he was a double agent. What did he give you in the plane? Secret messages? Or did you steal the radio from him, hmmm? Perhaps frequency papers that you've hidden? Now is the time to confess everything."

I didn't know what to say about this twist in the interrogation. What did the woman want me to say? When everything else fails, tell the truth . . .

"Look, I'm just an American missionary. I know nothing of spies or radios or—"

"Yet you were found with a Russian communication device," he said.

"The sergeant said they were searching for a saboteur. I came upon the radio and knew he would want it, so I was turning it in to the soldiers. Specifically, Sergeant Xing."

"Where did you come upon the radio?"

"Not far from where I met the soldiers."

"Did you use it?"

"No."

"Someone did. Who? We have transmission transcripts in code from the vicinity of your capture."

"I wasn't captured. I rode out to the road and offered the radio to a lieutenant with a letter to Sergeant Xing—which you guys have apparently lost."

"Who used the radio, Mr. Foworthy?"

"I never heard anyone use it."

"But you know who used it. Who?" He waited a moment for me to answer. When I remained silent, he walked to the briefcase on the table. "You claim to be a missionary, an honorable, selfless man, but you are a deceiver, Mr. Foworthy, with answers full of half-truths. Do you have a camp near where you were captured?"

"I was migrating south toward the Gobi. Both clans I was with were wiped out."

"Yes, I've read the reports. But there were survivors, right? One of the survivors used the radio? Is this possible?"

His back was to me. I glanced at the woman's face, but she gave me nothing. Maybe the guards behind me were watching her too closely.

"The clan people weren't educated enough to use the radio."

He turned toward me suddenly, a syringe of yellow liquid in his fingers.

"Who among these two clans, the survivors, spoke Russian?"

"I don't know who did or didn't. I'm only teaching Jesus." As he walked closer with the needle spouting liquid, I squirmed. "You have the radio. Why is this still an issue?"

"Because we don't have the spies." He knelt in front of me and pushed up my coat sleeve. With cold hands, he slapped my visible veins. "Identify them, Mr. Foworthy. Where are the survivors?"

The woman moved swiftly up to my other side. She reached for my shoulder to steady me as the captain inserted his needle. But as his needle plunged, the woman eased a second needle into my opposite shoulder where the man couldn't see. I flinched and looked up at her face, because I certainly felt the bite of the second needle. She withdrew her own syringe and slipped it into her pocket undetected.

My head suddenly wagged and my eyes blurred. The captain stepped back.

"That's it, Mr. Foworthy. Don't fight it. Listen to my voice. You'll tell me what I want to know. Everyone always does."

Trying to focus, my eyelids drooped, and a wave of warm passiveness washed over me. Two syringes—one hidden, and one obvious. *What had the woman injected me with? What did it mean?*

"Tell me, Mr. Foworthy, have you ever used the radio you had when we captured you?"

"No, I haven't," I said, slurring.

Frustrated, I fought the effects of the drug, but wasn't sure I cared anymore. My emotions and reasoning faculties were in a jumble. I began to cry uncontrollably.

"It's okay, Mr. Foworthy. Let it out. Now, you're not really a missionary, are you? You're a spy, aren't you?"

"I . . . don't know," I said, sobbing. "I try to do my best, but—"

"Your best at what, Mr. Foworthy? Who are you trying to please? Who are your employers?"

As fast as the drug had distorted my perceptions, it seemed to fade just as swiftly. I gained some of my composure, mentally at least, and realized I'd been given an antitoxin in the shoulder. *She had done that!* A war had taken place in my system—the antitoxin had battled the truth serum, and won! Understanding, I fell into the part.

"No employers," I slurred, intentionally now. "I work for Jesus. Can I tell you about Him?"

"Where did you get the radio?"

"From . . . the plain. Didn't I tell you that?"

"Where did you take the radio?"

"I took it to the, uh, soldiers on the plain."

"Before that. Where is your camp?"

"My camp . . ."

"Yes, Mr. Foworthy?"

". . . is in heaven. I have a mansion in heaven. Do you have a mansion in heaven?"

The captain scratched his head and spoke to the woman. He seemed concerned that his serum wasn't working. I probably wasn't that good of an actor.

"Mr. Foworthy, do you know the men who used the Russian communicator?"

"Men? They were men?" I asked hazily.

"What? They were women? Female spies?"

"I don't know . . ." Shrugging, my head wagged left and right. "They smelled like wet camels. Have you ever smelled a wet camel?"

"Will you show me on a map where your camp is? If you do, I'll give you food and freedom. Where's your camp? Show me on the map. See it here on the wall?"

He walked to the giant map of western Mongolia.

"It's a nice map." I sobbed. "I love maps."

"Do you see where my finger is?"

"Um, yeah. You need to trim your nails."

"Focus, Mr. Foworthy. Is the camp north or south of my finger?"

"Where my camp is?"

"Yes."

"Where I sleep?"

"Yes! Where you sleep!"

"North."

He moved his finger northward.

"Here?"

"More north. East now. East again. There. That's where I sleep."

Squinting, he studied the map. His finger had stopped over the town of Hasagt. Quickly, he whipped his hand to his side in frustration, and turned to me.

"Not where you slept last night, Mr. Foworthy! Where is the clan survivor camp?"

"Oh . . ." I pretended to drift off. So, we were in fact in Hasagt. At least I had confirmed that much, but now, what could I do with that information? "The clan survivor camp . . . I thought you found them."

"No, not yet, but with your help, we will. You're an honest man. You'll tell me, won't you?"

"Tell you what?"

"Tell me—!" Disgusted, he turned away, waving his hand at me, and spoke in Chinese to the woman. It was no use. His serum wasn't working on me. He returned to his briefcase and slammed it shut. "Next time, Mr. Foworthy, I promise you will speak to me with clarity. I have many other tools I can use to loosen your tongue."

With that said, he stalked out of the room. As soon as he was gone, the woman slapped me and grabbed my hair.

"You pathetic liar!" she hissed. "When more poison

comes from Beijing, you will talk! It takes one week for delivery from lab. Stupid man!" She slapped me again. "One week for me and you free. Stupid spy! I may need flee now with you. My time here not safe to help any longer. Be ready!"

She slapped me again and ordered me to be taken away. I guessed she turned her back to me so we didn't accidentally communicate through a final glance of mutual understanding.

Back in my cell, I lay on my back and tried moving my leg. It was stiff and painful. I still couldn't walk. How was I to escape?

"Andy!"

I crawled up the wall to my vent.

"Sembuuk!"

"You're back. Are you well?"

"Well enough. We escape within one week. Got it?"

"Yes, Andy. Can you walk?"

"No, but . . . Just be ready. God will work out the details, Sembuuk. You'd better be praying! Submit to God. That's the lesson through this."

"I believe you, Andy, and I'm praying. Jesus saves, right? Like Rahab and the spies?"

"That's right. The end is coming, my friend. Prepare your heart. You know what to do. We'll talk later."

Easing myself to the floor, I grimaced. My leg pained me with every bit of movement, but it didn't seem to be infected. Yes, just like Rehab and the spies, I thought with a chuckle. The Lord was working on hearts in Mongolia!

…✝…

CHAPTER TWENTY-SEVEN

The days ticked by and I was reminded more and more of my time spent in New York's finest institutions. That didn't make my time any easier, but the cold, cement cell did feel more familiar to me than it did to Sembuuk. The falconer had never spent a day or night in a building in his life, and this fine welcome to a stationary dwelling probably wasn't convincing him that civilization had the upper hand to comfort.

On day five, I received my daily ration of food and water like the previous days. However, inside the spoiled slab of beef that day, I found a rolled up note written in messy Mongolian, as if the writer had pulled the words straight out of the dictionary, interpreting from one language to another in choppy sentences. The message said:

"Once out of the town, you must take three persons to safety. Plan where to go."

Three persons. So, she had to escape with us. By freeing us, her cover would be blown. My life was in her hands. Soon, she would reach the limit of her abilities and she would put herself into my hands. She was warning me of this fact. Understandably, this meant her resources were limited outside the town of Hasagt. But were mine any better? I had no resources, except for Sembuuk. And I couldn't even walk!

At the vent, I called to Sembuuk.

320

"Yes, Andy?"

"How far are we from Three Rocks if we're in Hasagt?"

"Two hours, perhaps, by vehicle. I was awake when they brought us here. Why?"

"Just thinking, friend."

"Did you eat your fine meal, yet?"

"Not yet. Did you receive a side order of fruit or vegetables today?"

"Fruit."

"I'll trade you; I hate vegetables," I joked. "Send it up with the servants."

"And I suppose you want a flask of *airag*, too!"

Both of us laughed and then hushed ourselves for fear of being heard beyond the vent.

"Will we make it, Andy?"

"Yes, we will," I said. "Rahab has sent word. Any time now, Sembuuk."

"Do you believe they've found Three Rocks yet?"

I cringed at the thought of Zima falling into the hands of the Chinese. She had such Russian features; she'd be taken into custody without delay, maybe even executed.

"We must trust God," I said. "He can see all things and has all the answers. I can't even guess. Our enemy is strong. Their strength is from the devil. Of that, I'm certain. I'm also certain the devil is only a fallen angel, created by God Almighty, therefore, the Creator is stronger than His creation."

Back on the floor, I exercised my leg. It was so stiff! I finally shut out the pain and massaged the muscle to feel the femur beneath. If the bullet had grazed the bone, I thought

I'd be able to tell, but I couldn't.

"Lord, You know my infirmities. You could heal me in an instant, but You've given me this burden to . . . strengthen and humble me. Perhaps to cause me to trust You more. Help my faith, Lord. Please, don't let my anxiety surface to trip me when we're so close to the end. I'm nervous without much of a plan, with others depending on me. Take away my fear, Lord. And please lift me up as a leader. Above all, lift up the clan and open their hearts to Your power, Your Truth, the Gospel of Jesus Christ . . ."

That day closed, as did the sixth, without interruption. On the morning of the seventh day, Sembuuk and I each received an early meal of cornbread and cheese and water. *An extra meal?* I conversed with Sembuuk as to what it meant, and we decided the Chinese woman was strengthening us for what lay ahead. We both ate half the portion that morning. At noon, we received our normal daily ration, which we ate right away and felt overly full from the extra food. The butterflies in my stomach weren't helping, either.

Using the wall, I hobbled on my leg, tears of pain flowing from my eyes. Every few minutes, I collapsed on the floor to rest, and nibbled at what was left of my morning meal.

Any minute now, the door would open. What would be required of me? To Run? Fight? Attack a guard? I asked myself if violence was justified now. But my answer was simple—no. Compromise was unacceptable. If God desired to free me, He would provide a way that was void of sin.

The last of my food was gone. While sitting on the floor,

I stared at the door with my back against the wall. My waste bucket overflowed next to the drain, but I'd grown somewhat accustomed to the stench long ago. Human senses adjust to such things with time.

A door slammed shut somewhere. My breath caught. Hurried footsteps sounded outside my door—and they weren't the guards' heavy combat boots . . .

Slowly, a key turned in the lock. I climbed up the wall to stand on my good leg. The door swung open. The Chinese woman—my tormentor—stood there. No longer was her face a mask of cruelty or spite. She seemed more afraid than I, with the lines around her mouth trembling.

"Come!" she said in a hoarse voice, and waved at me.

"My leg. You'll have to help me."

Entering the cell, she pulled my arm over her shoulder to support my weight, which was twice her own. She thrust something leathery into my other hand. *My journal!* I tucked it inside my coat.

With more noise than either of us desired, she helped me hop out of my cell and down a narrow corridor to the left where she stopped at an intersection. I followed her gaze to the right and heard the sound of a television coming from some sort of guards' station. She put a finger to her lips, then we moved through the intersection to a steep flight of stairs. Waving her ahead, I used the railing to swing my leg down to the landing below.

"Where's Sembuuk?" I whispered at the next corridor.

She pointed ahead. For a small woman, she was supporting me remarkably well, but Sembuuk would be able to fully carry me if need be.

Like the floor above, we came to another intersection. The guard station here was now to our left. I smelled cigarette smoke. Down the corridor to the right were five cell doors. Sembuuk was in one of them.

"We . . . need . . . key." The woman mouthed to me and pointed toward the guard station.

More keys? Apparently, Sembuuk's cell required a different key. How were we supposed to get another key off the guard? I wondered how she'd gotten my cell key.

Suddenly, she forced me back against the left wall and joined me, flattening herself against me. She braced me so I wouldn't lose my balance on my one leg. The cigarette-smoking guard walked out of his booth and paused next to us. I could've tickled his ear. He stretched and yawned. In his peripheral vision, I hoped we stood as still as the wall. The guard finished stretching and turned his back to us. Lazily, he sauntered down the corridor toward the cells, lighting another cigarette as he went.

Without warning, the woman stepped around me and disappeared in the guard's station.

My wide eyes were glued on the guard's back. I prayed he didn't turn around—or smell me, since I reeked from my own filth and dried blood.

Stopping, the guard kicked his toe at a shard of something on the wall, then turned to his left out of sight.

The woman returned, a key held between her lips. She pulled my arm over her shoulder and we moved down the corridor. At the fourth cell door, she let me go. I fell against the wall and she gave me a glare for the noise as she fit the key quietly into the door. The tumblers clicked into place.

There was a scuff of boots in the corridor. I turned as the woman opened Sembuuk's door, and found that the guard had also returned behind us. He stood frozen in amazement, his cigarette dangling between two fingers. Using the element of surprise, I shot a hand out and grasped his uniform collar. With all my strength, I pulled him toward me, next to me, and then shoved him beyond me into the cell. Losing my balance, I tripped along unexpectedly, and fell through the cell door even before Sembuuk had exited the cell. Grabbing me by the shoulders, Sembuuk pulled me upright, then pushed the woman out of the way and slammed the door. Only then did we both look to the woman for direction.

"Outside," she said in English, and pointed straight ahead from where the man had entered only moments earlier. "Follow me."

I translated for Sembuuk, but he knew what to do. He pulled me halfway onto his back and dragged me forward after the Chinese woman. She opened a door. At first, I thought it was to a darkened room, but then I felt the chill of night air blowing into the building. We passed through the door as the guard locked in the cell behind us finally gained his faculties enough to start banging on the door and screaming for help.

Running between three vehicles, the woman checked for ignition keys. Beneath our feet there was a skiff of snow, but the sky was clear and starry.

"Here!" she yelled, no longer concerned about making noise.

She threw the door open to a tan, four-door recon

vehicle. Sembuuk boosted me into the front passenger seat then climbed into the back as she started the engine.

"Where do we go, Mr. Foworthy?" she asked in English.

"South."

"On highway?"

"No, on the incursion road."

Backing onto a desolate street, she started forward. As we got up to speed, a Jeep came into sight, passed us, and pulled into the jail parking lot behind us. We didn't have much of a head start.

I recognized Hasagt as we rushed west down its main avenue. There was the clinic, the grocery store, and a burned building. *That was new.* A pair of soldiers with rifles braved the cold and walked the street on our left. It was close to five degrees outside. No wonder not many invaders were out and about.

Turning left onto a street, she braked abruptly. We all saw it at the same time: a barricade with a checkpoint. I turned, looked behind us, and saw we were already on the incursion road. A convoy of four headlights drove toward us from behind, and others approached from the checkpoint's direction.

"Run through the roadblock!" Sembuuk said.

"There's no going back." I squinted, studying the checkpoint where there were two guards in uniform. One sat inside the tiny hut, probably with a heater, while the other stood outside waving vehicles through after they stopped and showed their papers. "Just go through the checkpoint," I said, instructing our driver, patting her hand on the steering wheel. "Go ahead. Just like normal. A lot of people are around. Don't do anything out of the ordinary."

Sembuuk didn't understand my English, but he felt the recon vehicle creep forward.

"Faster, Andy!" Sembuuk shouted in Mongolian. "They're armed! Faster!"

I ignored Sembuuk and eyed the two uniformed men as we approached. No doubt, when the guard outside grew cold, they rotated.

We stopped on the side of the road in front of the barricade to allow an ATV and a fuel trailer to pass us, heading in the opposite direction. As we waited, the convoy behind us caught up, announcing their presence by their frozen, squeaky brakes.

It was now our turn, but the woman hesitated. She glanced at me. *This will never work*, her look warned. A half-smile touched my lips and I nodded her forward. She licked her lips, maybe wanting to trust me, but she probably felt deep down that we'd never get through the checkpoint guarded by the Chinese. Even if we crashed our way through, there would be such a ruckus that we wouldn't get very far.

"This is insane, Andy!" Sembuuk gasped in fear. He reached for his door handle. "I'd rather run and die freezing on the steppe than go back to that—"

"Quiet!" I shouted at him in Mongolian, then changed to English for her. "Go ahead. If you don't trust me, then trust God that He'll get us through safely. Go."

The lines on her face trembled. She took a deep breath. The guard ahead waved us forward. Our vehicle crept toward the guard shack. The guard held up a hand as we drew abreast and he ducked his head into her driver's window.

"Travel pass and documentation," I understood the guard to say in Chinese. Then he saw me and switched to English. "New York!"

The sergeant grinned as the mouths of Sembuuk and the woman both dropped open.

"Sergeant Xing, what're you doing out here in the cold when your subordinate is in the warm hut?"

"Ah!" He waved at the jest. "Weaklings!" His eyes studied us more warily. "Is all well here?"

Just then, his radio crackled and a frantic call in Chinese rang out. He listened, his eyes focusing on each of our faces in turn. The radio was finally silent. The guard in the hut, who'd also heard the call, emerged from the hut, but Xing turned and snapped a sharp order that sent his soldier back inside. Xing faced us again. He asked my driver a question in Chinese and she nodded.

"It's not wise to stay on this road, Andy. They haven't found your people yet—if they're still in the woods there—but they are searching. It's just a matter of time, if they're where you and I first met."

He stepped back and raised his voice, ordering us casually through the checkpoint with a final wave.

"Thank you, New Jersey," I said through the open window. "I'll pray for you!"

We were well beyond the town, speeding at unsafe speeds on the frozen, rutty road when I urged the woman to slow down.

"I . . . must stop," she said.

"Fine. Turn off the headlights." I looked behind us. "We're clear. Pull way off to the right." She careened off the road and we rumbled across the open plain in darkness. Scrub brush whacked at our bumper. "Okay. This is good."

She slammed on the brakes and dove out of the vehicle. As she stumbled out of sight, I heard her retching. Sembuuk left the back seat to go comfort her in Chinese. A moment later, she was sobbing and mumbling against his chest. I couldn't imagine how deeply undercover she'd been, afraid for so many years that her faith would be found out. Now she was out and free, though on the run, which was still better than living her previous lie, I guessed. She'd saved us, and for that, I had few words to express my thanks.

By the time they returned, I'd climbed into the driver's seat and fired the motor to turn on the heater. The windchill was forcing the temperature below zero. The two sat in the back seat, indicating that I would drive, though we continued to shiver while the cab was heating up. Sembuuk put his arm around her shoulders for warmth and comfort.

Without turning on the headlights, I drive south again, parallel to the incursion road a half-mile to the east. By the moonlit sky, I caught the shape of timber along the mountains far to the west. Driving slowly, we rolled over hills and gullies where I'd once ridden my bike or a horse with Zima. My only gauge for direction was the moon and the occasional set of headlights to the east.

...✝...

CHAPTER TWENTY-EIGHT

An hour later, two motor bikes zoomed south on the incursion road. They were searching for us, but I said nothing to my two companions. Our foes would look in all directions, hopefully not considering we would be creeping along in the darkness nearby.

The engine sputtered.

"Uh, oh . . ." I tapped the fuel dial.

"No gas?" the woman asked, panic in her voice.

"Nope."

The engine died moments later. I couldn't help but chuckle and shake my head at all the challenges, yet God continued to pull me through. With a calm uncharacteristic for the moment, I determined to trust Him. My time on earth wasn't finished yet.

"We're far from Three Rocks, Andy," Sembuuk said. "What do you suggest?"

"Look in the back," I said to Sembuuk, turning in my seat. "See if there's extra fuel." As he turned around to look, I took the woman's hand. "I must know your name."

"Li. Li Chong. We three know not same language." She shook her head. "Now, no gas. My mess. My mess!"

"No fuel, Andy."

"It's God's mess to sort out," I said to Chong. "We step through the doors He opens. He takes care of the rest—and brings us home when He's ready and wills it."

She laughed through a sob. Chong was right about the languages, though. I spoke English and Mongolian; she spoke Chinese and some English; Sembuuk spoke Mongolian, Kazakh, and some Chinese. We were quite a trio—a missionary, a hunter, and an ex-torturer.

"How far away are those woods, Sembuuk?" I asked the outdoorsman.

"Maybe three kilometers."

"Let's pick this truck clean—tools, upholstery, whatever we can use. Does Chong have a watch?"

"Yes."

"Give it to me."

He unclipped a designer watch from her wrist and handed it to me. It was almost ten p.m.

"We'll sleep here for a few hours because it's the only shelter we have. But a couple hours before daylight, we need to set out for those woods."

"As soon as the sun rises, they'll find this vehicle," Sembuuk said.

"Nothing we can do about that." I shrugged. "The forest is near enough to reach in a couple hours—if you two help me along. After we reach the woods, we'll go south to join the clan."

"With the ground frozen as it is, we won't leave many tracks, though I doubt the Chinese can track like a true Kazakh."

"Yes, it's good the ground's frozen. I hadn't thought of that blessing."

"How we survive?" Chong asked after I explained the plan to her.

"Sembuuk's a master hunter, and whatever he can't figure out, the three of us can put our heads together. We need to sleep for now in what little heat we have remaining in here. I'll wake us in a few hours."

I didn't expect to sleep myself, but since I was bone-tired, I drifted off, having not slept comfortably on the concrete floor in the cell for more than a week. But the cold woke me. The windows of the recon vehicle were fogged and icy from our breathing. The watch said it was four o'clock. That was close enough. If I slept any longer, we might miss our trek over land while we still had cover of darkness as an advantage.

Behind me, Chong was curled up next to Sembuuk. In her sleep, she shuddered from a nightmare, or the cold, or both. Sembuuk's head was leaning back on the headrest and he was snoring lightly. I hated to wake them; it would probably be the last shut-eye we would get until we reached North Camp. That was a day's ride south by horseback. Without horses . . . It wasn't going to be easy.

"Chong, Sembuuk," I said softly.

They stirred. While they were rubbing the sleep from their eyes, I prayed for us, first in Mongolian for Sembuuk to witness the faith my God had graced me with, then in English for Chong's encouragement.

"Amen," Chong closed with me. She smiled and nodded at me, seeming to be a different woman than the one who'd been beating me days before. *What an actress!* "We do with God."

"Yes," I agreed. "We can do this with God's help."

It took us twenty minutes to gut the vehicle. We tore off

the upholstery, stuffing it inside our coats for extra warmth, and pulled out the maps and other papers from the glove compartment to use later for fire fuel. I found a flashlight, which I discarded after pocketing the batteries.

"No flint, Andy," Sembuuk grumbled. "No flint, no fire. Not even matches. And you don't have your lighter."

"I'll show you a little American trick I learned from prison," I said, patting the batteries bulging in my pocket. "We'll be okay."

With the seats' upholstery removed, I tore apart the foam cushioning until the thin coils of springs were exposed. I ripped out three of them to use with the batteries later.

"Sembuuk, I'm going to need a lot of help walking." We closed the doors of the vehicle. Chong carried a tire iron and a heavy wrench from the spare tire kit. "Come dawn, we need to be out of sight."

We set off at a crawling pace. Hopping on my one good leg was tiring and difficult, but the pain of holding my bad leg up so it didn't drag on the frozen ground was the worst agony I'd felt yet.

After ten minutes, I made a life-threatening announcement.

"I'm sweating," I said, and we all stopped. Sembuuk growled under his breath. At first, I hadn't thought anything of the trickle down my spine, but when I mopped my brow with my hand, I realized my error. In those temperatures, sweat was as good as death—icy death.

"Are you trying to kill us all?" Sembuuk fumed. Taking a couple breaths, he managed his anger. He'd been working so hard to help me, I was surprised he wasn't sweating, too.

"We'll go slower, but we have to keep moving."

But even in that pause, the wind found its way through my few layers of clothing and began to turn my innermost shirt into a thin sheet of ice.

We continued slower with fewer breaks. Chong walked quietly beside us, oblivious that I was as good as dead already. Sembuuk knew it, though. He knew I didn't have long, and stopping completely was the worst thing we could do. Once my body temperature began to drop, it was over. Icy sweat was the first step.

"If I can't be saved," I said, panting. "You have to leave me."

"Quiet! Save your energy. I'm not leaving you."

"She saved us," I said urgently. "Your priority is to save her."

So that Sembuuk didn't start sweating as well, we paused for a few breaths. Chong gazed longingly at the dark shadow of the forest that seemed too far away to reach by dawn.

Starting again, I shivered.

"One thing I'll admit," Sembuuk said, "we can't travel all the way to North Camp like this."

"Get me to the forest. I'll start a fire and—" My body jerked. "You two go for horses."

Though we were over halfway, I was declining fast. Chong noticed us both struggling. She abandoned the tire iron, but kept the wrench, and helped me on my other side. The wind whipped at our backs and on the right side, taking our breaths. I was freezing inside my clothes, my body heat sucked out by the ice that now sheathed my skin.

I fell onto the hard ground. My weight was too much for them in our weary condition. Sembuuk gave Chong instructions in Chinese, and she helped me climb onto his back, piggyback style. Through dazed eyes, I saw Chong run ahead of us.

"Chong, don't leave . . . us . . ." I mumbled deliriously.

"Quiet," Sembuuk said. "She's just going ahead. Hang on now. We're almost there."

But the forest still seemed miles away. I was tired of being optimistic. Hypothermia was already stealing my will to live. *Take me home, Lord. No more anguish. No more struggles.*

Sembuuk fell to his knees. I saw a bead of sweat fall from his brow. *He was sweating!* We were both doomed in this weather. Chang would be on her own, and without knowledge of the outdoors, she wouldn't last but a couple days.

"Go without me, Sembuuk," I pleaded weakly with him. "Please, go. I'm already starting to feel warm. I'll drift away, no more cold . . ."

"No. Just a little . . . farther! Where is your strength in God, coward! You never let me down! Don't do it now!"

"Sembuuk, no . . ."

Falling flat, we lay there, me covering him with my bulk, unable to move. We could've stayed there, could've died there peacefully, but he rolled me off with a grunt and dragged me forward. From somewhere within, I found a reserve of energy and rolled over onto my hands and knees. Together, we crawled, my bad leg dragging like the dead weight it was. I couldn't feel the pain any longer, and the muscles in my thigh wouldn't respond to my commands. Defeated, heartbroken, I realized I'd never see Zima again.

Chong's hands wrapped around my chest, under my arms, and helped me over a log. *A log?* I tumbled over the other side.

"Here! Wood!" she announced. "Make fire!"

My eyes focused.

"Too big. Need smaller. Twigs. Find small wood."

Understanding, she trotted away. A heavy weight fell on my legs. I turned around to see Sembuuk crawling on his elbows over me.

"Batteries . . ." he stuttered. "Show me . . . your fire trick now, Andy."

Chong returned. I nodded off to sleep until I was slapped awake with a familiar jolt from Chong. When I opened my eyes, Chong had the batteries from my pockets in her hands.

"What now? What now?"

"Springs." My words were slurring. "The springs . . . in my coat." She tore at my coat zipper with shaking hands. Sembuuk had passed out next to me. Chong found the springs. "Make . . . circuit. Both batteries. Get paper. Tap the spring. Rub it on one battery. Make . . . spark. Fire."

She fumbled to hold all the components together.

"I understand," she said. "Like starting engine."

Trembling, she aligned the springs after straightening them. She shredded a corner of the map and began to frantically strike at the battery.

"Slower," I said. "Start and stop the circuit. Scratch the wire."

The wind blew a mighty gust and the shreds of paper

disappeared. I hovered closer to protect her efforts.

"Again," I urged, and eyed Sembuuk. *Didn't he know how close we were to a fire?* There was hope!

But he didn't stir.

A flame leapt next to my pinky. Only then did I realize she had forced the batteries into my near-frozen hands as she held the wires. But with such thick wires, the batteries were sure to be nearly neutralized soon.

Another spark caught, and Chong added twigs. The fire snapped and grew. I rolled onto my side. We weren't in the clear yet, but I was feeling better just knowing that Chong would live. Unzipping my coat, I pulled it off and threw it aside as Chong piled on two oversized logs where the flame was tallest.

"Chong, build a wall to block the wind," I said. The wall would also shield the flickering flame from the steppe's observers.

She jumped up and began to pile and weave branches between the nearest trees and above the log over which Sembuuk and I had crawled.

"And take off Sembuuk's coat. He needs to feel this heat."

It wasn't easy, but the woman quickly did whatever was needed. The warmth drew me in as I crowded the blaze. I wondered if it was too big, that it would be seen from the steppe's road through the darkness, but I blinked and found that it was already daylight. To my right, Sembuuk was sitting upright, and I realized that I'd lost time when I'd shut my eyes. Chong held up my t-shirt, drying it by the smoke of the fire. My upper body was naked, my coat draped over my shoulders. The fire was hot and dry.

Chong knelt beside me, and helped me sit up and pull on my shirt. When finished, I admired the dense wall she'd built at my back to guard us from the wind and prying eyes.

"They haven't noticed our truck yet," Sembuuk said as he tied his shoe laces. "Or they have and they've not yet organized a search squad. We need to move, Andy."

"No." I faced him with my jaw set in determination. "The batteries won't start another fire, and if you take me with you, you'll never get to North Camp by sundown. We don't want a repeat of this morning, even if the temperature is a little milder."

"I told you last night, I'm not leaving you, Andy."

Chong asked what we were talking about, so Sembuuk explained in Chinese. They conversed and seemed to disagree. She stomped away to fetch more firewood.

"Her tongue is so sharp, I think she has Kazakh blood." Sembuuk chuckled.

"Don't change the subject," I said, pressing the issue. "Stay on the west side of the forest and go south. You know what to do. If you hurry, you can be back by midnight with horses."

"They'll find you by then," he argued.

He was right. Three kilometers east of us, the truck looked lonely and strange on the open plain—and a fair indicator as to the direction we'd taken. It had to be drawing every eye now that the sun was up. They would check the woods nearest the truck first, and I'd be found.

"Either we all stay here needlessly," I said, "or you two go, and I stay. They may not send out a search party until late; maybe they'll even wait until tomorrow."

"Andy, you know better!" Sembuuk said, shaking his head.

"You're risking Chong's life with every minute you stay here and fight with me! Take her and go!"

"I will not!"

Lunging, I grabbed his collar. Though I was crippled, I still had strength. I pulled him within inches of my face; he couldn't get away.

"Do you remember when Sergeant Xing was shooting at me?"

"Yes, I remember," he said with a gulp, probably knowing where I was taking the conversation.

"I should've died, right?"

"Yes."

"When my plane wrecked in the mountains, I should've died. A month ago, I nearly fell off a ledge. I should've died. Men and women who follow God's will don't meet untimely deaths, Sembuuk, not until God makes it so." Releasing him, I shoved him away. "Now go. God watches over us all." And to Chong I said, "Convince him to leave me. He can return with horses as soon as you reach the Kazakh camp. The longer you wait here, the more dangerous it is for all of us."

"He is not a Christian, is he, Mr. Foworthy?"

"Call me Andy. No, he's not a Christian. But he's seen God's hand in many ways. Some of his clan have become believers, but he's stubborn."

She put her hand on Sembuuk's shoulder and spoke pleadingly to him. It was common sense. They had to leave me. I was the weak link. It was unfortunate, but true.

"Sembuuk, go!" I ordered him again, and thrust my journal into his hand. "God is watching."

After a brief farewell, they marched southwest. Chong shed a couple of tears, but kept them mostly hidden, and Sembuuk looked as mad as a . . . Well, he was mad that he had to leave his American friend. We'd been through much together, and no one should ever have to leave an injured companion behind. It hurt him, and it hurt me because, regardless of my words to him, I considered the fact that perhaps my time had in fact come. God had used me. Now He could call me home.

...✝...

CHAPTER TWENTY-NINE

A s soon as I could no longer hear Sembuuk and Li Chong's footsteps, I diminished the size of the fire. I had plenty of wood to burn, but I wanted to keep to a minimum the amount of smoke that rose up through the wall of branches Chong had constructed. Without straining, I could see the truck. Still, no one had approached it. *Why not?* They had to be looking for the stolen recon vehicle. We had to be a priority since we were the army's only lead to the Russian radio's operation.

Though my stomach growled, I was content and plenty warm. I picked at dry grass and ate some of it. The fire was doing wonders on my leg, and I gently massaged the muscles around the wound. My end was approaching, and I readied my heart before the Lord. Prayerfully, I laughed and cried. So much happens in our lives, so many little things, things that shout of God's existence and His hand in small moments. It was these events that I recalled and praised Him for allowing me to glimpse. Of all the misery I'd witnessed, the kindness and love seemed to wipe all the bad away.

Gino, the man God had sent to reach me, was foremost in my thoughts. I would see him soon. After God had brought Gino into my life so many years ago, He'd given me a vision to reach out to others, to come to this place, and show them Jesus Christ. It was like a spider web, a fabric of

341

love and friendship that couldn't be equaled in any other facet of life. God reached whom He wanted to reach using whom He wanted to use—even me. He connected the dots of that web, and I was left in awe as I reflected upon His sovereignty.

Two hours passed before two dirt bikes left the incursion road and approached the truck we'd abandoned. I slapped my fire out to a small flame. Since I was downwind of them, they wouldn't smell my smoke. Watching closely, I wished I had my binoculars as they looked over the vehicle. In my pants pocket, I still had the ignition key. But it wouldn't slow down their search.

One of the soldiers moved away from the truck. For a moment, he gazed toward the distant woods in my direction. He wouldn't be able to see me from there, but I still held my breath.

My fire! From my pile of fuel, I added a few branches to the candle-sized flame. *Stupid!* I'd nearly let it go out. After that, I kept a closer eye on it as I also watched the unfolding events on the steppe.

The two soldiers left, and an hour later, a small platoon of soldiers came with a tow truck. With curiosity, I watched them, not realizing exactly what they were doing until the soldiers were already marching away from the recon truck toward me! They were still over two kilometers away, so I didn't panic. I had to hide or they would find me there. But moving and hiding through the cold with my injured leg meant I had to endure untold pain once again.

"Lord, please store the warmth of this flame in my bones. Watch over me, protect me . . ."

I smothered the fire, then picked at Chong's wall of branches and threw several boughs over the ashes and where the forest floor had been disturbed. It wouldn't fool a mountain tracker, but it was all I could do for now.

The group of soldiers drew nearer—near enough for me to count now—nine. And they were spreading out to enter the woods in a combing formation.

With my simple camp somewhat hidden, I walked like a three-legged dog on my hands and one foot deeper into the forest. The underbrush thinned out the farther I went, providing fewer places to hide, but there was no turning back. I heard a branch snap and knew they were entering the forest behind me, their rifles cradled and ready to fire.

Hopping over a log, I grimaced as my palm slipped on a rock and my chin slammed into the ground. Though my senses were rattled, I kept moving. My route was taking me uphill, straight through the forest belt to the mountain range beyond, though I didn't want to get caught on the bare slope. The forest was the place to hide. But where?

Breathing heavily, I rested against a leaning tree to survey my surroundings and nurse my bleeding chin. The brush there wasn't thick enough in which to hide. The edge of the forest had been the answer where the morning sun urged more vegetation to grow. I couldn't go much farther, not with my leg wound potentially opening up again. They were coming up behind me and I wouldn't be able to outrun them on three limbs! Where could I possibly—

The tree I leaned against was covered in brown mushrooms. And the tree was leaning against and intersecting with a tall cedar far above on which the branches were so high and thick, it hurt my neck to gaze upward. The leaner was especially rotten so I couldn't discern what type of tree it was, but the smelly mushrooms were like natural ladder rungs. It was my only chance.

I reached high with my hands, gripped tightly, and hopped upward on my good leg. When I placed my foot on a gnarled mushroom, it held. My hands reached higher and I focused on my next foot placement. *Hop!* Already, I was six feet off the ground. The leaning tree was much steeper than a forty-five degree angle, so I rose quickly. Of all the crazy stunts I'd pulled growing up, I'd had the sense to avoid unpredictable trees—until now. There was a measure of insecurity at every handhold or footstep where the limbs were cracked, the moss was slippery, and the bark was loose.

The climb made me dizzy, but I lied to my fear, trying to convince myself that it was the altitude's thinner air. There was truly something enchanting about the upper regions of the forest—any forest. It was a bird's eye view. But I wasn't sightseeing. My leg throbbed and my heart pounded.

Behind me, I heard voices. They'd be coming into view of me in seconds. Almost frantically, I hopped upward twice, my triceps and forearms burning from the strain as I held on. Stretching out my hand, I touched the giant cedar tree where the rotten log intersected at a height of thirty feet.

Dangerously, I stood upright on my good leg. A single, warty mushroom supported my two hundred pounds. I reached high and wrapped my hands around a branch as thick as my leg.

The mushroom on which I stood suddenly slipped away like jelly beneath my boot. I dangled from the branch and felt the blood drain from my face. Far below, the mushroom hit the ground with a thud. The sound brought several soldiers at a run toward my tree. Interlacing my fingers around the branch, I closed my eyes, daring not to move. As I was in my stained, filthy coat, I couldn't help but wonder if I blended into the foliage around me, just a tapestry of moss to be ignored . . . And I prayed.

I hung there for forty seconds, which was harder than I'd imagined. The soldiers turned in circles below me and asked each other, "*You heard it, too?* And, "*Yeah, I heard something around here, I think.*"

If I hung any longer, I wouldn't have the strength to pull myself up. And if I was going to do something besides fall, it had to be now, soldiers present or not. Back in the States, I'd known a boy who'd climbed a tall tree, but he'd fallen and broken his back. Falling out of a tree seemed worse than getting shot out of the tree at that moment, so I swung my good leg up around the branch on which I clung.

From my upside down position now, I saw the three soldiers below, their rifles at the ready. Farther back in the forest, a formed line of the other soldiers swept from east to west. None of them were searching the treetops for me, though.

Twisting around, I pulled and clawed at the tree itself to right myself on my branch. That's when I came face to face with the largest and smelliest owl I'd ever seen in my life. I imagined it hooting or emerging from within its massive burrow. If its body weight didn't knock me off my branch, the soldiers' attention would certainly be drawn by the commotion.

But nothing happened. The owl didn't move. It didn't even open its eyes. Peering down at the guards, I saw that more were gathering below me. In just a matter of time, one of them would look skyward, or check the sun's placement, and notice me. My options were limited: ascend into the tree higher, or fight the owl over its burrow. I decided I couldn't climb any higher. There was no cover above me like there was right there where the section of the tree was hollow.

With a finger, I poked the owl. Something wasn't right about the feathered creature. The owl didn't move at my nudging. It was winter. *Did owls hibernate?* I thought not. Feeling through the creature's feathers, I found him cold to the touch. Owls are warm-blooded. So the appropriate question to ask now was: *what happens to owls that die of old age?* This owl was two feet tall and part of the horned species. Though it hadn't been dead long, on closer examination, I noticed a few ants and beetles nosing about the feathers.

Carefully, I lifted the big bird aside. It was an easy eight or ten pounds. Then I climbed into the burrow next to it. I sat on a nest of animal bones and hair and feathers, and above me, the ceiling disappeared into darkness. With some exhaling and hushed grunting, I worked my shoulders around so I could pull my legs into the hole, though not without crowding the owl of its insect-infested space. My whole body was finally inside the burrow except for the toes of my right foot as I sat cross-legged.

I couldn't help but smile and mouth my thanks to the Creator. Somewhere around two hundred years ago, the tree had started to grow. The other leaning tree had been blown over and rotted with mushrooms. Fifty or more years ago, the owl had been born, perhaps in that very same tree. Something had built the nest. Then, the owl had died at a ripe old age, but right in time—evidently within days—of my arrival. Tell me God doesn't coordinate everything in creation!

Owl or no owl, God had put that burrow in that cedar for me, and I would've been a fool not to recognize God's handiwork then, as well as so many other times.

A shout rose up through the forest and I heard running feet. Peering out of my hole and down to the left, I saw the soldiers tromping to the east. I guessed they'd found the remains of my fire. *That was fast.* Perhaps there was a tracker among them, maybe even a Mongolian. They would know one of us was wounded and couldn't travel fast without transportation. How much of a trail had I left to my present location? Silently, I chastised myself for worrying about things I couldn't change now. In fact, I couldn't climb out of my cedar without falling over thirty feet down, that's how securely I was tucked away. The owl's burrow may as well have been my own coffin!

But I relaxed while the soldiers were gone—for now at least. In the Northern Hemisphere, owls make their homes facing south whenever possible, and I was grateful for this as the smallest sliver of sunlight shone through the heights above. As the cedars in the north, this one reached as high as two hundred feet. And though my hollow place was barely the size of a grown man, the trunk's base was larger than most round dining tables.

When I heard voices again, I dared not look out as the soldiers returned. They were tracking me, following sign across the forest floor. I hadn't been too crafty, lunging across the ground like a wounded dog. The soldiers would see everything I'd disturbed, if they knew what to look for—a trampled blade of dead grass, a handprint in soft moss . . . *A handprint?* That would confuse them, but it wouldn't slow their advance. There would be other sign, too, since Chong and Sembuuk had come that way. Was the tracker good enough to tell that our party had split up and I'd stayed behind?

The Chinese voices were close now—so close, they were sure to be at the bottom of the leaning tree. They would see my boot prints on the mushrooms, and they'd circle the cedar, staring up at its branches. The branches were so far apart, they could see nearly to the top of the tree and discern if I was up there or not. But, they couldn't know I was *inside* the tree. From below, the owl's home was out of sight, hidden by the thick branch just outside the opening.

I stared at the owl in silence, a smile on my lips like I was a toddler hiding in the closet from my peers, too excited to move lest my position be found.

My stomach growled and I picked at the moss inside the hole. I nibbled on the rot and reminded myself that health nuts in some civilizations made milkshakes out of such horrible tasting fungus.

The Chinese continued to discuss their plans below, yet even if I knew what they intended, I couldn't do anything about it, so it was best, for worry's sake, that I didn't understand much Chinese. Eventually, they parted, and I spied them noisily marching together back to the east.

But wait. My eyes narrowed. *It was a trap.* Two soldiers crept into different hiding places. One between three saplings and another in the ditch left behind by the roots of the leaning tree.

They felt so certain I was nearby, yet had no sense to realize they were hiding in such plain sight that I could count the buttons on their uniforms in the fading light. I decided to keep my nose inside my hole, though, and wait them out. After a couple of hours of silence, I assumed they'd be thoroughly chilled to the bone and depart, figuring whoever had been there was now gone. As long as they weren't there when Sembuuk returned to fetch me.

However, as the hours slipped past—with me dosing, nibbling on moss, and counting spots on the owl—I realized the two soldiers below weren't leaving any time soon. This was sure to become a problem for me since I had bodily needs. I couldn't move while they were down there listening to every sound the forest made.

The sun blinked, then faded behind the western range, and I watched the sun's rays diminish from the treetops until they were gone altogether. Almost instantly, the temperature dropped. If the owl wasn't crawling with its assortment of creepy-crawlies, I would've cuddled a little to stay warmer, its feathers making an excellent insulator for heat. As it was, I could only rotate my shoulders and twist my torso in an attempt to generate some heat and avoid cramping.

The wind whistled through the trees and I shivered. *Didn't owls know anything about doors?* Dusk settled, then the first stars winked above. The green and brown forest took on gray shades until it was nothing but shadows—and an owl that was still alive began to hoot.

Rustling below drew my attention. Leaning out, I stared at the ground. Someone was moving down there. The soldiers had to be getting cold. I was freezing. It was already below zero. Or was it not the soldiers moving at all, but Sembuuk and a couple of others returning with horses?

I noticed one of the saplings move. It was the soldiers getting restless. In hushed words, the two conversed. Then they slung their rifles over their shoulders and walked out of the forest to the east.

Not sixty seconds had passed before I heard a new sound. It was a snort, maybe a sneeze, from the south. Had other soldiers hidden themselves out there, too?

My eyes were well-adjusted to the dark and I trained them on a stand of trees to my right. *Movement!* Something dark, graceful, and of considerable bulk moved like an animal, but it wasn't an animal. It was a man who came into sight—silent, stalking, crouching, even sniffing the air. He knelt to listen and watch the forest for a minute before he moved toward my tree.

Gan-gaad. He'd moved like that when he'd prowled up the trail to the cave. The clan was wise in sending this man for me since his every skill was in demand for my recovery. The ex-clan leader stalked closer. He surely knew there were soldiers near. Maybe he could even smell them. The snort I'd heard was probably from his *aduu*, which he'd surely abandoned not far away.

Pressing himself against my cedar, he paused to measure every shadow, any bulk that could be a sulking enemy.

I dropped a chunk of bark down at him, nearly landing on his shoulder. His face turned upward. When I waved my white palm, he seemed momentarily stunned at my position, perhaps surprised to see me alive, then noticed the leaning tree and how I'd gotten up there. He motioned something I didn't understand, so I guessed.

"They went east a few minutes ago," I whispered just loud enough.

"Can you come down, Pond? There's no way I'm coming up there to get you."

"Um, I don't—" I'd been dreading this part. "We need rope!"

He waved at me, then like a ghost, he slipped through the woods and out of sight. My ears burned for any sound. *Where did he go?* A few minutes later, he walked back to me from the east. He'd prowled after the soldiers to make sure they were indeed gone. Without a word or glance upward, he crept below and beyond my tree in the direction from which he'd first arrived. While he seemed to take his time, my bladder was ready to burst. I needed to get out of the tree now!

Several forms approached the tree. Zima and others were on horseback. Gan-gaad pointed me out to them in silence. She waved frantically at me, her whole face a glowing smile. For nearly two weeks, they'd surely assumed Sembuuk and I had been killed. Sembuuk was below as well, though he was hunched over in the saddle, maybe dozing. It had been a long couple of days for us both.

Gan-gaad and Bolor connected reins and lead ropes together and threw one end up to me. After the third toss, I caught it. I hooked one knotted end into a crack of the owl's burrow, a place from which the rope could be freed when whipped hard enough from below.

My legs had fallen asleep hours before, and it took some coaxing to get them fired up again. Carefully, I climbed out onto the limb. Straddling the branch, I reached back and set the owl back into the center of its burrow. I nodded my thanks and farewell to my feathered friend, and slid down the rope.

Zima practically dove off her horse and tackled me, smothering me with kisses and hugs. Bolor had to pull her off as Gan-gaad whispered criticisms into my ear—because we were making too much noise and frightening the horses. But in moments, we were all on horseback riding south.

..✝...

CHAPTER THIRTY

"Ever since you two were captured, they've been searching the woods north and south—all around us," Kandal said as he poked a stick into the coals. "The only reasonable explanation why they haven't found and captured us is because God has hidden us from their eyes."

Kandal and I, and a few others, were gathered around the fire, forming an inner circle. Those who preferred to follow rather than lead sat behind us. And behind them, everyone else stood—the women and children, mostly—listening and biting their nails nervously. Duulgii stood in the back, having lost the right to speak at gatherings.

The entire clan from all three camps were there in Middle Camp, gathered the night after my return. I was rested and had a pair of crude crutches lying beside me.

"How long has Dusbhan been gone?" I asked.

Regardless of us initially keeping his mission hidden, the whole clan was now aware that Dusbhan had left to scout out a northwesterly passage that avoided the plain.

"Nearly two weeks." As the eldest, Kandal was best informed.

"Then he's on his way back now," I said, calculating.

"No one's ventured into the plain for days. Food is growing scarce. We may need to slaughter the older horses soon."

"My eagle, . . . has anyone seen her?" Sembuuk asked.

"Yes," Jugder said. "I'm sure it was your raptor, though I don't know where she's lighting. I think she looks for you."

"Instead of the plain, I'll go onto the mountain and try to draw her to me," Sembuuk said. "Our food stores will be replenished soon."

"When Dusbhan returns, we'll leave," I said. "God has been faithful to protect us while we were separated. We need not tempt capture."

"The journey will be hard," Kandal said. "The clan outnumbers the horses. But I agree: to stay much longer would mean disaster. We can see them coming this time, and if we do nothing to avoid the enemy, none of us may survive the next slaughter."

"Let me go hunt over the mountain before we leave," Gan-gaad requested from behind Sembuuk. "I know the land better than anyone."

"I'm not opposed to that," I said, since Gan-gaad was essentially under my watch.

"But only early in the morning when there are fewer soldiers about—in case there are patrols on foot or flying over," Kandal said. "That goes for any movement."

"Should we organize anything else before the journey?" I asked.

The instant I asked it, I realized what a foolish question it was. These people always knew what needed to be done. They were born ready to travel. Nevertheless, Kandal was thoughtful, and we all waited for the old man to speak.

"Perhaps . . . some will walk. Others will ride." He

looked at me as if to say, "*Is that enough organization for your Western mind?*"

I smiled and nodded. Yes, everyone knew what lay ahead. Their coordination was natural. The whole situation was foreign only to me and Chong, both of us having been born and raised in massive cities. But she was adjusting nicely, I'd heard from Olz, who lived in South Camp and spoke fluent Chinese. Naturally, Chong was preaching Christ to everyone through him as interpreter. After so many near-miraculous events witnessed by the clan, their eyes were open and their hearts were ready to have God's plan for their lives fully revealed. The Gospel was no longer foolishness to these people.

There was no question that we were leaving. Either that, or we'd be caught and probably killed, whichever came first. Everyone did their best to smile and lightheartedly attend their many chores, but our nerves were on edge. If I could have, I would've been out chopping wood just to pass the time—not that we needed any more wood, though. As it was, I was restricted to the camp on my crutches or on horseback in the woods. In camp, I was only in the way, and on horseback, there was a risk of straying into a Chinese search party. But riding into the mountains to the west was a relatively safe venture, and Manai escaped the camp on horseback with me to scout and explore the cave valley, and where Gan-gaad was hunting. Though Manai was barely six now, his horsemanship skills were better than mine. Kazakhs and Mongolians, during summer months, love to race their horses. Since horse racing is a test of the horse and not the rider, the youngsters are often used as jockeys—

the smaller and younger, the better.

While we rode through the mountains and threw rocks at pine cones, Sembuuk spent four days whistling and waving for his eagle, but it seemed the winged predator had returned to the wild, and we all felt Sembuuk's loss. The bird had been our sole source of meat at times. Now, we counted on Gan-gaad and a couple others who had set snares in the woods.

Gan-gaad didn't disappoint us. He brought in a buck on his second day out and a medium-sized doe on the fifth. Like Native Americans, the Kazakhs use every bit of the deer: skin, stomach, bladder, bones, and other parts.

After a week since my return, Sembuuk called me out of my *ger* before we'd even risen to stoke the fire that morning. I shushed him so Zima and Manai weren't disturbed, and quickly dressed. Judging by the urgency in his voice, something had happened. Maybe his eagle had returned, I hoped.

"The clan knows you and I do things for them that are too dangerous for anyone else, right?"

Smiling, I didn't like the way he'd started, but something told me I'd participate. I had already crutched my way over to him as he saddled two horses, so I knew he was up to something wild.

"Well? What's going on?"

"For hours I've been awake, so I walked out to Three Rocks to watch the Chinese. That's when I saw them." He met my eyes. A chill passed up my spine. "There's about twenty of them."

I frowned. *Twenty what?* Sembuuk didn't finish. He

slapped his leg and called Lucky Hunter to his side.

"Twenty?" I said, gulping. What could we do against twenty soldiers except sacrifice ourselves as decoys and hope the rest of the clan could ride like the wind on our too-few horses?

We mounted and rode out of camp just as Zima emerged from the *ger* to begin preparing the morning meal. She saw us heading east, but I couldn't meet her stern gaze, her disapproving eyes. Every time Sembuuk and I were together, something happened. It was expected, and she knew it could be nothing good yet again. I was worried as well. *Two men and Lucky Hunter against twenty?* Sembuuk and I had pulled some stunts together, but I hadn't thought he'd lost his mind completely!

Slowing our horses, we stopped at the edge of the forest. The sun was starting to peek above the golden Gobi.

"Have you been praying for the clan's deliverance?" he asked expectantly.

"Everyday, Sembuuk. Why?"

"Look!"

He pointed to the southeast. Halfway between Three Rocks and the incursion road, about twenty goats and sheep were grazing. I thought I was seeing things! Sembuuk grinned proudly. Climbing off his *aduu*, he aimed Lucky Hunter in the direction of the flock, then sent him out to herd the animals to us.

"These have to be ours," Sembuuk said, "and they got scattered during that first day. Evidently they've been grouped together by a watering hole somewhere. Wolves probably got a few of them. But something must've spooked them recently, sending them back toward us."

I just nodded, still speechless.

Lucky Hunter herded like he'd never herded before, darting left and right, barking and nipping at their flanks until they succumbed to his charge.

"Andy, I wanted to share this with you," Sembuuk said.

"Thank you, Sembuuk. This is a good day. I believe you're right: God has preserved us through yet another obstacle."

As Lucky Hunter and Sembuuk worked together to keep the strays in line, I led the flock through the forest. It was a stampede of little hooves that overtook North Camp that morning. There was screaming and laughing as everyone ran about to catch the animals and crowd them into the corral—then frantically hemmed them into the horse-sized fence to keep them in.

We kept six goats and lambs for ourselves and drove the rest to Middle Camp where a rider was quickly dispatched to South Camp to announce we had enough food to possibly last the winter. All three camps came together at Middle Camp where there was dancing and laughing. There was even rejoicing for God's continual preservation.

It was a wonderful day, a day of days, but it seemed to fade into just another day of heartache when, on the following afternoon, we were sorrowfully reminded of our mortality.

Sembuuk and Gan-gaad had been out hunting and had found no game when they caught up to me and Manai on our way back to camp from the mountains. Gan-gaad was responsibly hiding the rifle in the cave every day, and I'd witnessed a continued softening of the hard man's heart.

Halfway down the mountain's eastern slope, we halted our mounts to watch a horse limp from north to south just beyond the tree line. Frowning, I counted the horse's legs—it had six.

In quick understanding, Gan-gaad charged down the mountain at a breakneck speed. The limping, six-legged horse stopped at the next patch of snow it came to and chomped at the moisture. Gan-gaad arrived a little before us, and everyone but me leapt to the ground.

Dusbhan was on the far side of the horse. He'd been wounded. Too injured to mount his *aduu*, he'd tied himself to the saddle and walked or was dragged beside the horse along the way.

"He's alive!" Sembuuk announced.

Gan-gaad scooped his nephew into his arms, and since we were only two hundred yards outside camp, he carried him the rest of the way.

Kandal and I were the only two with any type of medical knowledge, but there was very little we could do for him now. Dusbhan had been shot twice at long range. Both entry wounds were from the back. One had shattered his hip on the right side. The other had lodged in his left lung. Each wound alone would've killed him in time. He was in God's hands. Just as discouraging was the infection in the hip injury, which I suspected had been there possibly for as long as a week.

In the morning, our friend and brother, Dusbhan, passed away. The only comfort I had was that he was a believer and we would see him again soon. Zima, upon picking through Dusbhan's pockets, found my binoculars and a number of pages that I'd given him from my journal before he'd left. Excitedly, I studied the pages, flipping through them with understanding. None of the others could identify Dusbhan's sketches and labels, but I knew what they were right away. I'd given him the pages for this very purpose.

"They're his wishes in death?" Bolor asked, peering over my shoulder.

My eyes sparkled.

"Remarkable!" I said. "Dusbhan's death wasn't in vain. He's mapped out an entire route west of the mountains!"

"West of the mountains?" Sembuuk picked up one page and examined it. "Has anyone ever been that far west?"

"I know it by other maps. Duulgii may make even more sense of all this," I said. "Dusbhan has shown us a low valley route between the mountains by which we can access the west side of the Altays. We'll be able to avoid the Chinese altogether. And if we find a good refuge with water along the way, we can stop and wait out the winter."

It was good news in the midst of a heartbreaking event. Everyone had appreciated Dusbhan's quiet and brief time with the clan, and he would be mourned as if he were one of the clan himself. Zima and I grieved him more than even Gan-gaad. Dusbhan had been one of the clan's first converts from the first people I'd met in Mongolia. But along with the bitterness, our grief was sweet as well. Soon, we would see him again.

...✝...

Beveg, Manai, and I spread the map of the world out on the floor of my *ger*. Zima looked on from against the wall as she sewed a *del* together of goat skins. Two days had passed since Dusbhan's funeral—a most somber occasion. And though we'd planned to leave and trek northwest, a savage cold spell had overtaken the mountain range. Both land and animals were silent and still. Thus, the map, and anything else we could think of to explore within the confines of the *gers*, helped to keep us distracted from the danger ahead of us.

"Don't tell us where we are, Pond!" Beveg instructed as she gazed at the colorful map with English words. Like Ziva, she preferred to call me by my miss-name. "I saw a map in my primer long ago." Those were bold words for a seven year old, but she stabbed a finger at east-central Asia right on the mark. "There's Mongolia, but it's in the wrong language."

"The language is English," Zima said. "It's what they speak and write in America where Pond is from."

But the children didn't seem to hear her.

"God made all of this," Manai said in awe, and swept his small hand over the oceans and continents.

"It took six days, Manai," Beveg taught him as the older sister she pretended to be.

"I know!" Manai pouted. "Beveg, I've been listening at night, too!"

A head poked through our felt door. It was Sembuuk. His cheeks were nearly frostbitten from being outside. He climbed in and nearly crumpled the map before Beveg moved it protectively aside.

"The weather is breaking." He rubbed his hands over our stove. "Kandal and Jugder agree."

"What does Gan-gaad think?" I asked. "He knows this region best."

"He says if the wild animals are about, we can be about."

"And have you seen any wild animals?" Zima asked.

"Not yet, but I've heard them along the north wall. Wolves, I think. They're hungry."

"Grrrrr!" Manai growled like a wolf and attacked Beveg, wrestling with her as she giggled and fought back.

"We'll see what it's like in the morning," I said for everyone. "I want to leave as badly as anyone. The soldiers will be out searching soon enough. Only by the grace of God have we not been found yet."

Two more days passed before the great cold spell broke. On the third day, we packed up, burdened our backs and our beasts, and met the other two camps on the mountain slope. Though the terrible cold of thirty below had passed, it was still colder than I was used to in New York. Five below was warm by Mongolian winter standards. Still, prolonged exposure of flesh to such a bite could cause frostbite. Thus, we all wore face masks with slits for eyes and only the nostrils fully exposed.

It was in this intense cold that we labored up the mountain slope so carefully. Muscles and bones are more susceptible to injury in such temperatures, and our goal of merely making it over the mountain was great enough for the first day.

Gan-gaad led the way on horseback, and as I had studied Dusbhan's maps and notes with him, he was the most adept man to take point. Jugder, Bolor, and Olz followed him, each leading their strings of horses that carried the heaviest *ger* structures and other supplies. Any riding horses available were for the elderly, the woman with a still-nursing infant from South Camp, a couple other men and women who were to trade walking for riding periodically, and myself. All but five goats had been slaughtered for meat and skins, including the sheep. The goats were the most sure-footed on the mountain shale with Lucky Hunter and the other dogs yelping for superior herding place. Those who walked were interspersed throughout the moving clan, though mostly in the rear, and Sembuuk and I came last, both on horseback, though Sembuuk and Kandal were to trade off and on.

Barely had Gan-gaad crested the top of the first ridge when the very distant rumble of a labored engine reached the animals' ears—the goats first and then the horses. They gazed back at the forest. Only then did we humans hear and follow their keen eyes. But keen eyes weren't needed to behold what terror we saw.

"Lord God, have mercy . . ." I whispered.

A muted puff of smoke from a twenty-five-millimeter cannon out on the plain announced the danger. An instant later, the report of artillery boomed with an explosion of rock and ice not far to our right. Tanks and armored personnel carriers had approached our section of the woods to search that very day. Upon seeing us over the trees from the steppe, they'd opened fire.

"Get up the mountain!" I shouted as a second round exploded to our left. They were sure to have us targeted now. "Run!"

But my words were ill-needed, for the scrambling had

already begun. Above, Gan-gaad rode back into my sight. He disappeared in a cloud of smoke, but he rode through it down the slope. Expertly, he leaned down and plucked up two children from the ground and plopped them, one in front and one behind him, on his horse. It was Manai and Beveg whom he'd rescued. Our eyes met over that distance in terrified understanding that it would be a slaughter again if we didn't get over the ridge and out of sight of the plain.

The pack horses lunged ahead—a chaotic scramble of near panic—and passed their three handlers. Sure-footing was no longer considered on the dangerous mountainside as we charged, crawled, and clawed upward.

"Why are they shooting at us?" I yelled as Sembuuk and I whipped our horses forward.

"They think we're a resistance!" he shouted back. "It's Duulgii's fault—and his radio!"

Yes, it was Duulgii's fault, but we'd all agreed to bring him back into the clan and now was hardly the time for casting blame.

Ahead, Li Chong scooped up a child and ran forward. An ordinance round landed between two pack horses and blew flesh and shrapnel in every direction. The other horses in the train were wounded but continued to drag torn carcasses behind them. Sembuuk drew a skinning knife and cut the lead rope with one slash to free the horses that weren't too badly wounded. In almost the same motion, he swung Kandal by the arm onto the horse behind him. Less gracefully, I swung Zima up with me as she clutched a kid goat.

Half of the clan had reached the ridge crest and were

spilling over the edge, but the rest of us were in disarray. The dogs and remainder of the goats were nearly trampled under hoof as Lucky Hunter and the others tried so loyally to maintain herding order. Bolor, Beveg's father and friend to all, died instantly in another explosion, a mare with him. Not a limb of either was left intact.

"Hiya!" I shrieked and whipped my mount.

A shell screamed overhead and blew up, peppering us with rocks and blinding us with burning hot shrapnel. My *aduu* screamed and reared, one side of her face singed and the eye blinded. Zima slid off the horse with her kid goat until I settled the terrified animal. Rounds burst around us. Screams and cries were everywhere. I searched for wounded clan members to help, but Zima and I were the last on the slope still alive. Zima mounted up again behind me.

In shock, and with only one eye, my *aduu* pranced sideways up the mountain. At the top of the ridge, she reared again, nearly spilling us. We danced in a circle and paused to gaze down upon the plain. The tanks had ceased their firing since their targets had passed out of sight. Only Zima and I were in their sights now. A few yards away from us lay the bodies of our dead.

...✝...

CHAPTER THIRTY-ONE

More movement at the base of the mountain caught my eye. Infantrymen on foot—and two on motorbikes—began to ascend the mountain with great haste. We were still out of their small arms range or they would've been shooting. As crippled as the clan was now, we could never outrun a pursuing force.

When the tank shells had first exploded, the birds in the vicinity had taken to the air in fright. Then they'd settled again in their rock or tree roosts. With a prayer on my lips, I saw them take flight again, though I wondered in wide-eyed horror what tragedy awaited us next that had caused them to escape once more into the sky.

It began as a low growl. Then, a trickle of rocks and pebbles vibrated around my horse's hooves. Our *aduu* reared again, but was quickly calmed without my urging, her ears flicking with curiosity.

Then, with ten times the force of a freight train, the mountain began to shake and bounce. The noise and motion of the ground moved more and more. Boulders buried under the frozen earth emerged from the snow as if pushed upward by a mighty hand. Our horse stood to balance itself as the ground shook even more violently. The boulders became so unsettled that they began to tumble like bowling balls down the slope. The soldiers below tried to escape death by the crushing, rolling granite, but the mountain heaved too severely for them to find their footing to run away. They crouched in place and tried to hide in crevices as the boulders tumbled over and through their ranks. Of fifty infantrymen, at least two dozen were crushed in the first minute.

The quake faded in sound and motion, and I patted my horse's neck and spoke soothing words as I urged her beyond the rim of the mountain and out of sight of the forest. Behind us, the remaining foot soldiers fled back into the woods and beyond to their vehicles.

I guided my *aduu* through the scattered remnant of the clan. Those not badly injured clung to the weeping and wounded on the western slope. The great rugged mountain valley lay below us, but we'd never reach its safer landscape if we froze to death here, where the wind tore at our clothing and took our breaths away. Almost all had wounds of some sort. Zima jumped to the ground to tend to a wounded woman from Middle Camp. Moving through the people, I found Gan-gaad at the front. One of his ears had been completely swiped off and his scalp was bleeding, skinned to the bone.

"Get us moving," I said to him. Sembuuk was near enough to hear. "We'll have to wait to lick our wounds at the cave, not out here."

He nodded. The cave was three hours away by horse. Those of us who'd explored the valley knew that, but the people didn't know. If they would've realized the distance to that night's shelter, they would've never started moving again.

Jugder approached me as the word to move reached him.

His shoulder was wounded and he limped terribly, but there was nothing but bravery on his face.

"Andy, if we start down the mountain and another earthquake occurs, we'll be caught in rock slides." He kept his voice low. The seven-fingered man held my reins and inspected my horse's eye. "Your mount is badly hurt as well."

"We all are. That's why we need to keep moving southwest to the cave—to keep our minds on the goal and not on our losses. The earthquake was an act of God," I said with bold assurance. "It pushed the soldiers back. God knows our plight. Let's go."

Everywhere I looked, my friends wept and held one another. No one was exempt from loss. Families were split, the dead were abandoned, but none were forgotten.

"Pond, take this one." Zima pushed a child of three into my arms. "He can't walk. I bandaged his leg. This cave . . . it will hold us all?"

"It'll do." I turned from her to find Sembuuk comforting Beveg, her father no longer with the living. "Sembuuk, take Manai and some tools and ride ahead. See if you can make a safer path along the mountain to the cave."

The child in my lap picked at my chest and I flinched as he held up a piece of metal the size and shape of a finger that had burned through my clothing and embedded itself in my flesh. *Shrapnel.* I smiled down at him as he held up his prize proudly.

"Good boy. There are others, too. See if you can find them."

I rode toward the back where the dogs warily guarded

the two remaining goats. Lucky Hunter trotted up to me with a third, dead goat in his jaws. He dropped it at my horse's feet.

"Good dog." Leaning down, I patted the loyal dog on the head. I'd discovered that he and the other canines preferred admiration more than edible treats. Then, I gripped the dead goat and tied it behind my saddle until it could be dressed.

"Andy," someone called.

Turning, I saw it was Duulgii with his Russian companion next to him. Duulgii lay on his back, his head on a rock, and a gashing wound across his abdomen. It was strange how quickly even the blood from our wounds was freezing into a thick Jello consistency.

"You have it bad, Duulgii," I said, finding no reason at this point to mince words.

"Are you taking them to the cave?" Panting, his voice was raspy as he spoke.

"Yes, Duulgii. The soldiers won't be postponed for long."

"Can it be said—" He groaned from his pain and his companion shook his head at me. "Can it be said that God, your God, allowed my sins against the clan so you would know there was a cave and a stream to escape to now?"

"It could be, Duulgii," I said. "But your sins aren't held in account by the clan inasmuch as they separate you from the living God, your Creator. You know His mighty hand. This life of yours will expire soon, friend. I trust you seek forgiveness through Jesus Christ so when you meet Him face-to-face, you are a child of His, and not a foe, as you've been your whole life."

"Leave me here and I'll find solace with the Creator, then." He rolled his head toward his friend and bid him to go on without him.

I couldn't linger, but Duulgii had grown up in Kazakhstan and he knew some of the basic truths of Jesus and the Cross. What he remembered from childhood had been emphasized during his time with us in camp. He had a knowledge, but he would only find everlasting life and peace if his heart was truly repentant.

"Mr. Foworthy! Come . . . to me!" someone called in English.

Only one person amongst us could speak English. I found Chong sitting on a rock with a hand on her side. She bore a cheek wound that had only recently stopped bleeding.

"Me not strong like Kazakhs, Mr. Foworthy." Her teeth were clenched in pain. "No more can continue."

"Let me see, Chong." I slid off my horse and knelt next to her.

"It no bother at start." She pulled back her coat. "But now, it too bad."

She had the worst of the wounds of the living, except for Duulgii. From her right armpit, shrapnel had cut her through to her ribs. Somehow, there wasn't much blood. The way the shrapnel had injured her, I found it surprising that her right arm was intact at all—and that she was still conscious.

"We'll take care of you." Turning, I looked for help. "Olz, boost Chong up with me!" I climbed back onto my horse, the boy still in front.

"But your wife!" Chong protested as she was launched

upward by strong Olz to sit behind me.

"It's okay. She won't mind and she's perfectly fine to walk."

Clinging to me with one arm, she held onto her wound with the other under her coat. After a few more minutes, the gear was rearranged and the wounded were seen to enough to start forward again—led by one-earred Gan-gaad who had Beveg riding behind him. With a parting nod to Duulgii, I brought up the rear with Chong as the clan descended from the ridge.

"Would you have left your post with us if you would've known you'd be joining us in these circumstances?" I asked the Chinese woman.

"If not leave, they torture me to death. I torture enough before I came to Christ, Mr. Foworthy, to know torture no way to die. If die now, die with friends. Not alone."

I looked up at the sky. It was so peaceful and blue above so much turmoil. If the trumpet sounded right then, no one else would need to die at all—no believers, anyway, and certainly not Chong.

...✝...

When Zima saw I was butchering the dead goat that Lucky Hunter had brought me, she took it from my hands. Firelight glinted off the walls of the cave.

"You're ruining the skin, Pond," she said as politely as possible. I was still a beginner when it came to skinning. "Here. You see to the dressings."

She handed me a wooden plate of steaming rags fresh from boiling. Naturally, the gaze of the clan members who waited for care now shifted to me. There were so many.

Gan-gaad knelt in front of me and offered the side of his head toward my reach. I grimaced at the earless scalp, and began to clean the dried blood and shrapnel from the wound. Infection would be our greatest adversary without medicine.

"Any man who leads a clan as you do should know how to gut a goat, Pond." The man grunted. "How did you survive in America?"

"Cockroaches." I set my hand on his shoulder. "You can go now, Gan-gaad. Come back to see me in the morning—and be sure to keep your wound clean, do you hear?"

"Huh?" he said, mocking as a deaf man and twisted his head with his one ear toward me. "I can't hear you."

He chuckled as he took up an axe and exited the cave. My next patient was the woman with the infant who'd first been at North Camp. The baby was the only one among us who was unscathed. The mother had taken shrapnel and rock in her back muscles that needed to be plucked out and the wounds cleaned.

And so, I doctored the clan that first evening of our exodus northwest. A fire had been our first priority upon arriving, and there'd been plenty of wood to gather to get it roaring. Next had come the cleaning of the wounded so everyone could get about their chores. Every able man was outside collecting more wood while the women saw to the evening meal or mended torn gear. The dogs would've normally been darting up and down the cave's narrow pathway, which Sembuuk had widened, but even the dogs limped, whined, and huddled against one wall, licking their wounds.

The limestone walls of the cave radiated the heat from the central fire, and in no time I'd stripped off my coat. I was only temporarily frustrated over not being able to cut wood with the men due to my leg, but I saw I was more necessary in the cave as a medic. Carefully, I rationed out the last of my first aid supplies to the worst of the injured, particularly Chong, who lay not far from the fire. There was nothing I knew to do for the woman who was missing so much of her side. She was surely in tremendous pain, yet she didn't complain.

I hobbled over to her and lifted her blanket. Every time I looked at her wound, I found new debris to remove.

"Your leg, Mr. Foworthy?" she asked weakly.

"It's healing fast. I'll be able to walk on it a little in a week, maybe less."

"What condition of clan?"

"Um . . ." I surveyed the cave. "We lost Bolor, Duulgii, and two others. Three horses didn't make it, and two others will have to be put down tonight. All the dogs made it, but only two goats are alive."

"The earthquake . . . was God," she said assuredly with a tear in her eye. "He save us."

"No doubt about it." I felt her fevered brow. "Rest, I'll be back in a few minutes."

Using my crutches, I walked to the mouth of the cave and peered through my binoculars at the ridgeline miles away to the east. There was no movement from the Chinese infantry, yet, but that's where they would first appear, on our back trail. Even if I saw them coming, there was little we could do. We were too crippled to move that night. The horses across the game trail below the cave were as wounded as the humans. I'd be surprised if we even mustered the strength to leave the next morning. Dusbhan's maps didn't show any natural shelters for another forty-five miles. That meant we'd be spending at least one night in our *gers* between here and there.

Lucky Hunter nudged my leg and I patted his head as he whined softly. He was missing a patch of fur high on his spine where he couldn't clean himself. Earlier, he'd come to me, knowing I could ease the burning. Like all the others, there was nothing more I could do for him after cleaning it gently.

"You'll be all right, boy."

His ears perked and he gazed to the east. My binoculars went to my eyes and I studied the mountain for any pursuers. Instead, I heard and felt a shallow rumble coming from the east. *Another earthquake or aftershock.* There'd been a dozen of them in the last few hours. God was keeping the soldiers at bay.

I tested my weight on my leg. If I started walking on it too soon, I'd tear the recently healed tissues. Maybe in a few more days . . .

"Mr. Foworthy! Mr. Foworthy . . ."

Quickly, I went to Chong's side.

"The Bible. Read Bible," she requested.

"It's in Mongolian, Chong."

"You translate, Mr. Foworthy. Read Psalm."

So, I read to Chong, but slowly, interpreting into English for her as I went. She closed her eyes and sighed, often repeating the same verse in Chinese as it came to her practiced memory. And this is how my Chinese torturer died, while I read her the Psalms, though I didn't know she'd passed for some time while I read. When she was silent for a long time, I closed my Bible.

"I'll see you soon," I said, and kissed her forehead. Then I chuckled and wiped my tear away. "No lies, no spies, sister."

As darkness approached, the cold became too bitter for the men to remain outside tending to the horses and wood. The two horses too injured to travel were slaughtered, and we ate well that night of horse meat, goat, and mare's milk.

The cave was just large enough for the survivors to crowd in with bed mats slightly overlapping in places. As everyone settled onto their mats for the night, Sembuuk insisted on keeping watch at the cave mouth. After midnight, I awoke to spell him.

"Wolves," he said, and I watched the snowy ground below for the dashing shadows in the night. "They smell the meat and blood, even our wounds. The pack already ate the snow where we slaughtered the two mares."

"Are they leaving the horses alone? The path is too narrow to bring them inside."

"So far, yes," he answered. "I think your half-blind *aduu* gave one the hoof an hour ago. The wolf crawled too close when he thought the hooved ladies were sleeping."

"Once Lucky Hunter is feeling better, he'll keep us better guarded," I said. "The horses know our dogs protect them, right?"

"Oh, yes." He laughed quietly. "They're probably mad that the dogs are up here relaxing in the warmth. But our dogs aren't shy of those range wolves, or of the Siberian timber wolves. Lucky Hunter outweighs any two of them, but a lot of that is his coat. He was Lugsalkhaan's best dog, you know."

"Yes, and I see why. He'll be better tomorrow. Go get some sleep, Sembuuk. I've got this watch."

Throughout the rest of the night, I prayed, wrote in my journal—from which you're reading now—and watched the wolves sulk about.

Below to the right of the cave, the men had buried Chong under a pile of rocks. The wolves weren't strong enough to move those rocks, but I listened to them whine hungrily for her frozen body.

...✝...

CHAPTER THIRTY-TWO

Morning dawned with a crack of a gunshot—but it was so far away that it sounded more like thunder. I'd heard it, though, and so had Gan-gaad, who was the only other early riser as he saw to our horses. My throat went dry as I watched through my binoculars soldier after soldier pour over the eastern ridge. They were on foot, and not knowing the way, it would take them the better part of the day to circle along the base of the mountain, find the game trail, cross the meadow, and discover the cave that was more or less out of sight to them still. The land was too rugged for their vehicles, which equalized us when it came to traveling.

"Now, we have no choice but to move," Jugder said as we discussed our options in a hushed circle, not wanting to cause fear among the others. "We can't help but leave a trail for them to follow, but we can at least try to stay ahead of them."

"If we can do twenty miles today, we'll be okay," Kandal said, almost too calmly. "Just because they made it over the ridge, doesn't mean God won't have more in store for them, right, Andy?"

Zima squeezed my hand, rejoicing with me as the clan elders trusted God.

"We have ten rounds left for the AK," Gan-gaad said. "I could stay behind and snipe at them."

"No," Sembuuk said, "we need to save those bullets for game when our meat runs low later. But we have feet, so we'll flee. And we have God, so we don't need to worry."

"You guys need to stop talking about God and give your hearts to Him, like Kandal and the others have," I said. "Recognition of God isn't enough. He desires to *know* you, each of you. Today, I want everyone to search their souls and ask why we're not all seeking God more. He's obviously shown us Himself over the past months."

They hung their heads.

"Some here died, though," Gan-gaad said. "Like Dusbhan."

"Dusbhan had received Christ, and God simply called him home after he completed his job for us—this route. There's a lesson in death for the living. God allows some to die, I believe, just to get others to recognize that we all go sometime—and we'd better get our hearts straight because it's too late after we die. I can't make the decision for you, but I know this much: even through this tragic time, the Spirit of God gives me peace that is beyond human understanding."

"It's true," Kandal testified. "I sense Him, too."

"We'll talk more tonight," I said. "Gan-gaad, take point, Manai with you. Sembuuk and I will take the rear. Let's get moving."

As we dispersed to gather the women and children, I tugged at Gan-gaad's arm.

"The shot we heard at dawn, why would they announce themselves like that?"

"They aren't clumsy." Gan-gaad shrugged his bulky

shoulders. "Maybe they shot at a wolf. Who's to say? But if they understood this terrain, they'd be on horseback. Since they're on foot and we're on foot, we have the advantage, Pond. We're more accustomed to traveling with burdens. If we keep moving, we won't have difficulty staying ahead of them. Everything they have is on their own shoulders."

"I'll keep that in mind."

"Pond?"

"Yes?"

His eyes searched mine.

"What you always say . . . that our sins must be washed away. I have done too many terrible things. You remember Tzegabor . . . And there were others, too, in my youth."

"There's no sin too great that God didn't take and put upon His Son on the Cross, Gan-gaad. King David, Moses, and even Paul in the Bible—they were murderers or criminals at times, but God changed their lives and hearts and used them after they repented. Some of us have darker pasts than others, but He can heal us. By faith, we must rely on His grace to save us through Jesus Christ." Before he knew what was happening, I gave him a brief embrace, a sturdy bear hug, clapped him twice on the back, then held him at arm's length. "I'll pray that God helps you sort this out, Gan-gaad. Since the day we met, I've prayed for you."

"You have?"

Smiling, I hobbled away.

Our stiff wounds were loosened in a few minutes of travel. Since our horses were few, most everyone was on foot now. Those of us who rode gave others rides periodically, or took turns. The youngest children were piled atop the gear on the horses' backs, sometimes two together, so we made good time all morning until we stopped at a frozen spring midday. Gan-gaad and I consulted Dusbhan's sketches of the route ahead while cinches were loosed and snow was melted for drinking.

"We're as far as I've ever hunted," Gan-gaad said. "Our greatest obstacle to leaving this valley now is through this pass . . . here."

"This is a steep pass. I hate to risk a fall, but Dusbhan says he searched a whole day for an alternate pass out of the valley." I sighed. "There has to be something else safer."

"There's this." Gan-gaad pointed at Dusbhan's scribbled marks. "To the west, another pass, but we would be too far west of the mountains then to take advantage of the better climate and natural shelters within the range that Dusbhan found for us along the way. That's why he didn't even check that route. If we did end up going west, we could circle around to the north to get back on track, but we'd lose a day. All that to avoid a steep pass?"

"How much would the steep pass hold us up?"

"It would be slow-going." He nodded in contemplation. "The Chinese may even come into sight there—maybe not within mortar range, but they may get a chance to catch us."

"Here's what we should do . . ."

I gathered Jugder, Olz, and Sembuuk together for my plan. Where the fork in the trail occurred, we would leave sign that made it appear that we'd turned west—obvious sign and tracks. But we would actually continue north to the steep pass and cover our tracks for a safe distance behind us to ensure we weren't followed right away. The Chinese would realize our trickery in time, but a delay was all we needed. If it worked well, we might stay ahead of them while climbing the steep pass, and maybe even leave them behind as they maneuvered the pass themselves. Lord willing, we would think of another scheme after that.

So, we cinched up and started away from our break spot. The three men who knew the plan rode far ahead to scout the western and northern routes to lay our scheme in place. The word spread of our plan and the clan's spirits were high as we hurried forward in anticipation of both the plan and the pass.

Zima clung to my stirrup as she walked alongside.

"If we come upon a lake, should we expect the water to part for us to cross?"

We laughed together as I considered a response.

"I'm not Moses, my wife, and we're not the Israelites, but we do serve the same God."

The dogs were feeling better that day and seemed to be themselves as they ran about nipping at each other when they weren't keeping the two goats in order. That is, all the dogs except Lucky Hunter. He'd been a loyal dog in the past, but since I'd cleaned his wound the night before, he displayed a sense of obligation to not leave my side now. I saw it in his eyes as he looked up at me on my horse every few seconds, and the way he growled and snapped at the other dogs when they ventured near—I was his.

Three hours later, we came to the fork where Sembuuk and the other two directed the clan to not stop, but to turn left and west without hesitation. We traveled that way for a hundred yards, then we were led to the right across a broad rock that would leave no sign. Minutes later, we were back on track, heading north, our misguidance fully intact.

Pausing with Lucky Hunter, I looked back. Jugder was using a tree bough to wipe out any sign we'd left, and Olz made sure enough sign was left to the west to mislead our pursuers. He even dropped horse manure and a couple ribbons of clothing. Once the Chinese trackers saw the sign and our suspected heading, we hoped they would confidently rush west to the wrong pass.

Lucky Hunter growled beside me.

"I hear you, boy. The bad guys'll be sorry to run into you."

Though I did hear him, I didn't see where he was gazing right away. He was looking off to the left where a thin forest was outlined by scrub brush. Suddenly, I saw a gray wolf run past. It stopped to cast me an icy, hungry glare, then it moved away like a drifting mist. There was a rule of thumb about wolves: they hunted in packs. If I saw one, that meant others were near.

"Easy, boy," I said, coaxing him aloud. Lucky Hunter glanced up at me. "I see them. Let them watch us. We're not going to give them any weakness to exploit."

But I knew the wolves wouldn't need much of a weakness in order to attack, not if they were starving. The cold weather had sent all other game deep into the forest or burrows. The wolves' stomachs would overwhelm their cautious minds and they could attack. Gan-gaad had told me that. In summer, a wolf might get close out of curiosity. In winter, curiosity gave way to hunger, and even people could become prey.

After waiting until Sembuuk and the others caught up to me, the four of us trotted to catch up with the determined clan. I didn't like being separated from Zima, but we each had our duties. As often as we could, we talked and prayed together. Usually, however, the children gave her little space.

The north pass now loomed above us, and I realized it was no lower in elevation than the ridge we'd climbed the day before. However, this pass had more snow suffocating its passageway. The others saw it, too, and though they said nothing of it, I wondered if we had made the right choice by coming this way. It was so steep! And with such little space to traverse between the rocky, vertical walls meant we'd have to tackle the climb nearly straight on.

That night, we set up camp at the base of the pass. I helped the others set up their *gers* as Gan-gaad and Jugder rode ahead to scout the pass that Dusbhan had recommended over the other. When they returned, we had the horses scrubbed down and grained, the *gers* were up, and the meat was being cooked.

"My nephew was right," Gan-gaad beamed. "We can make this pass. By tomorrow afternoon, we'll be in the lowlands, picking tropical fruit off green trees."

We laughed with him at his optimism. Exhausted, we crowded into the few *gers* we had. Two men were on watch, armed with gnarled clubs to whack the wolves should they venture too close. Any fire that burned through the night was sheltered behind the *gers* and brush so the flicker wouldn't be seen from afar.

I'd spoken with the men at dinner that evening about our

384 | D.I. TELBAT

earlier talk at the cave. A few wanted more time to think about taking God more seriously into their lives, and Gangaad said he would talk to me when we were alone in the morning.

Finally, Zima and I had a chance to speak privately, though we were crowded into the same *ger* with Beveg, Manai, and Kandal. Exhausted, they slept beside us.

"All day I watched the sky, longing for Jesus," Zima whispered. "Do you think it will be soon?"

"In his first letter to the Thessalonians, Paul explains how the saints will be spared the great wrath to come. The wrath is judgement and punishment intended for the wicked and unrepentant. While we have difficulties and persecutions now, we as believers—His saints—are being spared the great wrath and will continue to be spared the wrath to come. Look at how God has preserved a remnant the last few weeks. We have suffered through some of man's wrath, but soon, they will feel God's wrath. It's amazing, Zima, like He's allowing us to stay on earth up until the absolute last minute to give every last person a chance at salvation. That's why He leaves a few of us here, I believe. We must be close to the end. Nearly all of the clan has been saved."

"What if someone in the clan is left behind?"

I touched her sincere face.

"Tomorrow, we'll share Christ with those who have yet to profess. We'll challenge them with warnings as the Word instructs us: '*We who are alive and remain will be caught up together with them in the clouds to meet the Lord in the air.*' It doesn't get much clearer than that."

"Let the Chinese come upon our camp and find nothing except the dogs and horses!" she said, giggling excitedly.

"I love you, Zima." I kissed her.

"I love you, Pond."

...✝...

The next morning, I rose early to pray, read my Bible, and update my journal to the latest happenings, of which you read now. The Chinese were sure to realize the deception of our trail by now, but they would be at least another day behind us, if they'd followed the false trail for a few hours. And then they'd need to backtrack, doubling the hours they weren't on our real trail.

God also put it in my mind to be aware, if nothing else, that the Chinese might use their radios to call ahead for an intercepting force once they figured out where we were going. Should we expect an ambush on the other side of the pass in the next valley? Or could there be an air strike from one of the many bombers flying so burdened to and from Russia? Danger seemed inescapable. I kept these thoughts to myself and didn't share them even with Zima. God knew what lay ahead, and that was that.

"I've decided," Gan-gaad suddenly interrupted my journal writing.

The camp was coming to life around us as they packed and saw to the horses. Gan-gaad sat down beside me on a low rock.

"What have you decided?" I asked.

"It makes me nervous, but I have nothing else, you understand." He held up his palms. "Nothing left. So, I have decided to receive this Jesus as the God who delivers us—

the cross, the blood, heaven, all of it. He has really washed my sins away?"

"That's what the Bible says, and it has never misguided anyone yet."

"Then, what do I do? What did Dusbhan and Kandal and Zima do?"

"I thought you'd never ask."

Together, we prayed, and the whole camp saw us on the side of the camp with our heads bowed together, and our arms over each other's shoulders. Hard-hearted Gan-gaad, the murderer, received Christ that morning. He didn't weep, but he confessed, and I witnessed, as he pled sincerely for God to save him from the penalty of sin.

The camp tensed as we heard a galloping horse approach. It was Sembuuk. He'd ridden out before first light to check our back trail.

"They're two kilometers back!" he gasped. "To make up for lost time, they marched through the night!"

"That's madness!" Gan-gaad said. "They'll kill themselves from exhaustion!"

"We need to move now." I limped my way through the camp, helping where I could as everyone dashed about frantically.

My horse was saddled and Gan-gaad pulled the first string of pack animals up the pass where a grim game trail snaked. It looked as if it were accessible only for a mountain goat. The horses and those riding went up the narrow trail next since horses lunge and scramble almost recklessly up such inclines. Twice, a packhorse lead rope broke and the animal rolled backwards down the trail. But serious injury was avoided, and the animal jumped up and rushed forward through the pass, as if embarrassed it had ever lost its footing in the first place.

I sat on my mount at the top of the pass beside the trail as those on foot trekked past.

"Yes, that's what I told my wife last night," a man from Middle Camp said as he walked by with Zima. On his back was a child, his wife next to him. "If stubborn Gan-gaad prays to God for his sins, I told her, then we would, too!"

They moved on, then I heard Jugder and Kandal discussing salvation as well. And if I wasn't mistaken, I'd say they were cheery, even with smiles on their faces as they pushed forward.

Thankfully, none of the others looked back down the steep trail that had taken an hour to climb. But I looked back. At the site of our camp from the night before, two columns of men were marching. Once the soldiers reached the top of the pass behind us, with us descending below them, they'd be able to fire down at us at will. As if matters weren't bad enough, the sky was beginning to cloud up. Snow was in the air. The pursuing soldiers were probably marching themselves to death, but not before they sent us to a cold grave first. I suspected their gear and food was depleted by now. They had to catch us for our own supplies, or die trying.

Turning my back to the troops, I scurried up the trail to our pass. While the clan was busy traveling and talking of God's preservation, my own faith faltered. *Had we come through so much and so far to die horrible deaths below a mountain pass? Where was our deliverance?*

The clan suddenly stopped moving. *What now?*

I squeezed my horse down a gradual grade to meet Gan-gaad, panting and horseless, coming up to find me at the rear.

"Soldiers are at the bottom of the mountain, Pond! Looks like infantry." He shook his head as others gathered around. "There's no getting around them. We'll have to go back through the pass, maybe find another route on our back trail."

"We can't!" I gritted my teeth. "They're already starting up the trail behind us. Within the hour they'll be above us in the pass."

In silence, the clan of about fifteen watched and waited for me to make a decision as to our fate.

Eyeing the sky, I searched for direction. *Lord, what should we do?* It was growing darker by the minute and it wasn't but mid-morning. My eyes fell upon the faces of my friends, all of whom I believed to be brothers and sisters in Christ now.

"Look . . . a crevice . . . over there." I pointed to the right of the trail. "And an overhang. Everyone into it!"

"But the horses, Pond!" Beveg said, voicing everyone's concern.

"It's okay. Take what gear you can carry and turn the horses loose. The Chinese will eat the horses and maybe they'll leave us alone. Jugder, stay close to me so we can communicate with them if we have an opportunity."

"Everyone . . . into the rock!" Gan-gaad ordered and led the way.

We swatted the horses on the rumps and sent them

scattering. The clan filed into what could've been a rocky cave shaped like a tunnel, if the ceiling had connected all the way to the downhill slope. But since it didn't, a mean draft coursed through the incomplete hall of stone, a wind so cold from the north that we could only face it and shiver. Everyone crowded to the end of the ledge and took a seat, shoulder to shoulder. They passed out blankets and smoked meat and talked quietly amongst themselves.

I knelt before each member of the clan, one at a time, met each one's gaze, and grasped their hands.

"God sees us even now," I said, reassuring them and myself. "You have taken Christ's gift into your heart?"

Each one answered positively, even the children, and we prayed together as one, all of us, led first by me, then Zima, then Kandal.

With brave hearts and our backs against the rock, we sat in the crevice, and it's this final entry I believe I'll make before our end with the Chinese.

Seven-fingered Jugder, who speaks fluent Chinese, sits on my left. Lucky Hunter has draped himself across my legs. Zima's hands are wrapped around my arm, even now as I write. We have loved each other faithfully, as man and wife, though briefly. Beside her, Sembuuk, the hunter, dozes and mumbles in his sleep. I know he misses his eagle.

Next to Sembuuk sits Gan-gaad, who is talking to Manai. Manai is laughing as he listens to a hunting tale of a Gobi bear and a man in the desert who cuddle together for warmth during the nights. It's a fitting story for us here in this drafty crevice.

And so I close. Since the Chinese are nearly upon us, I

wish now I knew the Chinese language and my story was filled with their words here to read instead of my native language. Perhaps, somehow, this will be preserved. Perhaps a reader among them will be touched by the mighty hand of God in my life. He changed me, and I saw Him change so many others—this whole clan, in fact, *my clan*. And I'm joyful beyond words to have been so used.

If I could serve Him again, I would.

In His Name and service,
Andrew "Pond" Foworthy

...✝...

CONCLUSION

It so happens, I did find this journal, though not its writer. I knew Andy, so, following the orders of my superiors, I pursued the rebel band of Kazakhs and Mongols into the Gobi Altay Mountains. Near starvation ourselves, we marched through the night to overtake the band at a steep mountain pass.

We certainly had them trapped since we had the only known approaches and exits to the pass blocked, but what we found was not only confusing, it was downright haunting!

In a narrow crag, we found the last of the rebels' belongings, and a mangy dog that lay near boots I recognized. The Christians seemed to have abandoned all, even clothes and packs, in a last effort to flee up or down the cliffs and hide in the rocks. The troops with me killed their horses and ate the meager food they'd left behind. Thereafter, we searched for a week, whereupon we nearly starved to death a second time—and some did—but we never found a single rebel or even a fleeting trace of anyone.

Since I was the only one of my soldiers—and a sergeant at that—who reads and speaks English, I kept this journal without argument from the others. This journal is the second of two books that I now value beyond life itself, and both have changed my life since reading them.

The first is the Bible.

And, yes, having read both books, and having heard news reports from around the world that millions of others have vanished, I do now understand what has happened.

The world is in upheaval around me. The water turns crimson and the sun is blotted out by ash. Millions upon millions have died. But I'm still alive, for now. I've gone to great pains to see this book in print and distributed, regardless of the strife involved—and not only this book, but Bibles as well.

Once, in a drunken rage, I nearly killed Andy for his boots. Now, having only spoken to him two or three times, I count him a close friend—and even a brother. By his life, he led me to the One who saves souls.

Sincerely, Sergeant Xing

Dear Reader,

Thanks for reading *CALLED TO GOBI!* I pray it was a blessing to you. I thank the Lord that this novel was the 2016 Gold Medal Winner for the eLit Awards in Religious Fiction. If you liked it, I'd be grateful if you would leave a short comment or review wherever you bought the book. That would encourage others to read it as well. Thank you!

I've written other End Times books that you might enjoy. You can find links to them on my End Times Novels page at ditelbat.com/end-times-novels/. The page includes my latest futuristic novellas, *The Steadfast Series: America's Last Days*, as well as the upcoming series, *Last Dawn Trilogy*.

Again, thanks for reading. May the Lord be glorified.

David Telbat

Glossary

<u>Aduu</u> – stocky horse with large head, thick hair, and bushy mane; forages for food even when in domestic care

<u>Del</u> – ankle-length, loose-fitting felt or hide coat

<u>Genghis Khan</u> – 13th Century Mongolian Emperor

<u>Ger</u> – portable round tent; wood frame, covered in thick felt in winter, light canvas in summer

<u>Gobi</u> – an area of arid range land

<u>Mongolia</u> – three times the size of France, mostly high plateau, landlocked by China and Russia; known as Land of Blue Sky because of 257 cloudless days per year

<u>Morin-khuur</u> – two-stringed lute with wooden sound box and neck scroll carved in shape of a horse's head

<u>Steppe</u> – belt of grassland extending across the country.

<u>Tatlaga</u> – instrumental music with melody, rhythm, and timbre (tone quality) to tell a story

<u>Toono</u> - small hole in the ceiling of gers to expel smoke; also allows sun and air into the shelter

<u>Tugrik</u> – Mongolia's currency (1,000 tugriks = $1.00 USD)

<u>Ulaanbaater</u> – Mongolia's capital; means "Red Hero"

<u>Urtyn duu</u> – means "long song"; a song form with each syllable extended for long duration in guttural style, requiring great skill

ABOUT THE AUTHOR

D.I. Telbat desires to honor the Lord with his life and writing. Many of his books, such as his award-winning *COIL Series*, focus on persecuted Christians worldwide—their sacrifice, their suffering, and their rescues.

David studied writing in school and worked for a time in the newspaper field. As a young man, he found himself in serious trouble with the law, but God got hold of him and changed his life forever. He is now doing what he loves most—writing and Christian ministry. At this time, D.I. Telbat lives on the West Coast, but keeps his home base in the Northwest US. You can read his complete bio at ditelbat.com/about/.

On his Telbat's Tablet website, David Telbat offers FREE weekly Christian short stories, or related posts, which include his novel news, author reflections, book reviews, and challenges for today's Christian. Subscribe to his weekly blog at ditelbat.com to receive his posts in your inbox, along with occasional exclusive subscriber gifts.

Visit D.I. Telbat's site at ditelbat.com/all-d-i-telbat-novels/ to learn more and find links to all his paperbacks, eBooks, and audiobooks.

Please leave your comments wherever you bought this book. Reviews greatly help authors, and David Telbat would love to hear your thoughts on his works. He takes reader reviews into consideration as he makes his future publishing plans. Thanks for reading.

OTHER END TIMES NOVELS FROM D.I. TELBAT

In America's Last Days, only the Steadfast will prevail!

The STEADFAST Novella Series follows Christian survivalist Eric Radner through the heartache and heroism of living in the aftermath of America's collapse. The Meridia Virus has killed millions across North America and brought out the worst in the US. Bandits roam, and cities are left in charred ruins. Fear cripples and Christian persecution abounds.

But secluded deep in a Wyoming mountain range, Eric Radner hides alone, finding refuge in a small cabin. He has committed his life to a desperate survival, yet with a determined faith.

Emerging from the mountains to prove his faith in the face of a new breed of terror and persecution, God guides him to reach out to other broken lives. In the midst of America's Last Days, Eric Radner is . . . STEADFAST!

Visit *The Steadfast Series* at ditelbat.com/steadfast-series/.

GOD'S COLONEL: AN END TIMES CHRISTIAN NOVEL

America collapses and the Antichrist rises as supreme from the carnage. A broken family struggles to survive the devastation of the Final Tribulation. Caught in the crossfire of End Time plagues that strike the earth with fiery judgment, family mem-bers face hard choices and trials as they witness non-compliant Christians dragged to the guillo-tine. The future seems bleak, but the resolute few seek to salvage the faithful. A deeply-guarded secret may be the only hope to end the chaos for the remaining underground believers.

Visit *God's Colonel* at ditelbat.com/book/gods-colonel/.

OTHER BESTSELLING NOVELS FROM D.I. TELBAT

The COIL Series

International spies and Special Forces commandos are committed to saving at-risk Christians around the world. Join the Commission of International Laborers in covert ops and rescues—all with non-lethal weapons.

These novels of suspense, loss, love, and commitment to Christ will draw you, and you will see God is still in control even in the midst of chaos.

D.I. Telbat prays that your faith in Christ, our Savior, will be strengthened as you read *The COIL Series*.

The adventure begins with the Prequel, *Dark Edge*, followed by Book One, *Dark Liaison*.

Learn more about *The COIL Series*: ditelbat.com/coil-series/.

The COIL Legacy

With the suspense, *The COIL Legacy* includes an emphasis on family and practical faith. Corban Dowler is still running the Commission of International Laborers, but Titus Caspertein is back, making plenty of enemies. You'll find newly-developed COIL tech, drones, and more in the NL (non-lethal) weapon series.

Distant Boundary, the exciting Prequel, introduces this series. Agent Titus Caspertein, with his proud attitude, receives his first mission for COIL. He has left the criminal underground to carry the cross of Christ, but survival has never seemed more unlikely for this new Christian. Assumed dead after a botched humanitarian airdrop, Titus fights for his life against wild animals, rhino poachers, and the isolation of the African savannah.

Learn more about *The COIL Legacy* at ditelbat.com/coil-legacy/.

Made in the USA
Middletown, DE
04 November 2021